Greg Mitchell's storytelling mixes the modern pace and stripped-down narrative of a Ted Dekker with the spiritual tensions of a Frank Peretti. He draws us into the struggles of his flawed characters. *Enemies of the Cross* is an imaginative, sobering page-turner that reminds us of the spiritual battle we face and points us back to the cross.

—Eric Wilson
New York Times best-selling author of
Fireproof, *Valley of Bones*, and *One Step Away*

Greg Mitchell once again takes us on an unforgettable journey through the realm of evil and reminds us that faith and courage shine brightest in the blackest night.

—Alton Gansky
Novelist

Enemies of the Cross is a head-spinning, heart-thumping tale of good versus evil, full of breakneck action, surprising twists, and despicable villains—all guided by Greg Mitchell's exquisite storytelling skills. In other words, this is great stuff!

—Robert Liparulo
Author of *The 13th Tribe*
and *Comes a Horseman*

ENEMIES
OF THE
CROSS

THE COMING EVIL TRILOGY | BOOK TWO

GREG MITCHELL

REALMS

Most CHARISMA HOUSE BOOK GROUP products are available at special quantity discounts for bulk purchase for sales promotions, premiums, fund-raising, and educational needs. For details, write Charisma House Book Group, 600 Rinehart Road, Lake Mary, Florida 32746, or telephone (407) 333-0600.

ENEMIES OF THE CROSS by Greg Mitchell
Published by Realms
Charisma Media/Charisma House Book Group
600 Rinehart Road
Lake Mary, Florida 32746
www.charismahouse.com

Scripture quotations are from the New American Standard Bible, copyright © 1960, 1962, 1963, 1968, 1971, 1972, 1973, 1975, 1977, 1995 by The Lockman Foundation; used by permission (www.Lockman.org); and the Holy Bible, New International Version; copyright © 1973, 1978, 1984, International Bible Society; used by permission.

This is a work of fiction. The characters portrayed in this book are fictitious unless they are historical figures explicitly named. Otherwise, any resemblance to actual people, whether living or dead, is coincidental.

Cover design by Gearbox Studio
Design Director: Bill Johnson

Visit the author's website at www.thecomingevil.blogspot.com.

Library of Congress Cataloging-in-Publication Data:

Mitchell, Greg, 1978-
  Enemies of the cross / Greg Mitchell. -- 1st ed.
    p. cm. -- (The coming evil ; bk. 2)
  ISBN 978-1-61638-364-0 (trade paper) -- ISBN 978-1-61638-
638-2 (e-book)
  I. Title.
  PS3613.I8546E54 2012
  813'.6--dc23

                        2011042450

First edition

12 13 14 15 16 — 987654321
Printed in the United States of America

For Meghan, the Scully to my Mulder

PROLOGUE

Beware of the dogs, beware of the evil workers,
beware of the false circumcision…

—PHILIPPIANS 3:2

THE EMERGENCY ROOM doors slapped open as workers rushed Dras Weldon in on a stretcher. Paramedics hovered over him, their faces a picture of cold determination. At their sides, Jeff Weldon, his wife, Isabella, and Dras's best friend, Rosalyn Myers, hurried along, covered in Dras's blood and their faces stained by dried tears.

"It's going to be OK," Jeff whispered to his fallen brother. "It's going to be OK. I'm right here."

Despite his reassuring tone, Jeff held himself in contempt. *Why didn't I do anything to help him? I saw it coming.*

Last Saturday, when Jeff spotted the rolling clouds of the storm that threatened to consume Greensboro, he had an uneasy suspicion that bad times were coming on horseback. When he read about Lindsey McCormick's disappearance the following day, his anxiety grew. He didn't know how, but her disappearance was a part of the terrible pull he felt in the pit of his stomach as he watched the strange storm from inside the safety of his home. The winds and the rain had wrought their damage and retreated into the darkness, but he could not shake the mood that some great evil lingered.

"Give us some room!" the paramedics shouted at Jeff and the others.

A tall blonde nurse who answered to the name of Jill stood behind the front desk, her eyes wide. The paramedics stared at her impatiently as she struggled with the horrible sight.

"Where?" a member of the emergency team shouted at her, bringing her out of her stupor.

Stuttering, she pointed down the hall. "D–Doctor Brown will meet you in room 107."

The paramedics hustled Dras along as Isabella and Rosalyn drifted back, watching the parade leave them.

But not Jeff.

Keeping up with the paramedics' pace, Jeff stuck to the side of the stretcher. *I won't leave you, Dras. Not again.*

When Dras had pounded on his door not twenty-four hours earlier, he was more terrified than Jeff had ever seen him. Dras told Jeff that someone he called "the Strange Man" wanted Rosalyn, and Jeff dismissed it as one of his screwup little brother's ridiculous shenanigans. Jeff now made the connection. It was all because of that night and that awful, accursed storm.

Jeff had thought he'd done his part. As pastor at the Good Church of the Faithful, he always told his congregation to be on their guard. To read their Bibles, pray with fervor, and teach their children the ways of the Lord.

Yet, when Dras came to his front door and pleaded with Jeff to stand with him against the Strange Man, Jeff slammed the door in his face. *Serves him right,* Jeff had thought. He was mad at his brother for living like the devil during the week and sitting in a church pew smiling on Sunday morning. For being a blight on the face of the church. For being a hypocrite.

But now Jeff wondered if he wasn't the bigger hypocrite.

I turned him away.

The paramedics pushed Dras into the room, and Jeff moved to follow before a nurse intercepted him.

Jeff fought to break past her. "That's my brother!"

She nodded, well versed in the art of holding off angry and frightened family members. "You have to wait out here. We know what we're doing."

Doctor Herbert Brown, followed by two other doctors and a nurse, pushed his way into the room, shouting for assistance, and the nurse hurried to his side. The door behind him remained opened. Jeff peered in. Biting his lip, Jeff stood by helplessly as the doctors cut open Dras's sticky clothes, peeling the bloody layers away to expose the bruised and raw flesh. The evidence of the deputies' attack on him was a painful testimony to the gravity of the events that transpired earlier that evening.

Dras had marched off to face his bogeyman alone, to stand in its way and save Rosalyn from its clutches. By the time Jeff realized his mistake, he was too late to save him. He found Dras broken and bloody on the floor of The Rave Scene with a mob of crazed deputies

surrounding him, accusing him of murder, and Rosalyn in a traumatized daze at his side.

What happened? What came to Greensboro in that storm?

Rosalyn Myers remembered the last time Dras was in the hospital.
He was fourteen and had jumped off the roof of her home in Trysdale. There was this whole incident involving a trampoline and how
Dras thought he could attain maximum air if he cannonballed off
the roof and...well, he missed the trampoline. *Typical Dras.*

The stunt was intended as a kind gesture to cheer up Rosalyn, who
was in bed with the flu at the time, watching through her window.
Rosalyn got a huge smile from the ordeal, and in return for his kind-
ness Dras received a broken arm. But to Dras, it was an even trade.
Anything to make Rosalyn laugh.

Only now she wasn't laughing.

Now Rosalyn watched through the open door, frozen and helpless,
as doctors and nurses fought against death to bring back her best
friend. Her soul mate. The boy she had grown up with. The one who
made her laugh. The one who made her feel like she belonged.

"Clear!" the doctor shouted as the paddles of the defibrillator
pressed against Dras's chest.

A jolt surged through his body, lifting him off the table.

Jeff clenched his fists as Isabella braced herself on his arm.

"Again!" Doctor Brown shouted.

The nurse nodded—

ZZZT!

—and Dras's body jerked.

"Still no pulse."

Doctor Brown shook his head but refused to give in. "Do it again."

Rosalyn backed away from the sight, the sound of Dras's body
flopping on the bed too real for her to handle. Pressing her back to
the wall, she slowly slid to the floor and sat holding her legs together.

Clutched tightly in her grip was the note Dras gave her earlier at
The Rave Scene. She still hadn't mustered the strength to unfold it
and read it. This paper contained what might be the last words of
Dras Weldon—his final testament and his only good-bye.

Rosalyn couldn't accept the thought that he might die. She didn't
know how he got into this mess or why he was so afraid tonight at
the dance club. She didn't understand why he had changed without
warning and, out of nowhere, started talking about God and the devil.

More to the point, she didn't *want* to know.
She didn't want the responsibility.

Jeff watched with horror as the doctors fought to revive his brother. He wanted to run into the operating room and pound on his brother's chest until the little skeeve sprang up off the bed smiling and laughing, "Gotcha!"

Flatline.

Nothing. Only that terrible whine from the heart monitor.

Doctor Brown wiped the sweat from his brow and looked at the nurses and doctors. "Try it again."

As the nurse reset the defibrillator, a nearby orderly noticed Jeff and Isabella observing the bloody scene in breathless anticipation and closed the door for privacy.

Jeff stared at the door as if he could see through it. He heard the impact of his brother landing on the bed again. He wanted to tear through the door.

What then, Jeff?

I don't know! But I have to do something!

He spun on his heels and saw Rosalyn on the floor, her trembling hands draped over her knees, grasping something tightly—a folded sheet of paper, or something, but that mattered little.

"What happened?" he yelled at her. This wasn't her fault. Or was it? Dras said the bogeyman was after *Rosalyn*. Dras rushed out to save her. Now he was dying, and she was still here.

Rosalyn shook her head, her eyes glassy. "I–I don't know."

"What do you mean *you don't know*?" Jeff roared, throwing his hands up. "You were right there! It happened right in front of you!"

Rosalyn lowered her head, and Isabella firmly, but softly, spoke from behind her husband. "Jeff."

Jeff wanted to turn on her too. Turn on them all. He wanted to rage and roar and tear at the walls until his brother was all right and everyone who had a part in this nightmare paid for it.

Instead he paced, trying to cool down and make the shaking in his arms and clenched fists go away.

Isabella crouched beside Rosalyn, who turned the note over in her hand.

Isabella studied the girl. "Are you OK?"

Rosalyn shook her head.

A loud *smack* shook the hall, and both women looked up to see Jeff rubbing his knuckles and regarding a fresh dent in the plaster wall. Isabella frowned at her man's stubbornness. "Feel better?"

He shook his head, a near perfect mirror of how Rosalyn had shaken hers. Isabella somehow found the strength to smile at that. They were a lot alike, Jeff and Rosalyn. Angry. Strong.

Now they needed someone to be strong for them.

Jeff stopped pacing, a look of awful realization on his face.

"Oh, no…" he whispered. "I gotta call Mom."

Isabella stood and moved toward him, watching his eyes fill with tears.

"What am I going to tell her?" His voice cracked. "What will she say? Dad…"

Isabella slipped her hand in his and gave it a gentle squeeze, wanting desperately to take care of him. "I'll do it, OK, baby? I'll make the call. Just stay here, OK?"

She turned, eager to do something to ease her husband's worry, but before Isabella could step away, the door opened and Doctor Brown joined them in the hallway.

Jeff and Isabella hurried to him, and Rosalyn looked up. Isabella braced herself for the news.

Dras was dead.

"He's alive," Doctor Brown exhaled with great relief, or perhaps just exhaustion.

Isabella gasped then smiled. Jeff pushed onward. "How bad is it?"

Doctor Brown shook his head. "It's bad. We haven't had time to do a full workup. We need to do X-rays and probably an MRI. Still, my basic exam shows he has *numerous* broken bones, and his jaw will need to be wired shut for a while. He may even need reconstructive surgery, but it's too soon to tell."

Isabella's smile was now lost. "Oh, no."

Rosalyn lowered her head again, distant and dazed.

Jeff remained determined. "Can I see him?"

"Reverend Weldon, I don't think—"

"Herbert—" Jeff was firm but passionate. "—*please.*"

"We have a lot of work left to do, but…well…you can see him. *For a minute.* When your folks get here, we'll have a lot to talk about."

Jeff nodded, his face pained and worried. "OK."

Doctor Brown stepped aside, and Jeff moved for the door.

"Do you want me to call your mom?" Isabella asked, but Jeff had already left her behind, as if she had become invisible. She was hurt for a moment but considered the circumstances and quietly turned to make that call.

Rosalyn stood, stuffing the folded slip of paper in her back pocket, and wiped the streaked mascara from her eyes. Without a word she moved toward the exit.

Isabella stopped her. "Rosalyn? Are you leaving?"

Rosalyn froze, as if caught in the sights of a hunter. "Uh...I should probably go."

"What? No, stay."

"No, I really need to go. I've got...I've got a final left and..." She winced, on the verge of tears. "I mean, he's alive, right? That's what's important. You guys are going to be busy, and I don't want to be in the way."

"I'm sure they would want you here."

Rosalyn shook her head, chewing on her bottom lip, then turned toward the exit, her face harried by emotions Isabella could only guess at. She saw fear, guilt, sadness. *So much hurt.* Rosalyn forced a thin smile. "Tell Jeff I'll catch up with him later. I'm sure he'll want to check up on me and get all big brotherly."

Isabella sadly smiled at the sentiment. "I'm sure he will."

"Take care."

Isabella watched the hurting girl walk down the hall and waited until she disappeared outside.

"You too."

The automatic doors slid closed behind Rosalyn, and Isabella stood alone in the hallway. The space seemed enormous now.

"The cheese stands alone," she murmured. Gathering her strength, she headed to a cell phone friendly area to make the difficult call to Jeff's parents.

As Isabella moved away from room 107, Deputy Ryan Stevenson stepped out of the shadows. He watched her go, then frowned as he turned back to Dras's room, where he'd heard the doc inform Jeff Weldon that the boy was not yet dead.

Now Stevenson would have to inform his superiors.

With Dras's blood still tacky on his knuckles, Stevenson growled and reached into his pocket, pulling out his cell phone. Dialing an all too familiar number, he waited for a moment until the other party answered.

"It's me," the deputy dutifully reported. "The kid's alive. We'd better come up with Plan B."

CHAPTER ONE

Three months later

THERE WAS ALWAYS something special about Saturday mornings in the small town of Greensboro, and on that Saturday morning in August, it was no different. Children raced bikes down neighborhood streets while older boys played basketball in their driveways. Those who weren't spending their day off sleeping in were mowing their yards before the sun got too high in the sky. If his own childhood was any indication, Jeff imagined kids sat on living room floors all across town, still in their pajamas, eating bowls of sugary cereal and watching their favorite cartoons. Greensboro was at rest, recharging after another week.

But not Reverend Jeff Weldon.

He was in the process of moving a very heavy washing machine.

"You got it?" Jeff checked his partner as he strained to lift the appliance an inch higher. He and Isaac Monroe began to ascend the metal loading ramp into the U-Haul truck.

"Yeah, yeah." Isaac took a strained breath, breaking into a sweat. "I got it."

"It's heavy. Be careful."

It was at this time, with the washing machine cradled precariously between them, that the cell phone strapped to Jeff's side exploded in a cacophony of whirring bleeps. He yelped and nearly dropped his end of the washing machine.

Jeff was better prepared for the second ring, and the two managed to haul the machine to its destination. He wiped his brow with a sigh and reached for his phone. As he answered, he spied a grin on Isaac's face.

"Hello?"

"Reverend Weldon? It's me. Will."

Will Baxter. His assistant pastor. A very ambitious, nervous fellow, especially for someone just twenty years old. Ever since he was hired,

7

Will spent most of his time finding new emergencies, emergencies that only men answering to the name "Jeff Weldon" could manage.

"What is it, Will?"

"You're late, sir. Where are you?"

Jeff looked around and let his sarcastic side get the better of him. "Standing inside of a U-Haul truck. Why?"

"Did you forget the garage sale at the Duncan's today?"

"That's *today*?" Jeff looked at his watch. "What day is it?"

"The twenty-second, sir. Did you forget?"

The twenty-second.

Dras's birthday... How could I have forgotten?

"Sir?"

Jeff shook himself loose of painful memories, massaging his temple. "No, no. I'm on my way." He closed his phone and slipped it back into its holster then stood in silence, still trying to understand how he could have forgotten today of all days.

"Everything OK?"

"Yeah." Jeff nodded, coming to. "Just more work to do."

Isaac laughed. "You're going to work yourself into an early grave, my man."

"Yeah, yeah. When the world's a perfect place, I'll stop."

The two men smiled and looked around at what they had accomplished.

"I really appreciate you helping us move, Jeff. It's been a blessing."

"I'm just sorry to see you go, Isaac. The church won't be the same without you guys. We'll miss you. *I'll* miss you."

"You've been a good friend to my family."

"You too. I don't know if I could have gotten through the last three months without your prayers, what with the trial and..."

They shared a meaningful glance and extended hands. With a firm grip they shook on their friendship before pulling each other into a hug.

Outside the U-Haul, Isabella Weldon loaded some of the smaller boxes of the Monroe's belongings into the back of their Suburban. Elsa Monroe was right behind her with another box, when her son Matt sideswiped her in a giggle-riddled attempt to escape the tickling clutches of his older brother, Terry. Matt had just turned six and Terry was eight. Sixteen-month-old Cyan played in the playpen temporarily placed on the front lawn where she could witness first-hand all the moving day activity.

"Terry, quit chasing your brother and help with these boxes," Elsa snapped, before giving into a chuckle at their revelry. Terry managed to catch up to Matt and tackled him to the lawn, tickling him as they rolled around on the grass in raucous laughter.

Isabella grinned. "Boys will be boys."

She set her box in the back of the Suburban and Elsa followed suit, brandishing a smile and a raised eyebrow. "Yeah, let's hear you say that in ten years when it's *your* boys being boys."

The women laughed and closed the back of the Suburban.

Isabella threw a glance to the U-Haul. "You think they're about done in there?"

"They're getting old. We'd better give them a few more minutes."

Elsa sighed and looked back to the shell of her house. "Lot of good memories here."

Isabella remained quiet and allowed Elsa a moment. It was always hard saying good-bye to houses. And to friends.

Matt and Terry broke their roughhousing long enough to scurry to Isabella, each out of breath and holding wildflowers freshly pulled from the ground. They wore wide grins as they presented her their gifts.

"Here you go, Miss Isabella," Matt said.

"We wanted to give you a present," Terry elaborated.

Isabella wrinkled her forehead as her heart melted, and she knelt to accept her flowers. "That's so sweet. Thanks, you guys."

The boys continued grinning but ducked their heads, embarrassed. Isabella snickered and then tugged at Matt's belly. "I'm going to miss you guys in Sunday school. You'll have to draw some pictures at your new church and send them to me so I can put them on our walls, OK?"

Matt dug his toe in the dirt, glowing from the attention. "'K."

Terry nodded. "OK."

"Give me a hug," she ordered with a grin.

They reached out and hugged her neck for a moment. She pulled them to her and held them close, giving them a good squeeze, closing her eyes tight. *This is what it's like to have sons.*

Terry and Matt parted from Isabella's embrace, and before two seconds had passed, they were off again, chasing each other across the yard. Isabella smiled and turned her attention to little Cyan. She reached into the playpen and lifted the child out and into her arms.

"I'd better get one last hold in. I won't get to do this for much longer."

As Isabella held the girl, Elsa stroked her daughter's budding hair. "One day I'll be holding your baby."

Isabella fought back a wash of regret and managed a meek smile.

"Any luck?" Elsa asked.

Isabella shook her head. "The doctors are starting to think that it might not happen. They've said that before, but…I don't know. Maybe I'm just starting to believe them."

Elsa rubbed Isabella's arm. "I'm sorry, honey." Brightening, she added, "If God wants it to happen, it'll happen."

"Yeah," Isabella heaved a burdensome sigh. "The hard part is not knowing if it's what He wants or not."

Cyan cooed and Isabella was lost in her eyes, relishing the moment.

When Cyan started squirming to break free, Isabella chuckled. "I think it's time for Mommy to hold her now."

Elsa laughed as Isabella handed her the baby. Isabella held Cyan's delicate hand for a moment more.

"Everybody ready to go?" Isaac called, stepping down from the U-Haul truck. Immediately Terry and Matt shouted in excitement. Isabella knew from their energetic ramblings in Sunday school for the past few weeks that they were ready to move into their new house with their new *separate* rooms.

Jeff hopped down from the truck and closed everything tight. At last the two men approached their wives, preparing for the final good-byes.

"I think that's everything." Elsa huddled closer to her husband, and Isaac gently kissed the top of Cyan's head.

"Well, all right, then. Let's load up and go."

The boys were the first to hop into the Suburban, trading jabs along the way. Isaac broke down the playpen and packed it away in the vehicle. Then he took Cyan from Elsa and buckled her into her car seat.

"You take care of our girl," Elsa told Jeff, gesturing toward Isabella.

"You got it." The two shared a warm, friendly embrace.

They parted and Isabella was next in line for hugs. "Call us later to check in, OK?"

"It may be late. We want to get as many miles in as possible."

"No matter what time it is." Isabella held her friend tight, praying for her family's protection on the long trip.

"I love you, girl." Elsa kissed Isabella on the cheek.

"I love you."

Elsa stepped to the car and joined her husband. Isabella and Jeff followed. A moment later, Isabella wrapped her arms around Isaac's neck.

"See ya, Iz." He squeezed her tight.

They parted and she scratched her nose, holding back a sniffle. Jeff leaned forward and the two men shook hands again. "If you ever need anything, Jeff..." Isaac quietly promised.

"I know. Take care, you guys."

"You too. My Realtor friend in Arizona said the offer still stands if you guys want to come. You should really think about leaving Greensboro too."

Jeff grinned but remained resolute. "There's a lot in Greensboro that needs to be changed."

"Still think you'll be able to do it all?" Elsa laughed, folding her arms.

"I'm sure gonna try," Jeff said.

"I'm afraid for you, brother," Isaac added. "I've got a bad feeling about this town, man. Things haven't been the same here this summer. I'm serious. Get out while the getting's good."

A chill snaked up Isabella's spine, but Jeff seemed unfazed. "I think we'll take our chances."

"All right, buddy. Don't say I didn't warn you." Then, winking at Isabella, Isaac joked, "You don't let him work too hard."

"Believe me, I'm trying." Isabella playfully elbowed Jeff in the ribs.

Jeff slipped his arms around his wife's waist, and Isabella watched as Elsa got into the Suburban and Isaac took charge of the U-Haul truck. With a wave and a final farewell, the Monroes were gone.

Jeff and Isabella remained alone at the end of the driveway, silent for a long time, and Isabella could tell that Jeff was just as sad as she. At last he broke the silence. "What is that? Five families in two months? At this rate there won't *be* a congregation at the Good Church of the Faithful for much longer."

Isabella rested her head on his shoulder. "Have faith, Jeff. It'll all work out."

Jeff relaxed against her. It felt good to Isabella to be needed. Wanted.

Jeff's phone rang.

He reluctantly answered, pressing the SPEAKER button, no doubt to spare his ear another direct assault. "Yes?"

"Reverend Weldon? It's me. Will."

"I know, Will. What's wrong?"

"I'm sorry to bother you again. I had to leave the garage sale to drop off a present at the Mackenzie's baby shower. On the way I'm afraid I overheated. You know my car, sir."

Everyone does, Isabella mused. It was a jalopy, held together by rust and the mercy of God.

Will continued, "I was wondering if you could come pick me up on your way to the Duncan's. I'm on Fifth Street."

Jeff nodded, unable to say no when someone needed help. No matter how much he may have wanted to, Isabella knew. His father had taught him that. "OK, Will. I'm on my way."

Jeff hung up and slid the phone back into place. "I've gotta go," he announced with regret. Isabella smiled for his benefit, knowing he'd be able to see through her façade. "OK." He frowned and groaned, and Isabella tried to make the situation seem convenient. "I've gotta go get groceries anyway. We're low on milk."

"Again? You just bought that the other day."

"If you would cut down on your milk and cookies binges when you're up at all hours of the night…" She pulled at his shirt, playful. He smiled and brought her closer for a hug. They held each other, and she thought to remind him, "We're still on for tonight, right?"

"Tonight?"

She pushed him away, surprised, as he shrugged sheepishly.

"We were *supposed* to go out tonight. Dinner. Movie. Ringing any bells?"

"What movie?"

"Some new baseball movie with Kevin Costner. You'll love it."

He nodded, the arrangement becoming vaguely familiar. "Right. Tonight. Are we celebrating something? Did I miss it?"

She rolled her eyes. He did try so hard. "I haven't seen you all week, Jeff."

"What are you talking about? We just spent the whole morning together."

"Yeah. *Working.* The only time I see you anymore is when I sign up for volunteer work at the mission or if I get a flat tire. Not what I call quality husband-wife time."

Jeff glanced away, guilty looking. "I know. I'm sorry. I've been busy."

"I know, baby. I just miss you. And for one evening I would like to spend time with Jeff and not Reverend Weldon. OK?"

She rubbed the dark whiskers of the mustache and goatee he was starting to grow. She wasn't particularly fond of his new facial hair, but she understood that he was too distracted right now to worry about "silly" things like shaving.

He nodded. "Deal."

"Promise me you won't forget, Jeff."

He laughed it off, but she pulled him closer, forcing him to meet her eyes. "*Promise* me."

He put on his serious face, an amused grin creeping at the corners of his mouth. "My word is my bond."

"Yeah, yeah. Just make sure you're there at six."

She play-punched him in the stomach, and he feigned injury. Together they moved to where their cars were parked, she to her little maroon Oldsmobile and he to his beat-up work truck.

"Now that's *tomorrow* night, right?"

She spun on her heels to face him, trying to look mean, though she knew he was just being cute. "Jeff Weldon!" She slapped him on the arm and he laughed.

"Tonight, tonight! OK, I remember."

Isabella huffed and moved to unlock her car door, smiling to herself.

From the other side of her car, Jeff teased her, "I'm kidding. A joke. It was a joke."

She raised a sly eyebrow as she eased into the driver's seat.

He held out his arms with a boyish grin. "What? No kiss?"

Shaking her head, she taunted him. "I'm saving it for tonight. A little incentive to guarantee you show this time."

Without waiting for his reply, she giggled, got in her car, and drove away with a toot of her horn, watching his silly grin retreat in her rear view mirror.

CHAPTER TWO

THE ALARM BLARED, rattling Rosalyn's exhausted brain. Rosalyn Myers opened her eyes then winced at the onslaught of sun that penetrated the opening of her partially drawn curtains. Groaning, she rolled over, propped herself up, then smacked the alarm clock until it ceased its shrieking. With her enemy defeated, she crashed into her pillow and fought the urge to drift back to sleep. Although the thought of joining the waking world disgusted her, she had things to do today.

Rosalyn flung the comforter off and sat up in bed. Her pajamas—which consisted of a half-buttoned flannel shirt and a pair of Dras's boxers she stole before he ever had the chance to try them on—provided little protection against the cool air of the room. She felt a chill on her bare legs as she rose, brushing her tousled auburn locks away from her dark eyes, and scooted to the window to close the curtains, bathing the room in a soft hue of orange morning.

Grabbing a scrunchie as she passed her dresser, Rosalyn gathered her hair into a ponytail. She exited her bedroom and glanced at the cuckoo clock in the kitchen—12:05 p.m.

Ugh. Slept late again. Good job, Roz. At least it's Saturday.

Then the horrible realization hit her. It was Saturday. August twenty-second.

Their birthday.

We were five years old, and it was our birthday.

The emptiness of today fell away, and Rosalyn was five years old again. Dras was sitting on the floor, propping himself up with his arms, watching television after their much celebrated birthday party. With a mischievous smile Rosalyn sat facing Dras, propping herself up with her arms too, and perfectly placing her feet against his. She became his shadow, and everything that Dras did to shoo her away so he could watch his *G.I. Joe* cartoon in peace, she mimicked.

That was her first clear memory of Dras Weldon.

Now it was their birthday again. They were twenty-three today. Only this time they had stepped into some surreal bizarro world—

one in which Dras was in prison and Rosalyn was still stuck in Greensboro, chained to one more ghost.

How things change.

One thing hadn't changed, unfortunately. One tradition would still hold, despite Dras's absence this year. The annual birthday dinner at her mother's house in Trysdale. She snarled in loathing and massaged her forehead.

Rosalyn moved to her refrigerator and opened the door. She grabbed a bottle of water and screwed off the cap. As she chugged the fluid down, she retrieved a bag of corn chips from the cabinet.

Heading for her living room, she ignored the mess that her apartment had become. Between her and Dras, Rosalyn had been the neater of the two. Dras often paid her visits just so he could move something from its designated place. Of course, Rosalyn always noticed and promptly put it back. These days, though, she had abandoned such persnickety habits, and a part of her wondered if maybe it was her feeble attempt at keeping Dras's spirit alive.

Once upon a time she told Dras that she would fall apart without him. She had been joking at the time, but now…

The walls in her room were barren. Once, pictures of her, Dras, and the Weldon family decorated every square inch of free wall space. It only made life harder these days, though, when everywhere she turned, there were more reminders of him.

Why did he have to be such a big part of my life? Why does every photo I own have to hold his goofy grin somewhere in it?

Flopping on the couch, Rosalyn sat cross-legged and rested the bottled water in her lap. She flicked on the television, tried to forget Dras and the obligatory trip she would be taking later to see her mother, and dug around in the bag of chips, fetching a few broken pieces.

While one hand stuffed her drawn face, her other switched through channels at a dizzying pace. She was really in no mood for television this morning, but she felt too miserable to sit in silence. She craved the random bits of sound and images from the droning television set.

Then she saw Dras.

It wasn't until four channels later that she realized it was him. She knew it wasn't anything she hadn't seen before and would not want to see again, but she couldn't help herself. She hadn't seen or heard from him in three months.

It's your own fault.

Her heart racing with anxiety, she flipped back to the channel, hoping to see his face again.

There it was, superimposed over the county courthouse.

"In local news, multiple murderer Dras Weldon, pegged 'The Greensboro Ripper' was transported to Wexler State Penitentiary last night. Weldon was found guilty last week of the murders of both Terrence Joseph 'TJ' Walker and Deputy Dane Adams, seen here."

A photo of Deputy Adams and his little boy replaced Dras on the screen. The deputy was off-duty and decked out in camouflage, and he and the child wore big smiles as they prepared for a father-son hunting trip.

Rosalyn put the corn chips away.

"Authorities also suspect Weldon was responsible for the disappearance of twenty-two-year-old Lindsey McCormick, but there was not enough evidence to convict him on that charge. In fact, the only compelling lead in this rather bizarre case was the eyewitness account of five-year-old Millicent Walker, sister to TJ. She was in the house when Weldon broke into their home and murdered her brother. It was her testimony that sealed the guilty verdict."

Rosalyn felt the bile rise in her throat. The camera cut back to the courthouse.

"This was the scene one week ago at Weldon's sentencing."

The week-old footage showed Dras being escorted out of the courthouse by armed guards, who protected him from the mob of angry parents protesting on the front steps. Malice scarred the faces in the crowd as they clamored over each other to tear at the young man they believed responsible for their loss. Some held signs that bore the last pictures taken of TJ and Lindsey, bearing the slogan "REMEMBER OUR CHILDREN." Others carried homemade banners that read "BURN IN HELL."

The newscaster continued, "Reaction to the verdict seemed unanimous."

There was a quick cut to the elderly Miss Roberta Jenkins, a fixture at the Good Church of the Faithful. "I'm glad they're givin' him the chair!" She nodded in a *yessiree* manner.

"Eye for an eye!" Rosalyn recognized the man with the burly mustache that met his sideburns as Earl Canton. "He's gonna fry for this."

Then a couple of guys who graduated from high school with Rosalyn and Dras showed their grinning mugs. "Yeah," one of the guys said as he adjusted his Miller Gold Beer hat, "we're gonna get a keg, and when they throw that switch, we're gonna party. TJ was a friend of mine. I'd throw the switch myself if they'd let me."

Rosalyn couldn't listen anymore and clicked the television to MUTE.

It was absurd. This was *Dras* they were talking about. The guy couldn't even commit to sit through an entire episode of *Three's Company,* let alone contemplate and carry out an intricate murder plot.

They don't know him. Not like I do.

Do they?

The camera focused on the rage-filled faces in the crowd, and Rosalyn recognized so many of them. Their capacity for hatred astounded her.

Is this my town? Are these the same people who came to me at Dad's funeral and told me that some loving God had a plan?

Hypocrites.

Then one shining face broke through the masses. *Jeff.*

She smiled at the sight of him, a beacon of light in her dark world. The television remained muted as Jeff descended the steps to walk alongside his shackled brother on the long road to the awaiting squad car. And as the angry protestors spat and cursed and hurled their death threats onto Dras, Jeff faced them down. She didn't have to hear what he said. She already knew. It was the same thing he proclaimed to the gathered crowds all summer: Dras was innocent.

At least someone's still fighting for Dras.

The camera zoomed in on Dras as he was stuffed into the backseat of the squad car, confusion on his face, and Rosalyn turned off the television. She stared into the afterglow for a moment.

From its charger next to the couch, the cordless phone pierced the silence. Rosalyn set the bag of corn chips down and picked up the phone. Brushing a few stray strands of hair aside, she placed the receiver to her ear. "Hello?"

"Hey."

She smiled. "*Hey.* I just saw you on television."

"Oh yeah?" Jeff asked. "How'd I look?"

"Same as always."

"That bad, huh?"

She found the strength to smirk. She supposed there was something about the Weldon men that could always cheer her up.

"Listen," Jeff began, the static on his cell phone threatening to drown out his message. "I don't want to take up too much of your time. I just wanted to call and wish you a happy birthday."

17

"Thanks," she said softly. Sincerely. "I really appreciate that."

"Big plans today?"

"I think I'm going to Mom's."

"Ah." Jeff replied, staying clear of the topic.

"Yeah," Rosalyn agreed.

"Well, good luck with that."

"Thanks, I'll need it."

"I'm sure it'll be fine."

"Yeah, me too. Just so long as we don't argue. Or talk. Or look directly at each other for longer than three seconds."

The static was getting worse on Jeff's phone, and his voice took on a hurried tone. "Hey," he said, "there's this thing tomorrow."

"This *thing*?"

"A cookout. Whole town's going to be there. I was thinking maybe I could come pick you up after church and we could go."

Rosalyn got up off the couch and paced uncomfortably.

Jeff continued with a sudden playfulness in his voice, "Better yet, I could come pick you up before church, and you could hear me impart my wisdom to the masses."

She scratched the back of her neck, as if a good excuse for not going was somewhere back there, and if she could just scratch enough… "I don't know."

"Roz…" He was using his big brother voice. "We never see you anymore. Surely you can't stay in your apartment all the time."

"I don't," she defended weakly. "I get out. For work. Groceries."

"And fun? You get out for fun?"

"Not as of late." Then she exhaled. "Not really, no."

"Then, come on. I promise fun will be had by all."

"I…" Rosalyn winced, straining her brain for something she could be doing tomorrow.

The static worsened, and Jeff's voice barely broke through the noise. "Look, my connec…tion's get…ng weak. I'm goi…to have…o go. I'll st…p by after church to pick you up…'K?"

"Jeff," Rosalyn interjected, "I don't think that I—"

Too late. Disconnected.

There goes my Sunday afternoon.

With a groan, she tossed the phone to the couch. Sunday was still a day away, yet. She had enough to worry about today.

Time to go see her mother.

CHAPTER THREE

HELLO? ROSALYN? CAN you hear me?"

Finally, after a few seconds of dead air, Jeff closed his cell phone and hooked it to his belt. Already in a rush, he had no time to hunt down dropped calls. He would just have to trust that Rosalyn got the message.

Jeff hurried into Smokey's, dodging a couple on their way out. Smokey's was a small enough diner, but it served the best steak in town. He nodded to Clancy, the short and portly woman who had owned and operated Smokey's since her husband died in 1992. She waved in return.

"Running a little late today, eh, Reverend?"

He grinned, flushed. "Is he here?"

"In the back. Right on time. Like *usual*."

"Thanks, Clancy."

She turned back to her kitchen duties as Jeff shuffled through the lunch crowd toward the back of the restaurant. As he rounded the corner, he saw his lunch date, Sheriff Hank Berkley.

With the whole town finding reasons to hate the Weldon family these days, true friends were few and far between. Hank was one of the good guys. One of the only ones left in Greensboro, Jeff believed. Finding anyone who had something to say to him besides "Did you ever suspect your brother could do something like that?" was a rarity for Jeff anymore, and he really looked forward to his Saturday lunch meetings with Hank. He suspected they were a welcome break for the sheriff too.

Even when everyone didn't arrive on time.

"Sorry I'm late," Jeff broke the sheriff from eating.

Hank looked up, comically dumbfounded, before realizing his young friend had finally made it. "Oh, Reverend! Didn't see you there. Sit down, sit down."

With a friendly gesture, Hank leaned over and scooted a chair toward Jeff, who sank into it. "I went ahead and ordered your usual,"

Hank noted before dragging a lone fry through a mound of ketchup. "Beef tips and a baked potato."

Jeff laughed. "Thanks."

Hank winked and munched on his fry. "A man after my own heart."

Then Hank paused, looking Jeff over. Jeff had caught a quick glance of himself this morning in the mirror and knew that there were purple shadows under his green eyes and his beard was growing in. Disheveled was not a look that he sported often, and Jeff imagined it must have caught Hank by surprise as he took closer stock of him.

"Hope you don't mind me saying so, Jeff, but you look terrible. You getting enough sleep?"

Jeff settled deeper into his seat. "Uh…yeah. A little bit."

"Bad dreams keeping you up?"

Jeff hesitated and involuntarily glanced around the room. He adjusted his collar. "Yeah, you could say that."

"You know, I had a dream once that I was in a giant hotdog suit in a room full of Doberman pinschers. What does that say about a man?"

Jeff laughed hard. It felt good. The two men were still guffawing when a waiter came and deposited Jeff's meal in front of him.

Famished, Jeff prepared to dive into his food face first, abandoning all civilities. Eager to catch up to Hank, he shoved a forkful of meat into his mouth, barely aware that for the first time in a long time he'd begun eating without saying grace.

Hank must have noticed too. He looked aghast. "Busy day?"

Jeff looked up, his words barely escaping between chews. "Yeah. Me and Iz just got done moving the Monroes."

"They were good people. I hate to see them go."

"Also, it's the twenty-second, Hank. My brother's birthday and I almost *forgot*. Can you believe that?"

Another forkful of meat. More rapid gnawing. Hank snorted in amusement, and a second passed before Jeff realized that it was aimed at him. "Maybe you should slow down," Hank suggested. "Those beef tips aren't going anywhere."

Jeff came to a halt, slowly swallowing his last bite and wiping his mouth with a napkin. "Sorry. It's just that I had to go help Will Baxter with his car, and then we had to work the Duncans' garage sale together. I need to get back before too long, but I've got to go to a church elder meeting right after lunch."

"And how are things working out with your assistant pastor?"

"Fine." Jeff reflected before taking another bite. He chewed, *slowly* this time, swallowed, and continued, "He's still new, you know? Asks me about everything."

"The boy looks up to you."

"I guess. He's eager, I'll give him that. To tell the truth, though, I think I've had *more* work to do since I hired him. But having him around has given me more time to find a lawyer who'll get Dras's case appealed."

Jeff continued to eat. Hank took hold of another greasy fry and plowed it through the ketchup. He bit off the head, his countenance quiet. Jeff noticed the silence of the usually boisterous sheriff.

"What?"

Hank seemed reluctant to continue. "Ah, nothing, really. It's just…" Hank hesitated. "I was hoping that with the trial being over and all, that—"

Jeff set his fork down with a clank, his mood shifting quickly, growing defensive when no attack seemed imminent. "That what, Hank? That I'd slow down? That I'd give up? We talked about this. I thought you were on my side."

"I *am*, Jeff. But Isabella and I have been talking, and…"

Jeff sat back in his chair, feeling attacked. "Are you teaming up on me now?"

Hank waved him off. "No, no, that's not what I'm saying."

"I've been real busy lately, all right?"

"Oh, come on," Hank interjected with a friendly laugh. "You've *always* been a driven man, Jeff. You've got too much of Jack Weldon in you. But lately, it's been worse. You've shut us all out. You've been reclusive, and the only ones you seem interested in talking to are the lawyers. You should be home with Isabella and trying to move on with your lives, not rushing around town in your red cape, solving all of Greensboro's problems."

"Somebody has to," Jeff shot back. He wiped his mouth with his napkin, finished with his meal and the conversation. "The *police* aren't doing such a great job of it."

Hank averted his eyes, stung. "I know this town has let you down, Jeff, but some of us are still trying to do the right thing. Maybe if you would just work with us instead of trying to change Greensboro on your own, we'd get somewhere."

"Greensboro's not my problem anymore, Sheriff. The only thing I can think about right now is freeing my brother. Dras is innocent."

"I know you believe that, but—"

"He *is*. And it's not over until he's *proven* innocent."

Hank frowned at Jeff's clenched-jaw defiance. "Until *you* prove him innocent. Isn't that what you mean to say?"

Jeff had had enough. He stood rigid and fished for his wallet. "Thanks for the lunch, Hank."

Hank waved him off, a feeble attempt at saving their afternoon. "Nah, forget about it. Put your money away, Reverend. I'll get it."

Pride swallowing his heart, Jeff retracted a few bills from his wallet and set them on the table. "I'll get the tip. See you next Saturday," Jeff snapped, then left without a look back. Across the diner he spotted two older men, dressed in suits, watching his exit with interest. It struck him as strange, but he shoved the feeling aside.

CHAPTER FOUR

SOMEWHERE A PHONE rang. "Hello?"

"Our boy's at it again."

"Reverend Weldon?"

"He's causing trouble. Shaking things up."

"I wouldn't worry."

"*I* would. He's relentless. He's bound to find something. What if people start believing him?"

"We've buried the secret for this long. Have faith. Besides, he's only one man."

"He serves a big God."

A pause. "So do we."

CHAPTER FIVE

JEFF SAT, BITING his fingernails, as the meeting continued.

Greensboro was a primarily Christian town—in name, if not in deed—with many denominations sprinkled throughout the community offering a place for every Christian. Methodist, Baptist, Pentecostal, Church of God—every branch of the Christian faith was represented. The elders of each church in Greensboro met at regular meetings, discussing how best to reach their community. Rarely did they agree, but, at the very least, they put forth the effort to remain united.

Today, after the cursory discussions of after-school programs for the upcoming year and plans for Christmas celebrations, an uneasy quiet settled on the fifty gathered men.

"Now," began a balding man by the name of Thorn Parks, raising his voice to draw everyone's attention. He was a Methodist minister and served as the current chairman of the loosely organized board of elders. With all eyes on him, he continued in a quieter tone, "If we can talk a little bit about what's been going on at the Good Church of the Faithful."

Instantly the men turned in their seats, their curious and expectant eyes on Jeff, who continued to chew his fingernails, trying his best to remain invisible. For a brief second, his focus flashed to Leonard Fergus, the elder from his own church, who stood across the room, present to support his young pastor. He was a familiar and pleasant sight, the kind elderly fellow with a grayed goatee who was perpetually dressed in a sweater vest and golf cap. He'd started the church with Jeff's father, Jack, and even after Jack stepped down due to his ailing health, Leonard had stayed behind, a mentor to Jeff in times of trouble.

Help me, Leonard.

"What do you want me to say?" Jeff asked, already feeling defensive after his argument with Hank.

Parks clenched the back of his chair as he stood, fidgeting as if searching for a polite way to voice what they all were thinking. "We hear from Leonard that you're experiencing some problems over there. Losing a lot of your congregation, it sounds like."

"Yeah, we've taken a hit," Jeff replied, short. "But it's summer. We all have low attendance in the summer, right?"

I'm not responsible to these people. How I lead my church is between me and God.

"That's not it, Jeff," Old Moses Brennon, a retired Baptist preacher, shook his head, his jowls quivering. "Your congregation isn't just dwindling. They're leaving town."

"That's not my fault," Jeff said, perhaps too quickly.

"But it is your fault that you've been spending all your time defending your brother." Moses's face reddened.

"What would you have me do, sir? Abandon him? I think enough of us have done that already."

There was a rumble of protest, and Thorn held up his hand, quick to keep the peace. "Let's not get upset here. Jeff, we're just asking questions. We want to know how we can help."

"You could've helped by standing with me during the trial instead of using Dras in your sermons as an example of how not to be a Christian."

Wilford James, the head representative of the Pentecostals of Greensboro, raised a finger. "Can I just say something?" He directed the question at Thorn, still holding to the illusion that this meeting remained civil.

"Go ahead, Wilford," Thorn inclined his head respectfully.

"Jeff, I'm just as guilty of that as anyone, and I acknowledge that. But I won't apologize. Your brother was a notorious drunkard and foolhardy boy who insulted everything you and your father have done for this community."

Jeff seethed and gripped the arm of his chair.

Wilford continued, delicate but determined to make his point, "Now, on trial, he talks about God? About faith? We're just looking at his life, Jeff. The contradictions are there, and this trial has cost all of us members of our congregations. His ravings have hurt the validity of everything we stand for."

Jeff began to squirm in his seat, bouncing his knee. "He's changed," he said flatly. Harsh.

"But for how long?" Thorn finally spoke, revealing his true feelings about the subject. "There are no atheists in foxholes, Jeff. How can you be sure that all this talk of faith isn't just coming from the fact that he's on death row and is terrified? How genuine is this conversion?"

"He's making us look like hypocrites," Moses gruffly barked. "Giving off the wrong impression. You know as well as we all do that when a supposed Christian falls in the spotlight, it hurts everyone—"

"So what do you suggest?" Jeff cut in. "Do we just cut him off from the church? He needs our help."

"He got himself into this mess," Moses huffed and leaned back, holding up his hands in defense. "That's all I have to say about it."

Leonard spoke up, his voice low and soothing. "The church was established to care for those in need."

"*No,*" Moses sternly argued, his back to Leonard, "The church was established to get the gospel of the Lord Jesus Christ to the masses. We can't do that if we've got one of our own—he *says*—a no-good layabout in prison for murder, spouting nonsense about demons!"

Jeff shot forward in his seat, ready to interject, but Moses continued to huff and puff, "And as long as we stand behind a character like this, the community will continue to lose faith in us and people here will never darken the doors of a church again, and then what, Reverend Weldon? What do you suppose we do when that happens?"

"That's just about enough," Thorn reprimanded, visibly shaken by the heated turn of events. "We are not here for name-calling. We have a serious problem in our community, and it doesn't just affect the Good Church of the Faithful; it affects all of us." Thorn turned to the younger man and spoke in a careful, guarded tone. "Jeff, I know Dras is your brother, and you have every right to support him, but I urge you to do it privately, not from the pulpit. We need to be united, now more than ever, in repairing the damage that this trial has done to Greensboro."

"You don't believe him."

"Excuse me?"

Jeff sat straighter, eyeing each man with accusation. "My brother says that demons are in Greensboro, and you don't believe him. Weren't you all there that night when those...those *things* tore up half of Town Square?"

The men eyed the table, ashen faced.

Thorn carefully stated, "Jeff, nobody knows what happened for sure. No one really *saw* anything."

"Dras did."

"But did you?" Wilford asked.

Jeff faltered. No, he hadn't. Only heard the rumors: rumors that began with a pack of stray dogs and ventured into aliens from Mars.

But Dras *had* seen them. He knew the truth. Why wouldn't they listen?

"Dras said they were demons," Jeff glowered. "And the fact that you won't even *consider* it is a bit hypocritical to me, given that we talk about angels and demons, God and the devil, every Sunday."

"Of course we believe in demons, Jeff," Wilford corrected, exasperated. "But…not the kind you can see. Not real, physical creatures. That's just ludicrous."

Jeff made to retort, but before he could, a new voice filled the room.

"I believe him."

The men fell silent, their chairs creaking as they turned their attention to Father Joseph Molina. Father Joe was the priest at St. Dunstan's in Russellville. The Catholics in Greensboro were too few in number to form their own congregation and traveled to nearby Russellville for services. On behalf of his Greensboro parishioners, Father Joe faithfully attended these summit meetings, bearing a smile and a cup of coffee from the E-Z Mart on the old highway into town, ready to offer his assistance should it ever be needed. Most regarded him as the quiet priest in the back who spoke very little.

But today Father Joe had something to say.

Moses guffawed, "I never thought I'd see the day when the Catholics were more willing to believe in demons than the Pentecostals."

This incited laughter from everyone but Wilford, who looked flustered that his point had been missed, and Father Joe, who looked away as though embarrassed that he'd said anything at all.

Jeff wasn't laughing either. He looked appreciatively at Father Joe, his heart grateful that someone had taken his side. He, like most of the board of elders, rarely spoke to the priest beyond a polite "Hi, how's Russellville these days?" But now he found himself wanting to talk more with the father, just to have a conversation with someone who didn't think he was crazy.

The laughter in the room carried for a while, as the elders clung to the moment of good humor. When the mirth died down, Thorn began with a fading chuckle, "I think we've debated the issue enough. What's important is that we present the proper image to the community, to bring them in at all costs. If that means that some of us have to curb our tongues or stifle our own personal views, then I think that's a necessary sacrifice. We have to think of the town right now and help them to see that the church is a safe place with sane, rational people."

Jeff didn't wait for Thorn to dismiss them. He simply walked out, fed up with the lot of them. The others watched him go, no one attempting to stop him, until Thorn said, "All right, gentlemen. That's all."

Jeff had the blinding urge to smoke a cigarette. He hadn't had a cigarette since he was in high school, stealing smoke breaks with Kyle Rogers out behind the field house after third period. He'd been a different person then, rebellious and angry. But now, as he paced along the steps of the First Presbyterian Church's Fellowship Hall, he felt a bit of that old self resurfacing.

Kyle Rogers. He recalled the shaggy face of his old high school buddy. *Haven't thought of him in a long time.*

Despite his anger, his smile softened at the memory of old friends and simpler times.

"Jeff?"

Startled, Jeff turned to see Leonard Fergus leaning on his cane as he descended the steps.

"Mr. Fergus." Jeff sighed, his mind crashing back to the present and the rude impression he had left with the others.

"Surprised to see you're still here," the old man admitted.

"Just trying to blow off some steam before I go back to the Duncans' garage sale." Jeff hesitated, embarrassed to continue. "I'm sorry about that back there."

Leonard waved him off and kept walking, as if Jeff had made no great offense. "Nah. Forget about it. Those buzzards wouldn't be happy unless they had something to fuss about. You just made their day."

Jeff grinned, but he still felt regret over his behavior. "I guess I'd better get going before they all come out."

"The church will get through this, Jeff," Fergus smiled at his young charge. "Your father had his fair share of problems too, but we'll work something out."

It felt good to be compared to his father, to know that Jack Weldon had been through hard times and emerged victorious. It gave Jeff hope, which was something sadly lacking in his life ever since the judge declared Dras guilty and sentenced him to die.

"Thanks, Mr. Fergus."

Waving, Jeff moved to his truck and cranked the engine, pulling out of the parking lot just as the other church leaders emerged from the building. He caught sight of Father Joe exiting with the others, neglected and withdrawn, and thought to swing back around to speak to him privately. But fear of getting into another argument with the others stayed his hand, and he continued on, leaving the elders behind.

CHAPTER SIX

FOLLOWING HIS UPSETTING lunch date with the reverend, Sheriff Hank Berkley meandered into the sheriff's station to find the place in chaos. Deputies hurried around, filing paperwork, rushing out to calls, and shouting over each other. Before the Greensboro Ripper incident, the only cases these deputies had to worry about were someone stealing tomatoes out of a neighbor's yard or a DUI following the Big Game. Yet since that night three months ago, when the townspeople reported seeing "strange creatures"—the night Deputy Dane Adams was killed—things were getting progressively busier.

Before Hank had a chance to find his office and take a load off, Ray McCormick entered the building, eyes wild and searching. Hank marveled at how much Ray had changed since his daughter, Lindsey, disappeared. The poor man didn't appear as though he'd slept in days, perhaps weeks. His beard was growing in coarse and wild, and the incredibly dark circles under his eyes made him almost unrecognizable. Had he not made a weekly routine of checking up on his daughter's case every Saturday, Hank might not have known it was Ray at all.

"Sheriff Berkley," Ray gasped in urgent, breathless hysteria, reaching out with a trembling hand. "Have you heard any word on my daughter?"

Hank's heart broke. Lindsey was dead. They hadn't found a body when they pulled her car out of the thick mire of Greensboro Park Lake, but everyone knew she was dead. The trial was over. The case was closed. But Ray would not accept that. He had become a roaming phantom, tirelessly stapling more and more MISSING posters on storefronts and telephone poles, replacing those that had been torn down or destroyed by the elements.

Hank began as he had every Saturday afternoon since the beginning of the summer, "I wish I had something to tell you, but I don't."

And once again Hank watched Ray's face linger over the landscape of hope, until his words brought it crashing into the pit of despair.

"Oh," Ray said, playing his well-rehearsed part in the weekly tragedy. "I understand. Well…if you find out anything—"

"I'll let you know," Hank gently interrupted.

Ray nodded in remorse and began to move for the door. However, unlike the other times Ray visited, he stopped and turned to the sheriff, breaking from the expected.

"The man on the phone will help me."

Then Ray was gone, leaving Sheriff Berkley wondering what that was all about. He thought about it all the way to his office—

"Excuse me?"

Startled, Hank looked up to see a young man in his path.

"I'm looking for Sheriff Berkley."

The man was probably in his early to midthirties. Windswept hair. Bright blue eyes. Clean cut, though not so handsome that he appeared perfect. Hank thought he resembled a young Robert Redford. He wore a dark trench coat despite the summer's heat, and his smile seemed to warm Hank—who hadn't realized he was cold until that moment—down to his soul.

Hank, who never met a stranger, smiled in kind. "Well, you've found him. What can I do for you, son?"

The young man quickly extended a hand, eager to make a good first impression. "Special Agent Christopher Perdu. I've been assigned to the Greensboro Ripper case."

A Fed, Hank grimaced. Hank took Christopher's hand warily, and they shook on the introduction. "Sheriff Hank Berkley. Good to meet you."

Wow, what a grip. You can always tell a man by his handshake. He liked this Perdu already, although—

"Little late for an investigation, don't you think?"

Christopher smiled. "He hasn't been executed yet. I'd say there's still time."

"Yeah, well, that's a matter of opinion." Then, stepping aside to reveal the open door to his cluttered office, Sheriff Berkley gestured. "Come on in and have a seat."

"Thank you."

Hank closed the door behind them as Christopher sat down in the chair Deputy Adams used to occupy before he was ripped to pieces. Hank frowned in grim reflection, then rounded the corner to sit behind his desk. This kid seemed all right, but overcoats made him anxious. *Feds. Think they can come into my town and show me how things are done.*

"To tell you the truth," Sheriff Berkley began as he eased his large frame into the cracked leather seat that whistled as he made contact, "I wasn't expecting the FBI to send anyone down. I thought folks forgot all about Greensboro when they moved the highway."

The special agent turned to the blitzkrieg of officers on the other side of the Venetian blinds. "Lot of people upset around here. You can always tell when there's just been a murder trial."

"I never thought it'd tear up the folks like it has."

"People tend to lose their judgment when the ones they love are hurting."

The two men nodded in agreement, and then Christopher leaned closer as if to cut to the meat of the matter. "What *happened* here, Sheriff?"

Hank sighed, feeling solely responsible for the declining state of his community.

"I've asked myself that question a lot lately and can't rightly come up with a good enough answer."

"Why don't you give it your best shot?" Christopher urged, his face eager.

Hank paused, reluctant to delve into personal musings with a stranger, but found himself wanting to confide in this young man. *Guy's got a face you can trust.*

Even if he was a Fed.

"Greensboro wasn't always like this. We used to be good, decent people. As a matter of fact, I've seen most of these people headed for church on Sunday morning." Sadly, Hank reflected, "I guess folks aren't acting too Christian-like these days."

"Going to church makes you as much a Christian as going to a garage makes you a car."

Hank chuckled. "I guess."

"There's a lot more to being a child of God than most people understand."

"I wouldn't know," Hank chortled, uncomfortably.

Christopher ventured, "Do you mind if I ask why?"

"Look, friend, don't get me wrong. I've been to my share of church services on Easter and Christmas. I'm sure there is some God out there watching everything, but..." Hank trailed off, feeling he had already said too much.

Christopher only smiled. "You got it all wrong, Sheriff. He's not out there watching. He's right here with us."

Hank shifted awkwardly, put off by the man's overt religiosity. "To each his own, I guess."

There was a brief, awkward silence before Perdu's Fed mind

changed to all business. "Tell me about Dras Weldon. The Greensboro Ripper."

Relieved to be in more familiar and impersonal territory, Hank was all too happy to oblige. "The popular opinion is that he murdered his ex-girlfriend, Lindsey McCormick, and her boyfriend, TJ Walker, in some sort of jealous rage. He resisted arrest and, in the process, murdered my deputy." Hank paused at the memory of Dane. His friend, now gone.

Christopher nodded, taking it all in. "That's the official story. Now, what's the truth?"

"Dras did it. Just like the courts decided. Just like little Millie Walker said in her testimony." Then, in case the new guy was confused, Hank clarified, "TJ's little sister. She saw Dras murder her brother in their home and flee."

"Did they find any evidence on the brother's body?"

"They didn't find the body."

The agent raised his eyebrows, and Sheriff Berkley explained, "When we got there, all we found were signs of a struggle in the kitchen and that poor little girl rocking back and forth in the hallway, holding a flashlight." Hank looked away, feeling his throat tighten. "Merciful heavens, I hate to think what this has done to her. She's hardly spoken a word since it all happened..." Hank grew quiet, thinking of the Walker family, of Ray, of all the sadness that the people of Greensboro were carrying around.

Finally, breaking the intense silence, Christopher assured the old sheriff, "I don't want to cause any trouble, Sheriff Berkley."

Hank nodded with a friendly smile, though not too friendly. He still wasn't sure who this Perdu guy was or what exactly he was up to in Greensboro. However, it was better to be polite and play the "good ol' sheriff" than to earn the ire of the government variety.

Christopher continued calmly but with a certain enthusiasm. *Must be new to the Bureau. Great, they send some wet-behind-the-ears recruit down here to "help" my town.*

"I'm not here to impose or invade your jurisdiction. I just want to find the truth. I hope we can work together on this."

Hank agreed, seeing no immediate harm in allowing the kid to hang around. "All right. But I warn you. Folks around here don't take too kindly to having their 'popular opinions' challenged."

"Oh, don't worry," Christopher grinned, "neither does the rest of the world."

CHAPTER SEVEN

AFTER DRAGGING HERSELF through a shower and a quick fill-up at the E-Z Mart on the old highway, Rosalyn was on her way to Trysdale.

Little more than a neighborhood, Trysdale rested nine miles outside the Greensboro city limits, and if even a hundred people called it home, Rosalyn would have been surprised. There was absolutely nothing in Trysdale except a handful of houses, a one-pump gas station that went out of business six years ago, and a post office. Rosalyn grew up in one of Trysdale's rundown two-story farmhouses, something that, if restored, would have made a wonderful bed-and-breakfast. Despite the unkempt houses, it was beautiful country out here. Cows grazed and an old couple who lived down one of the county roads gave local kids horse rides. Rosalyn recalled that Isabella Weldon's father lived around here somewhere, fixing up old motorcycles.

Rosalyn passed Greensboro Park Lake where they said Lindsey McCormick was murdered. She shook off a chill and turned left off the old highway. Rounding the curve, she entered Trysdale. A whole new world. One she had longed to forget.

The historic houses that stood as monuments to the first settlers in Maribel County rotted in disrepair. Discarded appliances were strewn about the overgrown yards amidst lawn gnomes and weathered black-faced jockey statuettes. Broken windows that no one saw fit to repair stared back at her from abandoned buildings, and long dead cars rested eternally on cinder blocks outside vine-covered old sheds.

"Home sweet home," Rosalyn muttered as she looked into the faces of elderly ladies, perpetually in their nightgowns, watering their sun-yellowed lawns.

Was this to be her fate as well?

Trysdale Trash. That was what they always called her in town.

Trysdale Trash.

Rosalyn turned up the radio in her car, listening to the band

Hooverphonic, hoping to drown out the emotions a trip to Trysdale always stirred. *I'm making this harder than it has to be. It's just my birthday. All I have to do is go to Mom's, pretend like we're the best of girlfriends, eat some cake to humor Annie, and then I can go back to Greensboro.*

Did the sound of going back to Greensboro really lift her spirits? This was bad. She took a deep breath. *I can do this.*

She spotted her mother's old, imposing giant of a house looming before her. Thinking of the ghosts within its walls set her heart beating so violently it nearly tore open her sternum. A lump rose in her throat, and she swallowed hard.

"I can't do this."

But she had no choice. She was already in the driveway. She spotted the old tire swing that still hung from the oak tree in their front yard. Warm memories of pushing Annie in that swing reminded Rosalyn that life had not always been so hard. She remembered when she was young and waited every day for her father to come home from work. Little Rosalyn used to laugh as she jumped into his arms, and Daddy would whirl her around and ask her all about her day. And, of course, she answered all his questions, telling him more than he probably ever wanted to know, but he always listened. He always had time for her.

As Rosalyn turned off her car engine, resigned to try her best to be civil, Annie emerged from the house. "Roz!"

Rosalyn stepped out of the car and held out her arms, and Annie slammed into them. They held each other tight, and Rosalyn suddenly felt strangely glad to be home, despite her previous trepidations. Pulling Annie away at arm's length, Rosalyn took a good look at her sister.

Annie turned fourteen this year and was maturing from a little girl into a young woman. She stood two inches taller than Rosalyn and skinny as a beanpole. She wore a pink baby doll tee bearing a glittery butterfly and khaki shorts, revealing that her tastes in fashion had changed yet again. As always, her hair was untouched and hung to the small of her back. Her hazel eyes sparkled with dreams of the future, and her smile was infectious. Annie Myers was absolutely cuddle-worthy, braces and all, and Rosalyn couldn't have been more proud of her.

"Look at you. You're all grown up."

"Does that mean I can drive your car?"

Rosalyn laughed. "Not *that* grown up."

The two sisters giggled and hugged again, but their reunion was interrupted. "Rosalyn?"

Annie stepped out of the way, leaving Rosalyn face-to-face with her mother. There was a look of surprise on Meredith Myers's heavily made-up face, and Rosalyn wondered if maybe she had come a little early. Or maybe her mother was just surprised that she had come *at all*. Annie stood by tensely, looking to each woman. Meredith held out her arms and came closer to the birthday girl. "It's good to have you home."

She stopped, however, just before she reached Rosalyn, as if waiting for permission to touch her daughter. Rosalyn smiled awkwardly, and for Meredith that was enough. She drew closer, and Rosalyn allowed her a hug.

"Happy birthday, sweetheart."

Her mother squeezed, but Rosalyn did little more than just stand there. She felt bad for that and tried to feel warm inside. She wanted to enjoy being in her mother's loving arms, welcomed home even after the harsh words that had been said so often between the two. She wanted to be happy to be reunited with her family and to be loved.

Shouldn't this be making me feel something? It should be stirring my heart or something, right? Right?

But there was nothing. Rosalyn felt nothing at all.

Dinner went well, if barely eating one's dinner and only daring to glance at the others around the table for little more than a second could be considered "well."

Of course, her mother made spaghetti, Rosalyn's favorite. She always made spaghetti on B-Day. After Rosalyn finished off what little she was craving, she spent the rest of the meal chopping the remains of her noodles into tiny bits and scooping them into separate camps on the ceramic plate. The dinner table oddly mirrored the noodle bits as Rosalyn and her mother sat at opposite ends of the table with Annie caught in between, each woman keeping to herself.

It was good to see Annie again, and, all in all, her mother was looking better these days as well. Once upon a time, people said Meredith Myers was just as beautiful as Rosalyn was now—a five-foot-three, one-hundred-five-pound knockout with dark hair, wide, soulful eyes, and dangerous curves. But after bearing two children and establishing binge drinking as an Olympic sport, Rosalyn supposed time caught up with her. Still, the woman looked more put together than the last time Rosalyn saw her, and at least she was sober. Anyway, Rosalyn knew that it was never Meredith's beauty that garnered her a place among the elite of Greensboro's high society. She still had her wit and charm, and she was always fun at a party. *But no one ever really forgets that you're Trysdale Trash.*

And no matter how much Meredith seemed to fit in, that would be the name her rich friends would call her behind her back until the day she died.

The same name they called Rosalyn.

"Do you like the spaghetti?"

Rosalyn nearly jumped at the sound of her mother's voice. She looked up to see Meredith waiting anxiously for an answer. Rosalyn managed a weak smile. "It's fine."

Meredith tittered nervously, "I tried not to go overboard with the garlic. I know how you don't like too much garlic."

"It's fine, Mom. Really."

That seemed to do. Meredith lowered her head and went back to stirring her spaghetti around the plate. "So," she began, trying to sound casual, "how did your first session with Doctor Altman go? Well, I hope?"

Rosalyn shrugged. "I don't know. Maybe you should ask him. He's the shrink."

"A *therapist*. I think it could be really good for you, Rosalyn, if you let it."

Rosalyn remained quiet, refusing to continue the conversation. Finally, the pressure was too much for Meredith. She set her fork down abruptly and looked up, trying again to establish normality. "Maybe I should get the cake out."

Annie, who until now had silently watched her mother and older sister awkwardly attempt some semblance of a relationship, quickly finished her last mouthful of pasta and volunteered. "I'll help, Mom." She dabbed the corners of her mouth with her napkin and hopped out of her chair.

Their mother rose too, and she and Annie gathered up the dinner dishes. Rosalyn watched her little sister with a smile. Annie: the Dutiful Daughter. Always ready to be of help. Always there for her mother.

"I don't know how it will taste," Meredith teased. "Your sister helped me bake it."

Annie laughed and rolled her eyes. "*Mom.*"

The two of them shared in their private joke as they carried the dishes into the kitchen.

Rosalyn was happy for her sister. A part of her wished that she could be more supportive of their mother. Closer to her, like Annie was. But she was never very good at being a daughter.

"Did Annie tell you?" Meredith returned with the cake and Rosalyn looked up from her lap. "Annie's started babysitting for some of the couples from the club."

The Country Club, Rosalyn assumed. *Mom and her rich friends.* They didn't know the real Meredith Myers—the one who was always drunk and swore and talked bad about her husband for dying and leaving her alone with two daughters to raise. *You've got them fooled, Mom, but not me.*

Rosalyn shook her head, pondering her mother's duplicity, though Annie seemed pleased with herself for making a mark with the higher echelons of Greensboro's social ladder. She and Meredith exchanged an almost giddy smile, both proud.

Rosalyn smirked. "That's great, Annie. Maybe one day when I have some neglected children of my own, I'll let you babysit for me."

Meredith paused, disapproving of the rather off-color comment, but Annie didn't offer a retort. She continued to place candles on the birthday cake but kept a close eye on her mother, making sure things were still stable.

"Why do you always have to be so cynical, Rosalyn?" Meredith began to light the candles.

The remark hit a nerve, not because what her mother said was so terrible, but because Rosalyn was so sure she and her mother would fight. She was already prepared.

Maybe a bit *too* prepared. Maybe eager.

"Mom, it's OK." Annie placated.

"Consider my example, *Mother*," Rosalyn bit back, ignoring her sister.

Meredith slammed her hands on the table, causing Annie to jump. Rosalyn casually turned to face her mother, amused by the small outburst.

Meredith did not face her embittered daughter as she spoke. "I may not have been the world's greatest mother, but I did my best. I am *still* your mother, and I deserve some respect."

Rosalyn unsuccessfully fought back a sarcastic chuckle.

"Let's please not do this." Annie sounded much older than she was. "It's Roz's birthday. Let's just have a good time. *Please*?"

It was a desperate plea, and for a moment, the two women

conceded. After Annie finished properly placing and lighting the candles, Meredith set the cake before Rosalyn. Annie followed, struggling to keep the room in good spirits. She began to sing "Happy Birthday" and nudged her mother to join in. Rosalyn kept her eyes low and focused on the intensity of the candles' flames.

When the song ended at last, Annie chimed in, "Make a wish."

Rosalyn had to admire her sister's determination not to spoil the day and leaned into the candles to make good on the silly tradition.

That was about the time her mother breathed, "It doesn't quite seem the same without Dras here."

Rosalyn froze.

Abandoning her birthday wish, Rosalyn exhaled loudly and leaned back in her seat. "*Thanks*, Mom."

"What? I just meant—"

"I know what you meant."

"Is that so? You must be a pretty smart girl then. You seem to know an awful lot about what I mean and what I'm thinking."

"Whatever." Rosalyn looked away.

"No. I am tired of you waltzing in here with this chip on your shoulder, like the whole world's against you. Life isn't as bad as you'd like to make it out to be."

Rosalyn stood. "You know *nothing* about my life."

"Yes." Meredith seemed sincerely hurt. "I do. Because it was *my* life. And if you don't change something soon, you're going to turn out just like me."

"I'm nothing like you. If you knew me at all—"

"How could I? You haven't given me a chance to know you!"

"I gave you plenty of chances, Mom. Seventeen *years*."

"You keep pushing me away, Rosalyn."

"I push *everyone* away. What should make you so different?"

"I'm your mother."

"I'm not twelve, anymore, *Mom*. I can take care of myself."

"You seem to be doing a bang-up job of it. Look at you! You come in here dressed like a tramp. It's no wonder you're always getting into so much trouble."

Rosalyn regarded her attire, from her Mary Jane clodhoppers to her tight, hip-hugger jeans and on to the leather jacket that partially covered a rather revealing tank top.

"At least I only *look* like a tramp."

That was when her mother slapped her.

It wasn't until after the fact that Meredith realized what had happened. Instantly, as if her face had been the offended party, she shrank back in horror. Rosalyn set her jaw, holding in any kind of reaction. Mother and daughter stood frozen, both of them shocked into silence.

"Stop it!" Annie screamed, tears coming to her eyes. "Stop fighting! I hate it when you fight! I hate you! I *hate* you!"

Sobbing, Annie ran upstairs to her room.

Meredith and Rosalyn were left alone to face each other. Meredith remained quiet, as if paralyzed by fear and guilt.

"I'll go check on her," Rosalyn offered.

Annie slammed the door to her room and rushed to her stereo. She punched a button, and a screaming cacophony of teen angst shrieked over the speakers. She took the wicker chair from her small desk, faced it toward her window, and flopped down. Crossing her arms, she fumed with her back to her door and her family.

She hated them for always ruining things. For never trying to get along. For hating each other.

Look at me! I'm such a stupid little crybaby. Annie bit her lip until it hurt, punishing herself for crying. *Why can't I be stronger?* There was a knock at the door, and she rushed to wipe her tears away.

"Go away!"

"If you say so." Rosalyn's muffled voice came from the other side of the door.

The door opened and Rosalyn marched in. Annie rolled her eyes and spun to her sister. "I told you to go away."

"Oh." Rosalyn smirked. "I thought you said, 'Come in.'"

Annie shook her head in frustration, and Rosalyn cracked a smile. "Your music was too loud. I couldn't hear you."

In a huff Annie discarded the wicker chair and charged the stereo, mashing the power button. "*There.* Better?"

Rosalyn coolly replied, "Much. Thanks."

With a sigh loud enough to wake the dead, Annie sat on the bed while Rosalyn stood emotionless. Annie faced the wall, trying to blink back her tears as Rosalyn took a seat on the bed next to her.

Rosalyn said, "I'm sorry, Annie."

"It's *Anne*. No one calls me Annie anymore."

"This was all my fault. I shouldn't have—"

Annie swiveled to her sister. "Why do you have to be so mean to her?"

"I said I was sorry."

"She's really trying, Roz. She hasn't had a drink in six weeks. Did you know that?"

Rosalyn paused, frowning. "No. No, I didn't know that."

"Ever since…" Annie spoke carefully. "Ever since what happened to Dras…she's been trying to quit so that she could be there for you."

Rosalyn felt sick, humiliated by what she'd done. *Is Mom really trying to change? Is she really doing it for me?*

She held out her arms, and Annie climbed into them. She held Annie as the confused girl wept, and if she hadn't gone into the room expressly to be a comfort, Rosalyn would have cried too.

Moments later Rosalyn walked down the stairs, her arm around Annie. By now Annie's tears had dried, leaving her face red and puffy. Rosalyn still kept her emotions to herself.

Meredith Myers sat at the kitchen table, Rosalyn's lonely birthday cake shoved to the side. Her face was wet and pressed into her folded hands. Quiet sobs emanated from the room as Rosalyn carefully entered. She gestured for Annie to stay back for a second and approached their mother.

Gently she placed a hand on her mother's shoulder, ready to ease the woman's pain and maybe, just maybe, put their family back together. At her daughter's sudden touch, Meredith jerked to face her, then quickly wiped at her moist cheeks, embarrassed.

Rosalyn said, "Think we can try again?"

Meredith answered her with a wide smile, her brow cinching up as if she were about to cry all over again. "I'd like that."

Rosalyn grinned as Meredith jumped up from her seat, wiping tears away. She was filled with a new vigor that took ten years off her formerly worried face.

"I'll cut the cake," Meredith said.

Annie slid beside Rosalyn and gave her older sister a squeeze. It felt good. Who would have thought that, in the middle of this trying time, she'd find solace in her *family* of all places?

While she mused over this irony, Rosalyn glanced through the sheer embroidered drapes into the front yard.

And saw the man standing there.

For one heart-stopping moment she thought it was her father, back from the dead and ready for her to run out and jump into his arms again. Then, upon second glance, she realized that the reality of the situation was far more terrifying.

It was that strange man from The Rave Scene.

Dras's bogeyman. The Strange Man.

No...

He stood there, that cavalier grin stretched across his beautiful face, and in one fluid motion raised his hand, waved his fingers, then vanished from sight.

Rosalyn's blood ran cold.

"Honey?"

The sound of her mother's voice startled Rosalyn, but she quickly regained her composure.

"Are you all right?"

Rosalyn turned and met the expectant faces of her sister and mother. In a mad attempt at regaining the peace she experienced only a moment ago, Rosalyn grinned, flustered. "Yeah. I'm OK. It was nothing."

But in her heart she knew.

He found me.

CHAPTER EIGHT

THE SUN HAD begun to set as twilight usurped the sky. Jeff had just finished dropping off the last load of the unsold furniture from the Duncans' garage sale at the Mission Outreach, and now he and his beat-up truck were *ker-klunking* their way toward the last stop of the day: home.

Their *new* home, anyway.

As the congregation of the Good Church of the Faithful dwindled, Sunday offerings declined, and so did Jeff's salary, until at last he and Isabella were forced to sell their beloved house on Grover's Pond. Now they were living in a run-down brownstone on the East Side of town. Once, they were surrounded by the pond, oaks swaying in the breeze, and chirping nighttime insects; now they were boxed in by chain-link fences and barking dogs, teenage mothers and their yelling alcoholic boyfriends.

And The Rave Scene. The place that claimed his brother.

"It's OK," Isabella frequently told him. "It's not the best place to live, but if God put us here, it's for a reason. Maybe He put us here to reach out to these people before it's too late."

Too late. I was too late to help Dras.

A thought of Dras crept into his brain, but only briefly, before he refused to entertain it. Keeping his course, Jeff reflected on what a long day it had been. He wanted nothing more than to go to bed, but he and Isabella had a date tonight—their first date in ages—and he was determined not to miss it.

His cell phone rang.

He groaned and rested his head on the steering wheel in frustration before answering. Slipping the phone from its clip on his belt, he sighed, "Hello?"

"Reverend Weldon? It's me. Will."

Since Will had been hired as assistant pastor, he had been personally responsible for 95 percent of the calls to Jeff's cell phone, yet he still insisted on identifying himself.

"What is it, Will?"

"I'm afraid we have a bit of an emergency at the church, sir."

"What's wrong?"

"Tabitha Banks."

Jeff recognized the name. Tabitha was a single mother raising infant twins. Her boyfriend was in and out of her life and refused to pay child support, and she was still in the process of applying for government assistance. If she was at the church, it meant only one thing: she wanted money.

"Can't you handle it, Will? I've got plans tonight."

"I'm afraid she insists on speaking to *you*, sir."

Jeff pulled up to a STOP sign. He paused as he stopped his truck, thinking of what he should do. In a poetic twist of fate, to his right lay the road that led to Isabella. And to his left lay the road that would eventually lead him to the front doors of the Good Church of the Faithful.

Will waited for his decision on the other end. "Sir?"

Jeff was torn, so close to home. So close to his wife, who was waiting for him. He shut his eyes and mumbled, "I'm on my way."

"I'll tell her, sir. Thank you."

Will's appreciation did little to lift his spirits. He ended the call and turned left at the stop sign. As he began to pick up speed again, heading for the church, he dialed his house.

Isabella answered. "Hello?"

"Hey."

Isabella frowned, Jeff's light-hearted tone usually a good indication that something was about to go wrong with their plans. "Oh, no."

"No, wait. I didn't forget."

"But?"

"Something came up at the church."

"Jeff…"

"It'll only take a minute, and I'll be *right* home. I promise."

Isabella said nothing.

"You didn't already make supper, did you?"

She hesitated as her heart sank. "No."

"Great," Jeff brightened. "If I'm not there by the time the movie starts, go on to the theater without me and I'll meet you there, OK?"

She nodded before she finally replied, "Sure."

"OK. I'll see you in a minute."

Then he hung up.

Isabella quietly hung up the phone and turned toward the kitchen where a candlelit dinner was waiting on the table. With a heavy heart, she began to clear Jeff's place.

She was going to be eating alone tonight.

Jeff pulled into the church parking lot, his truck emitting a low groan as he shifted into PARK. Not wanting to keep Isabella waiting any longer than was absolutely necessary, Jeff hurried up the steps and through the doors.

Tabitha Banks—young and unattractive with bruised arms and dark roots peeking through her greasy, dishwater blonde hair—held her crying twin boys as she sat in one of the pews, facing outward. She had an expectant look on her face, waiting impatiently for her savior to arrive. Will stood next to her and rushed to Jeff when he saw his mentor make his entrance.

Will was a young, worried sort of man with white-blond hair and wire-rimmed glasses who always dressed more professionally than needed for his position. He met Jeff halfway, all business, as if they were going to discuss national security rather than Tabitha Banks.

"I'm glad you came, sir. Thank you."

Jeff patted Will on the shoulder as he pushed past him. He approached Tabitha and knelt in front of her. Her mascara streaked her thin face, and her eyes and nose were still red from crying.

"Are you OK?" Jeff said.

That was all the invitation she needed. She began to wail, trying to make her needs heard over her children's howls. "It's Danny!"

The boyfriend and father of the twins, if Jeff remembered correctly.

"We got into a big fight last night, and then he left, and I've looked everywhere for him all day, and I can't find him! Something's happened to him! I *know* it!"

Jeff took a deep breath. Either Danny was in serious trouble or he was just drunk and skipping town for a few days, as he was known to do, taking all of Tabitha's money with him. Money she didn't have. Money she kept "borrowing" from the church.

Jeff patiently listened as Tabitha finished. "He's got all my money, and now we don't have enough for formula or diapers or food! How are my babies supposed to *live*?"

He patted her knee and forced a smile. "It'll be OK, Tabitha. Just calm down."

She nodded, holding back dramatic tears, and Jeff stood to have an aside with his assistant pastor.

"What are we going to do?" Will spoke in hushed tones, watching as Tabitha hugged her crying babies to her as if their very fate hung in the balance.

Jeff rubbed his temples. "We give her the money."

"But, sir, she could be—"

"Lying? I know. And maybe she is. But those babies still need to eat. I have to do something."

Will pursed his lips, solemn.

"How much money do we have in benevolence?" Jeff asked, fearing the answer.

"I checked the books earlier. We don't even have enough to pay this month's bills. With Mr. and Mrs. Monroe leaving, we don't have anything extra."

Jeff sighed. The Good Church of the Faithful was going broke, and fast. He turned and gave Tabitha—who was wearing her best desperate look—a once-over before turning back to Will. Discreetly, so she could not see, Jeff pulled out his own wallet and took out his last twenty dollars. Will's eyes went wide.

"Sir? Are you sure?"

Jeff didn't even bother with an answer. He turned back to Tabitha and knelt before her again. He gave her the twenty-dollar bill, and she snatched it from his hand as if it had always belonged to her.

"Here you go," Jeff said as he smiled wanly. "This will be enough to buy diapers and some baby food. But that's it. Do you understand, Tabitha? Nothing else."

She nodded, getting his drift. "OK, Reverend. Thank you."

With her twenty dollars scored, Tabitha collected her children and left without a whimper, her tears instantly dried. Jeff watched her go, and Will joined his side.

"That was a good thing you did, sir."

"We do what has to be done." Jeff took no joy in the selfless deed.

Kevin Costner was all right. Not Isabella's favorite, though. Jeff was always a big fan. He even liked *Waterworld*.

Isabella checked her watch for the fifteenth time. The movie was nearing the half-hour mark, and still there was no sign of her husband. She was a beautiful woman sitting all alone on a Saturday night. Over the summer she cut her long hair and now sported a shorter 'do that stopped just above her shoulders. As summer lingered and she found herself out in the sun more, the natural highlights in her hair intensified. Her dark skin perfectly complimented the new burgundy dress she bought just for this very occasion.

But alas, no one was there to appreciate it in the darkened theater. No one but Kevin Costner, and he was enraptured by his red-headed love interest.

At this point Isabella really had no idea what the movie was about. She had spent thirty minutes watching it, but her mind was out wherever Jeff was. A crack of light, cast across the wall in front of her, told her that someone had entered the theater. She spun in her seat to see someone approaching her in the shadows. She could tell by the person's gait that it was a man. *Jeff.* Her lips formed a wide smile. Sure, he was late, but it didn't matter. She just wanted him here. With her.

The man was close now, but at just the time she was about to welcome him, he kept walking. And took a seat five rows in front of her.

Not Jeff. She frowned and slid down into her seat. Checked her watch again. Dug around in her popcorn. Wallowed in her disappointment.

After seeing that Tabitha's financial crisis was handled, Will left for the night, but Jeff couldn't resist the urge to peek into his office before he went to meet Isabella at the theater. The mail for the day had arrived and with it a barrage of bills for the church. Piles of unopened envelopes rested upon the other scattered papers cluttering the top of his desk, and he sat down for a moment to look them over. He checked the clock on the wall in his office—6:31. He had a good thirty minutes before he had to meet Isabella at the theater. With his sturdy letter opener in hand, Jeff went to the soul-sucking task of seeing how much was owed this month. The numbers blurred after a while, and only one thing remained certain: there was more demand than supply.

"Looks like I'm taking another pay cut," he mumbled. It was a wonder the church could afford to pay Will anything at all.

"Hello, Reverend." A deep, raspy voice broke the quiet.

Startled, Jeff looked to the door. Before him was the warm, cocoa-colored face of Leonard Fergus. With the help of his cane, Leonard entered the study, and Jeff relaxed, glad to see him for the second time today. "Mr. Fergus."

The old man shooed away the remark as he lazily took a seat in the chair opposite Jeff's desk. "How many times have I told you—"

Jeff laughed. "Leonard, Leonard. Right. I know."

Leonard Fergus had served as chairman of the board of deacons at the Good Church of the Faithful since Jeff's father, Jack Weldon, started the church. When Jeff was younger, Mr. Fergus always held conversations with the boy, talking to him as though he were an equal. That was something Jeff always loved about the old man. Yet despite the warm memories and the fact that he was now an adult, Jeff could never bring himself to comfortably call Mr. Fergus by his first name.

"Been looking for you," the man said.

Jeff tittered, anxious. "Am I in trouble?"

"Nah."

Jeff sorted through the mess on his desk, and Leonard pointed toward the bills. "Hard at it?"

"Actually I was just about to leave. I've got a date with Isabella tonight."

Leonard perked up in an interested but nonintrusive way. "And how are things with you and Isabella?"

Jeff lolled his head from side to side. "Busy. Been real busy."

"Puts a strain on a marriage. I know. Puts a strain on a man too. That's really the reason I stopped by."

Jeff looked puzzled.

Leonard took a deep breath, as if preparing for something difficult. "The other deacons and I think that you're spreading yourself too thin. What with the trial and all, you've been working 'round the clock, and I think you and I both know the church has suffered because of it."

Jeff looked at the bills, his heart picking up, feeling accused. "If this is about what happened at the elders' meeting today, I'm sorry. I was totally out of line."

Leonard stopped him with a tired laugh. "No, no, no. Don't apologize. You're trying to take care of family, and no matter what the elders say, your own deacons know how trying this has been for you. We understand, and we just…we want to help."

Leonard pulled a manila envelope from his side and laid it on the desk.

Jeff looked at it strangely. "What's this?"

He opened the envelope as Leonard answered, "Sermons. We've

already arranged them for you, to help you free up your time to help your brother."

The young pastor pulled out the papers, studying them. They were sermons, all right. Planned down to the prayers to open and close the service.

All mapped out.

Jeff felt flattered by the sentiment, though a trifle uneasy. "Wow...Mr. Fergus."

"Leonard."

Jeff corrected himself. "Leonard." He started to stuff the papers back into the envelope. "I don't know what to say. I appreciate the gesture, but I don't know if I can take these."

Leonard held out his hands, indicating that he would not take the envelope back. "Just look them over. Consider it another option. It's OK to ask for help. That's all this is. A little help until you get back on your feet and are able to prepare your own sermons again."

"Thanks." Jeff grinned, trying to be gracious to his old friend. "Thank you."

Mr. Fergus nodded in return, tipped his cap, and groaned as he stood on wobbly knees. He turned to leave. "Have a good night, Reverend."

"You too, Leonard."

And then the old man left. Jeff took a deep breath, setting the envelope on one of the many stacks of assorted papers on his desk. Just one more thing to worry about.

Always one more thing.

Suddenly Jeff felt very exhausted. He knew he needed to leave soon to make his date with Isabella, but he desperately needed a nap. Just a small power nap to give him that extra edge so he could be everything Isabella deserved tonight.

He checked the mounted clock on the wall—6:31. He had a couple of minutes. He only *needed* a couple of minutes. He settled on the couch against the wall and closed his eyes.

He fell asleep immediately and dreamed strange dreams.

In the woods again. He hears howling in the distance and pounding drum beats. He's been in these woods before. He knows what he'll find in the clearing. He'll see them, with their slick obsidian bodies, crowing to the stars. He'll be sickened by the sight of them, as he always is, but he must look. He must understand.

Nobody remembers how it began...how the town turned to monsters.

It didn't happen overnight—most were sure of that—but rather gradually. It started with the children, stealing them away one by one. Plucking them from the streets and consuming them in dark, thick oil. Then it moved on to the women, mothers desperate to find their children. Then it progressed to the men.

That's when it got worse.

The night was unusually cold for August. Isabella Weldon pulled into the parking lot of the Good Church of the Faithful. Jeff's truck was still there.

She shook her head as she parked the car. Gathering her things, tired from the evening's activities, or lack thereof, she walked up the steps and entered the sanctuary. In no immediate hurry, not seeing the point anymore, she meandered into Jeff's study upstairs.

He was asleep, lying face down on the couch in his office. The small lamp on top his desk offered just enough light for Isabella to see him, and she frowned at the sight. She wanted to be mad. To tell him off for not being with her tonight. For standing her up again.

But she was too tired to bother with it.

She bent closer. Watching him sleep and gently stroking his hair, she felt her tension melting away in spite of everything. "I love you, Jeff Weldon," she whispered into his ear. On he slept.

It was probably better that way. He needed to sleep; he hadn't done so in weeks. She could barely remember what he looked like clean-shaven and without bloodshot eyes. The stress was getting to him. If he wasn't careful, he was going to burn out.

But he won't listen to me.

Contemplating the crazy day, Isabella exhaled and wandered toward Jeff's desk to see what he had been working on. Next to a pile of unpaid bills was a large manila envelope she'd not seen before. Isabella took out the papers inside and looked at them curiously. They were neatly typed, well packaged, and easy to read. They looked like sermons.

That's odd.

Suddenly Jeff sprang up off the couch in a fright. The abrupt motion spooked Isabella, and she faced him with wide eyes. Frantically surveying the room like a frightened and caged animal, Jeff finally eased as he realized he was only in his study.

"Are you OK?" she asked.

He buried his face in his hands, trying to rub consciousness back into his head. "Just a…a nightmare."

Then he lifted his face, confused. "What are you doing here? I thought we were going to meet at the movie."

"We were." She raised an eyebrow. "*I* did."

"What?" Jeff stood up and looked at the clock on his wall. It read 6:31. "It's only six thirty-one…oh." With a moan he flopped back down on the couch. "The batteries must be dead."

She could tell he felt horrible, knowing he had let her down. Again.

"I'm sorry, honey. There was this emergency, and the church was a mess, and then there were all the bills, and I thought I could just lie down for a minute." He shook his head in shame.

Isabella didn't argue, but she didn't add to his self-condemnation either. Instead she changed the subject, gesturing to the manila envelope. "What's this?"

He glanced up, still looking guilty, and only mildly responded. "The deacons sent those over. They thought I could start using them."

Isabella winced, uncomfortable with the notion. "Prepackaged sermons? Isn't that kind of…?"

Jeff looked defensive. These days he seemed all too eager to take offense. "What?"

"Well, doesn't that kind of limit the Holy Spirit? What if He wants to say something that isn't on the schedule? And besides, what's wrong with *your* sermons?"

"Nothing. They just thought it would save some time. In case you haven't noticed, I've been pretty busy lately."

"Not too busy for God, though. Right?"

She waited for an answer. Jeff didn't offer one.

"You're still reading your Bible and studying, right?"

He ground his teeth, his earlobes reddening. "Well, *yeah*. When I can. But there's only so many hours in the day, and there are a lot of needs in the community. Not to mention all of our tithers are leaving. People just don't understand that we *live* off what they put in the offering plate. The bills are piling up here and at home, and no money is coming in to cover it. On top of that, I've been busting my chops trying to find a lawyer who will appeal Dras's case, but no one wants to fight a battle they know they'll lose. I'm really under a lot of pressure here, Iz, and I'm trying. But some things just have to be put on hold."

"But not God," she pleaded. "Not me."

"What do you *want* me to do?"

He was raising his voice, getting hot. She calmly reasoned, "I could get a job. I've told you that I have no problem getting a job."

"*No,*" he said flatly, barely letting her finish. "I can handle it. OK? I can do it. I just need to work a little harder and put in a few more hours. It won't kill me."

And that was that.

He cooled and began to absent-mindedly arrange some books on a nearby shelf. Isabella set down the envelope and clenched her fist. He was so stubborn, and he made her so mad sometimes. She'd held down jobs before and Jeff had never minded, but since they had tried to start having children, they both wanted her to be home—to prepare for staying at home and raising their family. It was what she wanted too. But they needed money right now, and she was willing to work. Jeff saw that as giving up on their dream of having kids or, worse yet, a slur on his manhood, an indication that he couldn't support their family by himself.

Quietly Jeff tried to make things normal again, as if hoping to redeem himself. "So...you wanna go try and catch the late show?"

"No. I just want to go home."

"OK. You want to leave your car here and come home with me in the truck?"

"I'd rather drive myself."

Isabella started out the door without another word.

Jeff reached out to her. "Iz..."

She only raised her hand, holding him off, her back still to him. Whatever it was he had to say, she didn't want to hear it.

CHAPTER NINE

I**T WAS A** night of unrest for Ray McCormick. A night of dreams, visions, and premonitions. An anxious itch scratched at his mind, and paradoxes promised something on the horizon but gave no indication as to its name. The night had brought torment and prophecies, anguish and pain, confusion, blindness, and despair—

"Ray? It's late."

Ray turned to his wife, mildly acknowledging her presence. "I know."

"Are you coming to bed?"

Lost in some other world, transfixed by the music of the stars, he replied in a hollow automation of the human voice, "Yes. Later. You go on without me, Caroline."

Caroline was hesitant to leave him. After the death of their daughter, Lindsey, Ray was...different. Caroline missed her husband. She missed their long talks of the day's events each night in bed, and she missed hearing him mumbling in his sleep after their conversations ended.

These days, however, she seemed doomed to sleep alone.

Now her husband paced the house at all hours of the night as if waiting for something. Expectantly he stood by the same window, night after night, looking out across their town, but Caroline didn't know what he thought he would see.

Unable to deter him from his steady watch, Caroline McCormick feigned a smile. "OK. Just...don't stay up too late."

He turned back to face the window, to look out on the neighborhood, yet *past* the neighborhood, as if he were seeing something else hidden in the depths of the darkness.

"OK."

Caroline waited a moment more, watching her husband's body

grow taut. He remained frozen in front of the window like a sentinel. Defeated, she made her way into the bedroom.

Ray continued to watch the blackness of the night sky, inhumanly patient, his mind disciplined and concentrating.

Not long after Caroline went to bed, the phone rang. As if activated, Ray sprang to life and quickly yanked the receiver from the hook, gripping the phone close to his ear, like an addict desperate for a fix.

Feeling wild and alive, he answered the call in a hurried hush, "*Yes*?"

"Are you ready to know the truth?"

Hope and joy bloomed in Ray's formerly graven heart. "Yes!"

"Meet me at Greensboro Park Lake." *Click.*

Ray held the phone a moment longer, the crazy grin refusing to fade from his face.

Finally his questions would be answered! His pain would end!

Without telling his wife good-bye, Ray grabbed his coat, opened the door, and disappeared into the darkness.

"Shut up, you stupid cow!" the raging young man hollered at the top of his lungs, his hateful remarks echoing through the deserted streets of the East Side.

"Please, Danny! I need you! Our babies need you!"

Tabitha Banks clung to her boyfriend—who had finally returned to her, only to retrieve a few more of his things—desperately pleading, but Danny Carpenter forged ahead, indifferent to her tears. "You should have been on the pill in the first place like I told you!"

She cried harder. "But I didn't have any *money* for birth control! You know that!"

He didn't stop to listen. Only moved. She cried once more, hoping to break through the hardened wall around his heart. "Please, Danny! Stop!"

"I told you I ain't gonna be no father!"

"Danny, please! *Stop*, will you!"

Finally he halted and spun to point a lone condemning finger to her nose. In a low harsh whisper, he sentenced her. "I told you when you first found out you were pregnant that you should have taken care of it then and there, but you wouldn't listen to me. So now you're stuck with them."

"But Danny…" Tabitha's vision blurred with tears. "I need you."

With a cruel laugh he pushed her to the paved street. "You need a hole in the head, Tabitha."

With a grim sneer Danny turned his back on the mother of his children and disappeared into the shadows, leaving Tabitha behind, her body shuddering with sobs.

Ray McCormick knelt in the crisp, desiccated grass by the water's edge. The dark placid waters of Greensboro Park Lake yawned before him, bringing to mind memories of family outings here. Trips with Lindsey…she used to love the water. But Lindsey was gone now, lost to this very lake. The town said she was dead, but Ray couldn't believe that. Not his daughter. God wouldn't be so cruel, would He? Ray had been a man of faith for so long, but his faith had yet to provide him answers or healing.

But the man on the phone will help me.

As he waited for his contact to arrive, Ray found himself increasingly drawn to the lake. He bent over the waters, fascinated by the black sheen absorbing the moonlight. Something rumbled beneath the surface, and his mind filled with a soft hum that beckoned him closer…tempting him with the answers he needed, promising him rest, peace—but only if he turned his back on his useless faith. He had put his trust in God, but Lindsey was gone and God was silent. Why hadn't He done something to save her? To avenge her if the worst were true and she was dead?

A cold pain churned in his chest, and Ray stooped closer, angry with a God who didn't answer His people.

Then he saw the water moving, slithering his way. He gasped and—

Danny Carpenter needed to get away.

Little more than twenty-one-years-old, with scruffy features, dirty brown hair that hung in his eyes, and a thin, compact body camouflaged in several layers of mismatched and loose-fitting clothing, Danny was a product of the streets, his once handsome face marred by a hard and misspent life on the East Side.

After dropping out of high school and having a big blowup

with Nana Loraine, the grandmother who raised him since he was about six, he left home to make it on his own. Sleeping beneath bridges and on friends' couches, he earned a living causing trouble and selling dime bags on street corners. All in all, Danny was just another cog in the gritty machine of dilapidated downtown Greensboro.

But right now, Greensboro was the last place Danny wanted to be.

He needed to blow off some steam and figure out what he was going to do. He thought to leave town for good this time, maybe even make his way in the City. Nobody would look for him. He could just disappear and get a new life far, far away from this stupid town and all its responsibilities.

Like raising babies. Babies he didn't want.

And Tabitha. Always clinging to him, wanting him to do everything for her. He never signed on for that. He thought that he might love Tabitha, but this family stuff, with commitment and kids, was too much. He was still a young guy. He had too many things to figure out—too much living to do—to give up his life for her.

And those babies. It always came back to those stupid babies.

He drove his Monte Carlo faster into the night, jamming out to AC/DC's "Highway to Hell," fighting hard to grip the curvy roads that led deep into the North Woods and onward toward Greensboro Park Lake, toward the old highway and the turnoff to the new interstate that had condemned Greensboro to obscurity and opened up the path to the City. Toward freedom.

Not many folks went in the direction of the North Woods these days. After the police found Lindsey McCormick's car in the lake, most parents stopped taking their children there to swim. Even though Lindsey's body was never recovered, everyone whispered that it was buried beneath the muddy water, and Greensboro Park Lake could not be separated from her tragic death in people's minds.

Plus, there were the creepy stories. All the fish died and the grass all yellowed and withered away around the water. The trees closest to the blackened muck were hollowed out by rot, and some even said they saw the lake eat a bird or two.

Yeah. *Eat* a bird or two.

Folks said old Greensboro Park Lake was cursed. Only Danny didn't believe in that garbage. Nana Loraine was a superstitious sort, always babbling about evil spirits and angels and the like. *What a bunch of nonsense*, Danny thought. It was all urban legends and ghost tales. The North Woods and Greensboro Park Lake were still the fastest way out of town, and no talk of a bird-eating body of devil water was going to keep him from the path to escape.

He drove faster, taking another drink. It was his fifth beer since getting into his fight with Tabitha, and he struggled against the alcohol and his anger to keep on the road. Out here traffic was rare, and deputies weren't too common either, so he had the whole road to himself to dodge pink elephants.

He sped on, indifferent to the risk of losing his own life. So what if he died? Seemed better than having to be a father or a husband. He wasn't ready for those things. Didn't *want* those things. He and Tabitha could barely get along and stay together, let alone raise a family.

It wasn't the life for him, just like it wasn't the life for his old man.

He drank the bottle empty then tossed it out the open window. After spiraling through the air, the bottle crashed to the pavement and shattered with a pop on impact. Satisfied, Danny hung his head out the window and crowed wildly, the wind whipping around his face. He felt liberated, like nothing could touch him. He had tried to leave Greensboro before, but he always came crawling back when he started missing Tabitha.

But this time he was going to get out for good.

He was still riding on his high as he brought his head back into the car, but his laughter trailed off when he saw a strange sight in the distance.

Slamming on his brakes, he stopped just inches shy of plowing into an unusual roadblock. Parked sideways in the middle of the street rested a car, apparently abandoned. The driver's side door hung open, and the headlights shone brightly into the void.

Danny frowned at the holdup, shut off his engine, and got out of the Monte. "Hey! Get out of the road!"

He moved closer to the car, lighting a cigarette and preparing to brawl with the idiot who was standing in his way. However, his anger became confusion when he observed that the car was empty.

"What in the…" Craning his head in both directions, he called out, "*Hey!*"

No response. With his eyes he followed the headlight trail into the tall, unkempt weeds that led to Greensboro Park Lake. Figuring the idiot was out there somewhere and in need of a good whuppin', Danny balled up his fists and left the road behind. Trudging through knee-high grass and wildflowers, he waded his way to the yellowed edge of the lake. Ghost stories aside, he was still reluctant to go traipsing any closer to the water just in case it was poisonous.

Cupping his hands to his mouth, he shifted the cigarette clenched in his teeth and called out into the darkened ruins of the North Woods. "Yo! Anybody out there?"

Again, no response.

His vision impaired by the night and alcohol, he struggled as he ventured closer to the lake. "Hey! Moron! Get your car outta the road before I move it for ya!"

Before trekking too far into the dark, he met a shadow, the shape of a man. With his back turned to Danny, the man was kneeling beside the thick, murky waters of the lake, his head inclined over the surface of the sludge.

As Danny watched, something like a slick, black arm reached out of the waters and fixed itself to the man's face.

Whoa. I think I had one too many beers.

Danny was startled at first, yet his irritation soon overwhelmed his initial shock. "Yo, moron! You deaf? I said move your car!"

The man did not move or speak as the slimy arm slowly retracted from his face and returned to the lake.

He only stood.

Danny came closer, reaching out a hand to tap the man on the shoulder. Firmly rapping, ready to pick a fight, Danny said, "Hey, *stupid*. I'm only gonna tell you one more time. Move. Your. Car."

Finally the man in the darkness turned around, and Danny caught full sight of him. It was Ray McCormick. A relieved smirk rose to Danny's face when he recognized the man as the local crazy who put those stupid MISSING posters all over town, but as he surveyed him more closely, his face fell. Something in Ray's hand gleamed in the moonlight.

It was an axe.

Terrified, Danny opened his mouth to scream.

CHAPTER TEN

THE CLEARING AGAIN. *Beasts dancing, pulling him closer with their tribal chanting.*

Nobody remembers how it began. How the town turned into monsters.

It didn't happen overnight—most were sure of that—but rather, gradually. It started with the children, stealing them away one by one. Plucking them from the streets and consuming them in dark, thick oil. Then it moved on to the women, mothers desperate to find their children. Then it progressed to the men.

That's when it got worse.

Before long everyone was infected with the black muck. They became a part of it. They became its eyes and ears, its arms and legs and muscle and skill. All the goodness in them was replaced by a sticky black substance that never let go of its own accord and could not be driven away by the will of man. Once it had them in its grasp, it became their master, and they degenerated into its mindless slaves.

They were dead, yet they walked.

That was how it happened in that town. Repentance never followed disobedience, and somehow Evil grew larger than it had ever grown before. So large, in fact, that it began to spread, to swell and consume the next town. Soon, the neighboring community was stricken with the disease, as well.

Yet, the evil would not be sated.

It wanted more victims to prey on. If left unattended, it would continue to grow, to pulsate with sickening, wicked life only to bring more death.

"It is coming."

Screams woke him. It was only after the screams stopped that Jeff realized they were his own. Catching his breath, he turned to his wife.

"You awake?"

She stirred, obviously not.

"Isabella," he tried again.

He gently placed his hand on her hip and peered over her shoulder to see if she had been wakened by his cries in the night. Nope. Sound as a rock, like usual.

Jeff Weldon sat back in his bed, drenched in cold sweat, his muscles still shaking from his nightmare. It was the same nightmare that had plagued him for the last three months—since the night of the big storm. Only the nightmare seemed to be getting worse.

Jeff got out of bed and moved into the adjoining bathroom. He flipped on the light switch and caught full sight of himself in the mirror. He looked awful. Haggard. Haunted.

He grimaced. Things had changed so much.

Instead of dwelling on it, he turned on the faucet, running cool water over his hands and splashing some on his face to wash the sweat away. Suddenly Jeff winced as a terrible pain shot through his brain, knocking him off balance. He urgently massaged his temples, but the pain wouldn't go away.

"Agh!" He doubled over and gripped the edge of the sink, nearly breaking the porcelain molding in half. He braced himself, grinding his teeth, trying to fight back the unbearable splitting in his head.

Jeff reached into the medicine cabinet and took out his bottle of painkillers. Using all his available concentration, he fought with the cap until he could remove it and retrieve a couple of pills. He popped them in his mouth, swallowed hard, and waited.

Breathing heavily, Jeff looked back to the mirror. The pain slowly began to subside, and he was thankful for it. Still leaning on the sink, he groaned.

"Not again..."

He shifted his gaze to the bedroom, where Isabella still slept, unaware of the scene. With a frown, he turned off the light and left the bathroom, the bedroom, and Isabella behind.

He hadn't told Isabella about the nightmares. If she had known, she most assuredly would have dogged him with questions until he revealed his innermost thoughts and concerns to her. And if that didn't work, she would move on to meat loaf.

It seemed that just when his mind was the most burdened, she always served meat loaf for dinner. Surely it was more than coincidence. Jeff was beginning to think that Isabella was trying to get something out of him by serving meat loaf, though he didn't know what. All he knew was that he hated meat loaf with a white-hot searing passion. He had *always* hated it, even back when his mother forced it upon his dinner plate. But would he ever tell Isabella that? *No. Of course not.* He could handle a meal he didn't like now and then. He was a big boy. *I can handle these dreams. If I told her about them she'd just worry about me. Or think I was crazy.*

Sometimes, in these moments just after the dreams ended, even he wondered if he was going insane. Every terrible nightmare was the same in that every one was excruciatingly horrible. Fortunately, there was something that, so far, was always able to make the fear go away.

It was time for milk and cookies.

It was a small thing, but he needed something sweet and familiar from his childhood to take his mind off the things he saw in his dreams. The nightmare was a blur of sickening screams. A mixture of pleasure and pain. Blood, blackness, and revelry in all kinds of unspeakable wickedness.

He didn't want to think about it. Especially not at three o'clock in the morning. Living out on Grover's Pond had been spooky in many ways. The house was isolated, there were no streetlights to illuminate the dark, and animals were always screeching about something. But living here on the East Side—where late-night noises included police sirens, yelling, and barking dogs—was downright terrifying.

As if on cue, reds and blues flooded the house. A blaring siren tore through the quiet night as Jeff entered the kitchen. He stepped to the window and peeked through the blinds to see a Jeep with the sheriff's crest wailing past.

Just another night in the East Side.

He made his way to the refrigerator, rubbing the sight back into his eyes. The appliance light momentarily blinded him, but he braved it long enough to take out the milk.

Sitting on a stool at the counter, he readied his glass of milk and retrieved the bag of Double Stuf Oreos from the cabinet. As he dunked, he had an uneasy feeling that he was being watched. He tried to ignore the sensation and enjoy his snack. The brownstones were packed pretty close together, but surely no one could see him.

Nevertheless, he kept a careful eye on the kitchen window, expecting some hideous, pale face of death to leer back at him. The bogeyman.

Dras said it was the bogeyman who set him up.

No. Stop.

Following his brother's arrest, Jeff had marched out into the North Woods one night, determined to find the monster that had caused all of this. He shouted and cursed and cried at the darkness, daring Dras's Strange Man to come after him.

It should have been me. I was the one God wanted to fight the monster.

Wasn't I?

He'd gone out there that night, ready for war, but the shadows mocked him with silence instead. He'd returned home, humiliated, defeated, and unfulfilled.

He never told Isabella about that night. It seemed he was keeping a lot of things from her lately.

Jeff put down the cookies and rubbed his face.

Now that the sirens had faded, Jeff found it sort of peaceful in the house, but still something was missing. Back at their house on the pond, when Jeff awoke in the middle of the night, he always felt as if God was sitting in the kitchen, waiting for him to come talk with Him. It was good to sense the presence of God so real and personal— as if the Creator of all things would hang out in Jeff Weldon's kitchen in the middle of the night, ready to share milk and cookies and long heartfelt talks. Maybe it was stupid, but it felt nice.

That wasn't the case here in the East Side, though. Things were different now, and Jeff knew the difference might be more than location. He fought hard to feel the presence of God at all these days.

He's still here, somewhere, Jeff thought. But in a moment of doubt, he wondered.

Either way, it was unnaturally still in the Weldon home, and Jeff felt a little emptier inside.

"Doomed!" Ray McCormick screamed insanely, his mind pregnant with visions of The Coming Evil. Monsters and ugly, curious things, slithering their way across yards and into houses. Fire and death and blood and that sticky black *thing* living in the shadows, waiting to strike. Nothing made sense, nor ever would again. Not for Ray. Reality, as he knew it, had finally unraveled, and little by little, the glue that held the mortal coil together was dissolving, his world slipping off into a thousand infinities of cosmic confusion.

Three nurses pinned him to the hospital bed, utilizing all their leverage to keep him from tossing them this way and that. His eyes squeezed shut, tears streaming down his hot face, he bellowed, "DOOM! DOOM!"

Consuela Margolis shared a worried expression with the two other nurses by her side. The three fought to keep their patient under control as he jerked, spitting as he proclaimed, "I've seen it! We're all doomed!" With a pitiful howl, Ray fell back on the bed, exhausted, and lay motionless.

Dr. Herbert Brown charged through the door, stern and ready for business. When he saw his patient, however, all blood drained from his face. He turned to Consuela. "Is that Ray McCormick?"

She nodded gravely. "Deputy Stevenson brought him in about five minutes ago. He found him wandering the streets with an axe, shouting and screaming like a crazy person and swinging at anyone who tried to come close enough to help him."

Brown felt for Ray's pulse, until Ray finally jerked to life again, his chest rising off the bed and his back arching impossibly. His knuckles popped as he flexed them. Consuela shivered, feeling unsafe.

"It's coming! The change is beginning! We're all doomed!"

Brown turned to her. "What's he saying?"

"He's been going on like this since they brought him in."

Ray interrupted, "No one is safe! We're all in danger! It's coming! *It's coming!*"

Brown took firm hold of Ray's arm, trying to break through the hysteria. "Get a hold of yourself! *What* is coming?"

Ray finally opened his eyes and stared at the doctor.

Consuela screamed and knocked over the tray of utensils, spilling them to the floor. Brown loosened his grip and slowly backed away. They stared horrified at the sight.

For Ray McCormick's eyes were solid black.

Consumed by some impenetrable darkness, the hollow, cold shark eyes gazed back at them. Ray calmed for a moment, and his eyes, devoid of humanity, glared with a strange recognition. "Repent," Ray whispered to Brown. "Turn from your sin before it gets you too."

Brown balked and tried to pull himself away from the awful eyes, but Ray held his focus. "There's not much time. The change has already started."

Bursting into coughing fits, Ray closed his gruesome eyes, much to Consuela's relief, and curled up, convulsing. She could not move, the image of the dark soul-eating orbs leaving her paralyzed with fear and foreboding. The other nurses struggled to control Ray again, but Brown looked on, helpless.

"Doctor Brown?" Consuela asked, finally joining in with her coworkers. "What do we do?"

But before Brown could respond, another nurse captured everyone's attention. "Look. Something's moving!"

Underneath Ray's shirt, something stirred, slithered, crawled, and contracted. Consuela shivered, hearing a slurping sound, as if something were feeding. Brown acted after a long pause, his face twisting in dread as he reached out one shaky hand toward Ray's shirt...and pulled it up.

His screams filled the room.

The elevator doors opened with a *ding*, and two gray-haired gentlemen in black stepped out. Dressed in complimenting suits, their footfalls echoing down the hall, they marched side by side, radiating power. One wore an unmistakable look of greed in his eyes and the condescending expectance of a crooked tax collector, while the other carried himself with cool intelligence.

They marched down the empty hospital hall, passing only the nurse behind the desk, too immersed in paperwork to acknowledge their presence. They moved with certainty toward their contact, Dr. Herbert Brown. He waited restlessly at the door to Ray's room. As the two men met him, he extended a hand in greeting.

"Mr. Hayden," he acknowledged the leader of the two, the one with the cool intelligence. "Thank you for coming."

"Of course."

Brown turned to the second, avaricious man with a worried glance. "You too, Mr. Simms."

Mr. Simms shook the doctor's hand, but the formality was brief. There were more pressing matters to attend to than introductions and hobnobbing.

"You have something to show us?" Mr. Hayden furthered the conversation, urgent.

"Yes, yes, sorry."

Brown fought to gather his senses as he discreetly led the men into the hospital room. "You said to give you a call if I saw anything that was...unusual. Without explanation. I believe I have."

Leading them to the only bed in the room, surrounded by blipping equipment, pumps, and IVs, Brown presented his latest patient and scientific find: a comatose Ray McCormick.

At the very sight of him, Mr. Simms stepped back and took a handkerchief from his inside coat pocket, placing it to his mouth to muffle a gag. Mr. Hayden stirred but stood his ground, appearing less disturbed by the gruesome sight.

Mr. Simms removed his handkerchief, horrified. "How long has this been going on?"

"I'm not sure. He was brought in tonight, but I don't know how far the virus got before then."

"*Virus*?" Mr. Hayden broke in. "Are we sure that's what this is?"

"I don't know. Not for sure. As you can see," Brown removed the sheet covering poor Ray's torso, revealing the ghastly truth in its entirety, "the...*infection* has spread to the majority of his body."

"Have you been able to treat it?" Mr. Simms asked with an undeniable hint of fear in his voice.

"No. It seems...impervious. Needles can't penetrate it; we can't X-ray it. And with each passing hour his dementia grows worse. He has fits of hysteria and then he passes out like this. When he's awake, we can barely contain him."

Mr. Hayden's eyes narrowed. "Has he...*said* anything? Given any indication as to how he got in this condition?"

"He's said quite a bit, actually."

"Oh? What?"

"Ravings, mostly. Nightmares. Prophetic claims of the end of the world."

The two mysterious gentlemen shared a glance.

"I'm not sure of anything at this point," Brown admitted, "but it appears he's gone mad."

Mr. Hayden gestured toward his associate. Mr. Simms took that as a cue and left the hospital room. Brown watched him go, curious, but Mr. Hayden stood in the gap and addressed him before any questions could be voiced. "Thank you for contacting us, Herbert. Your cooperation is always appreciated."

Brown beamed with pride at the commendation, and all thoughts of Mr. Simms' shadowy exit were gone. "Thank you, sir. I'll contact you if anything develops."

"Good. Until we know more..." Mr. Hayden stood taller over the good doctor, the authority behind his words unquestionable. "Let's keep this to ourselves."

Brown couldn't refuse a shudder. "Uh...yes, sir. Of course."

Mr. Simms stood in the hallway outside the hospital room. Conducting a cautious search of the surrounding hall and deeming it safe, he withdrew a cell phone from inside his coat and dialed.

After two rings the receiver was picked up. "Hello?"

"It's me. Call the others. We must meet."

The other voice sounded concerned. "What is it?"

Mr. Simms paused for a moment, letting the weight of his words settle in his own soul, knowing that the new development he had just witnessed meant serious changes for him.

For all of them.

"It's started."

CHAPTER ELEVEN

A S THE MORNING's light filled the bedroom, Isabella slowly opened her eyes. In the early days of their marriage, Jeff joked that Isabella was solar-powered and could only be awakened by the sun's rays. No alarm clock could do the trick. When Isabella was out, she was out, and nothing but the morning sun could change that.

Jeff and Isabella returned home last night to an awkward and uneventful evening. They stayed in opposite ends of the house, not speaking. Isabella quietly got ready for bed, while Jeff warmed up the leftovers of their would-be romantic dinner. The silence was only interrupted once when Elsa called, announcing that they had checked into a motel safely and were glad to be off the road. She and Isabella spent only a moment exchanging well wishes before both women decided it had been a long, tiring day. Agreeing to call once Elsa and Isaac were more settled in, Isabella hung up and went to sleep.

Now, the morning after, she sat up in bed and took a deep breath, last night's troubles still on her mind. Arching her back, she twisted, then exhaled. The thought of a new day did little to dispel the gloom from their tiff. She knew that she and Jeff couldn't keep up the silent treatment, and as much as it made her apprehensive to think of those first awkward words, she wanted to talk to him again, to mend last night's hurt. Resolved now, but uncertain how to begin, she turned over to see if her husband had awakened. He wasn't in bed.

Craning her head, she peered into the bathroom.

"Jeff?"

But he wasn't in there either. Then something else caught her attention.

She thought she smelled bacon.

The noisy sizzle of grease in a skillet filled the air as Isabella ventured downstairs, slipping on her robe. The bacon aroma was hard to ignore as she reached the first floor and rounded the corner into the kitchen. She was met with the sight of Jeff Weldon cooking breakfast. It was a first.

"What's this?" She was amused as well as confused.

He spun around, startled. "Well, in about fifteen minutes it would have been breakfast in bed. Now it's just a ruined surprise." He smiled wide and opened his arms. "Surprise."

Isabella couldn't refrain from grinning as she sat on a stool at the bar to watch him cook. "You made me breakfast in bed?" she asked, sincerely touched. "You've never made me breakfast in bed."

He flipped a strip of bacon, then turned from his cooking. He paused thoughtfully. "There are a lot of things I haven't done that maybe I should start doing."

Isabella's heart melted at the sentiment, and she discovered the depth of her love for Jeff all over again. He was a little absentminded sometimes, but sweet. She reached across the counter to take his hand, but as he began what was sure to be an apology, he looked away, vulnerable.

"Iz, about last night, I..."

"Jeff, it's OK."

He shook his head, resolute. "No. I've been a jerk to the *nth* degree lately. During my sleepless nights I've been thinking a lot about things, and I think that the reason I've been working so much lately is because I'm trying to keep myself busy."

Isabella knew that this kind of disclosure was hard for him, and she remained sympathetically attentive as he expressed himself.

"I'm afraid," he hesitated, struggling to get the words out, "that if I stop, then I'll realize that he's really gone. Dras is *gone*." He stopped, as if saying it aloud made the horrible truth all the more real. "He's gone...and there's nothing I can do to change that. I have to face that. I have to move on."

Jeff cautiously turned to his wife again, and Isabella rested her hand against his coarse cheek, showing her support for his difficult breakthrough. He took a deep breath, holding in whatever sob might want to escape.

"I have to focus on what's really important now. And believe me—" He paused and took her hand, his eyes seeking her forgiveness. "—you are everything to me. I just need a good kick in the head sometimes to remember that."

Leaning in, absolutely in love, Isabella tenderly kissed him. When they parted, Jeff smiled. "What was that for?"

"Because I love you. And because I owed you a kiss from last night."

"But that was if I showed. I didn't."

She smiled. "I think you just did."

"Better late than never, huh?"

They both chuckled and leaned in again to indulge in another, more passionate kiss that promised something more. Isabella pulled away after a moment, lingering close to his lips. With a wily smile she whispered, "You're on fire."

Playfully he replied, "See what you do to me?"

She giggled and pointed behind him. "No. I mean you're on *fire*."

He spun around to meet the blazing inferno that consumed his bacon. The smoke rose in thick plumes, and Isabella sat back and watched, entertained, as Jeff yelped and went to work to put the fire out.

After he managed to stop the spread of the conflagration, he turned to her, blushing. "So, you want skim or whole milk with your cereal?"

She laughed and stood. "I'll get it."

Jeff winced at his lack of cooking skills. As Isabella opened the refrigerator and stuck her head in, his cell phone, resting on the kitchen counter, came to life with a shrill ring. Irritated by the interruption, Jeff quickly answered before it had a chance to ring again, already thinking of reprimanding Will for calling him so early and interrupting what might have been a romantic breakfast.

"Hello?"

A man's voice answered, though it wasn't Will's. On the contrary, it was firm and full of authority. "'From the least to the greatest, all are greedy for gain; prophets and priests alike, all practice deceit. They dress the wound of my people as though it were not serious. "Peace, peace," they say, when there is no peace.'"

Jeff pulled back, baffled and a bit uneasy. "Who is this?"

The tone of his voice caught Isabella's attention, and she looked up from the refrigerator.

"Are you ready to know the truth?" the voice asked him.

"Who *is* this?"

The line went dead.

Jeff held the phone away from him and looked to the caller ID. It read: UNKNOWN. He folded the phone and stood lost in thought, rolling the cryptic message over in his mind.

"Who was it, Jeff?"

He hesitated, not quite sure what to think of the call. But he didn't want Isabella to worry, especially not now when things were so close to being good again. "Wrong number."

Jeff and Isabella made love for the first time in weeks before going to church that morning, and it seemed as though everything was finally going to be OK. The drive to the Good Church of the Faithful was filled with elbowing and snickering at private jokes and cuddling. There was a levity that they had not experienced in some time, and Jeff was resolved to keep it that way. The tension was gone and they could breathe again.

Still…

There was that strange call. The "Wrong Number."

Who was it? On the back burner of his mind Jeff simmered his questions about the odd intrusion into his otherwise wonderful morning. *And what did he mean, "Are you ready to know the truth?" What truth?*

After Dras's arrest their home received all sorts of calls of that kind. It seemed they were at the mercy of every Scripture-spouting psycho who could dial a phone. Most of the cryptic messages were about judgment and "the fires of hell" and how the wicked would be punished.

Of course, they were all referring to Dras.

But this call was different. The scripture sounded familiar, but Jeff couldn't place it. Intrigued, he took a moment before the service began to do a little cross-referencing in his study. Before long he learned it was Jeremiah 6:13–14:

> From the least to the greatest, all are greedy for gain;
> prophets and priests alike, all practice deceit. They dress
> the wound of my people as though it were not serious.
> "Peace, peace," they say, when there is no peace.

That was it, all right. But he had no idea how it applied to *him*. Needless to say, it was on his mind the whole morning. The case of the mysterious call, coupled with his sleepless nights, left him flustered and exhausted, and his sermon suffered. He wasn't as prepared as he should have been, but he probably could have bluffed his way through it if there weren't so many other things on his mind.

Especially this Wrong Number with "the truth."

The thoughts were still twisting around in his head like a Rubik's

Cube trying to solve itself as he gathered up his notes following his lackluster sermon. His entire congregation of twenty—over five times smaller than it was before Dras's trial—began to shuffle toward the doors as Isabella approached him. He saw her out of the corner of his eye.

"I really blew it today," he admitted, ashamed.

"You just lost your place a couple of times, that's all."

He grabbed his Bible and messy notes and tucked them haphazardly underneath his arm. "Iz, it took me five minutes to find my Bible passages."

She rolled her eyes. "It wasn't five minutes."

"And I said 'Jeremiah' when I meant 'John.'"

"I don't think anyone noticed."

"Well, they should have," Jeff said, frustrated. "They *should* notice. I shouldn't be able to stand in front of the church and preach from the book of Samson when there *isn't* a book of Samson. They've got to be sharper than that. How can they defend their faith if they don't even know what it is they claim to believe?"

As if to throw salt in the wound, Will walked by on his way to greet the leaving parishioners and offered an encouraging wave to the pastor. "Great sermon today, Reverend Weldon!"

What upset Jeff the most about the comment was that Will probably really believed that. His own assistant pastor hadn't noticed all the slipups. Jeff could have stood up there and rambled about...about *anything*, and his congregation would have just nodded and mumbled "Amen" every once in a while to appease his ego. They weren't even thinking about the words he was saying when he preached to them.

Jeff watched Will move to the doors to shake people's hands. He frowned, remembering when he used to do that. Now he seemed as much in a hurry as anyone else to get away.

Sorry, God...

"I'm off my game," Jeff confided in his wife, watching Will kiss Miss Jenkins on the cheek, bidding her a great afternoon.

Bearing a playful smile, Isabella nudged him. "Well, if you wouldn't stay up at all hours of the night..."

She was trying to lighten the situation, but Jeff wondered if this was God's way of opening up an opportunity for him to talk to her about the dreams and the migraines that followed.

His palms felt sweaty, and Jeff opened his mouth ready to tell her everything. Fear held him back—what he was afraid of, he didn't really know—but he fought against it, wanting to tell her what was in his heart. "Um, listen, I—"

Then Leonard Fergus approached, balancing himself on his cane. Jeff closed his mouth abruptly, admittedly relieved to put the conversation off until later.

"Leonard, hi," Isabella greeted.

The old man tipped his cap. "Hello, Isabella. Jeff."

Jeff nodded, feeling guilty—not for taking the easy way out of talking to Isabella, but for wanting to.

Leonard turned to Isabella kindly but with a definite sense of business. "Isabella, do you mind if I talk to Jeff alone?"

"Oh, no. Absolutely," Isabella perked up, helpful. She looked to Jeff as if wondering what he would've said if Leonard had waited thirty seconds more, then moved aside. She spoke to Jeff, "I'll be ready to leave when you are, babe."

Isabella left, and that nagging voice inside of Jeff repeated, *You should have told her. You should have asked Mr. Fergus to excuse you for a minute. You need to tell her.*

Later.

"What can I do for you, Mr. F— Leonard?"

The old man took a deep breath, preparing for something. Jeff grew tense, remembering his terrible sermon. "I couldn't help but notice you had a little trouble up there today," Leonard said in a gravelly voice that seemed perpetually filled with understanding.

Though his ears burned, Jeff was at least glad that *someone* had noticed. "I'm really sorry."

"Don't worry about it," Leonard encouraged him before Jeff could apologize any further. "Everyone has bad days. Even your father did." He finished with a wink that caused Jeff to feel like he used to in the presence of Mr. Fergus.

Leonard began again, his tone conversational, "Have you thought about what we discussed earlier? About those sermons we sent you?"

He had. Thought about them real hard. Again, another easy way out. But then he thought of Isabella. What she would have said if he'd gone through with it.

Jeff shook his head. "I have, but I…I need to be honest."

"Please do."

"I'm not really comfortable with the idea. It seems a little…staged." The words didn't come out as he intended, and Jeff cringed, hoping he hadn't offended Mr. Fergus.

"I understand completely. Your father never liked the idea of prepackaged sermons either. But things are different now. There are so many more resources out there to help you. Well, you just hang on to them. Just in case."

"OK," Jeff nodded. "Will do."

Leonard shifted his weight and headed for the doors. He turned his head and asked, "You going to the picnic today?"

The picnic! Jeff's mind raced. *Rosalyn was supposed to go with us! I forgot to call her for church! Oh, I'm losing it. Get it together, Jeff.*

"Yeah."

"Well, you let me know how it turns out."

"You're not going?"

The old man shook his head. "Nah. Got another meeting I gotta make. Miss Esther's Bridge Club. Deacon's job's never done."

"Oh," Jeff eased. "OK."

Leonard smiled and left Jeff behind. The young man emitted a desperate groan and dragged himself out to the car.

He just hoped Rosalyn was home.

CHAPTER TWELVE

T WAS NOT a good day to be Bill.

By now Rosalyn had spent the better half of an hour using him to vent her aggression. Each punch she delivered to poor Bill's face was more furious, more relentless than the last. She punched harder, oblivious to whatever pain he might feel, yet he remained silent as she beat at his visage, all in the name of therapy.

OK, so Bill was the speed bag that hung in the entryway to her kitchen.

It was a silly notion, really, to name one's punching bag, but Rosalyn felt ridiculous taking out her anger on a leather balloon. After all, she had nothing against the bag. It was an inanimate object, in no way the cause of any of her distress. But when she gave it a name, the bag seemed like someone she could blame.

Poor Bill would just have to forgive her.

With her hair pulled away from her face and boxing pads on her hands, Rosalyn unleashed her fury, trying to forget that the Strange Man found her yesterday. Saw her with her family. Saw *Annie*.

Another fist delivered to Bill.

She cried out, exhaling to make her hits more powerful. Harder and harder she pummeled the bag.

What does that man want with me? Her thoughts refused to put the subject aside. *If Dras was telling the truth—if that creep really did set him up—then why hasn't he skipped town? Why is he still here? Why won't he just leave me alone?*

Puzzling as they were, those were the easy questions. Rosalyn tried not to acknowledge the more disturbing ones, like, how the man disappeared. She didn't look away; she knew that with unwavering certainty. He disappeared right in front of her. One minute he was outside her mom's window, and then he was gone. It wasn't possible, but it happened. As insane as it sounded, either he was some kind of magician, or...

Or Dras was telling the truth. He was the devil.

"Stop it!" she roared, pounding Bill harder still. *The devil's not real, stupid! Maybe he's something else, but he can't be the devil.*

He can't be...

The sudden knock on the door ended her impromptu therapy session with Bill. She slid her workout gloves off and let them fall to the floor as she slowed her breathing, collecting herself for her visitor. Wiping her face, pushing aside a bead of sweat that was hanging on her eyebrow, she crossed the distance of her living room to the front door.

The knock again.

"I'm coming," she moaned, aggravated.

Again.

Rosalyn hurried to get to the door before the jerk on the other end had a chance to knock again. She reached for the doorknob and flung the door open, ready for a fight.

"*What?*"

The space in front of her door was empty.

She felt her muscles tense. Curious and confused, she walked into the hallway and searched the corridor, looking to the right, then the left. She saw nothing. Heard nothing, either. No shuffling footsteps signaling a hasty retreat. There was no one at all in the hallway.

Rosalyn paused and considered this: She *had* heard a knock at the door. *Right?* For a moment she swore that the space of the doorway grew colder. Her hot flesh chilled and goose bumps sprouted. Dismissing it, she eased back into her apartment.

Then she heard the sound.

It caught her off guard, but she wasn't frightened, only intrigued. Carelessly leaving her door open, she turned to face her living room.

There it is again.

It was a small sound. One that would have been completely inaudible if not for the fact that everything else in the room was dead silent. As it came to her ears once more, she held her breath and strained to listen. The sound was low, monotonous. *What is that?*

Then she realized. It was scratching. And it was coming from her window.

With her back to the door, she felt compelled to inch closer to the window, transfixed by the scratching. She made it a point over the summer to stay away from that window. When she returned home following Dras's arrest, she was shocked to find that her apartment had been broken into, this very window smashed. Later reports said that Dras murdered Deputy Adams on the street, two stories below the shattered glass. Rosalyn didn't know exactly what happened that night, and she felt it was best not to. The landlord paid for a new window, and she was careful to avoid it, fearful to investigate it too closely. Afraid it would tell her the truth about what happened here between Dras and the deputy. A truth that she might not like.

Her eyes never wavered as she stepped closer toward the window, all the while the scratching becoming a hard scraping.

Rosalyn edged closer as the whistling wind outside grew louder and the grating etched deep into her mind. Despite her nerves she forced herself to reach to the window. Her fingers moved closer.

Scratching.

Scratching.

Scratching.

She had to open the window. She reached for it. *Don't, Rosalyn…* Closer. *Closer.*

Her fingers raised the frame a hairline crack with a squeak. *Stop.*

"Hey."

Rosalyn screamed and jerked her hand back as if the window itself had addressed her. Frightened, she whirled on the man standing before her open door.

Jeff Weldon.

She had known him her whole life. He came with Dras as part of the package. He had been a big brother to her since forever. When Rosalyn was twelve and in braces, she even had a crush on him.

Right now she wanted to deck him.

"Sorry. I didn't mean to scare you. The door was open."

Rosalyn threw a quick glance back to the window. The scratching had stopped. Frustrated, she left the window behind, still barely cracked open. Shaking off her momentary jolt and regaining her cold demeanor, she huffed, "Yeah, well, knock next time."

She shrugged off the incident as if nothing in the world could scare Rosalyn Myers, but she knew Jeff would see right through that.

"Can I come in?" he said.

"You're already there as far as I can tell."

Jeff crossed the threshold and closed the door behind him. Rosalyn loosed her hair from the ponytail, shook her long locks, and made her way to the kitchen. She needed a drink. If Jeff hadn't been present she would have opted for something stronger to ease her nerves, but since the local pastor was here, she settled for water.

She reached into the refrigerator and brought out two water bottles. "Want one?"

"No, that's OK."

"Suit yourself."

Rosalyn placed one of the bottles back in the refrigerator, and Jeff took a moment to take stock of her apartment. The place looked awful. Clothes were strewn over her furniture, and dirty dishes were piled so high in her sink that Jeff thought the top one was trying to change the light bulb. Rosalyn had always shared in his often-labeled "compulsion" to clean. Now, though, it looked as though some other person was living here. This wasn't the Rosalyn he knew.

He frowned.

"How did it go at your mom's yesterday?"

Rosalyn screwed the top off her water, took a swig, and leaned against the counter in her kitchen area. "Not too bad, I guess. She's trying to go sober."

His spirits lifted. "That's *great*."

She shrugged. "Yeah, well, let's see how long it lasts before we start throwing her a party."

Jeff's happiness faded. "Oh. OK."

"So," she took a deep breath, cutting a path through niceties, "to what do I owe this visit?"

Jeff felt awkward, not really knowing what to say and certainly not wanting to be a bother. He was just worried about her. "How are you?"

"Yeah, well, you know. Busy." She took another drink.

He hung his head. "Right." Perking up, he began, "I know school's about to start. Have you given any more thought to Vermont?"

Rosalyn stared at the contents of her water bottle. "Not really. I'm thinking about taking a break from school for a while. Just doesn't really seem important anymore, you know?"

Jeff understood, but it hurt to see Rosalyn give up on something that once meant so much to her. Looking to lighten the mood, he noticed a speed bag and pointed. "I see something new has been added."

She rubbed at her brow, not sharing his enthusiasm. "My shrink—*therapist*—said it's cathartic. Whatever."

Jeff smiled as a memory came to mind, surprising himself by thinking back again to those old times with Kyle Rogers. "Remember when I got in that fight with Eddie Bornaz, senior year?"

He chuckled, still bearing the small scar from that eventful night across the bridge of his nose. Rosalyn couldn't suppress a smile for very long. "Idiot broke your nose. Me and Kyle Rogers had to keep you talking while the coach called your folks. You were all spazzing, thinking you were going to choke to death on your own blood."

Able to look back on the embarrassing drama in good humor, Jeff laughed, though he did feel his face flush. Rosalyn laughed too. It felt like old times. Rosalyn thawed a bit, leaving the kitchen to join him in the living room.

"Anyway, there was that cookout today, remember?"

She winced.

"You still going with us?"

She considered it for all of two and a half seconds. "I don't think so, Jeff."

"Come on." He turned on the charm. "It'll be fun. Besides, you said you'd go."

"No, *you* said I'd go. I thought it was a bad idea from the start."

"Why?"

"Look at us, Jeff. We don't belong in Greensboro anymore."

"What do you mean?"

"Every time they look at us, they just see Dras."

It was true. The people of Greensboro looked at his family differently these days. As if some psychotic disease had driven young Dras Weldon to murder, and it was hereditary. As if every associate of the Greensboro Ripper was one bad day away from turning into a monster. He'd even heard gossip that some members of his congregation had left the church for that very reason. Because they were afraid of him. Of his family.

"OK, we don't have to go to the cookout. We could go bowling or something. Just you, me, and Isabella."

She grinned. "You never give up, do you?"

"Not on family," he said, setting his face in stone. "No."

Rosalyn looked to the floor, hoping to hide the huge smile on her face. "You're sweet. Relentless, but sweet."

"It's just that we haven't seen you much lately and..."

Rosalyn's smile vanished. Although she knew he didn't mean anything by it—Jeff was never like that, at least not toward her—her guilty conscience spoke up for itself.

She set him straight, growing colder, "Look, if this is some kind of guilt trip because I haven't been by to see Dras since he got picked up or because I didn't sit with you and Isabella on the front row at his trial, you can save the gas. I've been up and down this road before. So many times, in fact, I'm thinking of buying some realty on it."

"No, Rosalyn. I didn't mean that. I'm just worried about you. We all are."

"Great. That's just great. Poor Rosalyn. Let's all watch to see if she cracks, right?"

She moved away from him, rolling her eyes, and took her water over to the window.

"You *know* that's not what I meant."

Exhaling, she chilled. "I know." And she *did* know. She was just being stupid and taking stuff out on Jeff instead of Bill.

Jeff took her sigh as an apology and moved behind her to look out over Greensboro.

Home, Rosalyn thought. *But it doesn't feel much like home these days.* Something squeezed her heart, and she wondered, *Where do I belong now?* Dras's face filled her mind, and this time she couldn't force it to go away.

"I miss him, Jeff. I really, really do."

It was the first time she allowed herself to say it, perhaps the first time she allowed herself to admit it.

"I do too. But I miss you too, Rosalyn." He braved a soft tug on her elbow. "Having you around... it makes it seem like he's not so far away, like he could walk in the door at any moment."

Rosalyn dwelled on that wonderful thought for a second. The possibility of Dras bursting in the door with a flourish of the arms, sporting that lopsided grin and brandishing a double feature of *Zombie Biker Mamas* and *Blood Farm Massacre*, was just about the most glorious surprise she could imagine. Yet she pulled back to spare them both the dissolution of that fantasy. "But he's *gone*. We can't pretend that we're going to wake up one morning and this will all be just a bad dream, Jeff."

"I know."

"And... that's why maybe you shouldn't come around so much anymore."

She hung her head, on the verge of tears. Jeff spun to her, hurt and confusion on his face. Rosalyn closed her eyes and fought to explain, "Because I'm trying to move on. I'm trying to stop thinking about him all the time and about how much I miss him. I love you and all, big brother, but I can't do that with you always coming here and reminding me."

When she opened her eyes, she saw Jeff slowly backing away, his own eyes watering. "Rosalyn."

"I'm sorry."

"We need to stick together now. We need each other. I need you."

But she shook her head. "Not this time, Jeff. It's time I start being on my own."

He nodded. "I understand." But she knew he was lying. She was lying to herself too.

It felt like the last remnants of their makeshift family were disintegrating. *Why are you doing this to yourself?*

"Anyway," he began clumsily, "I should probably get going then."

He moved for the door with a bittersweet half-grin, and Rosalyn watched him leave, a strange softness enveloping her. He was so tough and determined, but it was an act, just like hers. Inside they both had sorrow and fear and a need for comfort, no matter how much they would lie to each other about it. But Rosalyn wasn't ready to stop lying yet.

"Sure you don't want to come to the cookout?" he tried one last time, weakly. "You and Isabella could sit and make fun of me while I try not to strike out at the baseball game."

"As tempting as that sounds, I think I'll sit this one out."

"OK. But the offer still stands. And I *will* keep praying for you."

"I'll keep needing it."

Jeff waved and opened the door to make his exit. In a flash, seeing him about to leave—her last friend in the world—Rosalyn thought to stop him. "Jeff?"

He turned, an expectant hope on his face and a few tears escaping his eyes. A voice inside Rosalyn—a voice that sounded a lot like Dras's—screamed at her. *Tell him, Rosalyn! Tell him not to go! Tell him you need his help! Tell him that you saw the Strange Man! Tell him!*

She shushed the voice. "Nothin'. Have a good time."

Jeff's eyes dimmed. He nodded.

With that he was gone, and Rosalyn was finally alone.

CHAPTER THIRTEEN

TIMMY WHITAKER KNEW better than to play by the lake. His father used to take him to Greensboro Park Lake all the time. It was their private fishing hole, where the boy learned many things about life and what a man should be. One Sunday morning, about three months back, though, young Timmy raced ahead of his dad to the water's edge, eager to get a head start on the morning and show his dad how many fish he could catch on his own.

But that morning something was wrong with the fish.

They were all dead—bobbing and bumping into each other, all floating on the surface. Timmy's father, Franklin, placed a worried call, and the police came to check out the strange occurrence. In the process they found the remains of Lindsey McCormick's car, sans Lindsey.

The rumors started shortly thereafter that the lake was poisoned. The waters turned black and oily, more like a tar pit than a lake, now, and curious little boys were warned to stay far away, Timmy included.

But some little boys, like Timmy's buddy Sean Patrick, did not heed the warning.

"Sean, we're not supposed to be here," Timmy whined, yet he remained crouching in the dead grass with his older friend.

"Quiet, you baby," Sean hissed.

The picnic was in progress not far away, and it was Sean's idea to come out to the "haunted lake" to see if the stories were true. He caught a frog in the park and now held it as tightly as he could without killing it. Timmy kept back, having braved the venture this far but not wanting to get any closer to the banks of the dead water.

"Watch this." Sean grinned, edging closer to the dark mire.

Timmy didn't want to, but he did. If he didn't, Sean would think he was a coward, and at his age, no boy wanted to be known as a coward.

Sean dangled the frog over the surface of the muck. The frightened amphibian kicked and jerked, trying to break free, but Sean had him trapped. Timmy watched with silent dread, waiting.

THWIP!

Both boys jerked in surprise as the lake reached out and snatched the frog from Sean's hand with what looked like a sticky, black tongue. Sean laughed in delight as the frog was pulled into the tar, the surface barely disturbed. Timmy stepped back, repulsed.

"You shouldn't have done that."

Sean waved him off, already seeking what other little critters he could feed to the lake.

"Hey, you kids! Get away from there!"

Sean and Timmy spun around and saw old Miss Jenkins shooing them from the bank with her rather large and flowery purse. Both boys shot out like bullets, running from the scene of their crime without another word and hurrying back to the picnic.

The elderly woman watched them leave, disgruntled by their antics. Roberta Jenkins had never had children of her own, and for that she was grateful. She had enough on her hands keeping everyone else's children in line. That was the problem with the world today. No one watched their kids.

"Boys!" she huffed in disgust, then muttered more objections under her breath.

The lake gurgled once and she fell silent.

Then, before her stunned eyes, a little frog with the blackest of eyes hopped out of the dark slush and bounded away in an unnatural manner, as if in slow-motion. Miss Jenkins frowned at the odd sight, then hobbled back toward the picnic, glancing back once to see the frog watching her.

Just watching.

The picnic was in full swing as, everywhere across Greensboro Park, men manned their barbecue grills and shared stories while their rambunctious children ran freely in and around the main pavilion with mothers chasing after them chiding "don't touch that" and "stay out of that." The afternoon was at its climax, and those who were not keeping a close eye on their grills were at the obligatory community-wide baseball game. The call of the sport lured most of the menfolk away from their women long enough to try their skill—or luck, depending on how one looked at it—at a friendly competition.

A wood bat slapped against leather and the baseball zoomed across the field as Larry Sanderson ducked to preserve his head. A couple of his teammates moaned at the decision to save his own life rather than stop the ball, while the noncomplainers rushed off to chase the ball before the runner made it to second base.

Jeff Weldon was up to bat next. He took his place at home plate and stretched a bit, preparing for the swing. Sheriff Hank Berkley functioned as the catcher and attempted a little friendly chitchat with the reverend, as if hoping to make up for their fight yesterday at Smokey's. "Hit a homer."

"I'll try, Hank."

The two men smiled at each other, all trespasses forgotten, and Jeff braced for the pitch. Standing atop the pitcher's mound was Earl Canton. Earl was the town instigator, always pulling up a stool at the bar at Smokey's and spouting off about every topic under the sun, making sure no one left his presence without hearing his view.

Earl cracked a devious grin as he wound up for the pitch. With a heave he sent a spiraling baseball toward home plate. Jeff swung but missed by a mile.

"Strike one!" Hank called.

Jeff lowered his head and shook the knots out of his shoulder, loosening up. It'd been years since he'd played ball in school, but the feel of the bat in his hands brought back a thousand great memories of his childhood and adolescence. Once again he thought of Kyle Rogers. His nostalgic enjoyment was somewhat dampened, however, by Earl's zeal. Soft enough for only Hank to hear, Jeff muttered, "Throwing a little fast, isn't he?"

"That's Earl. Just trying to show off. Relax; you'll do fine."

Jeff nodded to the pitcher that he was ready for another one. Earl let go another shimmering zinger over home plate, forcing Jeff to scoot back to avoid being plowed down by the ball. The ball dug itself into Hank's mitt with a loud *thut* that reverberated over the field.

Earl chuckled. Jeff took a deep breath.

"Slow 'er down, Earl," Hank reprimanded lightheartedly. "We're not in the big leagues. Just a few old men trying to get some kicks."

Some of the men on the team laughed, sharing in the friendly good humor. Jeff took his position again. He was going to hit this one, and hit it hard. Right over the chain-link fence. Maybe, if he was lucky, it would bust out the windshield on Earl's truck.

Jeff squinted savagely.

Earl wound up and shot off a cannonball of fury, only this time a little to the right. Jeff turned to soften the blow, but that was all he could do as the ball struck him square in the back with a sickening *smack*. Hank stood and hurried to Jeff's aid. "You OK, Reverend?"

Jeff nodded, gnawing his bottom lip, nearly drawing blood. "I'm fine."

"That's a walk!" Hank shouted for all to hear.

He patted Jeff on the arm and sent him on his way to first base, where Will stood guard. Jeff, still massaging the sore area on his back, touched the base and leaned over, taking deep breaths.

"Sir, are you all right?" Will said.

"Yeah. I'm OK. Just forget it."

Will backed away, giving the man room to breathe. Jeff risked a look into the stands, where he met Isabella's worried eyes. Then he looked away. The game must go on.

The next batter took his place, and when Earl delivered a considerably softer throw, the bat thundered against the ball and sent it skyrocketing in the air. The crowd cheered as those on base ran. The man on third crossed home with Jeff on his heels. He checked the field to see the right fielder scooping up the ball and readying to throw it in, then turned back to his goal and lowered his head, racing ahead.

Everyone in the stands stood, cheering him on. Jeff was nearly safe, but somehow Earl managed to get the ball in his grip and shot toward the base. Growling, he charged into Jeff, sideswiping him and sending him sprawling to the ground. The spectators dropped to an awed hush.

Without missing a beat, Jeff sprang up and into Earl's smirking face. "What is your problem?"

"Maybe I just don't like your kind mixing with us regular folk!"

"My kind?"

The game crawled to a standstill, and the onlookers moved forward for a closer look at what was sure to be a fight. "Yeah." Earl's bushy handlebar mustache bristled. "*Christians*. That's what you church people call yourselves, isn't it?"

By now Isabella had fought her way through to be by Jeff's side, out of breath.

"You know," Earl spoke loudly, "your brother says he's a Christian too. Now, isn't that funny?" He stopped to look around at the crowd to see if they too saw the humor. "Dras was the biggest no-good punk who always ended up drunker than a skunk on Saturday nights but still managed to get himself to church first thing Sunday morning.

And he said *he* was a *Christian*? Now, how is that? What makes him any better than us?"

Jeff searched for the words to defend his brother, but Isabella beat him to it. "He's not like that anymore. He's changed."

"Oh, right!" Earl played it up for the crowd. "I almost forgot. Now, he's the Greensboro Ripper. A murdering monster who rants and raves like a crazy person saying that the devil killed those people and *framed* him. So, preacher," Earl redirected his taunts to Jeff, "which one is it? Which one is a Christian? The drunk who shows up on Sunday mornings or the loony who talks about hellfire and brimstone? If those are my options with your religion, I think I'll take my chances with the sinners. Ha!" He guffawed, and some in the crowd joined with him.

"You don't know the whole truth." Jeff forced the words through gritted teeth.

"Well, lay it on me, Reverend. What is *the whole truth*? The Good Book? Well now, I'm no saint, but I've been to my fair share of Sunday school. Doesn't it say in the Bible 'an eye for an eye'? You must not believe that's the truth, because you want mercy for your brother and not what he's got coming. I guess that 'eye for an eye' doesn't apply to you, does it?" Earl turned to the crowd, gesturing toward Jeff so all could see. "See how it is! He can't even keep his own house in order, but he's preaching to you about how to live and what to believe and how to raise your families! When even he proves that he doesn't believe what the Bible says about a simple thing like 'eye for an eye.'"

"That's Old Testament law," Jeff quietly explained, though knew it was a useless argument.

Isabella said, "Jesus taught about grace and said that we should have love for our enemies."

"Right." Earl's tone was condescending. "Love our enemies. So is that why you defend a convicted killer? *We're* the ones you should be defending. Poor Millie Walker has barely said three words since she watched your brother murder hers. *She's* the victim. *We're* the victims! You turned your back on your community to stand behind a monster!"

Jeff stopped to look at the faces of the crowd. They were visibly uncomfortable, but no one moved to protest. He wondered if they all felt this way.

Earl stabbed at Jeff again. "And now that Dras is on death row, now what does the reverend do? He scurries all over town, 'humbling' himself to be everyone's servant boy. Yard sales and baby showers and barn raisings. Just call the preacher, and he'll help you out! You know why, don't ya? He's trying to win back our good graces. He's trying to be one of us again." Then Earl turned to Jeff, his words cruel and venomous. "But we don't want you, Reverend! Maybe they'll take you over on the East Side with the other freaks and lowlifes, but stay away from the rest of us. Just go on back to defending that murdering brother of yours..." Earl trailed off, hesitating, but only to prepare for his final blow, "...*and* that Trysdale Trash he runs around with."

Rosalyn. Jeff saw red.

He swung a fist on reflex.

The crowd gasped in surprise as Earl and his newly busted lip crashed to the dirt. Isabella tried to hold Jeff back, and upon her touch, he retracted and staved off the desire to finish the job. Defiant, he stood over the crumpled body of Earl Canton, waiting for the loudmouth to regain his senses and get to his feet. Jeff's fist was still clenched, and he felt the sting where Earl's front teeth had cut his knuckle. The pain was exhilarating. He hadn't felt that strong and wild since his fight with Eddie Bornaz back in high school.

Something old and dark awoke in Jeff, and it was liberating.

Then he noticed the faces of the crowd staring in horror at what he'd just done. There were children among them. Some were in Isabella's Sunday school class before they left when all this mess with Dras started. They were children he shared Bible stories with, laughed with, and hugged. He bought them presents on their birthdays. These were children who looked up to him.

And now they stared at him like he'd become some kind of monster.

Suddenly, he wanted to run forever. To leave here and never show his face again. He could feel Isabella holding on to him, but he couldn't face her. He knew that he had disappointed her like never before, and the burden was so heavy and sharp that it felt like a mortal wound.

A couple of Earl's buddies helped him to his feet, but instead of burning with rage, the burly bully seemed glad to have been decked. With a laugh, still wiping the blood from his lip, he turned to the gathered. "You see! Is this how he 'loves his enemies'? By attacking them? Is this what he teaches up there at that church of his? Is this what a Christian is? They tell all us that they want freedom to believe what they want to believe, but they attack the first person who disagrees with them! Hypocrites!"

Jeff fought to hide his shame, but his face flushed hot, and he knew everyone could see it. Isabella turned to Will Baxter, who stood close by, and leaned into him, pleading, "Say something, Will."

Will only stuck his hands in his pockets and hung his head. Isabella searched the crowd until she saw the sheriff. Her tear-filled eyes fell upon him, and Jeff heard her whisper, *"Help him."*

Hank shifted uncertainly. Jeff knew Earl intimidated Hank, as he did almost every man here, lording over them all with his big talk. Hank's eyes showed signs of fear, but hoping to restore order, he stepped between the two warring factions. "All right, Earl," he said with a nervous chuckle, "I think we all need to just cool off. It's been a hard time for everybody, and we need to just—"

But a woman interrupted him. "No, Sheriff. Let him talk."

The crowd parted like the Red Sea to let the gray-haired woman through. Jeff recognized her as Dorothy Adams. Mother of the murdered Deputy Adams.

Trembling, she moved past the people to stand before the crowd. "I'd like to hear what Earl has to say." Then she turned her attention to Jeff. "You talk of a loving God? Where was your God when my son was torn to ribbons? Can you tell me?"

Her voice broke, and hot, bitter tears streaked her wrinkled cheeks. Jeff realized that he had no answers for her, and it sickened him. Where was God in all of this? Why didn't He ever do something instead of just standing around while so many people hurt?

He didn't know. And he didn't like it.

Isabella held a hand over her mouth to muffle her sobs. Jeff knew she wanted to help, to say something to make it all go away. But even Isabella didn't have any words of comfort or wisdom either. Not this time. Nothing would fill the hole in the grieving woman's heart.

Dorothy continued, her anger and pain escalating, "Why don't you go to my eight-year-old grandson—who will never hug his daddy again, Reverend Weldon—and tell him about your loving God?"

Jeff could only meet her with sadness and silence.

Then she slapped him.

He closed his eyes and embraced the sting. Isabella gasped and no longer concerned herself with hiding her cries.

"That's what I think of you and your God."

Dorothy left then, disappearing into the crowd. Earl gloated over Jeff, pleased with the end result of his outburst. Finally Isabella stood to face her husband and put a hand over his heart, as if to stop the bleeding of his inner wounds. "Let's go."

She took the lead, and the two of them walked off the field, the rest of Greensboro turning their backs on them.

Hank called out after them, sullen. "All right, folks. Show's over."

The picnic was ruined. Families solemnly packed up their blankets, baskets, and grills and dispersed, while Sheriff Hank Berkley reflected on the emotional scene. He was in the process of packing his Jeep and felt horribly torn. He hated to see Jeff hurt, but the boy just didn't know when to quit. Dras was in prison. The trial was long gone. It was over. *Let it lie, son.*

But he knew the young reverend well enough to know that he would not let it lie—not until he uncovered the truth, no matter who got hurt along the way.

Hank loaded up his cooler and closed the Jeep's rear door. He was alone again today, as always at such events. "*I'm tired, Hank. I've seen you play ball before,*" Doris would say each time he asked her to come along. As he moved around to the driver's side of his Jeep, Hank spotted a familiar face over by the lake.

Special Agent Perdu, still wearing his dark overcoat despite the heat, was down on his haunches examining the withered grass around the edge of the cloudy lake.

Hank frowned. There was another one who couldn't leave well enough alone.

"Might not want to get too close," Hank thundered across the field.

The federal agent dropped the blade of yellowed grass he was holding and faced Hank. His startled expression bloomed into a smile, and he stood, dusting himself off. "Why's that?"

Christopher approached the Jeep, and Hank met him halfway. "Lake's not been much good for fishing these days. Nothing can stay alive in it. Some folks even think that it's toxic now. Killing all the critters around it, grass, everything."

Special Agent Perdu nodded and glared studiously at the lake, mulling the information over. "I'll be careful."

Hank headed back to his Jeep and motioned for Perdu to follow him, hoping to lead him away from the accursed tar pit. "We found the McCormick girl in there," the sheriff began, then corrected himself. "Well, that is to say, we found her car. To tell the truth, we still don't know what became of that poor girl." He shook his head. "It's killing her father."

Perdu nodded in the attentive way he did, as if he were writing all this down somewhere on a mental notepad. Then he paused in his internal processing and regarded the sheriff thoughtfully. "Do you have any children, Sheriff?"

Hank stopped, not having expected the question. He had almost forgotten how to answer something so simple. "Yeah. I have a daughter. Becky."

Perdu nodded again, and Hank imagined Perdu jotting it down in that Fed-head of his: *Check. One daughter. Becky.*

"Sheriff, I look around your town, and you know what I see is the biggest problem?"

Hank kept walking alongside Perdu in a friendly manner, though inwardly he was pretty sure the federal agent was about to go traipsing outside his jurisdiction and all across that of the Maribel County Sheriff's Department. "Enlighten me."

"Nobody wants to ask the hard questions. Why was Dras jealous of TJ Walker? Dras and Lindsey broke up over a year ago, and she had been dating TJ for months. Why would Dras suddenly get so jealous it would drive him to murder? And where are the bodies? The only body found was your deputy's, and it was covered in teeth marks and scratches. He was nearly cut to strips, but a murder weapon was never found. Ever. In fact, it's hard to imagine a weapon that could have done something like that in the short amount of time Dras spent with the deputy. How could Dras have overpowered him in the first place?"

Hank listened uncomfortably as Christopher continued, "Maybe the court made its decision too soon. But we may never know because nobody is searching for the truth anymore. You have the popular opinion. But no one wants to find out the *truth*." This time Perdu stopped, his face twisted in consternation, his light blue eyes searching. Always searching. "What would you want your daughter to grow up believing, Sheriff Berkley? Popular opinion? Or the truth?"

Hank didn't answer. He didn't know if he was supposed to. It was a hard question. Sure, the truth would be nice, but what if the truth was dangerous? "Hard to be sure sometimes if the truth's always worth knowing."

"It's easy to go with the crowd, Sheriff. It's harder to stand for what's right, but more rewarding. I can promise you that."

But after seeing what the search for answers had done to Jeff Weldon, Hank had to wonder if that was so.

CHAPTER FOURTEEN

HIS FATHER CALLED it "God's Cliff." Like a proud and solemn giant, the precipice rested on the edge of Greensboro, overlooking the town. The sun set and twilight slowly descended, and from here the neighborhood lights twinkled like stars in a suburban galaxy. From here the casual observer could easily mistake Greensboro for a quiet, inviting town. *"A Nice Place to Live,"* just like it said on the sign at the city limits.

From here things still made sense.

Jeff hadn't been to this place in a long time. Almost twelve years, if he remembered right. *Has it really been that long?* He decided it must have been. That was when they moved into the new church in town. Half a mile from God's Cliff slumbered the old country church that once belonged to Jack Weldon. The original Good Church of the Faithful. Now it was a lopsided shack that sat amidst the North Woods as a monument to an all but forgotten era in Greensboro history. The vines grew around and through it, threatening to pull it into the ground—into its grave—but the old church refused to die.

Jeff loved his church in town, but there *was* a charm and a wisdom about his father's church and that special place he called God's Cliff that he always missed. And now, although the walls were moldy, the wood was rotted, the pews were uncomfortable, the spiders had taken up residence, and there was a cool, musty draft blowing through the missing patches in the ceiling, Jeff Weldon came to get a bit of that old magic back.

After spending some time looking over the abandoned church, Jeff made his way to God's Cliff and took a good look at the deceptively ordinary streets of Greensboro. Here he hoped to gain a better perspective on life. God's Cliff had brought a deep joy to his father long ago, but today Jeff felt cold to the touch of the Holy Spirit and could only remain silent and morose. He wondered if God was still here, if He was still in the business of answering prayers, or if He, like everyone else in Greensboro, had closed His doors to the needy.

Wind played in the blades of the unkempt grass, but no voice from heaven addressed his concerns. A big sigh escaped Jeff's lips as he sunk into the ground like a grim stone statue planted amidst the green fields and surrounding pink and purple skies. With his hands buried deep in his pockets, his broad shoulders taut, and a firm, unflinching set in his jaw, he remained a vigilant watchman over a town that no longer wanted him.

"Hey, you," Isabella spoke from behind. She hooked her arm in his and leaned her head against his shoulder. Together they looked out at the sunset.

"Hey," he responded mechanically.

"Are you OK?"

He continued to stand in silence next to her, burdened by his own guilt. She squeezed his arm gently, as if to coax him to come back to her. He knew he was shutting her out. He could feel her eyes on him, waiting for him to look at her. But still he couldn't. Not yet.

"My father used to bring us up here. Me, Dras, and Rosalyn." He chuckled at the memory of little Rosalyn Myers demanding to go anywhere Dras went. "He used to say that whenever anything was really wrong in his life, he could come up here and be reminded that God was watching over us."

However, Jeff's fond memories were short-lived. "But God's not here anymore."

Isabella turned to him, sharp. "Jeff, don't say that."

Jeff fought back the lump in his throat and the bitterness that darkened his heart. "I've prayed and I've fasted and I did everything I thought I was supposed to do." His teeth ground together, his body tensing. "And all I wanted was my brother. I waited on God to come and set everything straight. To clear Dras of all the crimes and show everyone that he's innocent. To bring justice like He's *supposed* to."

Jeff paused, defeated. "But He never came."

Isabella remained quiet, letting Jeff vent his angered thoughts. Finally, after a long moment, Jeff broke from the trance and shook his head with his eyes shut in regret. "I can't believe I hit him." Isabella cradled him, combing her fingers through his hair. He fought back a cry. "Did you see their faces? I can't imagine how the rest of the town is going to react when they hear about it."

Isabella did not respond. She just kept stroking his head, waiting for him to let it all go. Jeff sobbed suddenly and a tear escaped down one cheek. His heart broke at last, and Isabella held him tighter. "I let them all down. I should have never let him get to me like that."

"You just made a mistake, baby. It's OK."

"I can't afford to make mistakes, Isabella. I should have been—I'm supposed to be *better* than this. But I keep slipping, just like last time." Tears welled up in his eyes.

"You mean with Dras?"

"I–it's my fault. This is all my fault."

His eyes stung with hot tears, and he scrunched his face, helpless against his own sorrow. Isabella kissed his cheek and took his face in her hands, forcing him to focus on her dark, loving eyes. "You put too much pressure on yourself, Jeff. You are a great man. But you are *still* a man, a man who makes mistakes. But that's *OK*. It's *OK* to stumble and fall, as long as you don't stay down. You have to reach out to God and let Him pick you up."

A part of him wanted to hold on to her and her words. But another part told him he didn't deserve her sympathy or love. He had brought this ruin to his family. That night of the storm he felt as though God were telling him to do something—to stand against the coming evil—but he'd refused that call and Dras seemed chosen instead. Now Dras was as good as dead and Jeff was left behind. Had God left him as punishment for not being obedient in the beginning? What if this had been Jeff's purpose and he'd squandered it?

"Falling down doesn't make you a failure, Jeff. But *staying* down does." Isabella said, but he didn't want to listen to her anymore. Didn't want her pity. This was his problem to deal with.

Raising his head, Jeff turned his attention back to Greensboro and gestured toward the lights below them as the sun hid itself below the horizon, casting them into darkness. "Look around. All our friends are gone, Iz. They all left. Everyone left."

"I didn't." She stared at him, full of determination. "I'm still here, remember?" Jeff didn't reply, only glared at the town below them with contempt.

Isabella hung her head, then voiced, thoughtfully, "I wonder if this is how Habakkuk felt."

Jeff finally looked at her, perplexed. "What?"

"The prophet Habakkuk in the Old Testament. Remember? He said to God 'How long, O Lord, must I call for help, but you do not listen? Or cry out to you, "Violence!" but you do not save? Why do you make me look at injustice? Why do you tolerate wrong?'"

Jeff listened silently and Isabella finished, "But do you remember what God said? 'Look at the nations and watch—and be utterly amazed. For I am going to do something in your days that you would not believe, even if you were told.'"

Jeff grew quiet, feeling night approaching. The wind had chilled, and soon it'd be time for sleep. Time for the nightmares again. Isabella was pressed against him, ready to listen to whatever he had to say. Maybe now he should tell her about the things he saw in those terror visions...but he couldn't. He wasn't ready.

But something *had* to be said about the threat that had claimed Dras. "What if Dras is right? What if the demons are still—" He nodded toward the town below, quiet and unsuspecting. "—out there?"

It was Isabella's turn to pull away. Her face somber, her body tense, she turned toward town. Jeff watched her, seeing how frightened she was. It surprised him. Isabella never seemed frightened of anything. "I don't know," was all she said at first. "It's been three months and nothing. Maybe they're gone. Maybe they were just here to create panic and paranoia and resentment. Maybe they're *hoping* that people will finish the job. That's what demons do, isn't it?"

Jeff wanted to believe that. But there was no fairy-tale end for them. Whatever evil Dras had fought and lost against, it remained and would only grow stronger unchecked. No one was willing to help, to fight back. It was hopeless.

We're doomed.

Isabella snuggled up to him, earnest despite the levity in her tone. "God's still in control, Jeff. Things are looking pretty bad, but He's still on the throne, and if we just be patient and wait on Him, I know that He will be faithful to answer our prayers in even greater ways than we could have expected. He's *God*," she breathed, a sense of reverent wonder in her eyes.

Jeff knew that Isabella believed every word she was saying. But right now he didn't want to hear it. It only made him angrier. It seemed like God wasn't listening anymore, and if that were the case, Jeff would have to find his own solutions. He could fix this. He could fight the evil, save the town. He could—

"I could save Dras. I know I could. If I just—"

"You can't," Isabella stepped back, surprised. "You have to let go, Jeff. Let God be God. Turn it over to Him."

"What am I supposed to do in the meantime?" he growled.

"Trust Him," she said simply. "Have faith."

"What if that isn't enough?"

But before Isabella could answer, Jeff abruptly left her standing on the edge of God's Cliff. He couldn't talk about this anymore.

Isabella watched her husband stomp back to his truck, disciplining herself to be strong and not give in to the panic that nipped at her heels, ready to bring her down at any second.

"It has to be, Jeff," she whispered after his dark, retreating frame. "Otherwise, what hope do we have?"

Around a fine oak table in a secret meeting place at a secret hour, four of six leather upholstered wingback chairs were filled. Seated in them were educated men, influential and powerful business owners, cunning leaders. They were the molders of Greensboro's destiny, the makers of the small town's future and perhaps the engineers of its demise.

They were the Committee.

He'd never wanted any part in their dark business. He'd only been drafted because of his last name. Maybe in the beginning he thought he could have done something to stop this—affect change from the inside.

But now he knew better.

In silence he sat with the others in a cavernous room with no windows, surrounded by opulence. Works of art lined the walls, distracting from the gloom of the meeting place, and rare books of Greensboro's secret history and its lore lined a bookshelf in the corner. The warm light of candles did little to ward off the darkness that shrouded the aged men's faces as they waited for the remaining members of their brood to fill the two empty chairs at the table. The others sipped at brandy, murmuring solemnly amongst themselves, while he watched them in disgust, refusing to join in their conversations.

They think we're safe, but they're just fooling themselves.

At last the doors opened, and Mr. Hayden and Mr. Simms entered the room. Mr. Simms took a seat with the others, while Mr. Hayden took his rightful position at the head of the table, choosing to remain standing.

Looming over all those gathered, Hayden addressed them as one. "Gentlemen, we have much to discuss."

Mr. Simms, the counterpart to their leader, turned to face the Committee. "We have a new emergency, one that we did not anticipate at this stage."

The other men listened intently as the man at the head of the table spoke. "It appears that the change has started. Our Dr. Brown has discovered a..." Mr. Hayden paused, easing into the word, "...virus."

The Committee broke into an uproar of concern and fear, the men clamoring to be heard over one another. Mr. Hayden and Mr. Simms, however, remained perfectly composed and in control.

"A virus?" Lanky Mr. Gibson leaned forward to break away from the ranks of those seated. "Is it contagious?"

Mr. Hayden made a calming gesture. "As far as can be told, no. It does not spread as a normal virus."

Immediately sighs of relief reverberated in the chamber.

Mr. Simms continued, "Which gives us cause to think of this as something more...*supernatural.*"

Awed silence. Recognition in every eye. Suddenly their pact seemed all the more real. And terrifying.

That's it. I can't hold my tongue any longer.

"We should never have agreed to this," he stated from his place at the end of the table. All eyes turned on him as he clasped his hands over the handle of his cane.

"Now, now, Leonard," Mr. Hayden placated the old man coldly. "We have nothing to worry about. Our deal has granted us immunity when the change comes, remember?"

"But what about the others?" Leonard Fergus turned to his fellow Committee members, looking for support. "What about our families?"

"They too will be saved," Mr. Nigel, the bushy eyebrowed diminutive man in the tailor-made suit sitting across from Simms, reminded everyone. Yet he was unable to hide the doubt in his voice. "That was part of our arrangement, right?"

Leonard was fed up with the whole lot of them now. They just wouldn't see it. They didn't want to see it. "Forgive me, *gentlemen*, but I don't trust our 'benefactor,' Mr. Graves. He has proved lawless in the past, careless, and in no way cooperative with the Committee or our requests."

"It's a little late to try and revoke our bargain, Mr. Fergus." Mr. Gibson shot a scolding look to Fergus in an effort to end his traitorous words.

"It's only too late if we stand by and do nothing to repair the damage we've already done!" Fergus stood, using his cane for support, refusing to keep quiet. Gibson followed suit and rose to challenge him.

"The agreement has already been made, Fergus." Mr. Jacobson, at forty-seven, the youngest and most handsome of the gathered men, sighed in resignation.

Hayden and Simms shared a look, reaching a decision without either man saying a word, and Hayden spoke with authority. "Enough."

Fergus and Gibson cooled and turned to the leader of their order.

"We were told to await the Dark Hour, and now, whether we like it or not, that time is coming to fruition. There is little we can do now except to hide this latest development from the public at all costs until we receive further orders from Mr. Graves."

Hayden finished, and Simms took over. "The last thing we need is another incident like the Greensboro Ripper case. Fortunately, Mr. Jacobson and his men in the courts assure us there will be no room for an appeal."

Hayden picked up again. "Our secret is safe, and if we handle this new matter carefully, the town will return to normal, and no one will be the wiser."

With that Mr. Hayden paused, visually reprimanding Gibson and Fergus individually. "Am I understood?"

Like a rebuked child, Gibson hung his head and took his seat, but defiance remained in Leonard Fergus's soul.

There had to be another way.

He was determined to find it.

CHAPTER FIFTEEN

WITH THE SUN set and the day ended, Hank dwelled on the events of the afternoon over an order of french fries. He and Special Agent Perdu had managed to talk the day away. Perdu was an all right guy, Hank determined. Sure, he was a bit intense, but that was youth for you, and he seemed to have a good heart.

The two of them drove over to Beefy Burgers, a small outdoor hamburger joint, after the sun went down. It was the magic hour, and after the drama of the picnic, everyone had called it a day. Despite the fact that the curfew had been lifted after the Ripper case was closed, the streets were nevertheless bare and peaceful in Greensboro. It was a nice change of pace from the chaos that was always waiting for Hank back at the station these days.

Hank glanced at Perdu, who hadn't ordered. "Sure you don't want anything?"

Christopher, for the fourth time, chuckled. "That's OK. I'm not hungry."

Hank shrugged and continued to eat, but Christopher didn't allow him to stay quiet for long. His face focused, he titled his head forward. "Have you talked to the little Walker girl?"

Hank set his fry down, wondering if this guy ever relaxed. He looked up at the young man, tired and flustered. "What would be the point? She gave her testimony already. That's what convicted the Weldon kid. Look, why don't we just—"

"I know, but a courtroom can be a pretty scary place for an adult, let alone a little girl. Maybe if we could talk to her in a more comfortable environment—"

"Forget it, Perdu," Hank ended the notion. He respected the kid's eagerness, even admired it, but... "That family's been through enough already. We need to just let them move on with their lives. Try and get past this horrible thing."

"Why do I get the feeling that you don't want me poking around?

I'm just trying to make sure an innocent man doesn't get the electric chair, Sheriff."

"I know that," Hank said. "And I appreciate what you're trying to do." *But I'm an old man,* Hank thought. *I've got a family to think about. I'm too tired to be going on daredevil adventures and challenging the system.* He sighed as he popped another ketchup-drenched fry in his mouth. "I just want all of this to be over."

"The night you brought Dras in..." Christopher leaned in closer, lowering his voice to a whisper. "Did he say something? Something that scared you?"

Hank choked on the fry.

After he recovered, Perdu leaned back in his seat, pleased, as if his question had been answered. He regarded the sheriff expectantly, waiting for more. Hank checked over his shoulder, unwilling to continue, but Christopher urged him, "The truth needs to be told, Sheriff, no matter how unpopular it is. If we don't have the truth, then what do we have? Please, Sheriff."

Hank shifted, weighing his words before he finally answered. "The bogeyman."

Christopher listened.

"Dras mentioned the bogeyman. He called him 'the Strange Man.' He said that *he* was the one behind the murders."

Hank watched Special Agent Perdu take in the new information with a look of concern across his face. He was quiet. Hank worried he had said too much, and now this kid was thinking him a superstitious fool.

"Did you believe him?" Perdu was more serious than Hank had expected.

Hank considered for a moment. "I don't know." He laughed to break the tension. "I stopped believing in the bogeyman a long time ago."

Perdu was not laughing, and his solemn demeanor unnerved the old sheriff more than a little. "Maybe that's why he's back."

At about midnight Danny Carpenter returned to Greensboro. He had spent the daylight hours hiding in the woods. After nightfall he drove at breakneck speeds, trying to elude *them*, trying to find his way out of the maze of the North Woods, hoping that the police would not spot him and deter him from his mission. With every mile he drove in the ethereal green fog that settled over the dark, deserted streets, he could hear their multitudes growing nearer.

Hurried glances chanced behind him did nothing to calm his nerves. They were still hungry and getting closer by the second. He couldn't see them now, but he knew they were still out there somewhere.

Entering Greensboro, he veered down the first road he saw, losing a hubcap in the process. But he wouldn't slow down. This was too important. He accelerated in panic, clasping the steering wheel of his faded black '87 Monte Carlo tighter with each swerve, fighting a losing battle to keep control of the car as he wove his way around Greensboro. He couldn't resist the compulsion to cast one more look behind him. He jerked his head back, and only the darkness stared back at him. He allowed himself a moment to calm, but when he turned back around, he saw the end of the road. The Monte Carlo missed the turn and catapulted off the road and into an oak tree. Danny yelled and tugged the steering wheel, only succeeding in smashing the front right side of his car, wrapping it around the tree. The impact slammed him against the steering wheel, and his horn blared into the night.

After a moment, shaking himself alert, he staggered out of the car, bruised and sporting a minor cut on his forehead from the shattered windshield.

He ran. *I gotta find them.*

Two steps later he realized that his ankle was sprained, but he gritted his teeth and bore the pain. Trying to ignore the ache shooting up his leg like needles, he forced himself to run as fast as his new injury would allow. As he struggled, he heard their clicking in the shadows—like ten thousand cockroaches scurrying behind him, their nails scratching and scraping the concrete, asphalt, and brick. With frightened expectancy he watched the night around him, ready for an attack as he entered the East Side.

Demonic laughter filled the starless sky, a shrill squeal of ravenous delight. They were savoring the hunt. They planned to savor his death as well. But not now! Not when he was so close!

The old neighborhood was coming into view, and he nearly smiled despite the pain and blood and possible broken ribs. He hobbled along, hearing their twitching and scratching grow faster.

Ducking down an alley, Danny hunkered behind a Dumpster and watched as a blur of shapes, blacker than black and darker than the darkest night, fluttered past. His throat went dry. The churning, ambiguous mass carried on, taking the sounds of devilish giggling with it, and Danny thought he might be safe.

To his horror five tiny shapes broke loose from the herd of monsters and entered the alleyway. By the glow of the streetlight Danny glimpsed the creatures. They were child-sized, with charcoal skin. Their jagged needlelike teeth were too large for their football-shaped heads and glistened in the pale light. And those eyes—black and bulging, with animal intelligence.

The tiny beasts scouted the alleyway, searching for him. There was no way he could ever hope to outrun the thousands of those monsters that hunted him, but five? He might be able to outsmart five of them.

Better decide quick. They were closing in on his hiding place.

Keeping low, he made to sneak away—then knocked over a trash can.

He halted and pivoted to face them. One of them hopped on the Dumpster and lifted its head to the night. The critter clicked its teeth together, a shrill cicada sound.

Worse, the larger shape a block away returned the call.

They're talking to each other. Little freak just blew the whistle on me.

The five monsters turned on Danny, spreading their lips around their elongated fangs, and advanced, climbing the walls, skittering on the ground. Danny let fly a volley of obscenities and thought, *Ah, why not?*

He beat on his chest, laughing in their face. "Come on, suckers! Come and get me!"

He turned tail and ran, knocking another trash can out of his way, refusing to let any obstacle slow him down. Out of the corner of his eye he caught sight of reinforcements turning back and headed his way again. The five leaped into the air, pulled into the churning cloud. Challenged by an insignificant human, the amorphous blob spread through the neighborhood behind him, filling every crevice with their evil. He ran faster and faster, cutting a hard right and taking off through the backyards of his one-time neighbors, only able to catch a glimpse of the monsters over the roofs. He heard dogs, contained by chain-link fences, howling, defending their territory. As the twitching things in the darkness followed in pursuit, the angry dogs whimpered then grew silent.

Danny lost sight of the creatures in the maze of the East Side streets. With the coast clear for the moment, he bolted toward a broken-down trailer in the distance.

"Please be home…" he wheezed.

Unable to waste any time, he ran full force for the front door. He limped up the metal steps and grabbed the doorknob, ready to give it a twist and rush inside, but discovered the door was locked.

"Tabitha!" he called out, banging on the door. He shot quick looks behind him to make sure they had not tracked him here. "Tabitha! Let me in! Let me in!"

A light switched on inside the trailer, and he could hear the door being unlocked from the other side. When it opened, Tabitha Banks stood in the gap, freshly awakened and quite bewildered. "Danny?"

Allowing no time for explanation, Danny pushed her aside and barged into the trailer.

She stood back. "Danny, what's going on? You're bleeding!"

He slammed the door and bolted it. Without stopping, he ran to all of the windows, pulling the blinds closed and drawing the curtains.

"Where are the babies?" he stopped to ask her, desperation in his voice.

"They're asleep." She trembled, growing terrified. "What's happening?"

"They're here."

"*Who's* here?"

He hurried to the lights and shut them off, plunging the house into total darkness. He just hoped he wasn't too late. By now the things in the darkness would have realized they had been outsmarted. He could hear them getting closer again. Their incessant chattering and clicking. *They're here.*

Danny grabbed Tabitha and pulled her to the floor on the off chance that the creatures could see through the curtains and blinds. Together they crawled to a hidden corner of the trailer, and Danny crouched in total silence.

"I don't understand. What's happening?"

Danny clamped his hand over her mouth. Save for the pounding of their hearts, all was quiet. Danny could just make out the noise now as he forced Tabitha to listen. It was awful. Like a swarm of bees but with voices. He heard them talking in their weird, clicking language.

The sounds swallowed the trailer.

Scratching.

First it was at the windows. A small, taunting scratch. Then it grew louder, more frantic, as a thousand little animals tried to claw their way inside. Tabitha gasped, but Danny pulled her close, nearly suffo-cating her. He held his breath, praying they would not hear them.

There was a knock at the door. Danny and Tabitha flinched, and he expected the things to tear it off its hinges. The knocking turned into banging. The scratching turned into scraping. The beasts were determined to find a way inside. Like hungry jackals that smelled fresh kill, they pounded, squealing in hellish bliss.

Tears streamed down Tabitha's cheeks, but Danny remained firm and unmoving, resolved. The two shut their eyes and held each other, waiting for the terror to pass. Danny *hoped* it would pass.

It seemed like an eternity that the monsters labored to gain entry into their trailer, but at last the scratching began to fade. The banging at the door subsided, and the voices died to a dull whisper.

Danny opened his eyes, a warm calm spreading in his soul. He dared to believe the nightmare was over. He remained on the floor with Tabitha for another few moments, waiting to be sure. Finally he took a risk and moved for the window. Tabitha pulled at him, whis-pering pleas, "No. *No.*"

He shrugged her off and cautiously pulled the curtains back a crack, his eyes searching the night. He saw them. The imps were collecting again into their swarm and moving down the street. Either they had given up, or they had moved on to search other homes for their prey until some poor soul was foolish enough to answer their call.

Either way they were gone.

Danny let the curtains fall and rested his head on the wall. Taking a moment to collect himself, his first since leaving the North Woods and Greensboro Park Lake, he was finally able to feel like things would be OK. Tabitha rushed to him.

"They're gone," he told her.

Her eyes were wide and her hands trembled. "What *was* that?"

"I'm in trouble, Tabitha. Big trouble."

"What are we gonna do?"

"I don't know." His mind raced. "I don't know..."

He slumped to the floor, the pain in his ankle resurfacing as the adrenaline began to wane. As he sat there, Tabitha by his side, Danny tried to steady his breathing. But in the precious silence of the night there was one thought in his mind that rose above the rest. One terrifying fact.

His grandmother was right. The bogeyman was real.

"The babies!" Tabitha cried, wide-eyed.

Danny's panic returned. He stood and bolted down the hallway,

Tabitha following. Danny ran into one of the bedrooms and came upon the baby crib. He frightfully scanned the bed until his eyes settled on the small sleeping forms of two baby boys.

My sons.

With a gentleness that he never knew he had, he touched each son's head, careful not to disturb their deep sleep. He placed his hand on each stomach, feeling their tiny lungs fill with air and release deep, baby-sized sighs.

Wow, I love them.

Parental love might not come as a surprise to most fathers, but for Danny it did. It really did.

He smiled, elated by the revelation, feeling cozy as he watched the tiny bundles in the crib. "Danny?" Tabitha whispered at his side.

He turned to her, still caressing the Winnie the Pooh pajamas of his boys. She was staring at him strangely, as though she'd never seen him before.

"What happened to you?" she asked carefully. "Where did you go?"

His smile died. Tabitha winced, like she expected him to hit her again, but he only hung his head in sorrow. "We have to get out of town. It's not safe anymore."

"Why?"

"The Monte's busted. We have to find another way."

"What? How?"

"I don't know what to do." Danny felt cornered, and that infuriated him. He looked to Tabitha. He'd never asked her for help. He asked her for money but never her support, and he certainly never bothered to ask her about her ideas or opinions. But he had run out of answers. "Do you?"

Tabitha blinked at him, surprised. Put on the spot, she stammered. "We'll think of something."

He didn't feel encouraged. Nana Loraine was right. A thousand bad decisions passed his memory as he recalled all the times he shrugged off her warnings.

Danny slumped, faced with indecision. From somewhere in the kitchen, the phone rang, and they looked to each other, startled.

"Who's *that*?"

Tabitha shrugged, hurried into the kitchen, and picked up the phone. "Hello?"

Danny exited his boys' room and quietly closed the door, then met Tabitha as she held out the phone to him, her forehead creased.

"Who is it?" he asked.

She shook her head. Danny took the phone. "Yeah?"

"You've seen the truth," the voice on the other end uttered.

"Who is this?"

"But do you really know what you've seen?"

"Who are you?" Danny demanded, worried now that his little adventure at the lake had not gone unnoticed after all.

"Someone who can help."

"Who said I needed help?"

"They know what you've seen. Soon they'll come for you. The girl and your babies too."

Danny gripped the phone tighter, angry and scared. "Who *is* this?"

"There's a preacher who can help. His name is Jeff Weldon." Then the line went silent. A dial tone blared.

Danny slammed the phone back on the receiver, his hands shaking. He felt helpless. Tabitha stared at him.

"Danny? Who was it?"

He could not answer.

The call woke Jeff from another unsettling nightmare, and for that, he was grateful.

Isabella slept on, unaware of Jeff's beeping cell phone, taunting him from the nightstand next to his side of the bed. Rubbing the sleep out of his eyes and straining to see, he fumbled to retrieve the phone.

"Hello?" he muttered, barely intelligible.

"Reverend Weldon!" It was a woman's voice, one he didn't immediately recognize. And she was hysterical.

"Can I help you?"

"It's me! It's Tabitha!"

Tabitha Banks, he moaned. *Wonderful.* He had given her his cell phone number when he first met her. He was being helpful at the time. "Here, call me if you need anything." Little did he know she would use it so liberally.

"I need your help. Something's happened!"

"Tabitha," he tried to sound patient, "it's late. This really isn't a good time—"

"Please! It's Danny! He's in trouble! Can you meet us? It's important!"

Jeff wanted to tell her to leave him alone. He had his own problems to worry about and didn't need to bear someone else's burden too. But Jack Weldon taught him to be a better man than that.

"All right. Meet me at the church in ten minutes."

"Thank you! Thank you so much!" She hung up.

Jeff turned to Isabella, still asleep, and wondered if he should wake her. If she woke up in the night and found him gone, he knew she'd be worried. But if he woke her, she'd just want to come along, and he wasn't prepared for that.

Sorry, Iz.

Two minutes later he was dressed and out the door.

CHAPTER SIXTEEN

"OK, YOU WANNA run that by me one more time?"

After pulling up to the church and nearly being tackled by Tabitha and her two screaming children, Jeff met the famed boyfriend Danny Carpenter. The kid was rough but all talk. Jeff wasn't impressed.

He unlocked the church and escorted the young couple inside the sanctuary, then listened as Danny relayed a completely unbelievable story.

Danny paced back and forth like a caged animal, wringing his hands and watching as Jeff considered his tale. Judging the pastor's remark as an indication of disbelief, he gestured to Jeff. "I told you, Tabitha, a church type like him wouldn't believe me."

Tabitha sat in the same pew she occupied yesterday when she asked for money, rocking her babies, who were slowly drifting back to sleep. "Please, Danny, give him a chance."

When Jeff saw the sincerity in her eyes, he was reminded of the similar look in Dras's eyes when he came to him three months ago. The cold-water shock of it and the realization that he was about to repeat a past mistake forged Jeff to a sharp point. "Look, I'm just trying to understand. What you're telling me is that—"

"I saw the freaky lake come alive and it was, like, sucking on this guy's face!"

The babies, startled by their father's outburst, twitched and wailed. Tabitha readjusted their pacifiers, shooting Danny a reproachful look.

"What guy?" Jeff asked, his tone softer but just as urgent.

"The loony that's been walking all over town putting up posters about his missing kid." Danny rubbed at his knuckles. He jumped at every nighttime sound.

"Ray McCormick?"

"*Yeah*, that guy. I–It did something to him, man. I couldn't believe what I was seeing at first, but he was all hunched down over the lake and it was, like, attached to him. When he stood up, he was nuts! More nuts than usual. H–He *changed*."

Jeff hesitated, scenes from his horrific dreams flashing through his mind. "Changed into what?"

Danny continued to pace, massaging his arms. "I dunno. But it sort of...never mind. It's stupid."

"What?"

Danny looked to Tabitha, as if worried about what she would think of him. "I been having these dreams. Seeing some crazy things. Like guys—"

"Turning into monsters?" Jeff finished for him, his heart quickening.

Danny eased, giving the preacher a sidelong glance and thawing a bit. "How did you know?"

"Because I've been having the same dreams." *This can't be happening.*

The two men stared at each other, reaching a stalemate, and Jeff decided that Danny reminded him of Kyle Rogers. Both had the same aloofness and disregard for authority. Maybe this was why Jeff had been thinking of Kyle so much lately. Maybe God had been preparing him for this moment, to get him ready to accept this stranger. *Maybe this is my second chance.* The comparison to Kyle instantly changed Jeff's mind about the young man.

He had to help him.

"In my dreams I see them in a field," Jeff told him. Danny's face grew pale. "They're dancing. Singing to the stars. It...it scares me when they dance."

Danny shivered, chortling nervously. "Man, I thought I was going crazy."

"Maybe you are. Maybe we both are."

"What are the odds of two guys having the same dream?"

"Maybe they're not dreams. Maybe there's more to it."

"Now you're just creeping me out, preacher."

"Tell him about the gremlins," Tabitha interjected.

At the mention of gremlins, Jeff felt faint. "Gremlins." *They're still here, after all. I knew it.*

Danny raised a suspicious eyebrow. "You think I'm crazy, don't you?"

"No."

With grim assurance Danny revealed, "They don't want you to know about them, though."

Jeff's ears tingled. "They? They who?"

At that Danny stopped pacing and stepped closer to Jeff, keeping an eye out behind him farther along the sanctuary aisle. "I don't know if you've noticed, but this town's gotten *weird* in the last few months. You hear things out there, preacher. Talk about a secret group of guys running the show in Greensboro. They have their fingers in everything in this stinkin' town. They get things done, you know?" Danny lowered his voice to a near-whisper. "Or *un*done, if you know what I mean. Your brother—"

"What do you know about my brother?" Jeff blurted.

"Just what I seen on the news. But the judge what gave him the sentence? A couple of my buddies know *for a fact* he's not exactly on the up and up."

Jeff didn't understand, but he wanted to know more. "Who's in this secret group?"

"Don't know. Could be anyone, I guess. 'Spose that's why it's *secret*."

"How do you know *I'm* not one of them?"

Danny's eyes narrowed. "I *don't* know. I don't trust you." He paused and looked to his girlfriend, who sat very still while the two men talked so as not to disturb the babies any more. "But some guy called me and told me you could help, and Tabitha says you're all right."

Tabitha grinned at her boyfriend, nearly glowing. Jeff wondered who placed the phone call and was about to ask, but Danny interrupted his thoughts.

"I don't rightly want to know who they are. I just want to get out of this town. That's why I came to you."

"Why should I help you? The way I hear it, you're always running off and leaving Tabitha and your kids."

"This time I'm taking Tabitha and the babies with me." Danny explained, catching Jeff off guard. Jeff didn't picture Danny as the type of guy who answered to very many people in his life, and he certainly didn't need some Bible-beater's approval. "I don't want them here. Not with all that's going on. Whole town's going crazy. So, are you going to help us or not?"

Jeff couldn't suppress a grin at the young man's gruff countenance. He was a punk, and not only did he remind Jeff of his old buddy Kyle Rogers, but he also reminded him a lot of himself at that age.

Jeff liked him. But first—

"On one condition."

"Here it comes," he drawled. "You want us to join your church or something?"

"No. I want you to help me find out who these secret guys are. What they're up to."

"You're nuts."

"Maybe. But I'm the only help you've got. So, what's it going to be?"

Danny looked to Tabitha, unsure. She nodded. Finally, he relented. "You got a deal, preacher. Just try and not get me killed, all right?" Jeff extended his hand. "I'll give it my best shot." They shook on it, forming a partnership.

Atop a fire escape opposite the Good Church of the Faithful, Mr. Hayden and Mr. Simms watched Jeff, Danny, and Tabitha exit the church and go their separate ways.

Mr. Simms turned to his colleague. "What now? He knows everything."

Mr. Hayden remained calm. "Not everything."

"Should we tell *him*?"

The other man considered before replying. "No need to bother him with this right now. We can deal with the situation."

Simms nodded.

"Besides," Hayden began, his tone dripping with disapproval. "He has... *other* things to attend to."

At precisely four minutes past five, the stereo in Rosalyn's front room came to life, switching through channels of its own accord and selecting a song.

The Platters played at full volume: "Twilight Time."

The opening music began and Tony Williams crooned. In her bed, Rosalyn bolted upright and struggled to get her bearings. She pulled the chain on the lamp on the nightstand beside the bed, casting the room in a dim light. She scanned the room but saw no sign of anyone or anything out of the ordinary. Quickly she swung her legs over the edge of the bed and prepared to stand. Keeping her head low and eyes alert, she opened the nightstand drawer and retrieved a buck knife that Dras's dad gave her on one of their fishing trips years ago.

She opened the knife and clicked the blade into place.

Rosalyn gripped the knife firmly and held it high with the blade pointed to the ground, ready to bring it down on her intruder. She slipped from her bed. On tiptoes, holding in her breath, she searched the house. The music blared, and she couldn't believe angry neighbors weren't calling to complain. The melody continued to play, the soundtrack to her hunt.

She rounded a corner. Peeked into the spare bedroom. Nothing.

A quick scan of the kitchen next. Empty too.

The living room last. Nothing but darkness and the haunting ballad filled the room. She came face-to-face with her stereo, playing on its own. No one around to blame.

She moved closer to the stereo, her breath coming and going in slow, controlled puffs. She neared the machine, extending a shaky finger, and clicked it off. The music halted, and her ears rang with phantom noise.

She turned on every light and for the next few minutes checked everywhere in her apartment. Under every sizable appliance. In every nook, cranny, and corner. Everywhere. Looking for him.

The Strange Man.

After a thorough double-check, she deemed that her frenzy was unnecessary. There was no one in her apartment. No one had turned on the stereo. *Could be a loose wire.*

She eased and released a long, relaxing breath.

Get a grip, Roz. She felt herself calming as she walked back to her room, planning to call the police in the morning and file a report, just in case, but all in all feeling silly for her terror.

Fixed with his back to the ceiling and his arms spread like angel's wings, the Strange Man watched her from the unseen realm. His bait had proved effective. By playing the music, he had lured her into the living room so he could watch her move. Oh, how he loved to watch Rosalyn Myers move.

He floated down from the ceiling, creeping after her as she entered her bedroom and returned the knife to its hiding place in the drawer. He nearly licked his lips as she slid back under the covers.

She was even more beautiful than he remembered.

He had endured three long months without seeing her face, but in the past few days he found it harder and harder to remain apart from her. After the attention that idiot boy brought to him and the dark things of his world, the Strange Man had thought it wise to remain hidden, to lie dormant until the appointed time.

And now that time was here. The Dark Hour approached.

He salivated at the very thought of it.

The stars themselves were beginning to tremble in anticipation of events to come, and it gave him a new sense of boldness. Things were falling into place, being set into motion, and no one could stop it, even if they *did* see it coming, though he knew they never would.

It was too late for his defeat, and that left only victory to be enjoyed. Only *her* to be enjoyed.

Remaining invisible, he admired Rosalyn's form as she closed her eyes and drifted to sleep. He slinked to her sleeping frame and flicked his talons. Careful not to wake the girl, he traced the shape of her body, savoring every curve, every bend and fold. She was beautiful. Divine.

And so full of hatred.

Ah, yes. He sensed that in her most of all. Her rage was exquisite, and he knew that now, without that boy in the way, it would be easy for the girl to disappear into the shadows, where he would be waiting to embrace her with open arms.

Oh, how he wanted to take her, here and now! But still she was not ready. Not yet.

But she would be ready very soon.

It was difficult to tear himself away from her, but he knew that he must. There was other business to deal with. The Strange Man bid Rosalyn a wordless farewell and was swallowed up into the shadows.

CHAPTER SEVENTEEN

ISABELLA PADDED DOWNSTAIRS the next morning to find her husband asleep on the couch. Fully dressed, Jeff lay stretched out as if he simply fell back and never got up. His Bible and papers were strewn over the coffee table, and wild, frantic notes were scribbled on a number of small notepad sheets.

She hadn't realized that he wasn't in bed until she woke up that morning, and even then she never thought he would be up and dressed already. Once she realized he was wearing the same clothes and jacket from yesterday, though, she grew concerned, but she thought it best to let him sleep for a while longer.

Leaning over the back of the couch, she watched him rest, his mouth comically gaping like usual. A moment later something in the land of Nod startled him, and Jeff sprang up with a start. Isabella smiled down on him as he fought to regain his senses.

"Good morning."

He rubbed his eyes, disoriented. "Hey," he gruffly responded before sitting up on the couch. Taking a moment to look at his notes, shuffling through them as though he were worried that they'd vanished in the night, he finally stood to enter the kitchen. Lost in his thoughts, he didn't even seem to notice Isabella staring at him as he opened the refrigerator and grabbed the milk. He drank straight from the carton.

Now Isabella knew something was wrong.

Jeff Weldon would never drink straight from the carton. It was simply unheard of. Surely it had to be one of the signs of the apocalypse, right up there with red calves and the sea turning to blood.

She tried not to sound worried when she asked, "So...did you go somewhere last night?"

"Yeah," he replied briskly. "It was nothing."

He took another drink, closing his eyes, relishing.

Isabella turned to the notes on the table, looking at them more closely. She reached down and took a couple pages, reading over them, wondering what had been so important.

One verse she recognized as Jude, verse 4:

112

For certain men whose condemnation was written about long ago have secretly slipped in among you. They are godless men, who change the grace of our God into a license for immorality and deny Jesus Christ our only Sovereign and Lord.

The other verse was a cross-reference in Philippians 3:18–19:

For, as I have often told you before and now say again even with tears, many live as enemies of the cross of Christ. Their destiny is destruction, their god is their stomach, and their glory is in their shame. Their mind is on earthly things.

One verse in particular was circled. It was Joel 2:28, the prophecy concerning the Holy Spirit coming to the believers.

It will come about after this that I will pour out My Spirit on all mankind; and your sons and daughters will prophesy, your old men will dream dreams, your young men will see visions.

The last line of the verse was underlined multiple times, and a note off to the side in Jeff's hasty handwriting read: NO KIDDING.

What's this all about?

Isabella looked up to him, confused. "New sermon?"

He shook his head, sliding the carton back into the refrigerator. When he spoke, it was distant and automatic. "No."

What is inside that head of his? Why won't he look at me? Finally she could stand the mystery no longer. "Where were you last night?"

"Had to take care of something."

"Something that couldn't wait until this morning?"

"Look," he finally turned to face her, his face hard. "I just had to go out, OK? It's fine."

Fine. His answer for everything. Everything was always *fine.* Never "horrible" or "incredible." Never "I'm sad" or "I'm excited." Just "I'm fine. Everything's fine."

Well, everything was *not* fine.

Jeff brushed by Isabella, preoccupied, and began his trek up the stairs. "I'm gonna take a shower."

"You want me to make breakfast?"

"Not hungry," he managed before he was lost up the staircase.

Rolling her eyes in frustration, Isabella threw up her hands in surrender and wandered into the kitchen to make breakfast for herself.

Although she wasn't very hungry anymore.

Jeff stormed into the upstairs bathroom and locked himself in. His head pounded in a steady rhythm, and he felt a seething fury swirling inside of him, though he could not quite place its cause. It ate at him, pulsating in his mind until the pain was so intense he had to grip the edge of the sink to remain standing. Then, as if hit by a powerful blow, he flinched as the images of his most recent nightmare replayed in his mind.

He's running again, pulled to the clearing in the woods, where he already knows what terrible things he'll see. But he's unable to stop, unable to turn to the right or the left, unable to leave. So on he runs, pushing through the tangled branches and the soupy green mist, and with trembling hands he pushes away the foliage and sees it all. Just as he feared, things are worse.

The slick, black monstrosities that were once men have moved from the clearing in the woods to erect a bizarre monument in the town square. It bears a peculiar circular brand—the sigil of the sun. The town dances around the vile thing until their sins shine like a beacon for their dark god, beckoning it ever closer to their world, calling it from the infinite vistas of darkness where it slumbers and waits for the Dark Hour. When mankind is at its worst and finally ready for the change to begin, finally ready to worship it and call it "Master," they trust it will return to earth and swallow the world up in hell, murdering all things good, lovely, and pure and breeding new evils that have never before been seen or heard by men. New evils that will push the world into unending madness until the laws of everything holy and just are discarded in favor of chaos and gluttony.

Doom has come to the town, bringing horrors. Many came to prophesy to them. To warn them. To plead and beg and cry with them, promising God's forgiveness if only they would turn from their deceit and greed and monstrous intent.

But the people of that town chose to ignore the warnings and deny God, to live for themselves, to crow and shout, dancing and reveling in their wickedness as they murdered and found joy in detestable practices. They await the day when their new god will come to teach them new ways to shout and dance and revel in new kinds of more horrible wickedness and show them new ways to murder and find joy in it. They offer their children as sacrifices and defile themselves in anticipation of the Dark Hour, when their unholy Master will hear their call and come to reward them with all sorts of suffering and pain and pleasure.

And, as they reel in their iniquities, dancing under the pale moon's light, the people's minds swell with perverse visions of the Dark Master wakening from its sleep—beginning to stretch and yawn and open its awful, baleful eyes, turning a sickening, sentient gaze back on the earth that it was expelled from so long ago.

"It's coming for you, Jeff," their voices whisper to him. "You are all doomed."

Jeff jerked out of his waking nightmare to come face-to-face with himself in the mirror. His eyes were feral and scared, and he was sweating profusely. A thin line of scarlet trickled from his nose, startling him at first, then terrifying him. Grabbing a wad of toilet paper, he wiped the blood away quickly, as if doing so meant that it was never there. Next he opened the medicine cabinet, found his bottle of painkillers, and hurriedly unscrewed the cap. He popped down a couple and bade himself calm down.

Another pounding resounded in his skull, but this one was only a knock on the bathroom door.

"I made some scrambled eggs," Isabella weakly said from the other side. "There's some left if you want them."

"O–OK. Be down in a sec."

Listening to Isabella shuffle away, Jeff struggled to stifle his emotions. He needed to look presentable and composed so she would stop asking questions. He didn't want her to know about the nightmares. *Now there's nosebleeds.*

He would figure it out, just like everything else.

On his own.

CHAPTER EIGHTEEN

AFTER THE TOTAL waste of time she could only jokingly refer to as "therapy," Rosalyn Myers wanted nothing more than to go home and bathe repeatedly to wash away the filth that she knew must be oozing from her after being in the same room as Dr. Altman. Rosalyn only attended these miserable share-and-care sessions as a favor to her mother—who was also paying for it.

"Good afternoon," the receptionist smiled professionally.

Rosalyn nodded, disinterested. "Hey."

Pulling the ledger toward her, Rosalyn grabbed a pen and logged out. The clerk punched a few numbers on the computer keyboard before giving her the grand total. Inwardly gasping at Altman's exorbitant fee, Rosalyn pulled out her checkbook and filled in the amount in the little box, relieved that her mother would reimburse her. Once done, she ripped out the check and handed it to the clerk.

"Let me just get you a receipt."

Rosalyn nodded. *Yeah, yeah.* She waited, drumming her fingers on the desk, trying to kill the thirty seconds it took for a receipt to be printed, and happened to glance up.

Instantly her chest ached as hurried breaths left her body.

From across the hallway the Strange Man looked directly at Rosalyn. He smiled.

Rosalyn dropped her car keys.

"Ma'am? Are you all right?"

Rosalyn couldn't move. Other clients passed in front of and behind him, yet no one took notice of the strange, alluring man in their midst, his gaze locked on her.

"Who is that?" she demanded of the woman behind the counter.

Confused, the clerk asked, "Excuse me?"

"That guy! Who is that guy? What's his name?" She pointed madly behind her, but when she and the receptionist turned to look, the Strange Man had gone.

"Did you see him?"

"I didn't see anyone."

"Who was he?"

"I'm sure I don't know, ma'am. And even if I did, I'm sorry, but all patients' identities are kept confidential."

By now Rosalyn's outburst had drawn attention. Rosalyn lowered her eyes, trying to avoid their stares, and realized she had to go. She had to go now.

Grabbing her keys off the floor, she pushed through the lobby and left behind her receipt.

Rosalyn sped home, ignoring all speed limit signs. After hurriedly parking her car at a crooked angle, she raced up the stairs, unlocked her door, and crashed into her apartment. She slammed the door behind her and locked it. Flipped the deadbolt. Hooked the chain.

Stay out. Please stay out.

Her hands trembled. Her heart rattled inside her rib cage. She couldn't understand why she was so upset. It was just one guy. But the mystery surrounding him, which once seemed provocative, now was terrifying. He was the beautiful man who danced with her once three months ago. He was there at The Rave Scene on that awful night when Dras was arrested. Dras was trying to protect her from him, or so he said, but she didn't know why.

Who is he? What does he want from me?

"Hello, Rosalyn."

She screamed at the top of her lungs, all of her muscles tensing in one terrible moment. Rosalyn whirled around, already knowing he'd be standing there.

The Strange Man grinned.

"How did you get in here?" She breathed in horrified gasps, rummaging frantically through the drawer of the small table near the door.

His lips parted in a charming smile. "I used the front door like everyone else."

Inside the drawer, her hands finally found their targets and Rosalyn retrieved a string of garlic cloves and a two-inch-high wooden cross. The garlic she discreetly procured earlier at Larezzo's, the Italian restaurant where she worked as hostess, after she'd spotted the Strange Man at her mother's. The cross she received when she was eight, the one and only time she ever went to church camp with Dras. Violently she thrust them before her, waving the wards in the Strange Man's face.

"Stay back!" she screamed.

Catching a whiff of the pungent garlic odor, the Strange Man batted at the scent, laughing. "Whoa. How long have you had that in there?"

"I know what you are!"

Again he chuckled. "Do you now?"

"Yeah," she said in huffs, absently wondering why the beast wasn't shrieking at the sign of the cross. Come to think of it, he ought to be bursting into flames since he was standing in shafts of brilliant daylight pouring through the windows. "The smooth moves, the fancy clothes, seducing me...I went through my Anne Rice phase just like everyone else." She braced herself, preparing for the shocking revelation, worried that her mind would crumble when she voiced the thought. "You're a vampire."

At this the Strange Man threw his head back and exploded in genuine laughter. Rosalyn held her ground, still clinging to the cross, though she knew now that it would do her no good.

"No, no, no," he cooed after a moment, a tear of mirth still caught in the corner of his dark eye. "I'm not a vampire, Rosalyn. I'm something much, *much* worse."

Rosalyn balked and watched in horror as the Strange Man reached out, wrapped his long, slender fingers around the cross, and splintered the wood with ease. She released the ruined remains and the garlic cloves, and they fell to the floor. "You–you can't be here."

"Why not?" Still smiling.

She pushed past him, no longer concerned with who or what he was. She didn't want to know anymore. She just wanted him out.

At least she thought at first that she wanted him out.

But now, as she neared him, so close she could touch him—so close she could *kiss* him—she wasn't so sure.

"What do you want from me?" She nearly wept, confused by her own double-mindedness.

The Strange Man tilted his head, studying her. "Why are you upset? I thought you would be glad to see me."

"What do you want from me?" she yelled, then whimpered, "What are you? Really?"

The smirk fell from his face, and the light in his magnificent eyes faded. "What does your heart tell you?"

"The devil...Dras said on the news that you were like the devil or a–a demon."

She half-expected he would laugh again—*hoped* that he would laugh again. That he would tell her that she was being ridiculous and he was just as human as she. But somewhere in the cold expression on his paling face, past the beauty that had instantly attracted her to him, Rosalyn saw terrible things. A realm of nightmares existed beyond his smile, past the deceiving twinkle in his eyes. She didn't know how, but she sensed his true nature. There was death in his face.

Hell and damnation.

"Are you afraid?"

She hesitated, then finally shook her head.

"Demon. Devil…" He paced the room, his fingers trailing along her furniture and the bare places on her walls where Dras's face once hung in dozens of frames. He was so casual, so at ease with any situation. Rosalyn craved his confidence. He turned to her, regarding her with his deep, dark eyes. "What did I ever do to be called such names?"

Silence fell, as if the Strange Man was waiting for Rosalyn to answer. She had no answer to give. She could only watch him in awe, desperate to see his next move, to know his mind and heart and all the horrible things there.

Why am I thinking like this?

"Evil is a point of view, Rosalyn. The only evil I ever committed was in wanting to live my own life without the interference of God. Is that so wrong? Aren't there billions of people on this earth who want the same thing? And yet *I'm* called 'evil'? I'm called a monster?"

As the broken cross that lay scattered about her feet could attest, Rosalyn had been to church a handful of times in her childhood. In a church town like Greensboro, no one could escape the voice of a preacher for long. The odds of finding herself in a pew on Sunday morning were quadrupled when she moved in with Dras and his family in high school. His parents kindly insisted she join them for services, and, as a show of gratitude for everything they'd done for her, she obliged. She listened to Jack Weldon proclaim "the message" and underwent Louise Weldon's routine Sunday lunchtime probing session about what Rosalyn believed and if what she heard that morning "meant anything" to her.

Although she didn't always pay the closest attention in Sunday school, she understood that in Christian theology, a demon was nothing more than an angel who rebelled against God and got kicked out of heaven. If the guy standing in her living room wasn't crazy—and she didn't think he was, in the *traditional* sense—and he really was a demon…then that meant he had been, at one time, an angel.

And that meant God was real.

The thought worried her, maybe even more than the fact that she had a demon in her living room. It made her skin crawl to think that there was some God up in heaven looking down on her all the time and seeing everything she did. An uncomfortable paranoia seeped into her heart, and she had no desire to indulge the thought any longer. Instead she wanted to move closer to the stranger, the one who was so calm about everything. She wanted to draw on his power, to learn from him.

Forcing herself to brave the hard questions, desiring desperately to learn the truth, Rosalyn relaxed her breathing and took a fateful step forward. The Strange Man's face lit up in slight surprise, his eyes sparkling briefly.

"Dras was right then," Rosalyn said. "You set him up."

"To *save* him," the Strange Man rebutted without hesitation. "Christians mean well. They think it's their God-given duty to save the world from things like me. They think they're serving God, and that's commendable." The Strange Man turned from her, and the lights in the apartment began to flicker and dim. "But they don't know God like I do. They think He's benevolent. *Worthy* of their service. But God is just a kid with an ant farm, Rosalyn. He watches us scurry about, and when it pleases Him, He gives us a good shake, destroying everything we've built."

Rosalyn felt a chill cling to her bare arms, and the hairs on the back of her neck stood on end. The Strange Man swiveled toward her again, the light in the room becoming brighter and the warmth returning. "Dras thought he was doing the right thing. He thought he was protecting you. But there are things about the unseen realm that he doesn't understand. That he never could." The Strange Man touched Rosalyn's arm, sending thrills over her body. He pulled her close. "But *you* can. I can feel it in you. I sensed it in you the first moment I saw you in The Rave Scene. You're different from these simple people. You have the spark."

His lips moved wonderfully, forming each syllable in a hypnotic way that made her want to lean over and kiss him hard.

"But Dras—" The image of him emerged in her clouded mind.

"Shhh," the Strange Man spoke in a long and lasting whisper. "He only would have held you back. He was always holding you back."

"Don't say that…"

The man leaned down, his fragrant breath hot and soothing on Rosalyn's face, until his lips were only an inch from hers. Oh, she wanted to kiss him. She wanted to take him. To let him take her.

We were five years old, and it was our birthday.
She pushed the man back. "No." Firm. "I can't."

Pulling away quickly, making no room for any other protest, Rosalyn marched to the door, unlocked it, and swung it open for her guest.

The Strange Man, his hands still held out to her, looked on regretfully. Rosalyn averted her eyes as he approached her, moving toward the open door. "You've already started down the path, Rosalyn. It'll be dark and frightening, but the things I can show you...*far* outweigh the trials. Don't turn back now."

"Don't." But the command came out as a question. A plea. "I don't want to hear anymore. Don't come back. Please? Just go."

"Do you really mean that?"

Still she avoided his eyes, looking to the floor, a mixture of fear and excitement bubbling inside her. She was afraid of letting him get away with his secrets. He could be the one to lead her on her greatest adventure, out of Greensboro at last and into a future of possibilities. Rosalyn never believed that any man could completely fulfill her and make all her dreams come true, but if ever there *were* a guy like that...

It would be him.

"Yes," she told him. Told herself.

You don't need him, Roz. You don't need anybody.

The man nodded and quietly left. Rosalyn rushed to close the door, more to keep herself inside than to keep him out. She locked it just as quickly and took a deep breath.

Be strong. You don't need him.

I don't need him.

Do I?

CHAPTER NINETEEN

JEFF DECIDED TO pay Ray McCormick a visit.

According to Danny's story, his strange experiences started with Ray and whatever happened that night at the lake. However, a quick call to Ray's wife told Jeff that Ray was confined to room 322 at Greensboro Memorial.

Jeff put on his best Sunday smile as he addressed Trudy Doyle, the stern nurse at the desk in the third floor lobby. "Excuse me."

She looked up from a worn paperback novel, raising an eyebrow. "Yes?"

He smiled again, his charm in action, hoping to undo the dark stubble and haunted cast to his face. "I'm here to see Ray McCormick. I'm his pastor, and I just want to check in on him and make sure he's OK."

The nurse wavered. Hesitant to speak, Trudy scanned the corridors and appeared relieved as Dr. Herbert Brown approached.

"Can I help you?" Brown asked, professional. Then, with a look of surprise, "Oh, Jeff." The doctor gauged the young pastor, startled. "I didn't recognize you."

"Hey, Herbert. I'm trying to see Ray McCormick."

Brown paused and regarded the nurse, who met his eyes with uncertainty. Never losing his cool, he faced Jeff once more. "I'm sorry, Ray's not accepting any visitors at this time."

"Well, I just wanted to know how he was doing."

"Fine, fine. He's had quite an experience and—"

"That's what I heard," Jeff interrupted. "What exactly happened?"

"Now Jeff, you know I can't disclose that kind of information."

"Not even to his pastor?"

"Sorry."

"If I could just see him—"

"As I said, we're not accepting any visitors, but I'll tell him you stopped by."

Jeff ignored Brown and took a moment to glance over the doctor's shoulder. On the other side of a Plexiglas door marked AUTHORIZED

PERSONNEL ONLY in big red letters hunkered none other than Deputy Ryan Stevenson. Instantly images of the blue-eyed brute leading the band of deputies who tore at Dras's hair and beat his face flashed in Jeff's mind, and he felt a wave of fury flush over him.

Stevenson appeared to be standing guard outside a patient's room beyond the glass. Room 322.

Two distinguished-looking gentlemen quietly exited room 322, their faces solemn, and closed the door behind them. They looked familiar too. *Were they the ones watching me at Smokey's on Saturday?*

"If Ray can't have visitors, who are *they*?"

Brown threw a look behind him and caught sight of the two men. He reddened. "I...uh..."

The nurse behind the desk depressed a buzzing trigger, and the Plexiglas door unlocked. The two gentlemen and Deputy Stevenson, who trailed behind them like a gorilla bodyguard, stepped out of the private wing and into the main hallway and moved toward the scene for a closer look.

"Is everything OK here, Dr. Brown?" one of the men asked, his tone friendly.

Brown gladly backed away as the men took control of the situation. Jeff now recognized the leader of the duo and was shocked. His mind raced as he tried to imagine why the man was here and why the man had been spying on him at Smokey's.

Brown explained, "This is Reverend Jeff Weldon from the Good Church of the Faithful. He's here to make sure Ray McCormick's OK."

The leader of the two smiled. "Well, well. I'm glad at least one of the local ministers still makes hospital visits. A rare thing these days. Very noble. Mr. McCormick is ill and needs his rest. He's doing much better, though. We all expect a speedy recovery."

Jeff's eyes narrowed. "I didn't realize Ray was such a good friend of yours...Mayor Hayden."

Mr. Hayden eyed the pastor, his eyes narrowing over a composed grin. "Oh, yes. Ray and I are old friends."

Jeff nodded, disbelieving. *Right.*

"I've heard great things about you, Reverend Weldon. You're a valuable asset to this community." The mayor paused, letting the silence draw out. "When your focus is in the right place."

Deputy Stevenson snorted.

Jeff held in his mounting anger as Mr. Hayden turned to Brown. "We'll be leaving now, Herbert. Thank you for your time, and contact us if there's any change." Turning back to Jeff, he finished with, "We all want to see Mr. McCormick returned to good health."

The discussion finished, Mayor Hayden and his counterpart marched off in perfect step, leaving Deputy Stevenson behind. Jeff turned to watch the two men in suits leave, and his stomach twisted in knots. What was happening here? How was *Stevenson* involved?

As if hearing his own name in Jeff's thoughts, Deputy Stevenson smiled icily. "I think it's time you went home, Reverend."

"I'm just checking up on a parishioner, Deputy. No harm in that."

"Looks to me like you're just causing more trouble. Now, I'm asking you nicely to leave. Don't make this get ugly."

Just the sight of Stevenson's arrogant face caused Jeff to clench his hands into angry fists. His whole body trembled, his rage ready to be let loose. Back in high school Jeff got into his fair share of schoolyard fights. He was a hothead, even back then, and it had caused a lot of problems between him and his parents. They usually blamed Jeff's attitude on his friendship with Kyle Rogers, but Jeff knew better.

The beast was in *him*.

After all the trouble he got in during high school, Jeff learned to build walls to contain that anger. Isabella, his place in the church, his reputation in town—all safety checks to keep him in line. He clung to his new adult responsibilities and eventually forgot the true potential of his wrath.

But then yesterday he went and hit Earl Canton and found out that the beast never went away. It had only been lying dormant.

Now it was clawing to get out once more. Worse, Jeff *wanted* it to come out. After what Stevenson did to Dras, he deserved it.

Stevenson leered, raising his chin, daring Jeff to make a move, but Jeff remained firm, keeping his anger in place. A mounted wall camera was aimed right at him, and the last thing he needed was footage of the local pastor pounding a deputy on the nightly news. Finally Jeff headed for the doors, conceding the battle. Deputy Stevenson stayed behind, triumphantly taunting him, "Have a nice day."

Danny Carpenter waited in Jeff's truck, gnawing on his finger-nails, furtively watching for anything suspicious. When Jeff swung the door open and flopped down in the driver's seat, Danny nearly squealed in fright.

"Don't *do* that, man!"

"Scare you?"

Danny relaxed and shifted under the preacher's stare. "Well? What did you find?"

"Ray's in there, all right. They've got him locked up in a security wing."

"So what now?"

"Now we figure out how to break in."

"What? *We?*"

"I told you. You want my help, you gotta help me first. I just met our mayor in there, and I think he's in on the whole thing."

Danny blew a long sigh of exasperation, running his fingers through his tangled hair. "I told you it goes deep."

Jeff shook his head, overwhelmed. "My brother's trial was too fast. I always felt there wasn't something right about it. Like someone wanted it over and done with really quick. But what does Ray have to do with it?"

Danny shrugged. "Beats me, man. The whole thing is messed up."

"I'm going to find out what's going on, but I need your help. You do this for me, and we're even. I'll get you out of town, and you and Tabitha can start over."

Danny hesitated, picking at his nails. "What about you?"

Jeff looked back to the hospital uncertainly. "I don't know. I haven't thought that far ahead yet. I'm sort of just making this up as I go along."

"I can respect that."

"Right now, though, I've got to see Ray. I gotta find out what he knows."

The two sat in silence for a moment, staring down the hospital, until Danny said, "Well, then. Let's get this over with."

"No," Jeff said. "We'll wait until sundown."

From across the parking lot Deputy Ryan Stevenson exited the hospital, sipping a Styrofoam cup of coffee, watching as Jeff Weldon and some scruffy street kid drove off.

When Stevenson was a boy, his father took him out to kill his first deer. It was the waiting young Stevenson enjoyed the most, even more so than the kill itself. There was something thrilling about hiding, feeling invisible as he watched his prey carry on with its life, completely unaware that it was being stalked. And when the deer least expected it, when it felt the safest, one *thwip* of his bow and arrow, and its life was gone.

It made the boy feel like a god.

Now Stevenson's quarry was Reverend Jeff Weldon, himself little more than a nosy, bothersome animal that needed to be put down.

The deputy waited until Jeff's beat-up truck rounded the corner and disappeared before dialing his cell phone.

"Hello?"

"It's me," Stevenson reported.

"Well?"

"He's snooping around. He tried to see McCormick."

"He hasn't a clue what's really at stake here."

"Should I take care of him?" Stevenson asked hopefully.

"No. Arrangements have already been made."

"But—"

"He will no longer be a problem. Is that understood, Deputy Stevenson?"

Stevenson nodded, though he knew the other person couldn't see him. "Yes, sir."

Click.

Stevenson took another sip of his coffee as his prey escaped, seething with hatred. He would have to wait a little longer, but that was OK.

It was the waiting he loved the most.

Isabella leaned against the kitchen counter, cradling the phone between her chin and shoulder, listening to it ring on the other end. Ring. Ring. Ring.

Still no answer.

She gave up hoping Jeff would answer his cell and hung up with a heavy sigh. She had no idea where he was or when he would be home. But Isabella was patient; she just hoped she wouldn't have to wait long.

There was a knock at the door, and Isabella crossed the apartment to answer it.

"Oh," she greeted her visitor in surprise. "Leonard. I didn't expect you today."

Leonard Fergus nodded apologetically and removed his cap. "Sorry to drop by unannounced, Isabella. Is Jeff here?"

She grew flustered. "No, I'm afraid he's not."

"Mind if I wait awhile? I need to have a word with him."

"Uh...sure," Isabella agreed, stepping aside to let the old man through. As Leonard passed her, the air grew heavy, and Isabella sensed that her old friend brought bad news with him.

"You don't by any chance have some of that fine lemonade you always bring to the potluck suppers, do you?" Leonard inquired.

"Sure," she nodded politely, trying to ignore her inner sense of foreboding. "I can make some real quick."

"I'd like that. Thanks."

As Leonard sank wearily into the Weldon's couch, Isabella retreated into the kitchen, her mind troubled.

Jeff, where are you?

The Rave Scene was currently the hottest club in town, but long before its establishment, there were other less flashy bars in Greensboro serving alcohol to the masses.

One such bar was The Oasis. Tucked in between a pizza joint and a hair salon in a strip mall on the East Side, it was a complete dive. The beer was stale, the floor was sticky, and the bathroom perpetually smelled like vomit.

"Come here often?" Jeff asked as he and Danny took a booth in the darkened bar.

Danny shrugged defensively as he waved down a waitress. "Better than that Rave place. What do they serve there? *Light* beer?"

"I wouldn't know," Jeff admitted.

A waitress came over and took their order. Danny asked for a "man's beer," as he called it, while Jeff stuck with—

"Iced tea."

The waitress eyed him suspiciously. "You sure?"

"Yeah." He realized that for the first time in a long time, someone didn't immediately recognize him as Reverend Jeff Weldon. Here, in The Oasis, he was just another lost soul looking to pass the time.

It was really nice.

"Suit yourself," she said, eyeballing him before leaving.

Danny leaned across the table, embarrassed. "Come on, man, you're gonna give me a bad reputation."

Something about the irony of the statement made Jeff laugh out loud.

Outside the sun began to set, and workers were clocking out for the day. Soon this place would be packed with tired blue-collar folks looking to unwind before heading home. Day shifts would end, night shifts would begin, and somewhere in between Jeff would strike the hospital. But first he needed to kill some time. Get his head together.

His cell phone rang. He grabbed it from its holder on his belt clip and took a look at the caller ID: HOME.

Frowning, he let it ring unanswered. Danny noticed. "You gonna get that?"

Jeff shook his head. "No." Then, settling in his seat, he leaned forward. "OK let's walk through this again."

Danny rolled his eyes. "I'm the distraction, while you go and find Ray McCormick. It's not that difficult, Boss."

"It's my first covert operation, all right? Color me nervous. You got the gum?"

Danny patted the breast of his wrinkled coat, then eased back as the waitress brought them their drinks. Popping off the top and taking a deep chug, Danny seemed in his element. "A little breaking-and-entering is nothing. Believe me, I've done worse."

Jeff watched Danny confidently reclining in the booth, casually watching as the first of the after-work patrons showed up. "Yeah, about that."

"What?"

"I'm hoping that when you and Tabitha start over, you leave that stuff behind."

Danny shifted in his seat. "And do what? Get a real job?"

"You should try it. You might like earning an honest living."

The young man grinned, for a moment looking like the decent fellow he could become. "May be too late for me, preacher. I ain't got much practice at walking the straight and narrow. After all, ain't that why you got me hanging around? Face it; you need a criminal to do what you're doing."

The words came as a slap to Jeff's face. He felt very much the hypocrite, telling Danny to clean his act up as he himself sat in a bar, preparing to break into the hospital while lying to his wife.

"You know," Jeff began solemnly, leaning back in the booth, a mirror reflection of Danny, "you may be onto something there. Here's to the road less traveled." Jeff raised his tea, and Danny toasted him.

Danny gulped down his beer, turning to watch a couple of bikers enter the bar, then grew oddly quiet. "So...this is all about your brother, huh?"

Jeff sipped his tea and nodded, his jaw tense. "Yeah."

"You two close?"

"Ah, that's kinda iffy. We had our moments. Mainly he was just a pain in my butt. Good kid, just…misguided. He was headed down a rough road, and I tried to set him straight. I made my fair share of mistakes when I was younger, you know? I guess I was just trying to save him from it. But…I don't think he ever understood."

"Thought you were just a hard case?"

Jeff nodded again, this one accompanied by a smallish grin. "Yeah. Maybe I was too hard on him sometimes."

Jeff's smile widened as he thought of his brother and the relationship they were mending. Ironically, the trial had been good for both of them. It forced them to move beyond their petty bickering and brought them closer together. Jeff was grateful for the second chance. Things could have turned out so much worse that night at The Rave Scene.

Still, though, his brother was on death row unjustly, and he would not stand by while Dras was taken from him.

Danny thumbed his nose, an obvious attempt to mask his vulnerability. "I never had a big brother give me a hard time. I mean, I think I got some half brothers or half sisters out there somewhere. My old man bailed. Turns out he was pretty good at starting families, just not with the follow-through." His eyes dimmed and his face paled. Danny looked like he might be sick. "Guess I'm carrying on the family tradition, huh?"

Guilt-faced, Danny finished off his beer. Jeff dug at the table absently and muttered grimly, "Every son has his father's legacy to live with."

"I'll drink to that, man," Danny muttered, lifting his empty bottle morosely. "I'll drink to that."

CHAPTER TWENTY

JEFF PEEKED AROUND the corner. Trudy Doyle—the nurse from earlier—was still behind the counter, her nose buried in a paperback novel. He wondered what she was doing here, if maybe she were pulling a double shift. Regardless, her presence chucked Plan A out the window. While he and Danny came prepared for a little law-breaking, the preacher part of him had still hoped a new nurse would be on duty and he could charm his way into the secured wing. With Trudy still here, that would be impossible.

Have to do this the hard way.

A quick scan confirmed that there were three cameras in the hall. One was placed on the far right of the hallway, another on the far left, and one positioned directly behind Trudy's desk, aimed across the corridor at the secured door to the private wing. Three small black-and-white security monitors were at Trudy's side behind the counter. In order to get Jeff to Ray's room, Danny would have to depress the trigger, and that meant they had to get Trudy out of the way.

Jeff had a plan. It was completely ridiculous, and if it worked, he'd be amazed. But right now it was all they had.

"Havin' second thoughts, preacher?" Danny whispered, pressed against the wall, out of sight with Jeff.

Jeff regarded him with a grin, feeling untamed. "Actually, this is kind of fun."

"Welcome to my world."

The hospital was quiet and lonely, and Jeff had no fear of being spotted by a parishioner or well-to-do about town, but he could feel the security camera's presence right above his head. As it swerved back and forth, Jeff and Danny hugged the wall, keeping out of the lens' peripheral.

Jeff rubbed his moist hands together, nervous and thrilled at the same time. He turned to Danny, anxious to get started. "You about ready?"

Danny stood behind him, vigorously chewing three pieces of

bubble gum. His voice muffled by the mass in his mouth, he grumbled, "Give me a minute, will ya? It's not ready."

"Hurry up."

"I'm trying."

"Hey, Trudy," Jeff heard a man say.

Jeff braved a look around the corner. He saw a male nurse headed for the security doors, carrying a clipboard. The nurse smiled to the woman, and she set her book down. "Hey, Roger. Big day?"

"Just checking up on our mystery patient." He wiggled his eyebrows and made an "Oooohh" noise, eliciting a giggle from Trudy as she buzzed him through. With a smile of gratitude, he opened the door and Jeff watched as he crossed inside. The cry of the buzzer stopped abruptly as the Plexiglas door closed and locked behind the man.

Danny tapped Jeff on the shoulder. "All right, I'm ready."

Jeff held up his hand. "Hold on a sec. Someone just went in."

"Make up your mind already."

Jeff's heart quickened. This was it. He was so close to seeing Ray McCormick, to finding out what the secrecy was all about, he could taste it.

It tasted sweet.

Roger disappeared into Ray's room, his head down over his clipboard, and Jeff gave the signal to Danny.

"Go."

As Trudy returned to her novel, Danny plucked the sticky wad of chewed-up bubble gum from his mouth and waited for the security camera inches above their head to look the other way. Then he pushed the wad into the lens, rendering the camera eye blind.

He whispered to Jeff, "If you're going to do this, Boss, you'd better do it now."

Jeff ducked low to the ground and nearly crawled beneath Trudy's line of sight as she read. He tried to minimize the squeaking of his traitorous shoes as he inched closer to the security door. Careful to make sure Trudy was still enraptured by her novel, Jeff eased himself toward a nearby closet, the one closest to the security door.

Moving only a hair every second, Jeff slid himself into the closet and closed the door to all but a sliver of light shining in from the outside hallway.

Now he just had to wait for Danny.

Trudy read for a while, engrossed in her romance novel. She'd been married twice—both times to deadbeats allergic to regular employment—but she wanted to believe that true love was only a chance encounter away. If only she could get a few days of vacation, maybe get a makeover at her friend Freida's beauty parlor, head to the City, and check out the nightlife...Mr. Right was bound to be out there. Sighing, lost in her daydream, Trudy lifted her eyes from the book and stared at the monitors before her. She absently gazed at the monitor for the camera on the far right of the hallway while Roger exited Ray's room, headed back toward the security door. Then she turned to the monitor for the camera on the far left. The image jarred her back to reality.

The screen was black.

She frowned, perplexed. Banging the top of the monitor, she waited for the reception to clear. When it didn't, she looked up to the secured door and saw Roger waving at her, ready to be let back through.

She hit the buzzer and Roger pushed the door open, meeting her quizzical expression.

"What's wrong?"

"Take a look at this."

Danny got a glimpse of the nurse as she checked the wires on the back of the monitor, looking for loose connections. Roger looked equally stumped. Coming up empty, Trudy moved back behind her cubicle and picked up the phone. "This is Trudy. I got a camera down over here. Could you send someone to look at it?"

Fortunately she hadn't seen Danny down the hall, cutting the wire with his pocketknife.

Trudy waited impatiently, chewing her lip. Trying again, she spoke into the receiver, "There's a camera down in the hallway over here. Is anyone there?"

Silence again, thanks to Danny's sabotage skills. Trudy's frown deepened, and she looked to Roger.

"Want me to go find someone?" he offered.

"I'll go. Stay here."

"OK."

Roger stayed behind. Danny cursed to himself. *That* was not part of the plan. The preacher was stuck down the hall, mere feet from the closed security door, and it was up to Danny to find a way to hit the trigger and let Jeff inside.

And now he had to get by good ol' Roger to do it.

He could almost hear Jeff in his head, urging, "Do something!" So he did the only thing that came to mind.

"Hey!" Danny shouted, rounding the corner where he'd been hiding and coming right up to Roger. He put on his best someone-just-ran-over-my-dog face and pointed wildly toward the elevators.

"Can I help you?" Roger asked, a bit perturbed.

"You gotta help me, man!" Danny shouted, waving his arms and pacing like a fiend. "My girlfriend, man! She's in labor downstairs!"

Roger raised an eyebrow in the face of Danny's hysterics. "Sir, you should take her to the emergency room."

"No one will help her down there! You gotta come down!"

"Sir, if the doctors are busy, you need to just be patient—"

"No, *you* be patient, dude. My old lady is screaming down there..." he paused. He knew he had to turn up the dramatics, and fast. "She's bleeding! Yeah! All over the floor! I heard about things like this, man! I heard one guy died right on the emergency room floor and no one helped him!"

Roger stepped out of the cubicle, holding out steady hands. "Calm down, sir. Getting upset will not help anyone."

"Man, if something happens to her, I'm suing this place! What's your name?"

"My name is Roger."

Danny jabbed a wild finger at the nurse. "I'm telling them it was *you*. I'm telling them that I came to you and told you my pregnant girlfriend was dying and you didn't do nothing to help. You think you can live with that, Roger? Do *you*?"

Roger finally reached his breaking point. "All right, all right. Let's just call security—"

"Dude, I'm talking to you!"

Roger looked hesitantly at the downed security monitor behind him, then took a deep breath. "OK. I'll see what I can do. Come on."

Visibly aggravated, but no doubt trying to uphold a modicum of professionalism, Roger headed for the elevators. Danny hung back, suddenly worlds calmer. "Hey, I gotta hit the head, first," Danny said. "I'll catch up."

"But—"

Instantly he resumed his hysterics. "She's dying, man!"

"All right, all right," Roger held up his hands in surrender and entered the elevator as Danny rushed into the bathroom. A moment later the elevator carried Roger to the emergency room where he would find no bleeding pregnant woman. Danny slipped out of the bathroom, checking to make sure the coast was clear. He raced to the receptionist's counter and slid across. Jeff jerked the janitor's closet door open, his face beet red and covered in sweat.

"What took you so long?" Jeff hissed across the hall.

Danny gave him a sour look and jammed the button that activated the irritating buzzing. Jeff pushed open the newly unlocked door to the secured wing.

"Need me to come with?" Danny called after him.

Jeff nearly disappeared inside the security wing before he halted, holding the door open, and shook his head. "Head back to the truck. I can take it from here."

"You sure?" Danny asked with great disappointment.

But Jeff was already gone. Danny huffed and grumbled, "Makes me do all the work and doesn't let me see any of the good stuff…"

Jeff crept down the secured hallway and entered Ray McCormick's room, his body pulsing with excitement. Now he knew why people like Danny spent so much energy breaking the law—it was rather rewarding to know he had outsmarted the system.

With one leg of the journey over, Jeff took a good look at the sterile room, bathed in a sickening light green paint. He heard the steady beeps of the equipment and saw a plastic tent hanging over a bed in the center of the room. All the wires seemed to lead there.

Suddenly his excitement gave way to trepidation.

He didn't know what he expected to find, but it was certainly not this. He hadn't thought this far into the plan, period, and didn't stop to consider what would happen when he finally found Ray. Since meeting Danny, he hadn't stopped to consider a lot of things. He was simply reacting. Maybe Isabella could have thought of a better plan. Maybe she would have talked him out of it altogether.

Maybe that was why he left her at home.

"Ray?" he called tentatively.

Only silence from the anonymous patient behind the plastic veil.

With a shaky hand Jeff unzipped the tent and pulled back the curtain.

"Ray?"

Deputy Ryan Stevenson arrived at the hospital, prepared for a long night's watch. He'd gotten a bite to eat down at Smokey's and headed over on the Committee's orders. Ray McCormick—and whatever sickness afflicted him—was considered top priority, and Mr. Hayden wanted complete secrecy. No visitors, no questions, no exceptions. That nosy Reverend Weldon had already been by once today, poking around, and the Committee wanted Stevenson to stand guard lest Jeff try something stupid.

Jeff Weldon had been a thorn in the Committee's collective side all summer, doing his best to undo all their hard work in concealing the truth behind the Greensboro Ripper case. If Stevenson had his way, he just would have shot the man months ago. End of story. But the Committee was a pack of cowardly old timers, hunkered down in their secret hidey hole, content to talk big and feel important. They hid behind their demonic benefactor, expecting the enigmatic Mr. Graves to fight all their battles. But Stevenson knew better. Mr. Graves admired initiative. Plans were being set into motion. The world was on the brink of a new dawn, and Stevenson would settle for nothing less than to be a ruler in the new dark order.

He'd play the puppet for now, the Committee's muscle. But it was only a matter of time before he proved himself worthy of greater things.

Stevenson was still imagining his glorious future at the devil's side when he spotted Trudy Doyle at the front counter, talking to the head receptionist. Trudy was supposed to be up on the third floor, guarding the door to the security wing where Ray McCormick lay.

Flustered, Trudy gesticulated with her hands to the other woman, and her words became clearer as he approached. "Where's Jimmy? I tried calling, but the phones are down."

"Down?" The front desk receptionist picked up her phone. "I'm getting a dial tone here."

"What's wrong?" Stevenson asked, stepping up to Trudy. "Why aren't you at your post?"

Stevenson followed Trudy to the third floor. Their first stop was her cubicle. "See?" She pointed to the blacked-out screen. "Everything just went blank."

Something wasn't right. An uneasy feeling washed over him.

Stevenson didn't waste a second. He left the cubicle in long steps, with Trudy jogging to keep up. Stern, he marched toward the offending camera and looked up. Something was on the lens, he noticed. Scowling, he plucked it off and examined it.

Bubble gum.

Trudy asked, "What does it mean?"

To their side, the elevator dinged. Roger, the nurse on call tonight, flanked by two security guards, stormed out, looking peeved. Trudy spotted him. "Roger? I thought I told you to stay at my station."

Roger pushed past her, looking up and down the hall. He patted one of the guards on the chest and pointed toward the bathroom. "Check there," he ordered, then turned to Stevenson and Trudy. "Did you guys see some punk kid pass through here? About yay tall—" He held up a hand to indicate a height about six inches shorter that his own. "—dressed really shabby, and smelled like the bathroom at a bar?"

Deputy Stevenson slowly turned his gaze to the seemingly undisturbed door to the secured wing.

And beyond that, Ray McCormick's room.

With a low growl he headed for the door.

Jeff gasped at what he saw underneath the tent. It was shaped like a man but covered in gruesome black lesions that oozed and pulsed, seeping a thick, tar-like substance. Jeff put his hand over his mouth, nearly gagging at the sight.

Fumbling over himself, he zipped the plastic veil shut again, fighting the urge to vomit at the sight of what was once Ray McCormick.

"Ray...what happened to you—"

His cell phone rang.

He jumped, his knees about to buckle, and quickly answered the phone, not wanting his little escapade to be discovered.

"*Hello?*"

"Do me a favor." It was the Wrong Number.

"Who are you?"

"Duck out the window. Fast."

"*What?* Why?"

"You're about to have company." Wrong Number's tone was urgent. "Go. Now!"

This time Jeff didn't argue.

He raced for the window and threw open the latch. He stepped onto the ledge and felt the wind tugging at his coat, as if it wanted him to slip to his death.

"Better close that window, or they'll be right behind you."

Jeff struggled to hold onto his cell phone while closing the window at the same time. After managing to shut the glass, he heard Wrong Number say, "Wait here for a minute."

Jeff did as he was told, wondering how Wrong Number knew where he was and what he was doing.

Deputy Ryan Stevenson exploded into the room, pinning the door to the wall. Trudy and Roger were right behind him.

"What do you expect to find?" Trudy asked the behemoth.

Stevenson prowled like a big cat, searching everywhere. Underneath the bed, behind the curtains, in the bathroom, the closet. He didn't feel right about this. It had to be Weldon, doggedly pursuing his quest for answers. *We should have killed him already.* But the Committee underestimated Jeff. As it stood, the man was alive and quite possibly could have seen Ray. Could have seen everything.

When his search turned up nothing, Stevenson turned to Trudy and poked a finger at her round face. "Don't take your eyes off this room again."

"Yes, sir." Trudy muttered in a small, frightened voice.

Then the deputy left, Roger trailing behind him, mumbling, "I swear, he said his girlfriend was dying."

From his birdie's stoop outside, Jeff peered inside, doing his best to remain hidden. He spotted Roger and Stevenson leaving the room behind. Trudy Doyle remained a moment more, giving the room a thoughtful once-over, then closed the door behind her as she left. Jeff squeezed his eyes shut, his teeth chattering from the stress, and exhaled the breath he'd been holding. Even Wrong Number was quiet, waiting for the tense moment to pass.

Once it had, Wrong Number asked lightheartedly, "Friend of yours?"

"Deputy Ryan Stevenson. He's a thug. I'm not worried about him."

"He's not alone, though. He works for some very powerful people. You've been peeking in places you shouldn't, Weldon. You've gone and ticked off all the wrong people." Wrong Number paused, then continued, "'For certain men whose condemnation was written about long ago have secretly slipped in among you. They are godless men, who change the grace of our God into a license for immorality and deny Jesus Christ our only Sovereign and Lord.'"

Jeff recognized the scripture from Jude, verse 4. "Who *are* you?"

"Just a guy who wants the same thing you do."

"What's that?"

There was a pause. "To destroy them."

"Who?"

"You *know* who." Another pause. "The Committee."

The Committee. At last a name for the blurry faces Danny said were behind the strange things going on in their town. Maybe they were even the ones responsible for Dras's conviction...

The Committee. Jeff repeated it over and over in his mind, familiarizing himself with the enemy.

"Who are they?" He was ready to know more. Ready to learn all he could and go hunt them down and put an end to them.

"Do you really think this is a good conversation to be having while you're standing out there on the ledge?"

Jeff looked down, remembering again that he was three stories above the street.

"Climb down a story and crawl through the window," Wrong Number told him. "You can get out that way. Security's not as tight down there."

"*Climb down?* How do you expect me to do *that?*"

"Improvise."

"What about you?"

"I'll be in touch." The call ended.

"No! Wait!"

Jeff growled in frustration, then clipped the phone back to his belt and began his cumbersome descent, scaling the brickwork.

Once again on the ground floor, Jeff hurried from the hospital, trying not to look suspicious while at the same time wanting to be as far from the scene of his crime as possible.

Danny pulled Jeff's beat-up truck behind him with a cough and a sputter and leaned out of the driver's side window. "You ready or what?"

"Move over. I'm driving."

"What'd you see?" Danny asked in boyish anticipation as Jeff climbed in.

They pulled from the parking lot in silence while Jeff collected himself, trying to find the words to accurately describe the horror he saw on that hospital bed. "It was Ray. But he was different. He looked like..."

Unbidden, Jeff's nightmares flared up behind his eyes, and he realized that he'd seen the thing that Ray McCormick had become before.

In the clearing. Barking and gnashing and praying to their dark god.

Danny hung his head, as if somehow able to see the same terrible truth in Jeff's eyes. "He was one of them, wasn't he? One of those things from the dreams?"

Jeff nodded, unable to comprehend the gravity of the revelation.

"What's going on, preacher?"

"I don't know, but I'm going to find out."

"Reverend?"

Caroline McCormick stared, visibly surprised at the unexpected visitor.

Jeff stood on her front porch in the cool of evening with his hands in his pockets, feeling unsure and out of place. Behind him, sitting in the parked truck across the street, Danny waited, keeping out of sight.

Caroline looked awful. Her eyes were dark and lifeless, her hair disheveled, and she held a cigarette in a nervous hand. Jeff knew that Caroline quit smoking two years ago, but apparently she had picked it up again. Under the circumstances he supposed he couldn't blame her.

Perhaps thinking that maybe the cigarette would offend a man of the cloth, Caroline clumsily dropped it to the step and snuffed out its smoldering tip with her shoe, exhaling one last puff of smoke.

Jeff awkwardly greeted her. "Caroline. Hi."

She was hesitant to make eye contact. "What are you doing here? Wait, no, that came out rude."

"No, no," Jeff eased. "You're right, I should have called first. It's just...I tried to go see Ray."

Caroline's dull eyes brightened for an instant. "Oh?"

"I'm afraid I didn't get very far."

She frowned. "They're watching him pretty close. They haven't even let *me* see him yet. Finally I got fed up and decided to come home for a while."

"I'm sorry."

"Still, though, it means a lot that you tried," she said before stepping back into the house, her demeanor softening. "Come in."

"Sure. Thanks." Jeff crossed the threshold, throwing a quick glance over his shoulder at Danny before vanishing into the McCormick home.

Once inside, Jeff was bombarded by memories of holding Wednesday night Bible studies in the living room a few months ago. Familiar pictures of the family—of Lindsey—smiled back at him, reflections of a happy past that would never return. It hurt him to see old friends in such a broken state, and the pastor in him felt he ought to say something, to offer some kind of encouragement—especially since he knew what Ray had become while Caroline remained pitifully in the dark.

But he wasn't here to encourage. He was here to get answers.

Jeff was ashamed of his own coldness, but the shame did not thaw him.

"Do you want some coffee?" Caroline asked, still trying to get her bearings.

"No, I'm fine."

They stood without speaking for a moment, unable to look at each other. There was a strange sense of distance between them, what with his brother suspected of killing her daughter and all.

At last Jeff pushed onward, "How's Ray been feeling lately? I mean, what's wrong with him, Caroline? Is he sick?"

"I don't know. That's just it. The doctors won't tell me anything. I have no idea what to think."

She took a deep breath, her face anguished. "I know Ray and I haven't been to church as much as we should. Things just haven't been the same since Lindsey..."

She drew another cigarette from a pack on the coffee table, apparently no longer worried whether it was offensive or not, and lit it hurriedly. After a long drag to calm her nerves, she continued, "Things have been hard. Ray hasn't been able to let it go. He's becoming obsessed. Before he went into the hospital, he was quiet, withdrawn, didn't sleep for days. He's just...different."

Different. That's one of way of putting it.

Wary, Caroline said, "I want to show you something."

Jeff followed the distraught woman down the hall into Ray's study. Caroline pushed open the door, and Jeff felt instantly sick and terrified. Inside the study, loose sheets of notebook paper were taped and stapled all over the walls.

Every sheet bore the same strange circular sigil that appeared on the unholy monument in his nightmares.

Jeff's head throbbed, and he thought he might pass out.

Caroline stared at the floor. "I haven't shown anyone this, as you can imagine. They'd think Ray was crazy for sure."

Jeff left her side to examine the drawings on the wall more closely. While they were basically just drawings of circles, there was something maddening about the shapes. Scribbled in black charcoal, round and round and round, the etchings seemed to writhe like serpents. Jeff finally pulled himself away when he started to feel the sickening tug of the night terrors and the terrible whispering voices.

It's coming for you, Jeff.

Jeff closed his eyes, striving to drown out the screams of the black monsters echoing in his mind, and Caroline continued, "It got worse when he started getting the phone calls."

Sirens went off in Jeff's soul, and he broke free from his horrific dream-memories. "Phone calls?"

"Yes." She still refused to look at him, her face crimson. "Ray never said who it was or what they wanted, but every time he got one, he just seemed all the more...intense. They really began to bother him. He'd stay up all hours of the night, just waiting for that next one."

"Did he get a call before he went into the hospital?"

"I don't know. I went to bed." She sniffled, her heart breaking. "God help me, I went to bed and left him alone, and then Doc Brown is calling to tell me Ray's in the hospital for observation."

Nausea washed over Jeff, and he felt dizzy. He wanted to go home. This was all too much too soon. He needed time to think, to process what he'd seen in Ray's room and here in his house.

Caroline looked to the pastor, her eyes beseeching him. "Do you know what's happening, Jeff?"

Jeff answered her honestly, "No."

Her last shred of hope gone, Caroline hung her head again. "Ray's a good man. I know he hasn't been perfect, and we've both made mistakes, but he means well and I...I just want my husband back."

Jeff nodded sympathetically. "I'll keep him in my prayers."

That seemed to do little to ease her concern, and Jeff was shocked at how shallow it sounded coming out of his mouth. An uncomfortable hush settled until Jeff excused himself and left the McCormick home behind, entering into the night.

CHAPTER TWENTY-ONE

JEFF'S TRUCK COUGHED and wheezed its way down the East Side. After his talk with Caroline, he dropped Danny off at the trailer and called it a day. All Jeff wanted was to go home, curl up next to Isabella in bed, and fall asleep. He knew she would ask him where he'd been, and he was prepared to lie to her. He didn't want to, but the things he saw...there was no way he could tell her about them. He could talk to Danny about that stuff. Danny was seeing his fair share of monsters lately too. But there was no need to drag Isabella into it.

He needed to conduct an investigation without anyone looking over his shoulder. He needed to understand what his dreams meant, what was wrong with Ray McCormick, what the Committee was hiding, and what Dras and his "Strange Man" had to do with it all. If he could just solve this puzzle, then he and Isabella could go back to the way things used to be, and she would never have to be the wiser. He needed her to be safe, innocent of the deceit surrounding her. Knowing even the little that he did about the dark secrets kept in their town was starting to affect him. He could feel his heart filling with hatred for the people of Greensboro. Not just this new shadowy faction known as the Committee and not just that troglodyte Deputy Stevenson, but *everyone*. Everyone who abandoned him or turned on him during the last three months.

He'd given up everything for those people, spent his entire adult life being their champion. And now, when he needed them most, they refused him.

Well, he didn't need them anymore. He had Danny now, and the two of them would find a way to fight this thing.

Isabella would just have to understand.

With his mind weighed down by many burdens, Jeff pulled into his driveway, only to discover more bad news. They had company.

When Jeff entered his home, he saw Leonard Fergus sitting on the Weldon's couch, his wrinkled hands draped over the top of his cane. In the chair across from him, Isabella leaned on the edge of her seat and bounced her knees. It looked like a scene from his adolescence—his parents staying up after curfew waiting for their wayward son to return.

"Hey," he said quietly.

Isabella sprang up "Jeff, where *were* you? Are you OK? I tried calling and calling, but you never picked up."

"I'm fine. I turned off my phone."

Jeff's own words struck him. Yes, he *had* turned off his phone. In The Oasis.

Then how did Wrong Number call me?

"Leonard's here," Isabella announced apprehensively. Although she tried to smile as she introduced him, her voice wavered with uncertainty, and Jeff was immediately suspicious.

He managed a nod. "I can see that."

Fergus stood on shaky legs and straightened to his full height, his demeanor professional. "Evenin', Jeff."

"Leonard." Jeff was only dimly aware that, for the first time, he'd greeted the man by his first name.

"Can we talk?"

Jeff looked to Isabella, hoping to glean the purpose of Leonard's visit. She stood stiffly, biting her lip. Whatever Leonard had to say, Isabella had already heard it. And it was not good.

Jeff braced himself for bad news. "Sure."

"Jeff, the deacons have come to me. They heard about the meeting with the church elders, and a lot of them saw that incident at the park with Earl Canton. They're worried about you."

Since becoming pastor of the Good Church of the Faithful, Jeff lived under the scrutinizing stare of the church deacons, who never failed to remind him of how Jack Weldon used to run things. They were all old men with old ideas who'd been with the church since its days out in the North Woods near God's Cliff, and they saw Jeff as a young upstart, looking to change their traditions and shake things up.

And that was *before* the trial.

"You've been pushing yourself too hard for too long and we're all afraid that, with everything that's been going on, the stress is getting to you. It's hurting the ministry, Jeff. You heard it at the elders' meeting. It's affecting *all* the churches, and after your fight with Earl, the deacons think it's time to step in."

Leonard hung his head, releasing a deep sigh, then lifted his chin and spoke his next words. "This isn't easy for me, son, but...the church wants you to step down from the pulpit."

Jeff laughed unexpectedly. It was the laugh of a man who had lost everything and couldn't find the strength to cry. He turned to Isabella and saw the hurt in her eyes.

"Jeff..." she said, "this isn't funny."

Oh, but it was. It was all some sort of cosmic joke. God had let his brother get taken away, and now He was letting the Committee get away with taking his calling too. *Why aren't You doing something about all of this, God? If You won't, I will.*

Finding the truth was what was important now. Something evil was festering in Greensboro, and if God had decided to sit this one out, Jeff was prepared to finish the job himself and make the town clean again. *It doesn't matter anymore. Let them take everything away from me. I've got things to do, things to finish. Then I can cry over it all.*

"Who's my replacement?"

"The boy. Will."

Now Jeff felt as if a knife had been plunged deep into his back. Tears of pain and indignation welled up in his eyes, but he refused them. With a small, sad laugh he shook his head. "That figures. The deacons want a puppet, someone they can control. Well, they'll never find a better candidate than *Mr. Yes-Sir, No-Sir.*"

Isabella stared at her husband, shocked by his rudeness. "*Jeff.*"

He ignored her. His heart turned icy and mean as he focused on old Leonard Fergus. Something about everything he uncovered today didn't add up. First, he witnessed Ray's hideous transformation, then he learned about the Committee, and now he was demoted by deacons who wanted to get him out of the picture? There was only one explanation.

"I get it now," Jeff said, feeling a weight lift off his shoulders, his mind freed by the truth.

"What?" Isabella asked, confused.

Jeff put his hands on his hips, his eyes stern and calculating, as he sized up Leonard, wondering if everything this man had ever said to him was a lie. "This isn't about what happened with Earl. You're all in on it, aren't you?"

Isabella remained completely lost. "Jeff, what are you talking about?"

Fergus's shoulders sagged, and he exhaled through his nose, his lips tight. There was no shock on his face, and Jeff's worst fears were realized.

"Now the prepackaged sermons make sense. The Committee wanted to control my sermons, to use me to spread their propaganda. They wanted to make me a pawn in their conspiracy too, didn't they? But they planned ahead. They knew that might not work, so they brought in young, innocent Will Baxter, all the time preparing him to take my place."

Isabella's brow furrowed. "What? What's the Committee?"

Leonard leveled his gaze. He stood his ground, leaning on his cane, calmly taking the abuse.

Jeff kept going, on a roll, "'From the least to the greatest, all are greedy for gain; prophets and priests alike, all practice deceit. They dress the wound of my people as though it were not serious. "Peace, peace," they say, when there is no peace.'"

Fergus remained unfazed as Jeff advanced on him, his anger unleashed. "'For certain men whose condemnation was written about long ago have secretly slipped in among you. They are godless men, who change the grace of our God into a license for immorality and deny Jesus Christ our only Sovereign and Lord.'" As Jeff quoted the scripture that Wrong Number had given him, he was reminded of one like it in Philippians chapter 3 that called such men "enemies of the cross." "That's what he's been trying to warn me about, isn't it? The enemies of the cross. The Committee! They've got you in their pocket too, just like everybody else in this town!"

Fergus blinked back shame but did not avert his eyes.

Jeff raved, his voice growing louder. "I got too close to the truth tonight at the hospital, and they thought that if they took away my church, I would shut up, didn't they?"

"You went to the hospital?" Isabella asked.

Jeff ignored her, shouting, "They thought they could break me, *right*? Well, you go back to your boss and tell him or them or *whoever* that they're wrong! They can't break me. No matter *what* they do."

Isabella gawked at her husband. Jeff knew how this would look to her. Leonard Fergus had been a friend to both of their families since they were children. *It was all a lie, Iz. He lied to us!*

"How much was Will worth, Leonard? Did you hand him the keys to a shiny new car, or did he hold out for money too? Or maybe just the thought of taking my place and being pastor of the whole church was enough to turn him to your side. How much were *you* worth, Leonard?"

Isabella couldn't take it anymore. "Jeff! Stop! This is *Leonard*."

Jeff looked past her to Fergus, his adrenaline on fire. "Was it worth it? Was it worth my brother's life?"

Fergus finally looked away. Maintaining a gentlemanly composure, he reached into his coat, draped on the back of the Weldons' sofa, and pulled out an envelope. He handed it to Jeff. "I wanted to stop by and tell you in person and give you this. It's the phone that you gave Will and your last payment in cash. There's also a good recommendation from the church."

Jeff dumped the contents into his hands, including the cell phone that was the perfect twin to his own.

"You'd do good to read the recommendation, Jeff."

Jeff refused to acknowledge him further, recalling all the heartfelt talks he shared with Leonard over the years and realizing they were all part of the deception.

Fergus adjusted his cap, preparing to leave, and turned to Isabella with a soft smile, as if it were any other evening and he'd only come to pay them a neighborly visit. "I'd better go."

Isabella touched the old man's sleeve, sorrowful. "Leonard, don't."

"It's all right," he drawled, sadness in his voice. "Thanks for the lemonade, Isabella. It was wonderful as always."

Isabella forced a smile in return but did not attempt to hide her brokenhearted tears. Before he left, Fergus gave Jeff a wink, despite the young man's tirade. "I always did like lemons. A fascinating fruit. You can eat 'em, clean with 'em, even make invisible ink. You know, Jeff. Like in the movies?"

Jeff's bitterness was unshakable, and at last Fergus tipped his cap. The gesture was friendly, but his eyes were stern and focused. "Read the recommendation."

Giving Isabella one last half-hearted grin, Fergus wrapped himself snug in his coat and left the Weldon home. Jeff watched him go, feeling utterly enraged. He looked down to the cell phone in his hand, along with the rest of the contents of the envelope. His severance pay. Unable to resist, he thumbed through the bills, counting. It was a healthy sum. More than his regular paycheck. More than enough to pay the bills for the rest of the month, to last until he found another job. And the rest of the money?

A part of him knew it would be enough to help Danny get his family out of town.

No. Not yet. I still need him.

Now, after his monumental day, he just wanted to go upstairs and go to bed. Even the fear of his recurring nightmare did little to discourage the thought of even a moment's sleep. There was work to be done, but he just didn't have the strength to do it. Not tonight.

With an exhausted sigh, he turned but found himself face-to-face with Isabella.

Her eyes were red and wet. She watched Jeff closely, as if he were a total stranger. "What's wrong with you?" she finally asked, her voice broken by a sob.

"I don't want to talk about this."

Without waiting for her to respond, he moved for the kitchen and the carton of milk in the refrigerator. She watched, open-mouthed, as he drank casually as if the world had not just fallen down around him.

"We *need* to talk about this, Jeff."

He knew they did. They had needed to for the last three months, since this mess all started. But Jeff was in no mood for it right now. He just wanted to go to bed and sleep off the long, strange day. "We'll talk about it in the morning."

"No." Isabella was gentle but unmistakably firm. He hung his head and sighed.

Here we go.

"We need to talk about this now," she insisted.

Jeff waved her off. "I'll get a job, all right? Money will be tight for a while, but we'll manage—"

"I'm not talking about the money, *Jeff*. I don't care about the money! I care about *you*. What is happening to you? Why won't you tell me? You can't keep..."

Her hesitation betrayed her and put Jeff in the mood to fight. After avoiding her gaze all evening, now he chose to look at her. Directly at her. Challenging her. "'Can't keep' what?"

Isabella took a deep breath and met his eyes. "You can't keep pushing me away."

He turned away from her instantly. It had become almost a reflex now.

She leaned closer. "Why won't you let me in? Why won't you *talk* to me?" She sounded small and hurt, desperate to be a part of his life again.

"I can't talk to you, Iz."

"W–what?"

Jeff couldn't face her. "You're my wife. I'm supposed to take care of you. I'm supposed to protect you and I just…This is *my* problem, OK? I have to deal with it. If I talk to you about it, then that's like saying—"

"What? You're human? That you may possibly not be able to handle everything on your own? That you may need me? God forbid, right? Baby, there is no weakness in us needing each other."

Jeff shook his head, refusing to hear her.

"When are you going to get it? We're in this together," Isabella said.

"But you shouldn't have to be! Let me handle this."

His head throbbed the way it did after the nightmares, and he wanted his pills.

"No," Isabella interrupted him. "This is *our* life we're talking about."

He peered out the window above their kitchen sink and looked for the stars, hoping to find solace, only to find that the stars were all rendered invisible by the streetlights.

"Everything's falling apart, Iz. This whole town's gone crazy. There are things going on…but I can make it right again. I *know* I can."

She moved closer, wrapping her arms around him from behind and leaning her head on the back of his shoulders. "Is God not being God enough for you?"

In shock he pulled away from her, angered that she had named his sin so acutely. "What?"

"That's what this is about, isn't it? Baby, you've put all of this responsibility on your shoulders, and it's not even your responsibility. It's *God's*. It's *His* job to change hearts. You can't do it, Jeff. You're just a man. Stop fighting and let Him be God."

Jeff stepped back, looking at Isabella as if she had grown a third eye. *She doesn't believe in me.* "How can you say that? How can you expect me to just sit by and do nothing? Dras is out there! They're going to execute him for something he didn't even do. I'm not gonna stand by and do *nothing*. What is it with everybody? Don't you understand? Why am I the only one who sees that I have to *do* something about this mess?"

"He's not alone, Jeff," Isabella raised her voice too, something she was rarely known to do. "God is with him."

Jeff looked away, having heard enough. But his wife wasn't through. "Do you think they *took* Dras? Do you think they would have been able to touch him if God hadn't allowed it? Don't you see? God has a plan in all of this. He is working, even though you can't see it. You have to believe that." Isabella paused, her concern growing, and added, "You do still believe that, don't you?"

He remained quiet. He had heard Isabella give this speech before, and he was in no mood for the encore.

"Jeff...*please*."

He went back to looking at the suffocated starlight, more distant than ever before. "I don't know anymore. I thought He had a plan. When that storm first came to Greensboro, I felt called, you know? Like God was speaking directly to me. Like He was getting me ready for something. And then Dras came to me for help..." he trailed off, but forced himself to continue, "...and I turned him away. When I finally got back on board and went to save him, I was too late. I missed the calling. And ever since then it's like I can't get that calling back. I keep trying to show God that I can be trusted again, but—" He felt like he might cry, but he refused to surrender to the emotion. "I can't hear anything. Like God's not talking to me anymore. I missed my chance to serve Him and now—"

"Jeff..."

"He's forgotten us, Isabella. He's forgotten me."

"*No.*"

"He finally got tired of Greensboro, and now He's giving us what we deserve. He's left us here to rot."

"That's not true."

He spun around to face her. "Look around you! Where is He? If He's still here, why can't I see Him? I'm supposed to be a *pastor*! I'm supposed to lead His people, and how can I when *I* can't even find Him?"

"Maybe He's trying to show you where He is! Maybe you're looking in the wrong places!"

"See! *That's* what I'm talking about."

She retracted as if slapped. "What?"

"*That's* why I can't talk to you. You are always so calm and so together."

Hurt, she cried, "Would you rather I panic?"

"*Yes!* Anything would be better than you always having the answers. I need you to panic with me! But every time trouble comes our way, you have all of these words of wisdom!"

"You don't think I'm scared?"

"How can I? You're like some superhero of faith or something. Like Hebrews 11 should make a little more room for Isabella Weldon! It's like you are so above me! So much closer to God than I am. I–I feel so inadequate around you."

She froze in place. "I make you feel inadequate?"

"*I'm* supposed to be the one who keeps it together. Everyone is looking to me to figure out what to do."

"Who, Jeff? Who is looking to you?"

They were both in tears now, and neither tried to hide it any longer.

"*Me*?" she wept. "Do you think that of me? That I'm always counting on you to be perfect and to never make a mistake?"

He didn't know what to say, so he didn't say anything at all.

"Jeff, you have this idea in your head that you have to be Jack Weldon. I know your father is as good as a man can be, and I know he left big shoes to fill when he left the pulpit. But what makes your father so special is that he knows when to give up! He knows when to let go and trust God to do the rest. I know you think you have to be Superman. But you are *just* a man. A wonderful man, whom I love more than anything in this world, but I don't think you know when to *let it go*, Jeff. God doesn't expect you to do it all or to be perfect. He just wants you. In all of this, have you forgotten that? You are His *son*. Why can't that be enough for you?" And then the more personal question finally surfaced. "Why can't *I* be enough for you?"

Jeff shook his head again, stubbornly blinking back tears. "I'm doing this for you."

"*No.*" It was her turn to shake her head defiantly. "You're not. And you're not doing it for Dras either, despite what you keep telling yourself."

He turned to her, appalled that she would say such a thing.

"You're doing this for *you*. Because you're scared."

"I'm not scared of anything," he was quick to respond, like a little boy who'd been challenged to a fight.

"Yes, you are. I know you better than anyone. I know what this is really about. The night that they arrested Dras, you jumped in to save him, but the police held you back. They held you down, and you had to watch as they beat him. They took away your power, didn't they?" Isabella was nearly screaming. "You haven't been looking for God's calling to come back! You've been looking for that control. That power again. You are so afraid of not being in control over *everything* in your life! Well, reality check, you're not. God is. And until you realize that, your little quest or whatever you want to call it to make it sound noble will never be over because you will never be God. So you might as well give it up, because it's killing you and it's costing you everything."

She paused for a moment, terrible hurt marring her beautiful face. "Even me."

Having said her piece, Isabella walked away. Jeff didn't look up to see her go. He heard her jog up the stairs and close the bedroom door, shutting him out.

I'm losing her...

But that's OK, Jeff told himself. *I don't need her. I have work to do, and once I'm finished, she'll see why it had to be this way. They all will.*

"Dad?"

Jeff waited for the familiar voice to answer on the other end of the phone.

Jack Weldon responded, "Jeff? Is that you, son? You sound upset. Is everything OK?"

Jeff wanted to break down. To cry and confess that he was scared and confused, that he didn't know what he was doing anymore. Everything was slipping away, and he didn't know what to do to get it all back and make everything right again. *I'm a failure, Dad,* he wanted to cry.

But he held it in.

"They...uh...the church asked me to step down today, Dad. They...they fired me."

Jeff held his breath. His dad had been so excited when his son was elected to continue his work as pastor of the Good Church of the Faithful. He nervously waited to hear what the mighty Jack Weldon would say when he found out that his boy couldn't handle the job.

"That's too bad, Jeff." His father sounded sad but not disappointed. "I'm sorry to hear that."

Jeff ventured further and asked, "Dad? You...uh...you're still proud of me, right?"

He bit down hard on his bottom lip as tears stung his eyes and nose. His body trembled as he fearfully considered that his father might not affirm his worth. At the same time he was filled with shame as he admitted to himself that even now, as a grown man, he still needed to know that his father was proud of him. That his father still loved him no matter what.

Jack seemed surprised by the question. "Of course I am. It doesn't matter if you're the pastor or not, son. It doesn't matter what you do. It matters what kind of man you are. How you treat the people you love and that you serve the Lord the best that you can. I've always been proud of you, but it's because of the man you are."

But would his dad be proud to know the things Jeff had done lately? The things he'd said, the lies he'd told. *I'm not who you think I am, Dad. I never was.*

Jeff held the phone away, the tears starting to roll and not wanting his father to hear him weep.

"Are you all right?"

"Yes, sir," was all Jeff could manage before he felt a thick lump in his throat. "I need to go. I'll come see you guys soon, OK?"

"OK." His father's voice filled with concern, but Jeff didn't want to bring him any further into his problems. He quietly placed the phone back on its cradle and held his face in his hands.

The initial shock was beginning to subside and the bare truth was slowly sinking in.

I'm fired…

He'd never thought of a life beyond the pulpit, and he suddenly felt more lost than he ever had before. There was the possibility of leaving town, finding another church, starting over.

But I don't know if I can do that. Am I even meant to do that?

He noticed the manila envelope that Fergus gave him earlier staring back at him from the coffee table. Wondering what beautiful speech the Committee had constructed to make his dismissal sound less humiliating, Jeff sifted through the contents of the envelope until he found the recommendation. His eyes skimmed the page, seeing words like "good man" and "hard worker" and realized it didn't mean a thing. Not to him, anyway. He didn't know why Leonard had made such a big deal out of it. There was nothing spectacular there, and despite the potential it carried to help secure him a job pastoring in some other town, Jeff thought to throw the whole thing away.

But then he recalled something peculiar. Fergus gave him a strange wink when he told him to read the letter. And he went on and on about lemons and how they made great—

"Invisible ink," Jeff muttered, the letter still in his hand.

Jeff hurried to the kitchen. Flicking on the light and rummaging through one of the many junk-filled drawers, he finally came across a small, nearly empty BIC lighter. His heart racing in anticipation, he ignited the lighter and waved it beneath the recommendation letter, careful not to set the paper ablaze. A moment passed and nothing came of it, and Jeff worried that he was just being foolish, holding on to a false hope.

Then the incredible happened.

Slowly, ghostly letters began to form on the page as the lemon juice reacted to the lighter's heat. And there, with astonished eyes, Jeff read Leonard Fergus's secret message to him:

NOT SAFE. WILL CONTACT LATER. EXPLAIN EVERYTHING—LEONARD

Jeff set the note down, feeling a satisfied wolf's grin spread across his lips.

Bingo.

CHAPTER TWENTY-TWO

BY MIDNIGHT THE hospital was all but empty, with only the skeleton crew and overnight patients present. Dr. Herbert Brown was on duty, checking up on his latest, and by far most bizarre, patient: Ray McCormick.

Using his back to push open the door to Ray's room, Brown pressed his nose to his clipboard, reviewing his notes. "OK, Ray. Time for your morphine."

Putting on his best bedside smile, Brown glanced up from his clipboard to look at the patient.

Who was no longer there.

Brown's voice hitched as he stared at the mess of strewn sheets on the unoccupied bed. Ray was gone.

"Oh no." His heart picked up, his legs growing faint. "*Oh no*," he repeated, his voice faltering.

Frozen, he struggled to think of what to do, but his indecision did not last long, for a moment later he heard the slithering. It began as a low hissing. Like a snake. But not just one. Many hissing, slithering things. And the crawling, wet sound came from behind him.

Sssssss...

Brown choked and tried to regain his breath.

Sssssss...

The light from the hallway peeked in through the partially open door, casting shadows on the wall that reflected a tentacled monster lurking behind him. Slowly, cautiously, so as to not to upset what once was his patient, he tried to put forth a friendly voice. "Ray? Is that you?"

Sssssss...

Brown turned around, and what he saw hunkered in the corner of the hospital room filled him with such terror that he laughed uncontrollably. Louder and louder he howled with wild hilarity as warm tears streamed down his face. Cackling still, he watched as the awful, twitching thing stood to its full stature, raised its claws, and hissed.

Sssssssss!

Talons swooped down, ripping through the air and poor Dr. Brown. His laughter turned to screams as he fell back on the hospital bed, but the monster paid no heed to his cries. Lunging forward, it pinned Brown, using its razor-sharp tentacles like a flail to cut into him, reducing his doctor's coat and shirt to shreds and revealing a small, circular brand on his upper forearm. After shirt came skin, and blood flung across the room like splattered paint. Brown wailed, feeling the sting of one deep cut after another.

Trudy Doyle, upon hearing the racket, came barging into the room, backed by two security guards. The monster that used to be Ray McCormick stopped in its feral attack and turned to gaze upon the woman and guards. Trudy screamed, holding her hands to her eyes to shield them from the grisly scene, and the guards stuttered and stammered, trying to find the presence of mind to act.

Without giving them a chance to draw their guns, the monster leaped from Brown's filleted remains and burst past the three, knocking one security guard to the floor in the hallway and leaving the other bracing himself against the door frame for balance. The screams of the nurses in the hallway reached her ears as Trudy rushed to Brown, weeping hysterically.

"Dr. Brown! Dr. Brown!"

His whole body shaking, Brown calmly sat up on the bed in shock. His eyes were wide, and his body was covered with jagged, gaping cuts. Drenched in crimson, he clumsily pushed past the woman and walked into the hallway.

"Dr. Brown, where are you going! What are you doing?"

Fumbling his cell phone out of his tattered pants pocket, he limped into the hallway. With trembling, bloodied hands he dialed a number. When the receiver picked up, he spoke in a hollow, haunting voice, "It got out. It's loose…"

The phone fell to the floor and clattered against the tile.

Brown leaned against the wall, wide-eyed and dead.

All down the hallway behind him, staff and patients scurried and dodged as the former Ray McCormick blazed a trail of destruction to the front doors.

The monster was out.

Mr. Gibson clutched his coat collar as he hurried between two red-bricked buildings and down the dark alley. The cool breeze carried the thunderous music that flowed from the building to his left, and he reflected on what dreadful noise today's children listened to. It was appalling and disgusting, but this was where Mr. Graves—their benefactor—had chosen to locate his secret meeting place, so Gibson would have to bear it for another night.

Especially this night. He had urgent news that the others needed to hear.

Throwing a cautious look behind him every few steps to insure he had not been spotted by any curious onlooker or potential mugger, he quickly paced toward the door in the back. Covered in graffiti, it was barely recognizable as a door and thus served effectively as the secret entrance to the Committee's meeting hall. Scurrying up to the metal frame, he knocked twice, three times, then once more.

After a few seconds of nervous anticipation, the door creaked open and Mr. Gibson was ushered inside by a kindly butler. "Shall I take your coat?"

Mr. Gibson, too rushed for niceties, shooed the butler away and hurried farther into the stone labyrinth of the Committee's lair until finally the twists and turns led him to their inner sanctum.

The others were gathered, and already the ceremony had begun.

A shirtless Will Baxter knelt in the center of a circular stone room, fringed by shadowed faces and lit lamp stands. Mr. Nigel stood before the kneeling boy, his coat removed and his sleeves rolled up to reveal a circular mark on his upper forearm, a brand. Small but distinct, it was a dark circle with flames dancing around the radius.

The symbol of the sun.

Mr. Nigel performed the ceremony loudly so that all gathered could hear and be proud. "William Douglas Baxter, upon careful consideration of your record and deeds served for the Committee, I nominate you for membership in this, the most sacred of alliances. How does the Committee receive him?"

One by one the six men surrounding Will, including the tardy Mr. Gibson, showed their vote of confidence by answering, "We receive him as our brother."

Mr. Nigel turned to his pledge, and Mr. Jacobson came forth wearing heavy gloves and carrying a small stand of burning hot coals, an iron plunged deep into their fire. "William Douglas Baxter, once you take the mark of our covenant, you are sealed for life as a member and practitioner of the Secret. As an ally of the Committee, your loyalty to us must supersede all other duties. Work, friends, family, and even what faith you may hold must be forsaken for our cause and our cause alone."

Off to the side Mr. Gibson noticed that Leonard Fergus's face twisted with a tight grimace, yet he remained silent.

Mr. Gibson then spotted Mr. Hayden and Mr. Simms standing at a distance, away from their brood and under the shade of their favorite hireling, Deputy Stevenson, observing the rite like a sort of ruling triumvirate. Gibson hurried to them as Mr. Nigel continued.

"Do you submit yourself to the authority of the Committee?"

Will shakily replied, "I do."

With that, Mr. Jacobson took out the hot iron, and Will, with bowed head, caught sight of the brand on the end that glowed red. With one hand, Jacobson grasped Will's exposed right forearm. With the other, he pressed the iron brand to Will's skin. The young man's flesh sizzled, and Will ground his teeth in pain but endured.

"Then, with this mark, I declare you sanctified and set apart for the Dark Hour and our Master's coming. May he bless you with prosperity, and may you serve him well."

Jacobson pulled the iron away, and Will's forearm was left with a burning sun-shaped mark. The men applauded and one by one came forward to congratulate their newest member, except Leonard, who remained braced on his old cane.

With the ceremony finished, Mr. Gibson drew nearer to Mr. Hayden and Mr. Simms and whispered in their ears, "Doctor Brown has been murdered. It was Ray McCormick. The transformation is complete…and he's escaped."

Their faces grave, Hayden and Simms turned to one another and to Stevenson in concern.

"It has begun then," Hayden affirmed.

The phone rang after one in the morning, and Hank yawned and stretched, fighting back a curse as he reached over his side of the bed and picked up the phone. Groggy and annoyed, he bellowed, "Hello?"

"Sheriff?"

"Yeah?"

"This is Deputy Hollis."

On Deputy Andy Hollis's end, the wiry young man leaned against the squad car and talked into the phone with his finger in his free ear. Behind him a multitude of blues and reds flashed, as nearly every car on the force arrived on site. Deputies scrambled and hollered as Hollis tried to talk over the chaos. "Sir, we've got a situation down here at the train yard."

Just then Deputy Ortiz screamed in fright as he was thrown out of one of the many abandoned railcars by an unseen attacker in the shadows. The deputy bounced off the hood of the nearest car, and others rushed to his aid.

Hollis turned back to the phone with a wince. "You might want to hurry, sir. You'll want to see this."

By the time Sheriff Hank Berkley got out of bed, pulled his pants on, kissed his sleeping wife good-bye, and sped to the train yard, he was one unhappy camper.

Deputy Hollis noted his mood and rushed to explain. "We chased him into one of the cars, but none of us could get close enough to catch him. We've tried everything, and we can't get him out. He just stays in there and screams, and one of the boys said he was cutting himself with stones. What should we do?"

"OK, whoa," Hank rubbed the remaining sleep from his eyes. "From the beginning, Hollis."

"We got a call from the hospital that one of their patients escaped." Hollis paused. "It was Ray McCormick."

Hank scratched his head. "Ray?"

"He escaped the hospital and killed Dr. Brown and injured a few others in the process. We've been trying to hold him down, and Carter almost got him once. But he got away." Deputy Hollis's eyes widened in wonder. "There were five of us, Sheriff. Five capable men, and he threw us off of him like we were rag dolls."

Sheriff Berkley whistled in awe.

There loosed a scream behind them, and both turned to see an injured deputy stumbling out of a dark train car. He was cradling his bleeding left arm, and his face was ghostly white. Deputy Hollis left Hank's side to tend to his fallen friend, and other deputies followed. Sheriff Berkley watched the scene, his mind blank. The entire situation was way beyond what he felt equipped to handle.

"Need some help?"

Hank jumped and turned to see Special Agent Christopher Perdu at his side.

"Perdu? What are you doing here? I thought you would've left town by now."

Christopher examined the train car from a distance. "I'm still not convinced that all of this is over, Sheriff." The screams of the wounded deputy rang out sharply, and Perdu regarded Hank. "Looks like my hunch was right."

Hank looked back to the train car, his stomach knotting up. "What makes you think one escaped patient has anything to do with the Greensboro Ripper case?"

"It's been my experience that nothing happens by chance. Weird things are happening in Greensboro, and I would almost bet that they're coming from the same source."

Hank's brow cinched up. "And what source is that?"

"Can't say yet. But we should go check out that train car."

"Are you crazy? You saw what he did to that deputy, and Hollis says he's been flinging them left and right all night. They're decades younger than I am! I'm too old to go charging in there like John Wayne."

"Don't worry." Christopher turned to Hank with an adventurous smile. "I'll go with you."

Christopher's zeal was infectious, and Hank couldn't help but chuckle. "Perdu, you're one crazy son of a gun."

"I like to think I'm just curious."

The two men moved together toward the dilapidated train car. The deputies fell into an awed hush as their leader bravely approached the monster's lair. Leaning into the car, Hank peered inside the thick darkness and tried not to sound as scared out of his wits as he really was. "Ray?" he began, light and friendly. "You in there, bud? Why don't you come on out so we can talk?"

Silence.

Hank gulped and turned to Christopher, hoping to glean some courage from the young, fearless agent. Perdu nodded, encouraging him to continue, and Hank took a deep breath. Then, turning back to the darkness, he spoke again, "We don't want to hurt you. We just want to help."

Silence for a moment, then—

Sssssssss...

The deputies immediately fell behind the open doors of their patrol cars, their sidearms aimed at the dark opening. Hank waved them off, though their eagerness to open fire made him feel a little more secure. Deputy Hollis scurried up to his commander and handed him a flashlight. "Here you go, sir."

"Thanks, son."

And then the little deputy went back to hide.

Hank turned to Christopher, feeling uneasy. Quietly, so his deputies wouldn't hear and think less of him, Hank whispered, "Do you really want to do this?"

"No, but do we really have a choice?"

Releasing a deep sigh, Hank replied, "Nope. Guess not."

The sheriff carefully drew his gun, turned on his flashlight, and crossed his arms in front of him. Assuming the "enter" position, he and Perdu slowly eased their way into the train car, leaving the safety of the deputies' cover behind.

Once inside, Hank's heartbeat picked up, and he heard the blood rushing through his ears. He sensed Christopher's presence behind him, though, and it calmed him. It was nice having someone watch his back for a change. Deputy Adams used to play that role, and he would forever be missed. But Perdu was good stock, and the old sheriff was beginning to trust him.

Even if he was a Fed.

Hank shone the flashlight around the car, careful to cover every inch. "Ray? Where are you? I'm not going to hurt you. Just wanna talk."

Sssssssss...

Hank swallowed hard. Christopher leaned in with an encouraging whisper, "Easy now. Slow and easy."

Hank nodded, though in the dark he didn't think his buddy saw.

The two moved back to back, spreading the dim light of their flashlights. The sharp silence hurt Hank's ears. Then a new sound echoed in the quiet recesses of the car.

It was scraping. Scurrying. Like nails on metal.

Sssssss...

The hissing again, and close. Closer than a moment ago. Then the scurrying. It filled Hank's mind; it was all around them, but there was no way to pinpoint its origin. Hank sweat and his hands shook, but he continued to cast the flashlight's luminescence over the entire expanse of the railcar's floor. No sign of anyone. He moved the light up the walls but still saw nothing.

Sssssssss...

Now he was growing beyond nervous and moving into petrified. "Perdu?"

Sssssssss...

Scraping, scratching, scurrying, clawing. Like a rodent in the walls.

Hank listened intently, and he realized that the sound was not coming from either side of him.

But from above.

His mouth became dry, his tongue felt swollen, and for everything in the world Hank did not want to look up to the ceiling and see what he was afraid he would see. But still feeling Perdu's presence at his side and taking what courage he could from that, he slowly lifted the flashlight and shined it above.

There was the thing. Fixed to the ceiling on all fours.

Hank yelped as the thing shrieked, reacting to the light, and lashed out, knocking the sheriff backward and sending the flashlight spinning along the floor. The spiraling light cast a strobe effect across the walls, and continuous sporadic flashes revealed the monster dropping from the ceiling and landing again on all fours.

His heart pounding as the thing hissed, Hank fumbled in the dark until he retrieved his flashlight. Without wasting a second, he shined it toward the monster, and its full horrendous figure was exposed.

Hank could not hold back a gasp.

Deputy Hollis said that Ray McCormick was hiding in this car, but the thing standing before Hank barely resembled a man at all, let alone poor Ray. Like an animal, Ray—or the thing that used to be Ray—hunched over on its knuckles in a gorilla stance, its head hung low and menacing. His hospital gown was torn, exposing flesh. But it wasn't *human* flesh. It was something else. A kind of sticky, black oil contracted and pulsated as it slithered all over him like a live, thinking thing. It crawled all over his body, beneath his tattered garments and over the features of his face, smothering them and hiding them like a mask. On Ray's back, the slime flailed out like tentacles that tapered into razor-sharp talons. The tentacles moved about, rattling and creating the awful hiss, like a rattlesnake's tail when it's preparing to strike.

Hank backed away, appalled. His mind threatened to shut down as he remained unable to explain what he was seeing.

"Merciful heavens..." He held a hand to his mouth. "Perdu, you seeing this?"

"Yeah." Christopher was just as speechless but focused. "I'm seeing this."

The slime-encased thing covered its face, shielding itself from the light, and let loose a terrifying squeal.

"Wh–what's it doing?" Hank asked, watching the beast clawing and batting at the flashlight's intangible beam.

"I don't think it likes the light."

Suddenly the monster reared up on its hind legs and filled the car with a hellish, angry roar. The black goo began to vibrate, as if agitated. With a loud hiss from its snakelike arms, it sprang forward, headed right for Sheriff Berkley.

His nerves already shot, Hank let out a holler of his own as he opened fire on the misshapen creature. The bullets dug deep into the black goo with a sound like marbles thrown into mud, but they were simply consumed in its thick sea.

The thing kept moving.

Hank dodged just in time, and the monster flew past and stuck to the wall behind him. Turning itself around to get a better look at its intended catch, the slime-beast that had once been Ray McCormick circled, preparing for another attack. Hank fired again, his eyes wide with terror and surprise, but the bullets, although contacting, had no apparent effect.

"What is that thing?" Hank cried as the creature's hiss grew louder. Over and over Hank tried telling himself that it was Ray—that Ray needed his help—but he was unable to grasp the truth, only the stark terror that he felt in the face of the inhuman thing.

Finally the monster exploded forward and out of the train car, landing squarely on Deputy Hollis's patrol car. The car buckled under the weight, and Deputy Hollis looked up into a solid black void where a man's face should have been. The thing screamed and flailed about, knocking Hollis to the ground with the blunt side of its spindly arm.

Deputy Carter Ross roared to the troops, "*Fire!*"

The terrified deputies blasted a volley of thunder and smoke, their bullets ricocheting off the broad side of the train car and burrowing deep into the creature. With a loud scream that caused every deputy to clap their hands over their ears, the beast fled, leaping like a frog and disappearing into the tree line behind the train yard.

Making its way toward the North Woods.

"It's headed for the lake!" Perdu said with certainty in his voice. He and Sheriff Berkley emerged from the train car, following the creature as quickly as they could.

The deputies ceased their fire, and Deputy Roy Miller called out, "Sheriff, where are you going?"

But Hank did not have a chance to respond. Leaving his boys behind, he pushed onward, though not nearly as rapidly as Special

Agent Perdu. Christopher ran like a gazelle, bursting through the brush and bounding over fallen logs and thick, thorny bushes. Hank struggled to keep up, his age and affinity for french fries hindering him. "Perdu, wait up!"

But Christopher was a man on a mission. The monster led them on, nearly disappearing at times, bringing the two lawmen deeper into the heart of the wild woods. The trees grew thicker, hiding the moonlight until it was next to impossible to see. With his flashlight leading the way, Sheriff Berkley fought to stay in the chase. Pushing low-hanging branches out of his face and stumbling over entangling weeds, he huffed and puffed and cursed.

I'm too old for this.

Yet he pressed on. Wiping the sweat from his face, he forced himself to see through the darkness. In the distance he could hear Perdu beating away at the terrain, nothing able to stop him in his pursuit of the creature. Oh, what Hank would give to be young again.

"Sheriff!" Christopher called to him from somewhere up ahead. "I've found him!"

Encouraged by the development in the chase, Hank took a deep breath and ran just a little harder. He thought he felt a second wind coming.

Finally he spotted Christopher, his back to Hank and standing atop a small knob, looking at something. Hank, panting and exhausted from the race, bent and dragged his tired old body to his younger counterpart. His lungs burned and his side felt like he had a lead ball weighted inside. "Whatcha' got?"

Perdu's stern eyes narrowed. Watching. Hank reached the young agent's side and saw what had caught his attention.

The beast hunkered over, toiling away at some grueling task. In the blinding dark Hank's eyes took a moment to adjust, but when they did, he observed that the monster was holding jagged rocks and was—

"Oh my…"

The thing that used to be Ray McCormick was cutting away at the black goo—his second flesh—with the stones. Now the right side of his face was freed from the tar and exposed in a beam of moonlight, revealing a tortured man with haunting, human eyes that Hank recognized as belonging to the grieving father who came to the station house every Saturday looking for his lost little girl. Crying out in desperation, the man inside the monstrous shell clawed and scraped at his sticky prison.

"It really *is* Ray under there," Hank breathed, finally accepting the horrible truth. "What happened to him?"

Christopher's eyes saddened, and he made no response. Hank leaned closer to Ray, careful not to set him off again.

"Ray?"

Ray wept as he furiously dug into his flesh, trying to rid himself of the sticky, black mutation.

"Ray, put down the rocks."

"I can't..." he whimpered. "I can't make it go away. I can't get it off me."

Hank left Christopher's side and took a step closer to Ray, his heart going out to the man. "We need to get you some help. We need to get you back to the hospital."

Ray looked up with his one clear eye and stared at the sheriff. "No one can help me. I'm doomed. We're all doomed."

"That's not true, Ray. We can help."

But it was too late. The black goo, no longer held back by Ray's persistent scraping, slowly swallowed his face again and hid all humanity behind its empty countenance. Ray was lost once more. Slowly the tentacles in his back began to detach and peel away from the larger mass, raising and rattling.

"Hank," Christopher cautioned, "step back."

Hank wasn't going to argue with that. The monster stood tall and proud, fearing nothing. It moved boldly toward Hank, and the old sheriff gulped as he inched backward. Christopher remained still and quiet, on the edge of action. Hank took another step backward, and then another, as the imposing shape loomed. One more step he took, only this one sought to sabotage him. His ankle struck the exposed roots of a large oak. With a surprised shout he tumbled onto his backside as the beast approached. It hissed and screamed then leaped forward.

Throwing his hands up to shield himself from the gruesome attack that was sure to follow, Hank cowered on the ground. The attack never came. Hank dared to uncover his eyes. The beast hung suspended, midflight, then sprang backward, slamming against a tree. Hank watched in amazement as Christopher stepped over him and moved to the beast. With one hand outstretched, seemingly holding an invisible barrier between them, Special Agent Perdu pinned the monster to the tree.

Hank was too stunned to speak.

Christopher approached the creature as it wriggled wildly, trying to break free from the spell. Concentration deep on his face, Christopher, with boldness and authority, loudly pronounced, "In the name of Christ Jesus, Son of God, I command you to depart from this man!"

Just when Hank thought things couldn't get any stranger, the thick, black second flesh of Ray McCormick screamed within itself and trembled. With a rumbling tremor the black, gooey armor began to blast away, revealing more and more of Ray's body. Like old paint blown off the side of a house by a powerful water hose, it chipped away, piece by piece, until there was nothing left but Ray and a pool of blackness on the forest floor. Gathering into itself again, the goo took on serpentine form and slithered away, disappearing into the brush.

Ray McCormick collapsed, and Perdu stood over him, breathless and invigorated. Hank quickly got to his feet and clumsily stumbled to them. "What did you do? How did you do that?"

Christopher breathed heavily and stared into the forest where the parasitic beast had escaped. "You have to have faith."

"They teach you that at the Academy?"

Christopher turned his attention to Ray. Hank came back to his senses and knelt down beside the man. Ray was shaking, and his skin had turned a marble blue. Lifting the broken man's head, Hank spoke tenderly, "Ray, you OK?"

Ray's teeth chattered. "Thank...you..."

And then he shivered into death.

Christopher's face grew grim and Hank's slackened. He gently let Ray's head rest against the ground and closed the man's eyes forever. Standing, he took off his hat and held it to his chest.

"Perdu, what's going on in Greensboro?"

"That's what we need to find out—if you're finally ready."

Christopher turned to Sheriff Berkley, waiting for an answer. Hank opened his mouth to give one, but suddenly he heard something behind them.

It sounded like car engines turning over.

When Sheriff Berkley and Special Agent Perdu made it back to the train yard, they were just in time to see the entire fleet of deputies fleeing in the other direction with their lights and sirens off, quietly disappearing over the dark horizon.

"Where are they going?" Christopher wondered.

Hank's eyes fell upon a large dark van with no recognizable

markings and men in white biohazard suits standing by. Then he spotted a black sedan off to their left. Standing there were three figures.

Mr. Hayden, Mr. Simms, and Deputy Ryan Stevenson.

Hank's brow creased.

"Who are they?" Christopher asked.

"That's Richard Hayden. The mayor."

"What's the mayor doing out here?"

The two walked toward the sedan, approaching the mysterious trio. Mr. Hayden broke formation and stepped forward with the charismatic smile that won him the election. "Evening, Hank."

Hank was reluctant to respond but did so for politeness' sake. "Richie."

"We took the liberty of sending your deputies home. Their services were no longer needed here. We hope you don't mind."

He smiled again. Hank got chills.

"What are you doing out here? I didn't think the mayor came out to routine police calls."

"Ah, but this is hardly routine," Mr. Hayden replied. "We heard about Ray McCormick escaping tonight, and we think he might be infected with some sort of virus. We want to get him back to the hospital for careful observation."

"Virus?"

Mr. Simms stepped forward, obviously growing impatient. "Mr. McCormick is a very sick man."

"He's dead," Hank declared bluntly.

The news caught both Mr. Hayden and Mr. Simms by surprise. They briefly shared an uneasy expression, and then Mr. Simms nodded to Deputy Stevenson. Meanwhile Mr. Hayden distracted Sheriff Berkley, saying, "How unfortunate. We thank you for your efforts, Hank. We'll take it from here. We've called Deputy Stevenson in to assist us. What with your workload as of late, we thought he'd be a—" Mr. Hayden drew out a pause. "—suitable replacement. I know I should have checked with you, Hank, but this is an unusual situation. I trust there won't be a problem."

Stevenson, with the word from Mr. Simms, led the troop of men in white biohazard suits into the forest. Christopher stepped aside to let them through, though they looked fully prepared to walk right over him if need be, and Hank watched it all transpire, feeling helpless.

Mr. Hayden and Mr. Simms followed closely behind the men in white and only paused briefly to face Sheriff Berkley one last time.

"For the public's sake, we would like to keep this outbreak quiet until we discover if there's any need to panic," Mr. Hayden informed him. "You understand, of course."

Without giving Hank the opportunity to make a rebuttal, the two well-dressed men strolled on, each one's hands clasped behind his back, and entered the North Woods. Ahead, in the area where Ray McCormick lay dead, Hank spotted flames sprouting, consuming the "infected" patch of forest.

Hank didn't have to turn to Christopher to know the young man was watching him. And waiting. Waiting for his decision to uncover the truth.

But Hank couldn't. Not yet.

Not bothering to say good-bye, he left the agent behind and moped back to his car.

Christopher called, "You can't just walk away from this."

Hank didn't respond.

CHAPTER TWENTY-THREE

ROSALYN MYERS STOOD in the middle of the clothing department the next day shopping with her mother, something she had not done since she was fifteen, and even then those occasions ended in disaster. When Rosalyn was a kid and still felt she had something to prove, she often assembled various mismatched articles into garish, trend-challenging getups that were sure to turn a few heads and let people know that she was someone with a mind of her own who didn't want to be messed with. Her mother, however, had a subscription to every fashion magazine and maintained a steady watch on the pulse of modern America. Whatever was deemed the crème-de-la-crème of current style, Meredith Myers was willing to slap it on a charge card and worry about the price later. Their conflicting tastes always put them at odds, and the fights that they pitched in the middle of clothing stores all across town were the stuff of mother-daughter-angst-ridden legend.

Which was precisely why Rosalyn had no idea why her mother insisted on them going shopping again today.

Ever since their "truce" at Rosalyn's dramatic birthday dinner Saturday, Meredith had tried hard to rebuild her relationship with her eldest daughter. Rosalyn appreciated the gesture and was even touched by it, but by the time shopping entered the equation, she was beginning to get a bit worn out.

"This one is perfect," Meredith beamed, holding up a pink tank top that had lost a fight with a Bedazzler.

Rosalyn half-snarled. "I don't do pink."

"But you'd look lovely in it."

Lovely. Not a word Meredith used very often when Rosalyn was concerned.

It sounded nice.

Annie piped in, her arms loaded with her catch of the day. "I like it. I think it makes you look less scary."

Rosalyn spun to her sister, not sure if she was offended or wanted to laugh hysterically. "Watch it, you."

Annie stuck out her tongue playfully, and Rosalyn felt warm inside. This was what it was like to be a family.

Though she originally had her doubts, she decided that maybe this little outing was exactly what she needed right now.

"OK," she relented, trying to sound annoyed for image's sake. "I'll take the pink one."

"Maybe you can wear it when you come to dinner Friday night," Meredith suggested, her face full of light and life.

Rosalyn chuckled. "We'll see. I may have to work."

"OK," Meredith nodded, pleased with the possibility in her daughter's response.

"Ooh, Mom!" Annie shouted down another aisle. "Come quick! Look at this one!"

Meredith gave Rosalyn's hand a quick squeeze and threw a grateful smile. "Thanks for coming, by the way," she whispered, then hurried off to see what Annie had discovered.

Rosalyn watched her mother and sister "ooh" and "aah" over a burgundy skirt, unable to keep herself from smiling. *I must really look like an idiot.* But she didn't care. For the first time in a long time she felt good about things. There was no reason why she shouldn't enjoy—

"You'd look good in pink," a horribly familiar voice casually commented from behind.

Rosalyn started and faced the man, her eyes wide. "What are you doing here?"

The Strange Man, gorgeous as ever, dressed in a loose-fitting black shirt that opened wide on his tanned chest, grinned like a teenage boy sneaking out to see his girlfriend. "What? No one will see me. Even if they did, they wouldn't know who I am."

Checking to make sure the other Myers women hadn't spotted him, Rosalyn pushed the Strange Man into the nearest dressing room and locked the door behind them.

"I *like* this," the Strange Man remarked. "The direct approach."

"Stop it." She shoved a finger in his face. "You shouldn't be here. I don't want you here."

"Don't you?"

"Why do you always have to talk in circles? *No,* I don't want you. I want you out of my life."

"Right, because fashion is a much higher calling."

Rosalyn clasped her hands over her face and growled. "What do you want?"

"You keep asking me that, but I've already told you. You're too good for this town, Rosalyn. You've got better things in store for you."

"Like what?"

The Strange Man toyed, "It's one of those things you have to discover for yourself. I can't just tell you. Where would the fun in that be?"

Rosalyn huffed and turned to the door, growing worried. "I've gotta get back to my mom."

Her hand was on the latch, ready to unlock it, when the Strange Man asked wryly, "And how is dear Mother these days?"

"What's it to you?"

"You're close, the two of you. Closer than I've seen you in quite some time."

Rosalyn's heart stopped and she angrily spun on him. "How did you…forget it, I don't want to know."

"You think I just blew through town three months ago, Rosalyn? I've been here in Greensboro for a very, very long time. I've seen so many things and learned so many secrets. One secret, in particular, that you would take great interest in learning."

"I already know you framed Dras," she spat, not feeling any better having accepted the truth. She felt even worse. Although she knew he was responsible for her best friend's incarceration and impending death, she was still drawn to the Strange Man. Guilt tore through her.

"No, no, no. Not the boy. Forget the boy. This goes back further."

Rosalyn had no clue what he was talking about. More to the point, she didn't want to know. "I'm leaving."

Now she turned without hesitation and opened the door, but the Strange Man slammed it shut again with the palm of his hand. He gripped her arms forcefully and pulled her to him, nuzzling her.

"Not yet, my dear," he said without a hint of affection. "You can't hide in this life anymore. It's time you knew the truth. It's time to be set free and join me."

"What are you—"

He cracked the door open a bit, giving her enough room to see her mother and Annie shuffling through a rack of designer jeans.

"What do you really know about your mother, Rosalyn?"

Her heart punched harder in her chest, and she flushed with nervous anticipation. Whatever it was, she didn't want to know. Things were finally starting to get good again. Dras was gone, Jeff was gone, but she had her family. After all these years they were a *family* again.

Please, don't take that away from me.

The Strange Man combed her auburn hair from her face, revealing her soft pink neck, and bent down to whisper in her naked ear. "Do you trust her? Do you think she's told you the truth?"

"Please, stop," she begged, feeling her eyes tear up.

"I won't. You have to see that you live in a world of lies. I'm the only one who will be honest with you. I'm the only one you can trust."

Meredith was just outside, holding up a pair of jeans that belonged on a woman half her age, and Annie was teasing her for it. The two laughed, and Rosalyn wanted nothing more in all the world than to be out there with them and not in here with the devil.

"What has she told you about your father?" he asked, his voice a near hiss.

Rosalyn's lip trembled, and she bit down on it to keep it under control. Desperately she shook her head. "No, no. Please, stop."

"Did she ever tell you why he killed himself?"

"I don't want to know…" Her chest heaved with fresh sobs.

"Of course you do. It's always been in the back of your mind. You have every right to know."

"No, I don't. Please don't."

"She cheated on him, Rosalyn."

And there it was. Plain as day. A lifelong mystery, yet he had explained it tactlessly. The revelation sent Rosalyn's heart plummeting. She was crying now, caught in a twisted limbo between wanting to know everything and nothing more.

"That's not true," she sniffled. "She wouldn't."

"Ask her. When your father found out, it broke him. Paul was such a sensitive man. Troubled, some might say. That's when he took the gun and—"

Rosalyn wrenched free of his grip, turned on him, and slapped his beautiful face with all her strength. "*Shut your mouth.*"

The Strange Man flinched but stood his ground, his eyes intensely fixed on her. She searched them, found only malice and cruelty, and scolded herself for ever thinking she could love a monster like him.

"I hate you," she pronounced.

"Hate me, then. I'm not here to be your friend. I'm here to be your *teacher.* You're holding on to a life built on falsehoods. It's time you left it behind."

"If you ever come near me again, I'll—"

"What? What could you ever do to hurt me?"

At last Rosalyn understood. There was nothing she *could* do. She was utterly helpless to stand against the creature before her. She was the fly in his web, and as long as he had the mind to visit her—to torment her—she'd never be able to stop him.

Her only choice was to surrender to his will. It was inevitable.

He'll haunt me until I give in.

Rosalyn felt very much alone. Dras was gone. She had turned Jeff away. No one was left to stand for her. Words escaped her. Silently she hung her head, feeling what little light she had left inside die.

"What was his name?" she finally asked, defeated. "Who was it?"

"The name won't mean anything to you. After your father died, your mother broke off the affair. She hasn't spoken to the man since."

"His name."

"Arthur Pentil. He lived in the City. She met him—"

Rosalyn abruptly exited the dressing room, leaving her demon behind, and marched up to her mother.

Meredith Myers had retrieved her charge card from her Italian leather purse, and a very delighted Annie was snatching it from her fingers when Rosalyn approached. Meredith noticed her daughter, and her face brightened at once. "There you are. Annie thought we'd lost you."

Then she saw the tears.

Annie beat her mother to the question. "Roz, what's wrong?"

Rosalyn kept her tearful gaze fixed on her mother as she spoke. "Annie, will you give us a minute?"

Meredith regarded Annie, fearful of the separation, but Annie said, "Uh...sure," and left to pay for their new clothes.

When she was gone, Meredith ventured, "What's wrong, honey?"

Rosalyn clenched her jaw. "Who's Arthur Pentil?"

Meredith gasped.

Rosalyn pushed. "Is it true? Did you sleep with him? Did Dad find out? Is that why he killed himself?"

Meredith began to cry, hiding her face in shame. "Rosalyn...I never meant for it...you weren't supposed to find out..."

Rosalyn felt something cold swell inside her as she stood over her sobbing mother. She felt no remorse when she said, "Don't call me anymore."

Then Rosalyn Myers left her family behind for good.

The Strange Man remained in the dressing room and watched Rosalyn confront her mother, a giddy demonic leer distorting his otherwise flawless features, providing just a hint of the true creature beneath. Rosalyn walked away from her weeping mother, glorious in her hatred. There was a moment of tense conversation with baby sister Annie, who stood dumbfounded at the cashier's counter. Then Rosalyn threw the pink top her mother had bought her to the floor and stomped on it on her way out the door.

Meredith watched her daughter leave, a look of utter horror and bereavement marring her carefully painted face, before slumping to the ground as if stabbed in the heart.

"That was fun," the Strange Man cooed.

Still delighting in his dark deed for the day, he interlaced his long fingers and flickered out of sight.

CHAPTER TWENTY-FOUR

JEFF OPENED THE door, staring into the dark bedroom closet. He pushed aside his clothes, digging around in the back for a box he and Isabella had transferred from their house on Grover's Pond. He supposed he should have thrown the box out years ago—it was nothing but old junk. Just notebooks and doodles he'd made in high school. Letters from girls that weren't Isabella. Old snapshots of him and his friends smoking cigs and showing off for the camera with big, cocky grins on their faces. It wasn't a box he went to very often. Looking back on those times, riding with Kyle Rogers and chasing girls down the cruising strip, Jeff had often felt ashamed by his actions. He had been rebellious, living without a care toward his parents, least of all God. Life had belonged to him, each moment his to do with whatever he pleased.

But then he'd grown up. Had taken a job helping his dad serve the community, met Isabella, then seminary, marriage, a mortgage, and a position in the church. All in such a short time. All with so little effort.

Now it was disappearing. All in such a short time. All with so little effort.

He stared at himself in a photo, age seventeen, wearing a long black coat, fingerless gloves, and his hair jelled. A burning cigarette was held between two fingers, nails painted black. He was snarling at the camera, thinking he looked cool. What had he been so angry about then? What had he been trying to prove? Maybe that he was his own man and not just a clone of Jack Weldon. That he could make his own way in the world, fight his own battles, choose his own destiny.

But in the end he hadn't. In the end, he'd chosen his father's destiny instead.

Jack had been so sick. Leaving the pastorate had been heart-wrenching for him, and Jeff just wanted to fix that for the man in some small way—maybe in part to make up for the poor son he'd been. At the time he and Isabella were engaged, the town seemed to have forgotten the hell-raiser Jeff had become, and he was on his way to the good life. Everything was lined up, and he felt that God would be proud of him for doing the decent thing and taking over for his dad. But even in front of the congregation, Jeff had so often felt he was only doing his best Jack Weldon impersonation.

That's not me, Jeff feared, touching the photo, his dark youth smug and defiant.

Who was he now? Running with Danny these last couple days had been great. He felt seventeen again, ready to tackle the whole world, both fists swinging. He felt invincible, as though he had the power to reshape his life any way he saw fit. Only he didn't know what to do with that power. Pastoring had been his only identity of adulthood, his only anchor. Whether he really wanted to be Reverend Jeff Weldon or not, he couldn't imagine life without the honorific, without preparing sermons and Bible studies.

Life stretched before him now, mysterious and uncertain, every decision important and defining.

In the box, wrapped in a wrinkled roll, Jeff discovered the black coat that he'd worn in high school. He pulled it out, not surprised to find it still emanating the smell of cigarette smoke. With a flick he unfurled it, dusted off its creases, and held it up before him, as if gazing upon an old friend. Or perhaps, a window into his own past. In so many ways he wasn't that angry boy anymore. He had Isabella. He had his family. He had, well, up until three months ago, a good life.

But as he reflected on the jacket, even slipped it on, feeling transported back in time, he realized the things he didn't have. Self-respect, assurance, peace of mind. The things that mattered to him. With this coat on, he'd felt indomitable at seventeen, and now he tasted a sampling of that invulnerability again, just as he had by Danny's side. Maybe he'd cast off too much of the old Jeff in his quest to adulthood. Maybe there were things in his youth, valuable tools that he needed now, to rediscover who he was as a man. Maybe it was time to embrace his past, to learn from it, and to forge his future.

For now, though, Jeff crawled out of the inviting coat, returning to the present and all its troubles.

"I think Jeff's going crazy."

There was a laugh on the other end of the phone before Elsa Monroe finally answered, "Why do you say that?"

Isabella frowned as she cradled the phone between her cheek and shoulder while she scrubbed dishes. It was a beautiful afternoon. Calm, peaceful. A day that she would have enjoyed had a fight with her husband not preceded it. As it was, they had barely spoken since their row the night before, and it was killing her. Finally she had to talk to somebody.

"He's moody," Isabella said. "He hasn't been to bed in days. I don't even think he's been sleeping at all. He's pushing himself too hard—"

Elsa cut her friend off with a smile that was evident even from hundreds of miles away. "That sounds like our Jeff."

"But it's different, Elsa. He's different. Something's wrong."

"Well, maybe so. He practically lost his brother. It's a difficult thing. When my brother died five years ago, there were a lot of emotions I had to deal with before I could move on. Dras is sitting on death row, and Jeff's gotta know it's only a matter of time before he loses his brother forever."

"I know…he feels so helpless."

"Jeff's a fighter, girl. He'll get through this. You know he will. He just has some trials to go through, some demons to wrestle with."

Isabella had been scrubbing a ceramic plate vehemently, thinking about how much she missed her husband. Elsa's last words snapped her back to attention. She stood straighter. "What did you just say?"

"What? Demons to wrestle with?"

Isabella froze. A fear that she had never known before gripped her. Was that what this was about? Had the demons returned? Had they never left? What did they want? Were they after Jeff now? Prepared to take him away just like they took Dras?

"Demons," she muttered.

Elsa laughed. "You know. Of the personal kind? Like fear, regret, doubt?"

Relaxing, Isabella breathed easier. "Right."

"You and Jeff are the best couple I know. And that's myself and Isaac *included*. You guys will get through this. It's just going to take some time."

Her friend's encouraging words failed to rekindle the flame of hope that was beginning to die out in Isabella's heart. She barely smiled and sighed. "He's upstairs right now, doing who knows what. He's so secretive lately, with his notes and strange phone calls. I just don't know what to say to him anymore. What to do to help him."

She was met by laughter on the other end of the phone. "You two *deserve* each other."

Isabella frowned. "What?"

"Are you listening to yourself?" Elsa chuckled lightheartedly. "You sound just like him."

"Who?"

"*Jeff*. The two of you are like," Elsa sang out loud, "'Ba-b-Dah! The Weldons to the rescue!' You have a good heart, both of you. And you mean well. But there's not always an easy fix to a problem. There's not always something you *can* do. Sometimes people just have to face things alone. Sometimes that's the only way they'll learn. Jeff can't fix his brother's problems, and you can't fix all of *his*."

Isabella grew quiet, grappling with the hard truth. It was so difficult to let go. Elsa continued, "It's like the hero's trial. The hero has to face the dragon alone to find out what he's made of. It's the same in the Christian walk. God puts us through tests to see if we're ready to handle a bigger task that He has in store for us."

"So you think God is allowing Jeff to go through this because He has a greater purpose for him?"

"Not just Jeff, honey. *You*."

Isabella shook her head. "I'm not a hero."

Elsa sounded wise beyond her twenty-nine years. "That's something you'll never know unless you're tested."

As Isabella stood there, thinking her friend's words over, Jeff walked down the stairs. Stone-faced, he entered the kitchen and headed for the refrigerator. Isabella caught him in a glance, but both quickly looked away.

"I gotta go," Isabella quietly dismissed herself.

"I'll pray for you, girl."

"OK, bye."

She hung up and worked at drying dishes. Jeff was scrounging around inside the fridge and didn't seem as though he was going to say anything to her at all. Despite her fear of throwing more fuel on the fire, Isabella knew she had to say something. "Hey," was all she could muster.

Jeff took a drink from the milk carton and replaced it in the fridge. "Hey."

"What are you doing?" she asked casually, then quickly defended, "I mean, I'm not trying to be nosy, I'm just...I was just asking."

He turned to her, his eyes heavy and tired. "Just going through some of my old things in the closet."

His response surprised her. "Really?"

"I was looking at that old coat I used to wear back in high school."

"The long black one?" she asked with a smirk, remembering how sinister a young, angst-ridden Jeff had fancied himself in it.

He nodded, unaware of the humor in the nostalgia. "Still fits."

"Wow," she reached for another dish, hoping that busying her hands would take the edge off her nerves. "You haven't worn that since you ran around with Kyle, right?"

"I've been thinking about him a lot lately."

"That's odd. What brought that up?" Her heart pounded in excitement, thrilled to be carrying on a conversation without yelling. *Keep him talking, Iz.*

Jeff leaned against the refrigerator, tracing the lines on his palms, distracted. "Thinking about things I left undone when I was younger. I really screwed up with Kyle."

"Jeff, you were seventeen."

"I let him down. I let Dras down too." He grew morose. "Now I'm letting you down."

Isabella carefully set the dried plate on the counter and hesitated, trying to determine if she should reach for him or if that would only push him away.

She didn't get the chance to make that decision. Jeff's cell phone rang.

"Don't get that," she softly pleaded.

For a moment, he seemed uncertain. "I have to. I'm expecting a call." Jeff pulled the phone from his belt loop and clicked it open. "Hello?"

Isabella frowned, her eyes filling with tears, and watched Jeff exit out the back door for privacy.

Outside, Jeff heard a familiar greeting on the other end of the cell phone. "Reverend Weldon? It's me. Will."

He thought—hoped—that it was Leonard Fergus, finally ready to reveal his secrets to him. Disappointment filled him as Jeff shortly responded, "Will...what can I do for you?"

"Well, sir, I just wanted to begin by saying how sorry I am about what happened. And I hope that having me as your replacement in the pulpit doesn't cause any hard feelings between us."

It was a nice sentiment, and perhaps the young man meant it. But Jeff was in no mood for nice sentiments. "Get to it, Will."

Will cleared his throat. "Right." Jeff could hear a small intake of breath before Will began again. "I–I've found out some things, sir."

Jeff was only half-listening, thinking of Isabella and what he would have to do to win her back this time. He really didn't have time for Will's frightened attempts to get in his good graces. "What things?" Jeff asked, disinterested.

"I had no idea what they were doing," the young man said darkly.

Will was talking about *them*. The Committee. He was sure of it.

Now he was very curious.

Quieter now, he insisted, "The Committee? Tell me what happened."

"I can't," Will replied in a small voice that was almost a whisper. "Not over the phone."

"Do you want to meet?" Jeff didn't want an opportunity to get some answers to slip away.

"*No!*" Will shrieked. Recovering, he stammered, "No, no…we shouldn't do that. If they found out I was talking to you…"

"Easy, Will. It'll be OK. We can get you out of this," he said, though he had no concern for Will's safety. Right now he just wanted answers, and he was prepared to promise the moon to get them and worry about the consequences later.

Thankfully, Will didn't jump at the chance to be rescued from his new employers. "Listen. I have to make this quick. All I can tell you is this: You think it all started with the storm and what happened to Lindsey McCormick. It didn't."

"I don't understand."

"At the sheriff's station, Stevenson keeps a file."

Stevenson, Jeff glowered. "What's in it?" His mind raced with possibilities and explanations.

"Everything. The truth."

"How do I—"

Will cut him off hurriedly, as if he were suddenly interrupted. "That's all I can say. Be careful, sir." He hung up.

Jeff stared at his silent phone.

A file would be real, tangible evidence. If he could get his hands on that, it might be enough to appeal Dras's case.

It had to be enough.

Isabella reclined on the couch, mindlessly flipping through channels with one hand while resting her weary head on the other. She felt like a guest in her own home, out of place with her marriage. In the midst of her melancholy, Jeff rushed down the stairs wearing the long, dark coat they talked about earlier. Without giving her a second look, he made his way to the front door.

"Where are you going?"

Her voice broke him from his mission, and he turned to look at her, as if realizing for the first time that she was in the room. "Something came up."

"We were supposed to eat dinner at your parents' tonight," she reminded him, already knowing it was useless.

"Um..."

Disappointment swallowed Isabella whole, but she was too tired to fight anymore. "I'll make up something." With that she slumped deeper into the couch, defeated, and resumed channel surfing.

"Thanks, Iz. You're the best."

Without wasting another moment, Jeff opened the door to leave, but Isabella stood and spoke. "Jeff."

He stopped but did not face her. A persistent question nagged at the back of her mind. Isabella had fought hard to ignore her fears, but she had to know. One way or another.

"We're still friends, right?" she asked, hoping she wouldn't have to voice her worry in full.

"Of course we are."

"Then let's talk like friends."

He looked impatient, his hand still on the doorknob, his attention divided between her and the daylight outside. "OK, what do you want to talk about?"

"Who was on the phone?"

Jeff huffed. "It's nothing, all right? Just something I need to do."

That same bothersome question poked at her subconscious, and Isabella felt sick. *Do I really want to know?* At last she blurted out, "Are you having an affair?"

Jeff's eyes widened in surprise, then narrowed. "*What?* Of course not."

She took a breath, her body relaxing. "OK...good answer."

But he was on the defensive now. "How could you think I was having an affair?" he demanded, shutting the door.

"How could I *not*? You've been sneaking out of the house at all hours of the night, you hardly say three words to me, and now you're getting phone calls from someone and you won't even tell me who it is. What am I *supposed* to think?"

"I told you," he said through bared teeth. "I'm going through things, all right?"

With suspicions of a mistress felled, Isabella considered another possibility. "You're working Dras's case again, aren't you?"

His eyes cut to the door, evasive.

"Jeff..." she groaned.

"Dras is innocent!"

"Dras is *gone!*" she screamed, more forceful than she'd intended. Until this moment she hadn't realized how hurt and angry Jeff had made her, pushing her out of his life for his brother. Venting made her feel horrible. Jeff had lost a brother—how could she be so insensitive? Cooling, she tried to restore peace between them. "Baby, he's gone. It's not your fault."

"Yes it is," he snapped, his eyes like ice.

That was that. He turned the knob again, done with the conversation.

"We can't keep doing this," she called after him, wanting to beg him to stay. She said nothing else, but she hoped the hurt and fear in her voice told Jeff all he needed to know.

Their marriage was in trouble.

"Iz..." he began, and Isabella prayed he was trying to think of something that would mend the situation, something to show her he still cared and wanted their relationship to work.

But he didn't say anything. Nothing at all.

"Do whatever it is you need to do. But do it fast, Jeff. I don't know how much longer I can hold on."

"Good-bye, Iz."

And then he was gone.

Isabella waited for the door to click shut before she grabbed the nearest throw pillow, buried her face in it, and cried.

CHAPTER TWENTY-FIVE

NO WAY. FORGET it," Danny said, pacing across the floor of Tabitha's trailer. He'd done some dumb stuff in his time, but this was a whole new level of stupid.

Jeff remained seated on the edge of a wooden chair, watching Danny with dark intensity. "I need you."

"You wanna go breakin' into the sheriff's station? Are you *nuts*?"

"They've got our answers, Danny."

"*Your* answers," he pointed out, aiming an angry finger in Jeff's direction, still pacing. "I told you I don't want no part in this."

Tabitha sat on the couch across the room, watching him anxiously while dangling toys over their sons' giggling faces. Danny knew that she was scared. He had told her that he and Jeff snuck into the hospital yesterday. It was illegal, and Danny, who had quite an extensive criminal record, could get in serious trouble if caught. But Tabitha had reminded him of all the times Jeff helped her out. And he was a preacher, after all. "He wouldn't do anything that would put our family in danger," she had said. "Would he?"

Danny wanted to believe he could trust this guy, but now—

"It's just a little B & E," Jeff grinned. "Your specialty."

Danny picked up his pace, scratching his scalp. "Man..."

"I need you," Jeff said again.

"Why?" Danny suddenly stopped and faced Jeff. "To be your fall guy? You gonna leave me twisting in the wind while you make off with the file?"

Jeff stood, challenged. "Of course not. You'll run interference while I go for the goal. Just like last night."

"No! Not 'just like last night'. That was a *hospital*, dude. Slap on the wrist for suspicion to steal narcotics. What you're talking about now is sneaking into a whole room full of deputies—who hate my guts, I might add—to steal official classified police property."

"You're making it sound worse than it is." Jeff sat back down.

"Dude, you don't get it!" Danny pounded his chest for emphasis. "Man, I ain't like you. You're some hoity-toity preacher with a perfect life and a perfect family. I'm some dope dealer from the East Side. If we get caught—"

"We won't."

Danny grew louder, "*If we get caught*, it's my tail on the line! You get a stern talking-to, and I'm spending time in Wexler in a cell right next to your brother!"

Jeff's face hardened. "Don't talk about my brother."

Danny backed away, momentarily threatened, but when he saw that Jeff remained in his seat, his tirade continued. He stood straighter, waving his arms and taunting, "Oh, *excuuuse* me. How dare I talk about your wonderful, magnificent baby brother Dras Weldon, right?"

"You better shut your mouth, Danny."

Danny plowed on, "Let me ask you something, preacher. Would you have put your brother up to all of this? Give it to me straight. You've got me breaking in hospitals and driving you all over town; you've got me *toeing the line*, man. All I wanted was your help to get my kids somewhere safe, but you used me just so you could stick it to some old guys?"

Jeff slowly rose from his seat, glaring, but did not say a word.

Danny continued, not at all afraid but rather empowered by righteous anger. "The truth is, man, you don't care about me. You've got me doing things you'd never ask your brother to do, or somebody from your congregation. I'm just East Side trash to you, ain't I?" Danny turned to Tabitha for dramatic effect. "Use Danny as bait, yeah? What's he matter in the grand scheme of things? He's just gonna end up dead in the gutter anyway, right? *Right*?"

"Danny, don't say that," Tabitha begged.

"It's true, though, ain't it? That's all I am to you, preacher! I'm just your muscle. You weren't ever gonna help me, were you? You were just trailing me along."

Tabitha spun to Jeff. "That's not true, is it, Reverend Weldon?"

But Jeff ignored her. Caught in a maelstrom of fury, he reared back his fist, ready to explode all over Danny. Danny saw the punch coming but did not flinch. Instead he stuck out his chin and waved Jeff forward. "Come on! Do it! Prove me right!"

Jeff held back and lowered his fist. "I thought you understood," he said bitterly.

"The only thing that I understand is that you only care about yourself. We don't need your 'help' anymore, *preacher*. I'll get my kids out of town without you."

"Suit yourself."

Still fuming, Jeff threw open the door to Danny's trailer and marched out. Racing forward, Danny took firm hold of the door and slammed it as hard as he could. The twins started crying, and Tabitha started to do the same.

"What are we going to do now?" she pleaded.

Danny's face fell. "I don't know."

Tabitha frowned, walking off with their children. Danny rested his head against the closed door, his anger subsiding. Desperation remained in its place. *Hey, God. If You don't hate us too much, we could use a little help down here.*

CHAPTER TWENTY-SIX

SHADOWS PASSED BY the glass in the door to the file room. Maybe before, when Greensboro was just a sleepy, undisturbed town, a deputy or two might have been hanging around, passing time playing with the paper shredder. But in the new Greensboro, a place where evil lurked around every corner, all hands were needed on deck at all times. Under such conditions, the lawmen were too busy tonight trying to maintain the peace to notice a local and recently discharged pastor slipping into the file room.

The hydraulics softly hissed and the door shut behind him. He did it. He made it in.

And all without Danny's help.

Sneaking into the station wasn't as hard as Jeff had feared. With the deputies distracted by their piles of paperwork and unruly "guests," he simply walked toward the back of the station as if he were just coming to see Hank, like he used to. Then, at just the right moment, when attention was averted, he slipped off the main route and ducked down a lone hallway.

The one leading to the file room.

So far no one was on to him. He knew there were plenty of security cameras in the station, and there wasn't enough bubble gum in the pack to render him invisible to their electronic eyes. He would be spotted and caught, and then his troubles would just be beginning—unless he had a bargaining chip. He thought that perhaps having a secret file in his possession that laid bare the crooked dealings of Greensboro's leadership would be a pretty good start to staving off punishment.

He just had to find the file before the deputies found *him*.

Jeff thought of Isabella...wondered what she was doing right now. Somewhere inside a small voice pleaded with him to give up on his crusade and return to her, to hold her close, to make love to her as he had done only two days ago. Had it only been two days? Had so much gone wrong in their marriage in such a short amount of time? No, the truth was that this had been building over the summer.

Maybe even beyond that. *You're pushing her away, Jeff. You're going to lose her.*

The file can save your brother, another louder voice reminded him. And his own words to Will haunted him: *We do whatever has to be done.*

He was sure he was doing the right thing. Dras was innocent. He had a responsibility to save him—though he couldn't suppress the still, small voice that suggested that Isabella might be right, that it was God's plan all along for Dras to be arrested.

No. Dras is innocent. This isn't right. God has no right to do this to us.

I'm getting Dras back.

Alone in the darkened file room, with only the distorted light of the hallway shining through the frosted glass in the door's window to guide him, Jeff trod softly. The room was wall-to-wall filing cabinets, and he knew the search was not going to be easy. Quickly he pulled a tiny pocket light from inside his coat and twisted the end until the small bulb shone. Using it to guide him, Jeff scoured over the labels on the filing cabinet drawers.

Will only said that Stevenson kept a file in here, hidden from the public. Yet all of these cabinets were unlocked. Would an unfortified filing cabinet be trusted to guard the secrets of the Committee? Surely not. But this was the only place that the file could be. If it wasn't in one of the filing cabinets, then it had to be in...

He looked up and saw it in the corner of the room.

A miniature one-drawer filing cabinet with a key lock, sitting on a table in the back. Jeff crept toward it. He reached out to grab it and found that it was immovable. Beneath the shell of aluminum was what felt like solid concrete.

A safe.

Reaching into his long dark coat, he withdrew the crowbar he had brought along for this little adventure, just in case. Breaking into the sheriff's files with a crowbar wasn't befitting a pastor, but it was called for now.

And, besides, Jeff wasn't a pastor anymore.

Clenching the small pocket light in his teeth, he went to work on the lock. With a heavy pull, he broke open the drawer and slid it out to examine its secrets.

There it was, simple enough. Just like Will said. It was as big as the City's phone book and about as cumbersome too.

The secret file.

He took a moment to let the discovery sink in, a moment to

savor the victory. But he couldn't get carried away. No doubt he was only scant moments away from being arrested, and he couldn't leave empty-handed. Still, though, he *had* to see what was inside. To finally know what the Committee had been hiding. He would look at it all in more detail later, but right now he had to have a look at the evil that he was up against.

His hands reached out to pick up the mammoth text, and he found that his fingers shook as he anticipated the things he would learn. Dreadful things, he was sure, and once he knew them, he could never *unknow* them. He wasn't sure if he could handle that.

This means leaving my old life behind forever.

The phone rang, and he swore, cursing its timing. Snatching it out of its holder, he hissed into the receiver, *"What?"*

"Catch you at a bad time?"

It was Wrong Number. Jeff relaxed. "What do you want?"

"Please tell me you're not where I think you are."

"Could you hurry? I'm kind of in the middle of something."

"You found the file, didn't you?"

Jeff froze. "How did you know that?"

"The Committee aren't the only ones with spies, Jeff. I don't know what you think you'll find in that file—"

"Answers. I have to know what secret was so important that my brother was sentenced for a crime he didn't commit."

"I don't think you'll like what you find. Greensboro's not the safe, quiet place you thought it was, Reverend. There are dark truths buried underneath your little town. Dig too much, and they'll bite you."

"That's a risk I'm willing to take."

"Consider what you're doing, Jeff. Do you want to stop these men? There's another way."

"I'm listening."

"There's God's way."

"Yeah. Well, God and I aren't so much on speaking terms these days."

"Don't rush ahead of Him, Reverend. You'll just trip and fall."

"Then I'll take them all down with me when I do."

"Jeff—"

Jeff hung up, no longer interested in what his mysterious source had to say. Without further interruption, he firmly placed his hands on the secret file and cracked it open.

It was time to learn the truth.

He turned to the first report and saw a photo of eleven-year-old

Billy Potter. Billy and his family used to live across Grover's Pond from Jeff and Isabella before moving to a larger home deep in the North Woods. According to the file, last year Billy was out playing with plastic army men in the backyard, enjoying the quiet evening, when his mother heard Billy holler something about a shape moving in the shadows.

The words "BLACKER THAN BLACK" were written on the report.

When the hour grew late and Billy's parents went to call him in for the night, all they found were his toys. There was a search of the woods—Jeff remembered that—but the boy was never found.

Jeff relived that night in his mind. Billy's parents came over, frantic, begging him to go before God and pray their son out of danger. He and Isabella tried to comfort them then and again after the police found nothing. They weren't members of the church, or any church for that matter, but they were friends and Billy was just a boy. It had been hard to deal with his disappearance and watch his parents suffer. Jeff remembered, with some agony, preaching the boy's funeral and standing before his little grave.

But what does Billy have to do with the Committee?

It was tragic, sure, but Jeff never considered that little Billy's death could be connected to what happened to Dras. Jeff flipped to the next report. It concerned Charlie Canton. *Earl's son.*

Eighteen years old. An arrogant pitcher with a real shot at the majors, if it hadn't been for that chip on his shoulder. Charlie died two days after Billy's parents called to report the disappearance of their son. Charlie was reportedly drinking with a few of his friends at the river in the North Woods when they decided to go diving off the cliffs, goofing around like boys do. Charlie jumped in too shallow water and broke his neck. That was the story Jeff heard and the story that ran in the paper.

However, in this secret file locked in the darkened halls of the sheriff's station, it said that there was more to the tale that no one was privy to. Not even Earl. Here it said that Charlie's friends reported seeing "something" in the woods. "Some *things*," one boy went so far as to say. According to the file, the boys were running from "monsters" when Charlie slipped and fell into the water.

The boys were told not to repeat the truth to anyone else, and the "official" story was that a stupid, drunken stunt took Charlie's life.

It was unbelievable. Shockingly, after Charlie, there were more. Strange reports of "black shapes" in the shadows of the North Woods. The file went on and on. More disappearances, more unexplained events. All the way up to a homeless man named Eldon Granger and Lindsey McCormick three months ago—the day of the storm.

Then, as if everything else were building up to it, there was the report on Dras.

It was painful to look at it, but Jeff forced himself to read on.

The account made mention of over a dozen reports of "scurrying things" chasing after Dras.

Jeff grimaced. "Gremlins." The Strange Man's little henchmen. Just like Dras said. Just like *Danny* said. They were real, documented right here in front of him. All of it was real. The stories from his youth. The Strange Man. Devils. Demons. Everything, just like Dras told him about that fateful night. They were here among the citizens of Greensboro, picking them off one by one, but no one noticed.

No, someone did notice, Jeff realized. The Committee was aware of the connection all along and was working to conceal it. They buried the truth here, in this file, while the monsters roamed free and stole children from the sides of their unsuspecting parents.

It filled Jeff with a righteous fury.

He searched the file, unable to quench his thirst for more knowledge. How much had gone on underneath his nose? How much had gone unnoticed by the entire town? *How could we have been so blind?*

He was enraged but ashamed, for he had not known either. He had done nothing when Dras gave him the perfect opportunity to fight against the coming evil.

As he looked through the file, growing sadder as he read about death after death, he came across an interesting note. Billy Potter disappeared a year and a half ago. About the same time as the highway was moved.

It was an odd coincidence and one Jeff did not dwell on for too long. The words in the reports blurred together, and he was unsure of where to go next.

Then something caught his attention. He didn't recognize it at first in the dim light of the room, but now he noticed that there was a signature resting at the bottom of every one of the reports. In every investigation the same officer had been in charge. At every crime scene the same man covered things up, locking away more and more evidence to keep the truth hidden. This was the link to the inside. The Committee's man hiding behind a badge.

No...

He flipped through the reports, as many as he could grasp, hoping to prove himself wrong, but they were all the same. All held the same name: the officer in charge was Sheriff Hank Berkley.

Hank resigned himself to another evening of toiling endlessly through the overwhelming amount of paperwork on his cluttered desk. With Ray dead and the secret of the strange sludge apparently gone with him, Hank hoped that the nightmare, which began when the Strange Man first made contact and struck his pact with the Committee, would fade into the background once more.

But before Hank could even slide a fresh report before him, Jeff Weldon burst through his office door.

Judging by the fire and determination in his eyes, Hank knew immediately that his friend was here on business. Then he saw the large file in Jeff's hand.

Hank's mouth grew dry. His eyes widened.

"Oh, no," he muttered under his breath.

Racing to get ahead of Jeff, pointing wildly and shouting, the receptionist clamored for the sheriff's attention. "Sheriff! Sheriff! He was in the file room! He broke into the file room!"

Jeff ignored the tattletale and focused only on Hank. The sheriff stood and kindly waved the woman aside. "It's OK, Pat. I'll handle this." It was time to have the inevitable conversation that he had feared for over a year.

Pat huffed and crossed her arms before marching the other way.

"You knew," was all Jeff said.

"Jeff," Hank tried to begin, calm and slow, "let me explain."

Jeff, his eyes burning with a quiet rage, threw the file across the room to the sheriff's feet, busting it wide open and sending a mess of loose papers everywhere. Hank closed his eyes and hung his head.

"You *knew*!"

Suddenly every noise in the overcrowded sheriff's station halted abruptly. Some of the deputies turned to see what the commotion was about. Hank cleared his throat, throwing a threatening look to his men before closing the door to give him and Jeff some much-needed privacy.

"Jeff..." Hank attempted once more, knowing no explanation he could offer would ever suffice for the crimes he had committed.

"You lied to me. I trusted you. Out of everyone in this town, you were the only one left that I trusted!"

Hank released a sigh, growing hot under his skin.

"I saw Ray McCormick, Hank. I've seen the files too. I know the truth."

Hank's stomach twisted and lunged, and he fought hard not to shake. Shame overtook him. He could not look at Jeff.

Jeff, bold as a lion, roared, "I know. I know what really happened. Not just with Dras. I know about the others. All the people who disappeared over the last year and a half and how *you* kept it quiet."

"I…" Hank didn't know where he was going with the sentence, and Jeff never gave him the chance to find out. Instead he posed to him a difficult question.

"How much were *you* worth, Hank?"

Hank turned away, growing more uncomfortable.

"How much was it worth to you to sell out my brother?"

The tired old sheriff paused for a long moment. "I just wanted my family to be safe. I didn't know what it would cost," Hank finally confessed, hoping his treacherous act would be forgiven. "I didn't know what they would do to Dras."

"You covered it up. He's innocent, and you *lied* for them. Do you understand that? His blood is on your hands!"

"Hey!" Hank spun around to the cocky preacher, shoving a chubby finger toward his chest. "I tried to save your brother, all right? I didn't mean for this to happen. I didn't start this!"

"No. But you aren't trying to stop it, either. And if you're not part of the solution…"

Jeff ended there, and Hank could fill in the blanks.

"The Committee. Who are they? I want names. Are you one of the prime members, or do you just run errands for them?"

"I can't." Hank held his ground. Admitting his own sin was one thing, but he had no right to point out the others.

"Is it the mayor? Is he the one behind all this? What does he have on you? Did he threaten Doris or Becky?"

"The mayor? Is *that* who you think I'm afraid of?"

Jeff's confidence faltered. "What?"

"It's the *other* one that terrifies me. The one they say has the yellow eyes and the claws. I've never seen him, but—"

"The Strange Man," Jeff blurted. "What does he want, Hank?"

"I hope you never have to find out. You don't know what you're dealing with."

"I'm not afraid," Jeff claimed, though the hesitation in his voice suggested otherwise.

"You *should* be afraid," Hank spoke from wisdom and regret.

"Help me, Hank." It was the plea of a man desperate to fight his demons and find himself again. "Help me fight them. It's not too late. We can save this town."

"I'm an old man, Jeff. I don't have too many fights left in me. I've got a family to think about. If something happens to me, they'll be the ones who will have to live with the things I've done."

Hank trailed off at that, thinking of his wife and daughter. Would they have to pay for the things he'd *already* done? He shuddered to think that the Committee could do to them what they had done to Dras or any one of the others who had uncovered the dark truth for nearly two years.

"Come on, Hank." Jeff pushed, his eyes beseeching, "Take a stand for once in your life! You can't let people push you around forever. You helped the Committee, but you don't have to keep helping them. You're going to have to make a decision and pick a side. It's time to fish or cut bait."

Hank remained silent.

Jeff's lip curled in disgust. "You've already made your decision, haven't you?"

Silence again.

Jeff never broke eye contact with Hank as he moved to leave. "Then I'll find another way."

Bitterness masked the young man's face as he slammed the door behind him.

Sheriff Hank Berkley slumped in his chair, his spirit broken.

CHAPTER TWENTY-SEVEN

ISSUS LORELAI AINLEY had taught him to play the piano when he was a boy. She believed that any well-rounded young man ought to appreciate the classics. *Even a colored*, she had once said, innocently enough, if not a bit crass. Mozart. Beethoven. They were masters of capturing the human soul in song, she told him, and deserved our respect and admiration.

And so Leonard Fergus studied Mozart and Beethoven, though he also picked up a little blues and jazz along the way, much to the dismay of Missus Lorelai Ainley.

As Leonard sat at the piano now, however, he found himself playing a mournful song rather than the chirpy, rollicking jive of his youth. It had been a long time since Leonard felt happy enough to jam to one of those old tunes. Maybe not since Eleanor died.

She was his wife for nearly sixty years before the good Lord took her home. And Leonard knew that he was going to see her soon.

His gnarled fingers caressed the piano keys, and he wondered what kind of life he would have to present to the Lord as He sat on that old Great Throne. Leonard was once a man of great faith, Jack Weldon's right-hand man, shouting and praising and fighting to get the gospel spread throughout the town. But now...he had allowed himself to forget the passion he once possessed. He sat idly by while a sinister force marched into Greensboro and took control. He turned a blind eye while people he knew suffered and died. Perhaps worse, he stopped relying on God to guide them out of this black hole.

But not anymore.

As soon as he got the phone call, he knew what to do. He believed that the Lord made it clear that He was giving him a chance to do something right. A chance to make amends. The phone call was simple. It was Simms, the second in command.

"Ray McCormick is dead," he had said. "Things are moving faster than we expected. We must meet tonight." And then he hung up.

Leonard began to play the sad tune on his aged piano. Thinking. Just thinking. Thinking of Eleanor and how he missed her. Thinking of their son and daughter, both grown now with children of their own. He was a "grampa." Leonard smiled at the thought of his five little grandchildren, his eyes heavy with happy tears. He'd miss them most of all, he thought.

But mostly he thought about heaven and wondered if it had room for an old man who loved to play a little Roosevelt Sykes from time to time.

Daylight had all but retreated by the time Jeff's truck pulled up to the Walker residence. Jeff was still unsure about this course of action, but he didn't know what else to do. He didn't have the secret file anymore to use as leverage against the Committee; in his anger he left it lying in a heap at Hank's feet. But what he read in the file was plain. Dras was innocent, and the investigation had been tampered with—staged—to prove otherwise, which meant that there was one person outside the Committee's web who knew the truth. The only other person who was there when TJ Walker was murdered. The only person who could come forward and save Dras.

Millie Walker was the key.

Jeff stepped out of the dusty pickup and marched to the front door of the Walker house, taking one last breath of courage before he knocked. Rebecca Walker answered.

Rebecca used to be an attractive woman, but these days she looked pale and unkempt.

"Hey, Rebecca," Jeff's tone was already apologetic.

"Reverend Weldon, what can I do for you?"

Jeff thought to correct her on his title but knew that the charade would carry him further than the truth. He feigned reluctance as he made his request, but inside he was as anxious as a kid on Christmas Eve. "I hate to bother you after all that's happened. You've been through so much already, but I was hoping that I could talk to Millie for a minute. It's just that … " His mind raced, trying to find the right combination that would grant him access into her home. To Millie and the truth she had locked away in her mind. "Isabella and I have been thinking about you guys a lot lately, and I just wanted to stop by and make sure she was OK."

Rebecca cracked a sad grin. *"OK?* How do *you* think she is?"

Jeff flushed. "Right. That was stupid."

She sighed, cooling. "No, I'm sorry. You and Isabella have been a real help over the summer, and you didn't have to be. I'm just tired. Come on in."

Managing a ghost of a friendly smile, Rebecca stood aside, letting him through. Jeff felt a strange sense of déjà vu as he stepped inside, realizing this was the second family he'd visited in as many days that had reportedly lost children to his brother.

Rebecca observed her messy living room. "If I'd known you were coming, I'd have cleaned up the place."

"That's not necessary," he tried to sound caring and not as rushed as he really felt.

"Watching Millie is a full-time job these days. She…she has nightmares, keeps us both up all night. During the day she just sits in her room. She won't even eat unless I spoon-feed her."

Jeff grew uncomfortable hearing the details, fearing Rebecca partly blamed him for the devastation she believed his brother had caused. "I'm sorry," Jeff said, and meant it.

She continued, "I lost my job at the hospital, so we're just getting by on Steve's child support and unemployment, which, you know, isn't much. But," she huffed, with a defeated sense of finality, "that's how we're doing here. How's *your* life these days, Jeff?"

She made no effort to hold in her sarcasm and purposely dropped the "Reverend." Friend or not, Rebecca Walker was a hurting woman who had more pressing matters to deal with than preachers who got a whim to be concerned.

Jeff let her tone roll off his back. She was entitled to her anger, and she didn't know the truth. That wasn't her fault. That was all down to the Committee.

To Hank.

"Rebecca, I'm sorry. But I really need to talk to Millie."

"Why?"

"I told you. We're worried about her."

Rebecca crossed her arms and stood facing the front window, watching the bright life outside that was continually denied her family. "Everyone's so worried. Reporters show up every day, wanting to interview 'the grieving mother' or the 'traumatized little girl.' And if it's not the reporters, it's the parent groups promising me they'll get justice for TJ. They all want a piece of the tragedy, but it's *my* tragedy." Tears traveled down her cheeks as Rebecca shook with rage and despair. "This happened to *my* family. Not theirs. It's not their child's face posted on every street corner with the word 'Remember' in big bold letters underneath it. It's not their burden, but they all fight like it's their cause. That's all it is to them. A cause."

Jeff moved to speak, but Rebecca faced him, her countenance twisted with pain. "I didn't know Dras, Jeff, and I don't care. I don't care what drove him to kill my son. To be honest, I don't even care if he lives or dies at this point. All I care about is my little girl and what the rest of her life is going to be like."

Jeff began to wonder if Rebecca had only let him in to vent her frustration. He supposed he couldn't blame her. He was probably the first person other than Millie she'd spoken to in weeks. Her hostility, though, did not negate the importance of his visit. He *had* to talk to Millie. And in order to do so, he was willing to do anything. Lie. Cheat. Steal.

Even tell the truth.

"Rebecca, I know I'm the last person you want to see right now, and this is the last thing you want to hear, but you have to listen to me. Dras is innocent."

"So you've said all over the news." Rebecca breathed deep, dropping down on an ottoman, exhausted by her emotions.

"I know my brother. He's many things, but he's not a killer. He couldn't have done this. He *didn't* do this."

"Are you saying Millie lied?"

"No. I'm saying I think she was scared into giving a false testimony."

"By who?"

"The real killer."

Rebecca abruptly stood and marched to the door. She opened it for him. "I think you should leave, Reverend Weldon."

Jeff did not budge but quickly elaborated, "I've come across certain evidence that points to another killer."

Rebecca wasn't buying it.

"Sheriff Berkley and I have been investigating leads."

This caught her attention, though, just as Jeff knew it would. It was a lie, of course, but it was his only hope. *Sorry, Hank.*

"The sheriff is helping you?"

"Yes." Then, more truthfully, Jeff said, "I promise you, Rebecca, I will tell you everything I know. You probably won't believe half of it, but I'll tell you if that's what you really want. But please, I *have* to talk to Millie."

The concerned mother slowly closed the door and folded her arms, remaining skeptical. Jeff felt so close to his goal now, he could hardly stand still.

"Please, Rebecca. Don't you want to know the truth?"

"Hi, Millie."

The tiny child sat silently, brushing the knotted synthetic hair of one of her dolls. Her attention set, there seemed to be no hope of deterring her from her work.

Jeff tucked his hands in his pockets, trying to find the words to say. He threw an encouraging look to Rebecca, who stood at the doorway, to indicate that he and Millie would be all right alone. "Think you could get me a glass of water?" It was a way to remove Rebecca from the equation.

She seemed hesitant but finally nodded and left the room. Jeff eased in closer to Millie. He wanted to get the information he needed as quickly as possible, but he knew that he had to be careful. The little girl was so fragile that one wrong word could shatter her into a million pieces. He sat on her bed, directly behind the chair where she played with her dolls. "How're you doing?"

She began to sing "Mary Had a Little Lamb." Jeff couldn't help but shiver. She continued to brush the doll's hair diligently as she sang.

"I…" Jeff paused, trying to contain his desperation, not wanting to scare the child away. "See, Millie, I've got this problem, and nobody can help me with it except you. You're a very special girl, and I need you to help me. Can you do that? Will you help me?"

She kept singing and brushing her doll's hair.

He hung his head and ventured once more, "I need to talk about your brother and what happened."

Her silence was unnerving.

"Can you tell me what happened, Millie?"

A long pause. Then, suddenly, she flung her finger to her lips and spun her doll around to face her.

"Shush, Abigail!" she ordered her plastic friend. "Don't say anything. Remember? We have to be good girls and not say anything."

Picking her song up again, only this time in a quiet hum, she resumed brushing the doll's hair. Jeff backed up a moment, his hackles rising. His heart pounding, he leaned in gently. "Why can't you say anything, Millie? Did someone tell you that you would be a bad girl if you did?"

No response.

He tried again, feeling so close to the answer he'd been seeking for three months. "You won't be a bad girl, Millie. You're a *good* girl. The best little girl I know. I know it's hard, but you've got to tell me what happened. I *need* to know the truth."

Without warning Millie stopped brushing her doll's hair, as if something important had suddenly crossed her mind. She looked to another doll and grabbed its legs, slinging it across the room violently. "No more tea for you, Miss Nancy! The bogeyman will come if you say any more! Be quiet! Quiet!"

She reached out and began attacking other dolls and stuffed animals, tears welling up in her eyes. Upon hearing the commotion, Rebecca rushed into the room. "What's happening? What are you doing to my daughter!"

Millie crashed into Jeff's arms, and he held her close as she buried her face in his chest, surprised that she had come to him. All at once his obsession subsided, and he realized he held a small life in his hands—a little girl who had been severely hurt by the very same monsters who hurt Dras. The way he had viewed her only moments before, as a tool that was necessary to accomplish a task, startled him now, and he was painfully aware that his search for answers was turning him into a monster as well.

What am I doing?

With Millie's warm, trembling body in his arms, weeping against his chest, Jeff's heart softened, and he thought of the children that he and Isabella hoped to have someday.

Isabella...she was almost like a distant memory now. *What have I done to her?*

"It's OK, Millie," Jeff stroked her soft hair, feeling lost and full of newfound regret. "It's OK. No one's going to get you."

Millie pushed herself away and looked him dead in the eyes, shaking her head. Fear consumed her, as though she wanted to believe what the nice man said but was unable to do so.

"TJ said the bogeyman comes for bad little boys and girls. Mommy said the candle keeps him away. I lit the candle, but it didn't work! He hurt TJ, and he said if I told, I would be a bad girl and he would come back for me." Her lips puckered and quivered as the guilt nearly crushed her.

Rebecca moved for her daughter, wide-eyed and open-mouthed. "*Who* came? Who came, honey?"

Millie spun to her. "The bogeyman! It was him!" She turned back to Jeff. "I saw him at my window, but Mommy didn't believe me. He was here! I'm sorry I lied..." Her eyes reddened. She started to cry again, broken and repentant. "I'm a bad girl. I lied."

Jeff found forgiveness in his heart, despite the fact that her testimony had been the final nail in Dras's coffin. He knew that it wasn't her fault, and right now he just wanted to take care of this little girl. His mind drifted back to the secret file at the station. So many lives lost, so many families shattered by the Strange Man and the Committee. Jeff realized that he had been selfish in thinking his family was the only one suffering. *Greensboro* was suffering, plagued by an evil the people were kept blind to, with no way to defend themselves.

Jeff felt emboldened. *I'll defend them.*

"The bogeyman said that I had to tell everyone that Dras hurt TJ. He said if I did, he wouldn't hurt Mommy or me. So I lied. I lied..."

Tears rolled down her round cheeks, and she lowered her face to hide her shame. Then she turned to her mother, who was also in tears. "Am I a bad girl, Mommy?"

Rebecca cried out, dropping to her knees beside her daughter. Millie left Jeff's side and fell into her mother's arms. "No, honey. Oh, baby, no. You're not a bad girl, Millie. Don't you ever think that."

Rebecca embraced her daughter as Millie wept, liberated and forgiven, and the curse was broken. Mother and daughter held each other close in a way they had probably not since that horrible night three months ago. The two of them cried together, reunited at last.

Rebecca had her daughter back.

She looked to Jeff, stunned, but grateful beyond words. Her eyes, soaked by love and hope, said it all. Jeff was dumbfounded by what had transpired, both in Millie's heart and in his own, and sat back on Millie's bed. "You did it," Rebecca pronounced in awe. "You saved her, Jeff."

He smiled, but there was an emptiness in him that he could not shake. "The truth is the craziest thing, Rebecca." He paused to marvel as Rebecca hugged her weeping daughter tightly. With an exhausted grin he finished, "It'll set you free every time."

Jeff left the Walker residence unfulfilled. He had learned so much. Uncovered so much.

But there was still more to do.

Worse yet, he had no idea where to start. He didn't know how to fight the bogeyman, or even where to find him. The answer came to him in the form of a note tucked under his windshield wiper blade. He pulled it out, curious, and unfolded it.

It was blank.

Knowing what needed to be done, Jeff looked over his shoulder, then quickly withdrew the BIC lighter he now kept in his coat pocket in anticipation of such a moment. Igniting the small flame, he carefully held it under the paper until he could read Leonard Fergus's secret message.

Sure enough, as before, the lemon juice changed color and the words became clear:

MEET ME AT THE LAKE AT 7:00 TONIGHT—LEONARD

The message internalized, Jeff held the flame up to the page until the paper caught fire. Holding the note out with his thumb and forefinger, he watched with grim satisfaction as the fire consumed the page. Just as the heat became uncomfortable, Jeff dropped the paper and watched it burn to ash on the ground. He stomped it out, destroying every shred of evidence.

He wondered if this could be a setup. It was impossible to know if Leonard really wanted to help him or if he was just baiting him for the Committee. Or maybe it wasn't Leonard who wrote the note at all. Maybe someone on the inside had discovered Fergus's disappearing ink idea and was using it against Jeff.

He couldn't be sure, and after all he learned from the secret file, he felt he needed a little extra insurance. He needed someone he could trust to back him up and protect him. A partner.

A friend.

"It's really great to have you back."

Tabitha Banks soothed her son's hunger pains, which he made known by wailing loudly. She shoved a spoonful of strained carrots into his mouth, giving her a moment of quiet in which to finish her thought. "I was really worried that something would happen to you."

Danny slouched on the couch, playing with their other son. His mind remained distant. Try as he might to occupy himself otherwise, he kept thinking of Jeff and wondering what trouble the preacher was getting himself into.

I should be there with him.

The baby cooed, happy to be with his daddy. Danny's expression softened, and he looked into his son's big blue eyes and found himself smiling. The thought struck him that he'd never taken a good, long look at his boys before. If he had, he surely wouldn't have left them. They were so beautiful, untouched by all the stupid mistakes Danny had wasted his life making. They were clean, their whole lives ahead of them. They could be anything in the world. Doctors, teachers, *good* people. These were his sons. *His sons.* His chance to leave something good behind in the world.

His own father had given up that chance. The only memories Danny had of his father were drunken fights with his mother. Danny crying as Pop slapped Ma or flicked lit cigarettes at her, telling her to "clean up around here." The day Danny's dad left with another woman was probably the greatest day of his young life.

It terrified Danny to think his own children might think the same of him someday.

He rubbed the fuzzy head of the child before him, marveling at the gift he took for granted before. "I'm gonna be a good father to you," he whispered. "You'll see. I'll make you proud."

A knock at the door interrupted his moment with his son. Tabitha looked curiously at the door, pausing with a spoonful of carrots just out of the other baby's reach. "Do you think it's safe?"

Danny froze. Paranoia took hold, and he set his son down in the playpen and marched to the front door.

"Should you answer it?" Tabitha asked.

Danny turned the knob and opened the door to find Jeff Weldon. He cooled and relaxed. Then he hardened, squinting as he suspiciously eyed the preacher, remembering their last meeting hours earlier. "What are you doing here?"

"I found the file," Jeff said.

"And?" Danny asked, trying not to reveal how interested he really was.

"It's bigger than I thought. The Strange Man's been killing for over a year and the Committee's been covering it up."

Danny looked back to his children, one playing with toys in the crib, the other kicking his chubby legs in excitement at another bite headed his way. What kind of world had he brought them into? How could he not do something to make it better for them?

Suddenly he felt the urge to start a war with the Committee himself.

Jeff continued, "They framed my brother to help divert attention from what they've been doing. They're using him to hide their secrets. I'm going to meet someone tonight. Someone...well, someone I hope I can trust. But I don't want to go alone. I need your help."

Despite Danny's inner willingness to do anything in his power to stop the Committee, he crossed his arms indignantly. He was still mad at Jeff, after all. "Yeah, I bet."

"You were right," Jeff admitted. "I used you. I'm sorry. Now I'm asking you, as a friend. Please. Help me."

A pause. "Why should I trust you?"

Jeff reached into his jacket and pulled out a thick envelope. He handed it to Danny, and the young man thumbed through it, startled to find a stack of twenty-dollar bills.

"That's the last of my severance pay. Just enough for bus tickets out of Greensboro and a little money to get started whenever you settle down."

Danny looked up, shocked, and Jeff grinned apologetically. "Trust me yet?"

Danny warmed, before he realized that his soft side was showing. He affected a grimace. "It's a start."

Tabitha headed to the door, a twin in her arms. She looked worried, but Danny hoped she realized how important this was. Jeff informed Danny, "We're going into uncharted territory. We might even find some monsters."

Danny considered it, his heart wrenched at the thought of never seeing his sons again. *Not now. I was just getting used to the idea of being around.* But he knew that if someone didn't do something, a lot more people would be losing their babies.

Having settled the issue in his mind, Danny cracked a sly sneer. "Sounds dangerous."

"It is," Jeff returned, smiling. "To tell you the truth, I can't even guarantee we'll live through it."

Tabitha nervously looked to Danny, waiting for his reply. Jeff waited as well, though he seemed confident that he had his friend back. Now he was ready to take on the forces of hell with Danny at his side.

Danny kept still for a moment, then shrugged.

"Let me get my coat."

CHAPTER TWENTY-EIGHT

SABELLA SAT IN the porch swing at her in-laws' house, her legs crossed and her arms tucked close to her, looking across the horizon as the sun faded away. She stared hard into the purple and red clouds, as if hoping they might tell her where her husband was. Here she was, at his parents' house without him, eating dinner and laughing and talking, carrying on as if nothing were the matter with her marriage.

Inside, Louise Weldon stood at the kitchen sink, finishing up the dishes, while Jack sat at the table nursing a cup of after-dinner coffee. Normally Isabella would have been there with them, helping Louise with the dishes or talking to Jack.

No, that was wrong. Normally she *and* Jeff would have been in there.

Without him here, though, she felt out of place and quietly excused herself, telling Jack and Louise that she was going outside to wait for Jeff to arrive, though she was losing hope that he'd show.

She wondered where he was. Who he was with. Maybe he'd found someone he could talk to about the flood of emotions he was experiencing lately, someone he could confide in and trust. But that was supposed to be her role.

Jack started coughing in the house behind her, a wet hacking. Isabella turned her head to look through the screen door. She saw Louise lay down her dishtowel and move toward her husband. "Are you OK?"

He nodded and shooed her away, embarrassed. "Fine, fine. Can't a man have a cough? I just need to lie down for a minute."

Louise gave him room, though she stayed close in case he needed a guiding hand to help him. Jack managed to stand on his own. Hunched over, he hobbled away from the table and into the living room. Once he was safely on his way, Louise approached Isabella on the front porch, her expression cheerless.

"It's always hard letting go," Louise said after a moment's reflection. She joined Isabella, looking across the twilight landscape. "He's not getting any better," the older woman commented quietly. "I know he doesn't have much time left in this world. He's made peace with it. He's ready to move on." Louise took in a deep breath and let it out. "But I'm not ready to let him."

Louise turned to Isabella. "You're thinking about our boy, aren't you?"

Isabella faintly smiled, feeling guilty, and turned back to face the quiet neighborhood that surrounded the Weldon's home. "Yeah."

Louise nodded and sat beside Isabella on the porch swing. Isabella loved this swing. It reminded her of the one she and Jeff used to share at their house on Grover's Pond. The best part of the day was always when Jeff came home and the two of them sat on that swing, watching the still waters of the pond and talking about the day or their plans for the next. They would talk for hours some nights, listening to the birds and feeling the cool spring breeze.

But that was then. Now things were different.

The two women sat in silence. Isabella's mother left when she was still a newborn without so much as a good-bye note for her children. Growing up in a house of four rough-and-tumble brothers and a taciturn father left Isabella with a sense of isolation among women. Her childhood had been one of catching frogs, firing guns, and gutting deer.

Sadly, she reflected that she had very little in common with Louise save the fact that they both loved Jeff. Louise certainly made every attempt to grow closer to Isabella and break the curse of the "dreaded mother-in-law," and for that, Isabella was appreciative. But progress was slow. A part of Isabella felt guilty for the few times that she had opened up to Louise. Guilty for telling her things that she would never be able to tell her own mother, sharing things she would never be able to share with the woman who birthed her. Like her wedding, or Jeff's sleepless nights, or burning the casserole. Those were things that she wanted to share with *her* mother. And although she liked Louise and was thankful to have a woman like her for her mother-in-law, it just wasn't the same.

At a time when her marriage looked to be crumbling, Isabella wanted to talk to a mommy of her own. But, she reminded herself, that wasn't going to happen.

"He loves you very much," Louise broke the long silence.

"I know." Isabella let go a sigh that had been held in for too long. "And I know he's going through a lot, but I am too. He lost a brother—" She stopped and turned to Louise respectfully. "—and you lost a son."

She then looked back at the stars that were beginning to appear. "But I feel like I'm losing my husband."

"Why do you say that?"

Isabella leaned back in the porch swing. "We had a fight."

"Oh." Louise giggled, wisely. "Jack and I have had a few of those over the years."

"I mean, we've had fights before, but..."

"This one was different."

"Yes. Well, you know Jeff. He always has this tendency to..." Isabella searched for kinder words than those that came to mind. After all, she was talking to the man's mother. A little tact might be in order.

But Louise laughed, knowing her son all too well. "Has a tendency to overreact? To fly off the deep end?"

Isabella relaxed and smirked. She waited for a moment, digging deep inside herself to find the source of her heartache. When she found the words to express what she was feeling, she looked up to the stars again, finding it difficult to face Louise as she confessed the fears of her heart. "He's pushing me away. He's always doing that. Like he's trying to spare my feelings or protect me, or whatever, and he will never let me in. It's like..." She thought about it, then grimaced, embarrassed. "OK, this is really stupid."

"What?" Louise's interest was piqued.

"Meat loaf."

"Meat loaf? Jeff *hates* meat loaf."

Isabella faced her mother-in-law, excited. "Exactly! That's what I'm talking about. But instead of *telling* me he hates meat loaf, he'll just sit there and eat it and tell me I did a good job. It worries me, you know? If he can't even tell me a simple thing like he hates meat loaf, then how will he tell me when something really serious is bothering him? That's the worst part of it. I *know* something is wrong, but he won't even tell me what it is. He won't let me help. So I just have to sit back and watch him ruin his life, and my hands are tied." She fumed, "It drives me crazy!"

Louise nodded. "I know what you mean about feeling helpless. My youngest son is in prison, my oldest son is having a nervous break-down, and my husband is slowly dying of an illness that can't be treated no matter how many specialists we take him to. I can't do anything about any of it, and it drives me crazy too. It sure does."

Louise grew quiet, and suddenly Isabella feared she had offended the woman by going on about her problems that, really, paled in comparison.

"But," Louise continued, "what else can we do? Except wait. Pray."

"I don't know." Isabella hung her head. She believed that once. Had even told Jeff that was the solution just the other day. But now...she still believed God could help Jeff, but the question remained if Jeff *wanted* to be helped.

"When Jeff first moved away from home, I wanted to be over at his apartment every night to make sure he ate supper and that he went to bed early enough that he wouldn't be exhausted the next day. I would have been there every night too if Jack hadn't stopped me." Louise chuckled at the memory. "I loved him and I wanted to take care of his every need, but there came a point where I had to let him go and trust God to raise him and to watch out for him. I know you love him too, and I know you have that instinct in you to take care of him, but you can't fulfill his every need. And if you spend all of your energy trying, you'll only kill yourself. It's hard. I would be lying if I said it wasn't, but you have to let go sometimes and just trust God to be God."

A gentle smile tickled the corner of Isabella's lips, and she found the woman's words ironic. *Let God be God.* That was what she'd been telling Jeff to do this whole time. Could it be that she needed to learn that lesson too?

Louise ventured, "Do you know what it is that Jeff needs?"

Isabella thought a moment. "He wants an answer."

"An answer you can't give him, right? One that he'll have to find on his own?"

"Yes."

"I think it's a test that the Lord is putting us *all* through. I think what He wants to know is how far we're willing to follow Him *without* having all of the answers. That's the essence of faith."

Isabella nodded and remembered her earlier conversation with Elsa. "You're the second person today who's told me that God is putting me through a test of faith."

Louise smiled, like a sage teacher. "Funny how the Lord works, isn't it?"

Isabella looked away, but her spirit felt lighter.

"I believe God has the power to bring Jeff around. Jeff is a stubborn man." Louise leaned in and her eyes brightened as she whispered, "He got that from his father. Just have faith. Let God be God, and you just work on being Isabella."

Isabella replied, "Deal."

Comfortable silence settled between them again, as the two women were left with warm smiles on their faces and less estranged than before. Isabella realized that Louise wasn't her mother, and she never could be. But she could be the next best thing.

Isabella couldn't help but squeeze the woman tight. "Thank you."

Louise returned the hug. "You are the answer to a mother's prayer, Isabella. Never forget that."

Isabella released her mother-in-law and stood, straightening her clothes, prepared to fight for her marriage once again. "I'd better get home. He's probably already back."

"Probably so." Louise winked.

Isabella left the porch and walked to her car. She pulled from the driveway with a little wave good-bye.

Louise waved back kindly, yet the warmth of the moment was replaced by a cool in the Greensboro night air that she hadn't felt in a while. She sensed the shadow of something passing overhead, and it chilled her to the bone.

Quickly she gathered herself and went inside.

CHAPTER TWENTY-NINE

THE NORTH WOODS had a reputation for all things spooky, but Jeff paid no heed to the countless warnings of ghost stories and the superstitions of his youth. After parking his truck by the old highway, he and Danny waded through the tall grass and wildflowers, headed toward the lake. The sun had gone down and the moon took its place in the sky, replacing the soft colors of day with the deeper blues of night. The breeze picked up, upset at the two interlopers disturbing Greensboro Park Lake's dark secret. Jeff pulled his long coat just a bit tighter around him, trying to shut out the grisly tales he had heard of the monsters in the North Woods. They had scared him as a boy, but all the more now, for now he understood that they were true.

The bogeyman was real, and he could be out here tonight. Jeff wasn't ready to face him. He did his best to avoid the notion, but somewhere inside he understood this path he was on would eventually lead to the Strange Man. Right now, though, he was after the flesh-and-blood men behind the deceit that was corrupting his hometown.

He would ruin them. Tear down their house of cards around them. It wouldn't be pretty. If the betrayal and murder that occurred in the shadows of Greensboro came to light, it would render the whole community rubble, but it would be the truth. And right now that was all Jeff cared about.

He looked to Danny. "You know what to do."

Danny nodded, "Got it, Boss," and trudged off into the brush.

Jeff noticed the moonlit clouds swiftly forming overhead as he brought out his flashlight. Shining it to illuminate his path in the treacherous weeds, he came across the lake. Though a light wind whipped the grass and the branches of the nearby trees, the water never stirred. Instead it remained placid and thick. The black surface glistened with a gooey, oily consistency that unnerved Jeff down to his spirit. Surrounding him, a host of crows perched in the dead limbs of the trees growing close to the diseased lake.

But the crows uttered no caws. They just silently stared with their blinking black orbs, watching Jeff. They sat without motion, decorating the withered remains of the lake's haunted garden. The sight bothered him.

He tapped the small earpiece that was connected to the cell phone on his belt.

"See anything?" His eyes surveyed the creepy landscape.

Danny, who was investigating another portion of the woods, spoke into the headset on Will Baxter's former phone, "Not yet. You really think the Committee will try anything?"

By the lake, still searching the area with his flashlight, Jeff shrugged. "I don't know. But I wouldn't put anything past them. Just keep a lookout. Be ready for anything."

On Danny's end, the young man nodded. "All right."

The beam of Danny's flashlight happened upon a wooden sign bound by weeds. The paint was faded and the wood rotted after years of exposure, but Danny could make out the faint words: OLD GREENESBORO.

He'd somehow come upon the old ruins. Like any young ne'er-do-well, Danny had spent much of his adolescence sneaking out to the old ruins to party. In a town the size of Greensboro, entertainment was hard to come by, so back in the days before The Rave Scene was available to cater to their fleshly appetites, the youth of Greensboro had come to the old ruins to drink, dance, and do other things parents didn't want to think about.

The ruins were a familiar sight to Danny and reminded him of days gone by. Fearful to journey too deep into the charred foundations and whatever animal dangers lurked in the tall grass, Danny kept his distance, choosing instead to run his hand over the coarse, cracked wooden sign, careful so as not to earn any splinters for his nostalgia. He trailed his flashlight along the sign, wondering how long it'd been out here. He knew little of the history he was taught in school and even less of the history of his town. He didn't know how the ruins came to be or why Greensboro had moved in the first place. The only things he knew about the ruins were memories from his wild youth.

The light from his flashlight danced over what could have been a century's worth of carvings on the old sign, obscenities and messages declaring short-lived teenage love. Danny grinned, remembering that his name was on here too.

Sure enough, he soon found DANNY & KRISTI 4-EVER.

Kristi. He couldn't even recall her face now.

Kneeling to touch his name, as if doing so would help him connect with a less complicated past, he noticed another message carved beside it. This one appeared older and stood out somehow from the other names and phrases decorating the old sign.

"Deuteronomy 8:19."

Danny didn't know much about the Bible. He hadn't cracked one open in…well, he'd never cracked one open. But he knew enough to recognize a scripture when he saw one. Nana Loraine used to have a couple of paintings of Jesus or somebody. The paintings had Scripture verses on them. He had no idea what this Deuteronomy thing meant or why someone went to the trouble to engrave it on the sign, but it intrigued him all the same. He stood, about to radio in to ask the preacher if he knew the reference when—

BOCK!

From the shadows, a blunt object knocked the flashlight out of Danny's hand, then delivered another hard blow to the back of his neck. Danny doubled over, winded, and was dragged off into the darkness.

By the pavilion in the park, Jeff searched the picnic areas, his pulse beating in his fingertips as he looked for his mysterious contact. A whisper over his left shoulder drew his attention back to the distant lake. His eyes wildly searching the darkness, he called in a hushed voice, "Leonard?"

He was answered by more whispers in the dark. Growing nervous, knowing he could be stepping into an ambush, he swallowed hard and pushed onward toward the sound.

The whispers surrounded him again, like someone beckoning, but Jeff couldn't distinguish the words.

"Who's there?" His feet inched ever closer to the black waters of the lake.

Whispers once more, hurried now. Growing louder but still unintelligible. Jeff grew numb with cold, and his breath left his body in frosty puffs. Louder and louder the voices called, whispering words he couldn't quite make out, until he was standing in the withered grass right beside Greensboro Park Lake.

Then he realized that the voices were coming *from* the lake.

He strained his eyes, bathing the lake's still surface in his flashlight's glare, skimming the horizon for a boat or swimmer.

"Is someone out there?"

Unable to see anyone, he knelt on the yellowed bank.

The whispers were furious now, hissing at him, and Jeff felt along the grass, leaning over and shining his light, trying to find the source of the sound on the water.

"Hello?" His body trembled in the odd cold that had settled on the shore.

Then, without provocation, the whispers silenced.

Without their presence, the lake went totally silent. Jeff sat stunned, listening to the nothingness. No birds, no nighttime insects, not even the distant rustling of the leaves.

Dead silence.

"Ah—" He caught his breath as his fingers brushed against the thick, black waters of the lake. It felt as though something reached out and grabbed his fingertips in an attempt to pull him underwater, to suck him in.

"Get away from there," a gravelly voice commanded from behind.

Jeff jumped to his feet with a fright, spinning around and wiping the remains of the sticky black goo on his coat. He shone the light in the direction of the voice and found Danny, held by the scruff of his shirt. The dark shape tossed Danny forward, but the young man caught himself and rubbed at the back of his neck, wincing.

"Danny?"

Danny moved forward, and his captor stepped into the light, supporting himself on a cane.

"We have a lot to talk about," said Leonard Fergus.

"Leonard," Jeff replied with a nod. The familiar sight of Fergus calmed him.

Danny looked to Jeff with surprise. "You know this guy?"

"I'm sorry if I startled you," Leonard explained. "I had to make sure we were alone."

Jeff approached his old friend and mentor, leaving Danny to massage his neck in confusion. Leonard met Jeff's eyes. "We've had our eye on you for quite some time."

"The Committee?"

"Yes," Leonard replied grimly.

"Tell me everything."

However, Leonard looked at the crows; they weren't the only ones observing them. Already Jeff spotted some frogs in the dead grass, lending their ears as well. Frogs, crows, insects, snakes…the lake had gotten to them all. Now they all worked for *him*. The Strange Man.

"Not here. The lake's…bad. Follow me." Leonard led the two men away from the lake and its spying eyes.

"It started a year and a half ago," Leonard began as Jeff and Danny followed him through the twisted trees of the North Woods and farther away from the lake. "Though I suspect all this madness goes back lot farther than that. All the way back to Old Greenesboro. You don't know much about the history of this town, do you?"

Jeff shook his head. His father used to show him the land out in the country, naming the families who first settled there and whose kin owned which property and where the lines were drawn for so-and-so's farm. It was kind of a thing with him. Jack Weldon was a man who longed for simpler times of hard labor and quiet country living. Usually his historical anecdotes bored Jeff, but now Jeff was ready to listen.

"All this country was worked by the Greene family, back in the late 1880s. Before that, they lived in the City, back when folks called it by name, I suppose. But things in the City started gettin' strange. The City seemed to draw a lot of shady characters, with a lot of…dark beliefs. Didn't take long 'fore families like the Greenes, they wanted out. They got together with a few like-minded Christian families and decided to pick up and set their tents farther down the path. They came to the North Woods and started Old Greenesboro."

Jeff remained silent as Fergus relayed the story of his town's forgotten heritage.

"Things were good for a time, I suppose. They lived off this land, raising their families, not harming a soul. But I guess some of that strangeness in the City got restless; trickled down here. Folks started disappearing. Those left behind took to blaming each other. It ended…badly."

"What happened?" Danny asked, and Jeff was surprised to find the young man so interested.

"Don't know. What happened is something that no one ever spoke about in great detail. All I could find was an old newspaper clipping that said, in the winter of eighteen eighty-four, there were riots after Everett Greene set fire to the town hall, claiming it had been overrun by demons."

Jeff felt a shiver crawl over him. "'Give me strength, O Lord, for

I am surrounded by devils...' That was an inscription that Greene wrote in his Bible. I saw it. It was dated December eighty-four."

"Papers called it 'Greenesboro Madness.' It ended with the whole town burning to the ground. After that, those who made it out alive founded the Greensboro we know today. Generations passed, and history became tall tales we used to tell our kids for a lark. But then the highway moved, and the madness started all over again."

"The highway?" Jeff asked.

"You know as well as anyone. With the highway gone, there wasn't reason for anyone to come through Greensboro anymore. We were facing extinction almost overnight."

Jeff listened intently, waiting for the man to continue. Leonard drew a deep, sad breath and came to the twist in his story, "One day a stranger set up a meeting with the town elders. Called himself 'John Graves.' He offered us a chance to take our fate into our own hands."

Leonard trailed off, as if remembering the horror he and the others had committed to concealing, but Jeff brought him back. "Then what?"

"The Committee was formed. A group of six men. Lawmakers, educators, old money types. The descendants of those who survived Old Greenesboro. Hayden, the least of the six founding families, was put in charge of the Committee. Looking back, he knew more than he was letting on. Most folks 'round here heard the stories of the monsters in the North Woods, but Hayden *believed* because the Haydens have been keeping an eye on these woods for genera-tions—ever since Old Greenesboro. They believed those monsters tore through here once, and they were waiting for them to come again."

"Why would they do that?" Jeff asked.

"Maybe the same reason you and I are waiting for Christ to return." Jeff blanched.

Leonard didn't elaborate, clearly bothered by the notion as well. "The others didn't believe as Hayden did. Not at first, though I knew that the stranger wasn't right, and I don't mean that he was just a crook. No, I felt it, in my heart. Just like you did, Jeff, when you talked to me after you saw the storm that night. You said you felt like it was demonic, like it didn't sit well in your soul. That's what I felt whenever we went into the woods to meet with Graves."

Leonard forged ahead, his brow drooped. "We agreed to let Mr. Graves help us, even though we understood we were dabbling in something dark. I wish I could tell you that it was all Hayden, that he convinced us to listen to the stranger. But…we all have to answer for saying yes. We were fearful old men, lying to ourselves thinking we were doing what we were for the town, when we were just scared of dying.

"For his part, Graves helped us. Greensboro got back on its feet again, and the people were happy." Leonard softened and then spoke again in a dismal tone. "But then folks started going missing. Bodies started piling up in the North Woods. That's when Greensboro's nightmare began." The old man paused briefly and confessed, "We couldn't deny then who we were dealing with."

"The bogeyman," Jeff said.

Fergus nodded, his lips a thin line. With trembling fingers he reached into his coat, pulled out a yellowed photo, and handed it to Jeff. "I looked through the county records after our trouble started. I read the accounts of the families that survived that night back in eighteen eighty-four, and I tracked all of Old Greenesboro's problems to the arrival of *this* man."

Fergus tapped the sepia photo from long ago. The man in the picture was dressed in fine, tailored clothes, with a distinguished top hat and trimmed beard. But his eyes were dark and cunning.

"It's him, Jeff. John Graves. The Strange Man."

His breathing becoming ragged, Jeff was filled with numerous questions, but he hadn't the heart to ask them. This went beyond anything he could understand, and he felt like Alice, spiraling down the rabbit hole.

Fergus said, "The accursed thing had come and made his deal with us. He'd been spying on our town for decades, finding our weak spots, testing our defenses, and then, finally, he made his move. And we…" the old man broke off, ashamed. "We just invited him right on in."

"What about my brother?"

Leonard winced and shook his head. "That was an accident. Somehow your brother found out about Mr. Graves—the Strange Man—what he really was. Dras didn't know about the Committee. He was just in the wrong place at the right time."

"And the trial?" Jeff already knew the answer, but he wanted to hear Leonard say it, once and for all.

"It was orchestrated by the Committee, using their players."

"A cover-up."

Leonard nodded. "Yes, it was."

At last, Jeff thought. Three months of searching finished. Now, with the secret file, Millie's firsthand account, and Leonard Fergus's profession, Jeff knew the truth he had sacrificed his life to find.

Knowing didn't make him feel as vindicated as he'd hoped it would. It only made him feel very, very small.

Careful what you wish for, Weldon. You just might get it.

CHAPTER THIRTY

HANK BERKLEY MOPED into Smokey's, weary with life. He hoped the next few weeks would be smoother than the last few months. Soon, school would start back up. With all the activities of the new school year, people already seemed to be distracted from the gruesome events of the past summer. The Greensboro Ripper trial was over, leaving the protestors bored and looking for new things to occupy their time. The steps of the courthouse were again abandoned. Even the press packed up their camera crews and left to find new stories, coming up dry with any fresh angles to take on the tragedies of the small town's ordeal. Dras Weldon was starting to fade into the annals of urban myth and campfire ghost stories, and all the while the truth remained hidden. *Now, things should be getting back to normal.*

Smokey's boasted of the best wings in town, and the pool table was always beckoning company. It was a good place to go after hours, to drink with the fellas, watch the game, and get away from it all. It was the perfect place for Hank to unwind before he went home. Doris and Becky didn't need to deal with his problems. When he walked through the front door at home, they wanted him to be a husband and a father—not a sheriff.

As he had many nights before, Hank came to Smokey's this evening to be alone and reflect on the day. Mayor Hayden was leaning on him to keep quiet, and he knew that to speak outside certain circles about what he had witnessed with Ray McCormick in the North Woods would spell certain doom for his career.

Possibly his life.

Hank was largely kept out of the Committee's loop. They were content to deal with Stevenson, no doubt shaping him up to be Hank's replacement as soon as he stepped out of line or became expendable. Three months back Hank had been just as surprised as anyone to discover Lindsey McCormick's missing car. What surprised him most was TJ's report that Lindsey had seen the Strange Man at The Rave Scene. *In city limits.*

Up until then, the terror had been confined to the woods. For over a year, after Hayden had convinced him to swear his secrecy until they discovered how to deal with this John Graves character, Hank had kept the "mysterious deaths" in the woods under wraps. It was a labyrinth out there—lots of things to blame for disappearances. But hearing that the Strange Man was *in town* had filled Hank with a terrible fear. After that, Dras discovered the truth, and the secrets that Hayden and his brotherhood had worked so hard to keep under wraps were unraveling.

Hank pleaded with the Committee to be reasonable. Folks were dying.

That was when the subtle threats on his daughter started. Hank kept quiet after Dras's arrest, just like he was keeping quiet about the creature that Ray had changed into.

It looked as though the conspirators had won. Again.

He sighed, took a hard drink from his sweet tea, and thought about his family.

Doris...How he longed to tell her the truth. But he was scared, and he told himself things were calming down. The trouble would pass, this town would get better, and no one would have to know about the hard decisions he'd had to make. *Don't stir the waters, Hank. Just let the storm blow over.*

But deep inside Hank knew if someone didn't do something, and soon, Greensboro was going to slip right off the face of the planet and into the straining throat of hell.

If someone didn't do something...

Someone—anyone—other than a tired old sheriff.

"Hello, Sheriff."

Hank opened his eyes and looked up. Special Agent Christopher Perdu.

"Perdu? I wasn't expecting to see you tonight."

Perdu took a seat at the sheriff's two-seater table. "I've been working the case."

Hank tried to muffle a chuckle but wasn't very successful. "*What* case? Ray's dead. The medical reports have been sealed. We'll never know what was wrong with him."

He took another drink of his tea. Perdu wasn't shaken. "You give up too easily."

Hank set his drink down and leaned across the table. Something about the young agent had itched at him since he first walked into the station, and now he was unable to contain his curiosity any longer. "How do you do it, Perdu?"

"Do what?"

"Keep positive. I mean, for crying out loud, the whole world's gone to pot around us. How can you stay straight in all this?"

"Because I understand something that most people don't."

"What's that?"

Perdu said with a straight face, "That Jesus Christ is Lord."

Hank shifted uncomfortably in his seat, just as he had the last time Perdu started in on religion. He wasn't asking for a sermon, just some solid-headed advice. "What's that got to do with anything?"

"It has everything to do with everything, Sheriff. God isn't just in control on Sunday mornings. He's in control all the time. Nothing can happen without Him permitting it. It's absolutely impossible. Even when things seem chaotic, He is in control. Once you can hold on to that, nothing else matters. There's nothing left to fear."

Hank looked suspiciously over his shoulder, then leaned in. "Is that how you did that thing to Ray? How you made him better? That was incredible, what you did."

Now it was Perdu's turn to look shaken, as though caught.

"I mean, you're not just an ordinary G-man, are ya, Perdu?"

Christopher's jaw tensed, and he faced Hank, his eyes piercing. "I have a lot of experience in...these kinds of cases."

"What kind?" Hank asked.

"The strange ones."

Hank felt his heart twitter, skirting on the edge of talk he'd not shared with anyone outside the Committee. *He knows. I don't know how, but he does.* "So what do you think is wrong with Greensboro?"

Christopher's blue eyes never wavered. "You know what's wrong, Hank. You've known from the start; I've just been waiting for you to finally admit it."

Hank sipped at his tea. "I don't know—"

"Demons, Sheriff."

Hank spit out his tea, but Perdu did not falter.

"The wolves aren't just at the gate, Hank. They're in the camp. I need you to help me fight them."

Hank tittered. "You're crazy, Perdu."

"You know I'm not." Christopher leaned in, with that same soft urgency he had about him. With a simple look he cut through Hank's bluster, seeing right into him. "If we don't, who will?"

"And work that magic you used on Ray?" Hank laughed, not able to picture himself so fearless and powerful.

"Not magic, Sheriff. Faith. God does the work; you just have to be an open channel."

Hank frowned. "I guess I just don't have that kind of faith."

"You *could*."

"Well, if He's here, where is He? If you're right and we've got some kind of—" Hank lowered his voice. "—demon infestation, then why doesn't He just show Himself?"

"He did once," Christopher said, and for the first time since Hank had met him, Special Agent Perdu became absolutely bleak. "They crucified Him."

"You're talking about Jesus, aren't you?" Hank gave him a sidelong glance. Perdu nodded. "But how do you *know*, Perdu? How do you really know that any of this is true? There are a lot of religions in the world. Even people who claim to be Christians can't seem to agree on very many things. It's been two thousand years since the Bible was written. That leaves a lot of room for error. What if, over the years, it got changed and now it's nothing like it was? What if—"

"I think everyone has asked those questions at one point or another, and it simply comes down to faith."

"That's a lot to accept on blind faith."

"But it's not blind. God *does* reveal Himself. I'm telling you, He wants to show Himself to you more than you could ever want it for yourself."

"Then why doesn't He just show us?" Hank asked, legitimately interested.

"Because He's waiting for you to be ready to accept Him on His terms, not your own."

Hank pondered the statement, but he couldn't quite wrap his head around it. Perdu saw him struggling and started anew. "Sheriff, let me ask you something. You love your daughter, right?"

"Of course."

"Would you want your daughter to only speak to you, to only hug you, to only tell you that she loves you when you bought her something?"

Having a teenage daughter, Hank Berkley understood full well what the young man was saying. Becky *had* been like that lately, and, *no*, it wasn't what he wanted. He shook his head.

"God is the same way. If we only accepted Him and loved Him when He did miracles and wonders to prove to us that He existed, that wouldn't be much of a love, now would it?"

Hank felt a little bogged down by all the theology and took another thoughtful sip of his sweet tea. "That's pretty powerful stuff."

"It's all about faith, Sheriff."

"But I do believe, Perdu. I *do* believe there's a God."

"The *devil* believes in God. Do you think that will save him? You can say you believe in God all you want, but if you never show it through your actions, how true is your faith?"

Hank blushed at the direct question, but he had no answer.

"Faith draws us to God, and in Him there is protection. The faith of this town has shriveled up. Is it any wonder the things that have slipped in? But God hasn't given up on Greensboro, Hank. He's just waiting for Greensboro to return to Him."

In some strange way Hank was comforted by Perdu's faith, though he didn't know if he could ever possess it. Before he had a chance to consider it further, Earl Canton walked into the diner. The urgent expression on his bearded face made it instantly obvious that everyone at Smokey's was about to get an earful.

"Listen up, everybody." He raised his voice over the din. Even the people playing pool stopped their game to listen to Earl's newest tantrum.

"I just heard the incredible." His tone dripped with sarcasm as he placed his hairy knuckles on his waist. "I just heard that little Millie Walker wants to change her testimony."

There were a few gasps in the crowd. Bewildered stares all around, but none so bewildered as Sheriff Hank Berkley. Shocked, he turned to Perdu, who looked as confused as he was.

A lone voice called out, "But it was her testimony that put Weldon away!"

"That's right," Earl agreed. "And now she wants to go and change her story."

"To what?" hollered someone from the bar.

"I don't know. Nobody's telling us anything."

Then Earl saw Hank.

Sensing trouble, Hank lowered his head and averted his gaze, but it was too late. Earl had found a target. "Maybe *you* can tell us, Sheriff Berkley."

Instantly, expectant glares fell upon the weary sheriff, demanding answers.

"I don't know anything about that, Earl," Hank quietly replied, and that was the truth.

Earl walked over to the sheriff and rested his fists on the table as he leaned in, towering over Hank, as if scolding a child. "I think the people have a right to know."

The room clamored in agreement. Hank's face flushed.

"After all," Earl fanned the flame, "what if she *does* change her testimony? What then? Will they let the Greensboro Ripper back on our streets? You all remember three months back. Those…those *things* he had with him! You want him bringing those critters back to get his revenge? I know the paper wants us to think those were a bunch of rabid dogs or something, but you all know that ain't true." Surveying the crowd, gauging their expressions, Earl sought backup.

"Didn't *you* see them, Regina?" he called out to a redheaded woman sitting in the back with her husband. She immediately blushed as eyes turned on her. "Didn't you tell me they were more like bats or something?"

"It was dark, Earl," she said quietly, throwing a fearful look at the sheriff. "There was a lot of confusion. I can't be sure what I saw."

"Well, I remember," Earl bellowed, and he pointed to Smokey's front window. "I was standing right *there* when I saw one bang up against the glass, and it weren't no dog or bird or bat, like ol' Hank here would have us believe. It was some kinda *monster*, and they were following that Weldon kid like he was the Pied Piper!"

"All right, all right, Earl," Clancy shooed him. "Just simmer down."

"I won't!" Earl retorted. "Don't you know all them serial killers dabble in the occult? And we all *know* Dras was a weirdo with his head always buried in some monster magazine! He was some kinda Satan-worshiping nut-job, babbling about how the devil made him commit those crimes! Now we've got Millie Walker wantin' to change her story and set him *loose* again?" Earl turned to Sheriff Berkley, his face full of rage and desperation. "We have families that we have to protect here."

Hank finally scooted his chair back and slowly rose, unable to sit any longer. He didn't want to appear as though he was threatening Earl, but he was fed up with sitting under the loudmouth's nose. "I know that, Earl. I have a family to think about too."

"Then why aren't you doing something?"

"It's not for me to decide anymore. The courts are handling it."

Earl turned to his makeshift congregation and continued his sermon. "You know what *I* think? *I* think it's that Holy Roller reverend behind all this."

"Jeff Weldon?" asked a surprised voice from the crowd.

"I heard he was out at the Walker house today. I'm betting he convinced her to change her story. He's the Ripper's brother, after all. I'm sure he would just love to get him out of prison. Back on the streets. With our families!"

Hank reached out a calming arm. "Now, Earl. We don't know that."

This was the first Hank had heard about this, and he could only imagine what Hayden would do in retaliation.

Hide, Jeff. Hide.

No one even noticed the sheriff's gesture. All attention remained upon Earl's big mouth as he said, "He probably even *threatened* that poor little girl just to scare her into changing her story! You saw what he did to me at the ball game!"

He was winning them over. Hank searched the crowd, failing to come up with any course of action that could fix the mess Earl had created. He turned to Perdu, hoping for an encouraging scripture or something useful, but Perdu appeared just as uneasy as he was.

"*I* think we should have a little talk with the good reverend! If he gets his way, that animal will be free! We cannot have that killer loose in our neighborhoods. We have to think about our children! We have to stop Jeff Weldon and his meddling any way we can!"

"It's either him or us!" added a feisty old timer.

The mob roared in response.

"Then let's go!" Earl called out.

"Now, hold on just a minute!" Hank stepped in as some of the people closest to the door were already on their way out of Smokey's, ready to follow Earl into battle.

"Listen to yourselves! What are you going to do? You going to lynch an innocent man based on rumors and gossip? What's next? Hanging ropes? Pitch forks?"

"What do you suggest we do, *Sheriff*?" Earl pushed himself right into Hank's face, nose to nose.

"We let the courts decide."

"Oh, right. Let the *courts* decide!" Earl laughed, and a few of his new converts joined in. "'Cause we all know we have a flawless judicial system. You've played by the rules, Sheriff Berkley. But the rules don't cut it anymore. We have to do something *now*! There's a madman on our streets and—"

Now it was Hank's turn to interrupt. "That's right. In fact, we've got one in this very room, and I'm looking at him." He stared accusingly across the diner. "You're ready to attack Reverend Weldon based on fears of things that may never happen. You don't really know that Millie wants to change her testimony. If she did, you don't know if it would change anything. And more importantly, you don't even know that Dras Weldon killed those people!"

The air seemed sucked out of the room, leaving nothing but stunned silence. The crowd gawked at Hank as if he had just committed the most profane blasphemy. By now, it was gospel truth in Greensboro that Dras killed Lindsey McCormick, TJ Walker, and Deputy Dane Adams. No one dared challenge that anymore.

No one except one tired old sheriff who suddenly realized he was getting in way over his head.

"What are you saying, Hank? You saying you think that boy is innocent?" Earl goaded, his tone at the edge of rage.

Perdu watched Hank closely, waiting with bated breath. But Hank, having stood in the spotlight longer than he liked already, could only lower his gaze. "I'm not saying one way or the other."

Perdu's face dimmed.

"I'm just saying you can't take the law into your own hands."

"Well, we sure as anything ain't gonna sit around here and wait for *you* to do something. We'll solve this problem on our own."

Hank was defeated, and Earl Canton knew it. He kept a steady gaze on his fallen foe for a tense moment, making sure he was going to stay dead. When he was satisfied, Earl raised his voice and called out to his brand-new lynch mob. "You ready?"

He was met by their battle cries.

"Come on!"

Whooping and hollering, Earl led his troops out of Smokey's. Hank was caught up in the sea of people, nearly knocked over as he stood helpless and sullen. Perdu watched them all rush out in a frenzy and turned to his friend with panic in his voice. "You can't let them go out there! They'll kill him!"

Overwhelmed, a very ashamed Hank lied, "There's nothing I can do."

"But they're going to hang an *innocent man!*"

Earl was crazy enough to do just that, and Hank knew it. But he remained silent as the bar cleared out. Once the mob was gone and the damage done, Hank looked up to face the young agent, took a deep breath, and left Smokey's behind, shouldering his regret.

"You wanna fight the monsters in this town, Perdu? Be my guest. I'm done."

CHAPTER THIRTY-ONE

IT HAD BEEN a quiet few days for Rosalyn Myers. She hadn't left her apartment except to cover her shifts at Larezzo's. During her off-time she sat in the dark, reliving her father's death and the terrible look of horror that overtook her mother's face when she told her she knew the truth. She expected another visit from the Strange Man, her new dark guardian, but so far he remained silent too. Instead her only company was a case of Corona she bought on her last venture into civilization, and even that was cold comfort.

Simply put, Rosalyn wanted to die.

But for now she had to work. Were it not for her loyalty to her boss, Max, she would have blown off her shift at Larezzo's. But he trusted and respected her, unlike most people in Greensboro, and she felt like she owed it to him. So tonight she put away the bottle and the depression that clung to her now like a wet cloak, slapped on her best smile, and worked the dining room at Larezzo's Italian Restaurant.

"Right this way." She led another respectable-looking couple in dressed-up duds to their reserved table. Despite her unarguable dislike for people as a whole, Rosalyn performed her hostess duties flawlessly. She could be quite the lady when she put forth a little effort.

As she handed the seated customers their leather-bound menus, Rosalyn's attention was snared by the seemingly endless parade of pickup trucks driving by the all-glass front of Larezzo's. Diners and servers alike took notice of the sight as the caravan of speeding vehicles, filled to the brim with beer-guzzling country boys, raced down the center of town, blaring their horns and cheering.

Wonder what's going on. A part of her felt like she ought to know, and the hairs on the back of her neck stood at attention.

"Miss?"

The snooty voice broke Rosalyn from her trance. She turned to a rather impatient gentleman who looked hungry. "We're ready to order now."

"I'll find your waitress," Rosalyn replied automatically. She couldn't shake a horrible sense of foreboding. *Where are they going? Is someone in trouble?*

For a second, she heard a small voice inside whisper, *Jeff.*

But the obnoxious clatter of the gentleman's voice and his demand for quick service pushed the voice aside. She motioned for one of the new girls to attend to the ravenous couple as she headed for the kitchen.

Rosalyn pushed her way into the kitchen as another young hostess met the next group of customers at the door. Larezzo's seemed especially busy tonight. The elementary school was hosting an introductory PTA meeting to kick off the new academic year, and everyone had arrived to fill up before they hit the school's buffet line of Kool-Aid and cookies.

In the kitchen Rosalyn passed by Max, the owner and head cook at Larezzo's. The man stood no taller than five-five and weighed at least three hundred pounds, his body covered in a carpet of hair. He was a short grizzly man who smoked like a freight train.

When Rosalyn saw him, he was finishing off a cigarette and rolling Larezzo's famous handmade meatballs in his fat, sweaty palms. Max took a moment to wipe his filthy hands on his greasy apron before fishing around in his pockets. "Hey, girl," he huffed, retrieving the lighter and pack of cigarettes that were never absent from his apron. "How are things holding up out there?" he asked, lighting up another smoke.

Max liked Rosalyn. He'd often told her she was a hard worker, always pleasant to the clientele, and was one of his only employees who wasn't endlessly sneaking away to the back room to text message a boyfriend or girlfriend.

Rosalyn had a soft spot for Max too. While some of her coworkers began sidestepping her at the onset of the Greensboro Ripper trial, Max never brought it up, and for that Rosalyn would be eternally grateful.

"Just needed a quick breather."

"Something bothering you, kid?" Max asked, patting together a healthy chunk of raw ground sausage in his hands. A bit of ash from the cigarette that he clenched nimbly in his teeth snowed onto the meat as he worked.

Rosalyn smirked at the sight. "You, uh, dropped a little there."

Max guffawed, never slowing in his task. "Ah, it's good for the flavor."

Rosalyn patted Max on the back. "I'll be all right. Just need to sit down for a sec." He happily returned to his meatballs, adding his special brand of seasoning, as Rosalyn slipped into the wonderful quiet of the break room. Once inside, Rosalyn took a sip of a soda she had stashed under a counter. After standing on her feet all night, it felt good to sit down and massage her ankles. As she rested, Carrie Garner, one of her fellow hostesses, entered into the break area carrying a folded note and frowning curiously.

"Hey, some guy at one of the tables wanted me to give this to you."

Carrie handed off the note and waited expectantly, no doubt hoping that Rosalyn would share some details. Rosalyn was as confused as Carrie, but she took the note and looked at the front. In beautifully crafted handwriting, it simply read: ROSALYN.

Rosalyn unfolded the paper and stared at the words. As her eyes pored over the message once, then again, rage replaced her interest, and her face felt on fire. She fought back anger long enough to stare up at the messenger.

"Who sent this?"

"Just some guy."

Rosalyn was on her feet. "Did you see him? Where is he?"

Carrie shrugged and pointed into the crowded dining area. Rosalyn, still clutching the note, shoved Carrie aside and raced through the break area and kitchen. Carrie called out, "What is it? What's it say?"

Rosalyn slipped by Max but never slowed. Exploding through the kitchen doors, she nearly smacked right into an unsuspecting server with a bowl full of salad. With her blood running hot, she searched the crowd with determined eyes. As a large party of twelve was seated, Rosalyn pushed herself deeper into the crowd, still frantically scanning the scene.

Finally, she spotted someone quietly stealing away from a table, dressed like Hollywood royalty, not a typical sight in Greensboro. She only saw the back of his head, covered with dark, unruly locks.

"Hey!" Rosalyn trekked across the crowded restaurant while he tossed a wad of bills on the table and headed for the door. All ladylike attempts were quickly forsaken as she shoved and elbowed her way with the best of unkempt brutes.

Finally, she neared the man, but he made his exit through the doors of Larezzo's. After pushing her way through an eternal stretch of hungry pasta lovers waiting to be seated, Rosalyn managed to break free, bursting out of the restaurant and into the night outside. In blind wrath she searched the streets, bracing herself for whatever monster she might find. What she found was worse than anything she'd expected.

The streets were deserted. She was alone out here. Just her and the note, a new present from her secret admirer. Braving another look, she unfolded the paper and reread its message, hoping that the sickening pull in her stomach might not be so strong. She was wrong.

The pull was worse.

The bold, black word stared back at her: SOON.

With a throaty roar she screamed into the night, "What do you want from me?"

The night did not answer.

Isabella entered Smokey's about a quarter after seven to find the place empty. Only Clancy remained, still in her apron, wiping down the tables. Despite the obvious barrenness of the establishment, Isabella still gave the place a once-over, just to be sure her husband wasn't there.

Finally she moved over to Clancy, who noticed her and broke from her chore, her eyes friendly and bright. "Well, hey there, Isabella. What are you doing out here?"

Isabella offered a polite smile but quickly moved on to business. "Hey, Clancy. I'm looking for Jeff. He wasn't at home, and he's not answering his cell. I've been looking every place I thought he could be."

"And you thought he might be here?"

"Not really a thought. Just a hope."

Clancy braced her towel hand on her waist and shook her head at the floor as if she'd just found a nasty mess down there. "Can't say that I've seen him. And I gotta say it's probably for the better."

"Why's that?"

Clancy leaned in closer, as if to prevent eavesdropping, even though they were alone. "Talk's all over town that he scared that poor little Walker girl into changing her testimony."

"*What?*" Isabella's heart pounded.

"Yes, ma'am. Folks are pretty mad over it."

Isabella felt like sitting down but knew there was no time. She had no idea where Jeff was, and it sounded like he could be in trouble. What had he been doing? "I don't understand."

"Earl came in here gettin' everybody riled up. Saying that Millie wants to change her testimony to say that Dras was innocent. But if it wasn't Dras, I don't know who it could have been." She blushed and amended, "No offense meant to your family."

A startling thought formed in the back of Isabella's mind. "The bogeyman," she whispered, remembering the look of terror that was etched on Dras's face that fateful night three months ago when he came to Jeff for help.

Clancy giggled, "Oh, my! I haven't heard anyone talk about the bogeyman since I was a little girl."

Isabella felt dizzy. Gears were turning; things were starting. No, things had already started without her. Whatever was going on, it was picking up like a bad storm, and Jeff was out there in it somewhere.

"The bogeyman came for Dras," Isabella murmured to herself, piecing things together. "He tried to tell us the truth, and he was nearly killed."

"What's that?" Clancy asked, her face twisted in confusion.

"If Millie knows something too... if she tells people the truth about the bogeyman—"

Isabella rushed for the doors. Clancy called out after her, "Are you all right?"

But Isabella was already gone. *Hold on, Millie. I'm coming.*

"So, why are you telling me all this?"

After he finished his long, shameful tale, Leonard Fergus continued to lead Jeff and Danny away from the lake and all the eyes, feeling lighter somehow, now that the truth was coming out. He'd worked to keep it secret for so long, it seemed effortless now to undo all that hard work.

Jeff kept pace with the old man and rephrased his question, "I mean, if the Committee hates me so much, why come to me?"

Leonard felt old and powerless. "Because events are coming to a head. The Strange Man is gathering his forces, and whatever that dark beast has planned, it's going to happen soon." He took a breath for emphasis and explained, "Three nights ago Ray McCormick was brought to the emergency room. He was found roaming the streets, waving an axe, and shouting something about the end being near."

Jeff turned to Danny, and the two traded a significant look. Then Jeff faced Leonard again and confessed, "I know. We saw him."

Intrigued, Leonard asked, "You did?"

Jeff nodded gravely. "He was covered in this...*slime*. This black slime. What was it, Leonard?"

Leonard shook his head. "Don't rightly know. We may never know, now."

"Why?"

"Ray's dead, I'm afraid."

"Poor Caroline," Jeff rubbed at his haggard face. "But there was something else," Jeff said after a moment to collect himself. Leonard turned back to the young man, all ears.

"The oil that covered Ray. It moved on him like it was…" Jeff struggled for description, "…feeding. I saw it."

"Feeding?" It was Danny's turn to chime in. "Like feeding *off* of him?"

"Or feeding *him*."

Leonard spoke up. "We don't know what the Dark Hour entails, but anyone with any intuition at all can sense it's coming fast and soon. The truth of the matter is, we don't know what infected Ray McCormick, and we are all afraid. The Committee is falling apart, and I'm afraid once that happens, Graves will assume full control of this town. God only knows what will happen then."

"Then why don't you stop it?" Jeff spat. "You invited this thing here; it's your mess. Why don't you fix it?"

Leonard hung his head, the disgrace of his decisions and the decisions of the Committee wearing on him. "Because I'm afraid." Leonard turned and looked into the darkened woods, unable to face his charge. Jeff calmed, much to Leonard's surprise. Maybe the young man was beginning to feel compassion for him. Maybe Jeff would counsel him, tell the old man that it was not too late to get things right with God. That Christ would still forgive him.

But a coldness seized Jeff's face, and his eyes hardened. The man had changed, Leonard saw, and whatever compassion had warmed him, it dissipated. Dark shadows formed under Jeff's green eyes, and he nearly growled, "The Committee. Where are they?"

Leonard didn't like the direction the boy was headed. "Give it up, Jeff. Just let it go. You know the truth now. I told you so that you could have some peace. So you'd stop poking the lion with a stick. But to go any further…you don't know what you're doing. Get out of town while you still got a chance. Before whatever happened to Old Greenesboro happens again."

"I can't let them *win*. The Committee has to pay for what they've done!"

"They will." Leonard said, weary and frail. "But in God's timing, not *yours*, Jeff Weldon."

"I want justice."

"Oh, stop kidding yourself, boy." Leonard raised his voice, cutting through Jeff's rationalization. "It's not justice you're after. It's *revenge*, and you know it! You should be getting your family out of here while there's still time, not acting like some spoiled child throwing a tantrum!"

"Maybe he's right," Danny cut in, at Jeff's side. "Maybe we should just leave."

"I'm not running." Jeff either ignored his own feelings or was too thickheaded to feel anything in the first place.

Leonard shouted, his body trembling with anger. "Don't you see what this is doing to you? You're losing your soul. And for what? For *pride*, that's what. You know what the difference between you and your brother is?"

At the mention of Dras, Jeff turned away. "I'm not listening to this."

"You'd better!" The old man shook his fist. "There was one thing your brother understood. When he stood up to the Strange Man for that girl of his, he knew it would cost him his life, but he trusted God to bring something good out of it."

Jeff turned a deaf ear, refusing to hear…refusing to change.

But Leonard was not done. "*You* are still stuck on yourself, boy! You still think that the power is inside you. You think you are too good to need God because you're a third-generation pastor. You hide behind your strength, and it will be your downfall if you're not careful! You hate the Committee, but you're just *like* them! Enemies of the cross—all a'ya! Only Jesus can save us now, but you're not convinced of that. You still think you can do it. The Committee thought they could control this thing, and look what's happened! Don't fall into the same trap they did!"

Jeff spun to face him, outraged and offended, but Leonard was past the point of worrying about stepping on toes. The truth had to be spoken. At last the old man was starting to understand that.

A hush fell between the two, and Danny looked expectantly as if waiting to see which one would break the silence first.

"I have to go." Jeff finally spoke. "I'm giving you one last chance to tell me where they meet, or I'll tear this town apart until I find it myself."

"You'll never make it out of there, Jeff. Please listen to me."

"I've listened long enough. Where?"

Leonard thought to resist but ultimately gave in. Jeff would not be dissuaded, and as much as he wanted to protect his old friend's son, Leonard knew the man had to make his own decisions. "The Rave

Scene. There's a secret maze underneath a room. Been in Hayden's family for generations. They meet there."

At first Jeff's fury was replaced with a look of surprise. Within seconds, however, his countenance hardened, and darkness threatened to swallow him.

"Come on," he growled to Danny, and the boy nodded, dutifully following close behind him, reluctantly.

Leonard called out after them desperately, "Please don't, Jeff! What does it profit a man if he gains the whole world but loses his soul?"

Danny kept walking, but Jeff stopped for a moment and turned around. "My soul's not worth a lot these days, Leonard. Not to me, anyway."

Leonard saw something alarming in the moment before Jeff whirled to leave. Just a flicker of black in the boy's eyes. Something that moved. Twitched.

"God, help him." He shook his head. "God, forgive me."

Once Jeff was out of sight, Leonard detected a rustling behind him. Snickers. Scurrying.

Leonard spun, using his cane for support. Then he turned back to call out for Jeff and Danny, only when he did, the young men were gone and the trees looked...different. Gnarled. Perverse.

The snickers grew louder. A chuckle. A guffaw.

Leonard felt rivers of sweat forming on his forehead and wiped them away with his arm. The rustling became more violent, and the leaves on the trees came to life with lunacy, writhing and trembling.

Soon an ethereal green mist rolled along the ground, circling him.

Leonard ran, propelled by something primal inside. Using his cane as a third leg, feeling the arthritis eat up his right leg, he limped as fast as he could. The guffaw became a screaming, like the sounds of wild animals, but nothing indigenous to the area. Nothing indigenous to this world. Perhaps the next one.

"Help..." he wheezed. "Help..."

The things were behind him, and now he heard the snapping of small tree trunks as they pushed them over in pursuit of him. The green fog built into a wall of impenetrable mist, closing in.

"Jeff!" he shouted, praying the young man was still close by. "Jeff! Jeff!" But his cries were only met with more laughing and shrieking and snapping.

They were right behind him.

He cried out, and his mind raced with memories. Eleanor on their wedding day. How his friends dared him to shove cake in her mouth at the reception, but he refused because he respected his lady and didn't want her to look like a fool on their special day.

I miss you, Eleanor. I'll see you soon.

He hobbled deeper into the North Woods while eyes watched him. Crows in the mutated trees and possessed frogs *ribbiting* in the yellowed grass glared at him as he moved closer and closer to the lake.

No! I don't want to go there!

But that was where they were herding him. Leading him like a lamb to the slaughter.

Leonard ran full force into something solid and fell back with a *whump* onto the hard ground, and the mist grabbed at his wrists, his ankles. The impact knocked the breath out of him and robbed him of his cane. He fumbled for it in the darkness and fog, knowing the things would be upon him soon. He had to run.

"Hello, Leonard."

Leonard Fergus looked up and saw the Strange Man emerging from the glowing emerald vapor.

The monster stood in his handsome form, though Leonard had seen his true face before. The fact that the beast was using his illusory visage now seemed like an insult.

"If you're gonna kill me, you ol' devil, do it with your real face on."

"You've been tattling on me, Leonard," the Strange Man drawled in his singsong voice. "You think you can come into *my* woods and tell my secrets and I not know about it?"

Leonard crawled through the dead leaves, searching for his cane.

The Strange Man stepped around him, watching him fumble. "It seems I've been neglecting my flank as of late. You're not the only one telling on me. It looks like I have some housecleaning to do tonight."

Leonard found his cane and used it to stand tall, as tall as he could, in the face of the monster. He refused to be afraid anymore. This time he would try having faith instead.

If You'd still have me, Lord.

And somewhere inside his heart he felt a warm peace... a welcome acceptance.

Leonard felt the faintest hint of tears at the corners of his eyes, but they had nothing to do with sadness.

"You have no power over me, devil," Leonard declared. "You can't harm me unless you've got permission from the Lord Almighty, and even if y'do, it just means He's ready to bring me home. You can kill my body, but you'll never get your claws on my soul."

The Strange Man crossed his arms and cocked his head to the side. "Anything else, old man?"

"I should never have kept my mouth shut about you." Leonard pointed a trembling finger into the Strange Man's face. "I should've stood up to you from the beginning!" Then he smiled softly, comforted by his inner peace. "I guess it's never too late to start doing the right thing."

The Strange Man deflated a bit when he saw the old man's smile and raised an eyebrow. "Are you finished? Feel better?"

Old Leonard Fergus adjusted his cap, straightened his jacket, and stood just a little bit prouder. "As a matter of fact, you old buzzard," he stuck out his chin and finished, "I *do*."

"Good."

The monster snapped his fingers, and gremlins exploded from the fog, tearing Leonard Fergus to pieces in the blink of an eye.

At last he saw Eleanor again.

CHAPTER THIRTY-TWO

THERE WASN'T MUCH to this babysitting business, Annie Myers decided. All she had to do was make sure the little ankle biter didn't burn the house down. Other than that, her night was free for doing her homework. Free for watching television.

Free for talking on the phone.

Making full avail of that last freedom, Annie mindlessly gabbed with her best friend, Ginny Hutton—same age, same hair color, same taste in clothes. They were twins of style and were never seen apart in the halls at school, especially since starting ninth grade this year. Freshmen at last! Between boys, fashion, and that new Robert Pattinson movie, there was much for the two girls to talk about.

At the moment Annie cradled the phone on her shoulder, practically dancing through the stranger's house, jabbering away. She checked out the home as she moved from room to room and judged it to be quite nice. Nicer than her house at any rate. The paint wasn't chipped, the steps didn't creak, and the floors were carpet rather than cold, hard wood. *This* house was sturdy, unlike her home, where the halls were filled with shouts and anger that lingered long after the source of such cries had gone. A home filled with the ghost of her father, a mother drowning in guilt and self-pity, and the memory of the rebellious daughter tearing up roots and soft soil alike to leave.

To the average Greensboro citizen the Walkers' home might have looked mundane, but compared to Annie's decrepit old house in Trysdale, it was beautiful.

Her young charge for the evening was Millie Walker. Annie had heard all the stories but refused to join in the defamation of the Walker family. She too belonged to a family marred by tragedy, and she knew, firsthand, that the whispers of nosy, ignorant neighbors did little to ease the pain. Although the town's collective finger pointed accusingly at Dras Weldon and Millie testified that he was, indeed, her brother's killer, Annie had a hard time believing. Could a guy who had played Barbie dolls with her to distract her from that case of the flu she had when she was six honestly be the Greensboro Ripper?

Annie didn't have any theories to the contrary, but she refused to listen to the hushed chattering of the girls at school who somehow associated Annie with the horrible acts, all because her big sis was the Greensboro Ripper's best friend. Instead she kept quiet and continued to walk the halls with her head held high, despite the cutting remarks and the gawking stares trailing behind her.

She knew that, for poor Millie, escaping the public wasn't so easy. All in the name of morbid curiosity, Millie and her mother had been captured by the news and dissected by reporters, then turned over to the starving, cannibalistic townspeople who longed to relish someone else's misery, celebrating that it wasn't their own.

Rumors. Gossip. *Why can't they leave us all alone?*

Millie sat in her room, silhouetted by the moonlight that shone in through her grand bay window. She hummed an unrecognizable tune as Annie poked her head in. Despite her initial reluctance, Rebecca Walker was en route to her first PTA meeting in her kindergarten-bound daughter's honor, leaving Annie here to eat Rebecca's munchies, talk on her phone, and check on her daughter.

"Hey, Millie."

Annie tiptoed into the little girl's room, hesitant to break the silence Millie had so carefully constructed around herself. A small clown lamp illuminated the better half of the room in its soft glow, and Annie smiled as Millie wriggled around in her cotton pajamas, working tirelessly at something by the window.

"Watcha doin?" Annie softened her voice, speaking the language of a child.

"Nothing."

Millie was quiet. Concentrating. Annie grinned. "You having fun?"

"Mhm."

Unable to resist a peek at what could so hold a five-year-old's attention, Annie held the phone away from her and ventured a glance over Millie's shoulder. "What's that?"

"Butterfly."

Annie brightened as the butterfly came into view. It was large with blue, orange-spotted wings. Millie carefully petted the insect, humming a lullaby as if to lull the tiny creature to sleep.

"It's pretty," Annie said.

"It's dead."

Annie stiffened, taken aback. "Oh."

Millie continued to hum.

Annie thought to seize the winged corpse and dispose of it, but Millie seemed to have taken a liking to the dead thing, and it was only a butterfly. It wasn't as if she were picking at a cat split in two by a truck on the side of the road.

Yuck! Annie flinched in revulsion brought on by her overactive imagination and slid from Millie's room. Still trying to get the imagery of the splattered cat out of her mind, she turned back to the phone. "Morbid," she commented, unsure whether she was referring to herself or Millie.

"Well, *duh*," Ginny Hutton laughed at the obvious. "She watched her brother get butchered. I'm sure that has to screw you up."

Annie frowned with compassion for Millie and threw one last helpless glance to the little girl petting the dead butterfly and guiding its little insect spirit to the afterlife with her song. "Yeah."

"So, her mom's gone for the night?"

Ginny's friendly voice beckoned Annie back from such upsetting thoughts, and she headed downstairs into the spacious and well-lit living room. "She's at the PTA meeting Mom's organizing."

"Your mother is involved with *everything*," Ginny drawled. Annie could almost hear her eyes rolling on the other end of the phone.

"Tell me about it. You don't know how often I wish we could have time to eat a home-cooked meal. My mom's favorite recipe is the Yellow Page Special."

"What's that?"

Annie giggled. "When she looks in the yellow pages and orders takeout."

Ginny laughed. "No wonder you're always over at my house at supper time."

"Well, sometimes you just want to eat something without a wrapper, you know?"

The two snickered as Annie flopped down on the Walkers' comfy couch and sprawled her long, slender legs over the arm, dangling her feet.

"So, anyway…" Ginny's voice grew intense, a precursor to juicy news to come. "Guess who was talking about you today."

"Who?"

"Ben Harper."

Annie sat up off the couch in a hurry. "Shut the front door!"

"I kid you not," Ginny sang.

"What did he say?" Annie listened closer, as if such wonderful news would surely be whispered.

"That you're cute. And he *loves* your hair."

Annie immediately twirled the locks in question. She was too excited to contain her smile. She tried to recall if she'd done something different to her hair in the past few days. Then, again, maybe he liked it just the way it always was.

Maybe he liked *her* just the way she always was. *Oh, could it be?*

"Really?" This was too good to be true.

But Ginny assured her, "Yep." Then she waited a moment before confessing, "I told him you thought he was cute too."

Annie stood. "What? Oh, Ginny, you didn't."

"Well, it's the truth, isn't it?"

"Yeah, but you're not supposed to *tell* him that," Annie whined. "Where's the element of mystique? A girl's gotta have mystique." She learned such wisdom from the July issue of *Seventeen*.

"You've been hanging around your sister too long," Ginny groaned. "If you *like* a guy, you should just *tell* him. That 'hide-and-seek' routine is sooo immature."

"Ginny, I'm *fourteen*. I'm *supposed* to be immature."

"Yeah, yeah," Ginny laughed.

Ginny was right, though. Every time she was around Rosalyn, Annie wished a little bit more that she could be like her. Rosalyn was so amazing, so beautiful and mysterious. Every guy strained his neck to get even a fleeting glimpse of her when she walked into the room. Legendary fights had broken out at The Rave Scene between her would-be suitors, who duked it out for the chance to dance close to her. And yet Rosalyn just laughed and batted her eyes, only giving the boys a taste before she pulled away and was lost in the crowd.

That was how it was done. That was the surefire way to have every boy noticing you and leave him wanting you. It was every girl's dream.

Well, it was *Annie's* dream. Sure, she was noticed. She was "the little sister." Never old enough. Never pretty enough. Never as strong and self-assured as Rosalyn. But she swore that one day she would prove herself. She wasn't just some kid. She knew stuff. She had a lot to offer a guy.

Especially if he's Ben Harper.

Her toes tingled at the thought of his name, but Call Waiting's rude noise emitted from the phone, abruptly interrupting her fantasies. "Grr. Hold on. I got a beep."

"'K."

Annie held the receiver away and pressed the button to put her through to whoever's call was so urgent it had to interrupt visions of dreamy Ben Harper. "Hello?"

"*Who is this?*" It was a woman's voice. Out of breath and hurried. Frightened. It didn't sound like Rebecca.

"Annie Myers," she answered matter-of-factly. "Who's *this?*"

"Annie, you have to get out of the house!"

"Who is this?" Annie demanded, her eyes shifting to the night sky just beyond the windows.

"This is Isabella Weldon! Jeff's wife!"

Annie had met Isabella on only a handful of occasions. Times like that last Thanksgiving before Rosalyn moved out, when the Weldons and Myerses combined their hungry stomachs for a single turkey feast. She smiled at the funny memory of Dras and Rosalyn fighting over the last spoonful of stuffing and Dras's dad reprimanding them both like little puppies.

"Oh, hey, Isabella. I didn't recognize your—"

"Listen to me!" Static began to break up Isabella's words. "There isn't…much time…you have to get…Milli…out of…house…I'm…ming to…but you ha…ve to get…t…"

Annie moved through the living room to find a clearer signal, struggling to decipher Isabella's fractured message. Frustration consumed her, and to make matters worse, the phone's Call Waiting function beeped at her again. She shook her head, overwhelmed. "Could you hold on a minute? I've got a call on the other line."

"*NO!*" Isabella protested as Annie held the phone away, reaching for the button. "*Annie, wait!*"

Click. "Hello?" Annie asked, hesitant.

"You hung up on me."

Ginny. Annie smiled, relieved. "I did? Sorry. This phone has weird buttons."

"Well, who was it?"

Annie felt a strange uneasiness creeping up her spine, slithering like a snake, flicking its tongue and tickling the hair on the back of her neck.

She heard dogs barking outside.

"It was Isabella Weldon. A friend of my sister's."

"What did she want?"

"I don't know." The dogs barked. Bayed. "I could barely hear her. I hate cell phones."

"I know what you mean," Ginny laughed.

The beep again. This time, Annie jumped.

The dogs outside howled.

"Wait, I'm getting another beep."

Without waiting for Ginny to respond, Annie tossed her hair to one side and released her chin's hold on the receiver. Once the button had been pressed, she dared quietly, "Hello?"

"Annie!"

Static distorted Isabella's voice again. Annie felt her heart thumping loudly in her chest and wondered if Isabella heard it too. "Sorry, Isabella, my phone's messing up. I can barely hear you." Annie strained, placing her free hand against her other ear, trying to isolate all other noises to focus on Isabella's voice.

"You have to listen very carefully," Isabella spoke.

A knock at the door.

The phone dropped to the floor with a plastic *crack*. Annie sucked in her breath and turned wide-eyed to the door.

The dogs barked, yipped, bayed, cried, warned.

"Annie?" Isabella's hollow voice dimly called from the phone's position on the nicely carpeted floor, not like Annie's cold, hard wooden floor. This was such a nice house. No holes in the screen door. No screen door at all, in fact. Only one very solid door.

Where the knocking continued.

Annie's hand trembled, but she rebuked it. *You baby*, she chided herself. *Stupid kid sister who will never be anything else! Get a grip.* She knelt and snatched the phone, pressing it painfully to her ear as if she could cram herself into it to hide. "Isabella? There's someone at the door."

The knocking again. Slowly. Forcefully. Rap. Rap. Rap. Solid knocking. Tight-fisted. Rap. Rap. Rap. Sweat cooled on her forehead. Her hand shook, and with it, the phone and Isabella's voice.

"Annie, don't open the door!"

Rap. Rap. Rap.

Annie's eyes widened further. A tear fell lifelessly from her long, dark lashes and rolled down her cheek into its grave.

Rap. Rap.

Stop it! Please go to someone else's door! Please bother someone else! Not me! NOT ME!

Rap.

Annie *had* to move closer to the door.

"I have to open the door," she announced, trancelike.

"No, Annie!"

Against every instinct, Annie reached for the doorknob, flexing her fingers.

"Wait!"

Her cold, numb fingertips brushed against the metal.

"Whatever you do—"

Gripping the knob tight, Annie turned it with a click.

"—*don't open the door!*"

Annie pulled the door open and heard the sound of dying old men shriveling to dust, the sound of fate come and death triumphant, the sound of kid sisters tricked and traps sprung. The phone line went dead, immediately followed by every light in the house. Silence. Cold. Dark.

Annie dropped the phone to the floor, expecting to see the devil on the other side of the door, but only starless sky awaited her, covered with clouds that suffocated the moon, preventing it from shining any light to comfort her. She was alone with the darkness. Alone at the door.

But not alone in the house.

Millie!

The spell had been broken, and Annie felt in control of her own body once more. Haphazardly kicking the phone across the floor, she groped her way through the darkness toward the little girl's room. "Millie!"

Clawing at the night, she turned over an end table and a floor lamp, knocking everything out of her way to find the stairs that would lead her to the young girl. Stumbling in the dark, she cried, "Millie! Where are you?"

A cold shrill wind surrounded her. Strange, green mist coiled into the room, glowing as it rolled along the carpet. A dark shape only reaching Annie's knee tripped her in mid-dash, and she tumbled forward onto the ground, feeling the rough carpet burn her bare elbow. Carpet, not cold, hard wood floor. *Stupid carpet!* With a yelp she scrambled to her feet to dodge the dwarfed creature but found the shape whimpered like a little girl.

"Millie?"

"It's too dark," the shape whined. "I can't see."

Feeling her fright loosen its grip on her heart, Annie scooted across the floor to the shape that had tripped her and found that it was only Millie, tiny and confused.

"What happened to all the lights?" Millie asked.

"It's going to be OK, Millie. It's going to be OK."

Won't it? Annie wondered with great fear. Taking hold of Millie, Annie pulled her cuddly body close and held her, clinging to her as if she were a stuffed animal and Annie herself were the five-year-old girl.

"Something's wrong, isn't it?"

"Shh." Annie combed the little girl's hair with her fingers, her own heart jackhammering. Her mind raced, and she wished Isabella were here rather than on the other end of a dead phone lying on the living room floor.

The two of them sat there, unmoving, with only Annie's hurried breathing filling the still night until Millie finally said, "He's here, isn't he?"

He, here? No! Not here! Who is he? Please don't be here! Be somewhere else, whoever you are! Whatever you are! Stay away!

"Shh...just be still, Millie."

"It's my fault. He said I shouldn't tell what really happened to TJ. He said he would come back for me if I told." Millie paused, then stated plainly, without any tremor or sob in her voice, "Now he's back."

Annie cried out as frigid green mist encircled her ankles. Tears spilled from her eyes, and she clutched Millie tighter as the first sounds of scratching echoed from the walls and all atop the shingled roof. Annie cupped her hands over her ears, hoping to drown out the horrible noises like the flapping of raven's wings and the squealing of angry hogs. The darkness came alive around them, twitching and jerking, and she heard the chattering of hungry teeth and razor pincers sharpening. The twitching things laughed and trilled and whinnied, and the dogs in the distance howled all the more.

Annie held her head high as if to cry out to God, but she was met by the blinking eyes of gremlins on the ceiling, hissing at her with black tongues.

"AHH!"

Millie said not a single word or made a whimper. Annie hated herself for falling apart while Millie remained so collected. *If Rosalyn were here, she'd know what to do.*

But Annie wasn't tough like Rosalyn. She was only the good sister who did what she was told; she never asked questions and never did anything so wrong to merit these creatures coming to kill her on the darkest of nights in a stranger's house. She wanted to leave Millie and run into the night alone, screaming until she arrived at Trysdale and fell into her mother's arms, but fear had broken her legs at the kneecaps, crippling her.

The air in the room changed, and suddenly the repugnant smell of dead fish in a hot July sun filled Annie's nostrils and burned. The twitching monsters in the darkness turned and looked in unison like one dark, despicable body toward the open door.

Backed by the starless skies, the shadows escorted a new visitor into the house. Clad all in black, he stood, no, *hung*, in the air, his pointy toes dragging across the ground. He wrung his bony, inflamed skeletal fingers together, causing his tapered talons to click against each other as Annie looked up at him.

The black leather wrapped taut around his decayed body glistened in what little light the streetlights provided. Chains and hooks and belts wrapped all around him, as if only they could keep his true evil bound in one concentrated form. The suit, which seemed to be designed as a prison, covered him to his neck, where his head, even more horrible than his body, blossomed like a sickly flower. The shadows parted before him, revealing a green-yellow smile stretched grotesquely tight across his skull-white face. His pointy and bald head bore a crooked nose, and two glowing orbs of hellfire at the bottom of the twin dark wells served as his eyes. In his expression was condemnation and threat. Terror and heartache. Nothing good and all things evil.

Annie screamed and squeezed her little friend, feeling their heart-beats melding into one throb. Despite his blackened, curled lips, the monster poured forth a most pleasant voice that sounded like it would be wonderful for telling bedtime stories.

"Hello, Millie."

Shocked and sickened that such a beast would know an innocent child's name, Annie looked at Millie, whose eyes were closed and whose tiny, chubby digits were wrapped into fists.

"Millie," the Strange Man repeated in a lilting voice, as if he were oh-so-tired of these silly games, "you disobeyed me. I told you what would happen if you broke your promise. Now—" He flicked his knotted hand, and the twitching, clicking creatures in the darkness frenzied until Annie could feel the slobber of the ones above her drip down and stain her hair.

"—you must find out what happens to bad little girls."

With incredible strength for such a small frame, Millie pulled away from Annie and broke free. She ran, full force, toward the Strange Man. "Millie! No! Stop!"

But Millie did not. She stood face-to-face with the Strange Man and directed a finger at his crooked nose. "*No!*" she protested. "I'm a good girl! My mommy told me so!"

The Strange Man seemed charmed by the rebellion and somewhat impressed that one so small could stand against him. He smiled at her courage. With one plump little finger she held him at bay.

But for how long? Annie did not waste time to find out. Instead she rushed behind the miniature titan and pulled her from danger. With the legions of gremlins licking her heels, the teenager seized up the tot and rolled to the side. The Strange Man grinned.

"We shall see, little one. We shall see how long you last."

The shadows of night encircled him again and carried him off.

Left alone with the army of tiny executioners, Annie and Millie held each other close, and the older of the two let out one final screech, which she felt certain would be her death cry.

It was over.

Without warning, a gremlin crashed against the wall before slumping to the ground with a dull moan.

A loud *clang* sounded and another creature, sideswiped by some blunt flying object, spiraled backward and collapsed in a heap.

Annie looked up through teary eyes to see her salvation.

"Isabella!"

Standing over the two frightened girls, sweaty and breathless as though she'd run a great distance, Isabella Weldon held an iron skillet from the Walker family's kitchen, the wrath of God in her eyes.

Gritting her teeth, she heaved the skillet, and it flipped end over end before catching one of the gremlins between the eyes. The skillet ricocheted and bonked another goblin on the misshapen cranium before both went tumbling to the floor. Isabella reached down with one hand and jerked both Annie and her charge to their feet, shoving them behind her. "Get out of here!"

"What?" Annie asked, not knowing where they could go or how far they could get with these things after them.

Isabella grabbed for the knives in the butcher's block on the center island in the adjoining kitchenette and hurled one, edge first, into a critter's shoulder, sticking him to the door. The force of the impact sent the door teetering open, and the gremlin's shocked whine could be heard as the door swung closed, then open, closed, then open. It would have been comical under different circumstances.

Isabella pulled another knife and turned to the girls, her expression grim. "I said *go!*"

This time Annie did not wait. She hoisted Millie, and the child wrapped her legs around her caretaker like a monkey as Annie rushed out the open front door.

Isabella watched just long enough to see that they made it through, then turned back to her quarry. What felt like a large spider landed and crept on her shoulder, but she soon realized it was, in fact, the hand of one of the raving creatures. Shocked, she shoved the knife into its chest, and the gremlin howled but did not die.

Two gremlins jumped on her back and pulled at her hair. Twirling around the room, trying to fight them although she could not see them, Isabella banged into cabinets and walls, trying to break free of their hold. Finally, grabbing one by its long, pointed ears, she wrenched the thing off her and kicked it across the hallway. With psychotic glee it cheered as it sailed across the hallway and vanished into another room. Isabella thrust her head back and smashed the second gremlin's broad nose. It yelped and fell faint, and she took the second of liberation to fight her way through the sea of little monsters and out the front door.

"Help us!" Annie screamed at the top of her lungs as she, holding Millie close to her flat bosom, stumbled across the yard of the Walker home. No one came out to see what the yelling was about. No lights blinked on. No curious onlookers stepped out on porches. "Help!"

No one cares. Hopelessness seized her throat and ended her cries.

Isabella sprinted from the Walkers' house and joined Annie. Chancing only a second's look back, Isabella looked relieved to see nothing behind them.

"Are we safe?" Annie asked.

Isabella took her gently, turning her around. "Are you hurt? Are you OK?"

Annie nodded, tears rolling down her cheeks as Isabella checked over her and Millie. Isabella smiled faintly and gave the girl a small hug. "It's going to be OK. We'll get through this."

Annie allowed herself to believe that for the moment, yet she didn't know how it could be true.

"But right now," Isabella pulled away from the embrace, "we have to get out of here and go to somewhere safe."

"But *where*? What are we going to do? Where will we go?"

In the distance, Annie heard the gremlins growing stronger. The wind picked up, and she knew that they were coming for them. She panicked. "Oh *no!*"

Isabella jerked Annie by the arm, dragging her and Millie across the yard. Fumbling in her jacket pocket, Isabella led the girls to her car. Annie screamed again, and Isabella abandoned her search and looked up and into the face of a grinning, chattering gremlin.

Twenty of them.

Like a flock of vultures, they tore Isabella's car asunder, piece by piece, tossing doors aside and slashing tires with sharpened claws, ripping out stuffing in the seats and yanking wires out of place.

Annie continued to scream until Millie pressed a soft hand over her guardian's mouth to muffle the noise. Isabella hurriedly pushed the girls onward. Over the tops of the neighborhood homes, the creatures—thousands upon thousands of trembling things—collected into a swarm of hideous evil to form a blitzkrieg, rocking every house in their path and shaking every tree to its roots. Even the scavengers that had stripped the car to its skeleton were now caught up in the air and joined their legions. As a single awful shape they moved. With one mind. One will. One purpose.

To devour everything in their path.

Annie wept and turned to her protector, but Isabella's face fell in desperation. "There's too many…I can't…"

Headlights nearly blinded Annie. She turned to the source and saw a Jeep slow to a stop before them.

Sheriff Hank Berkley tipped his hat as he poked his head out of the driver's side window and barked, "Get in!"

CHAPTER THIRTY-THREE

HIS NAME WAS Brad.

Or Chad, or Chet, or Bret, or Brent.

Rosalyn couldn't remember, and for all practical purposes, his name was of little consequence. She just didn't want to be alone anymore.

He had been one of the many standing outside The Rave Scene. She had gone to the club in a vengeful last stand against it and its ghosts. However, once she approached the doors and Pete, the bouncer, waved her in, she couldn't go through with it. She wasn't ready. All she saw was Dras, bloodied and near death on the floor.

All for me. He did that for me.

She couldn't go in, so she brought a piece of The Rave Scene home instead.

They kissed fervently as she struggled to unlock the door to her empty apartment. She broke from him for a moment to close the door behind them and haphazardly dropped her keys on the floor. He chuckled, and his breath smelled like stale beer. He disgusted her. The whole fling disgusted her. But she couldn't see any other alternative to her loneliness.

Isn't this better than being with the Strange Man?

Rosalyn kissed him again as they moved toward the couch. She tried to close her eyes in passion, but there was no passion to be found and her eyes remained open.

This will make it better. Won't it?

They continued to go at each other, and she held him close, wanting the worthless make-out session to be over but wanting even more than that to feel again. Everything inside her had just shut down. Her heart felt cracked. She didn't know what to believe or who to trust. And the emptiness! *Why won't it go away? Why can't I feel anything?* She couldn't even cry anymore, and since the final dissolution of her relationship with her mother, she felt utterly damaged. Something had broken inside, and she had no idea how to fix it.

But maybe the Strange Man could.

She wished tears could form in her wide-open eyes so that she might drown the doubts and worries that haunted her. She kissed her mystery beau harder, forcing him closer, praying to any god who would listen that she would feel something. Some kind of warmth from him. Some kind of proof that she was alive.

But there was nothing.

Brad or Chad or Chet or Bret or Brent pulled away from her face and began to kiss her neck. He didn't see the vacant stare in her eyes.

What's happening to me? What's wrong with me?

The only thing she felt was shame. She felt cheap. Hollow.

Memories that she had fought so hard to bury broke free…

We were five years old, and it was our birthday.

"No," she whimpered.

It was their fifth birthday, and Dras was sitting on the floor, propping himself up with his arms, watching television. With a mischievous smile, five-year-old Rosalyn sat down facing Dras, propping herself up with her arms too and perfectly placing her feet against his. She became his shadow, and everything that Dras did to shoo her away so he could watch his *G.I. Joe* cartoon in peace, she mimicked.

That was her first clear memory of Dras Weldon.

"No!" Rosalyn screamed as she shoved the man off her. He reared back, shocked.

"What's wrong?"

Sniffling and wiping away tears with the back of her hand, she scrambled to get as far away from him as possible. "Get out."

"Hey, chick. You picked me up, remember?"

"*Get out!*" she screamed at him.

He got up and marched to the door, flinging it open. "You're crazy, you know that!"

Then he slammed the door, letting the horrible harshness generated by his force reverberate throughout the empty apartment. Rosalyn curled up on the couch and hid her face in her hands as she finally wept, feeling the dam break free.

She was losing her mind. Nothing seemed real. What was she *doing* with her life? Dras had been ready to die for her. Now she was wasting the very thing he had been ready to make the ultimate sacrifice to save. She *hated* him for that! She hated him for going away! He was the only one she wanted to be with. He was the only one who made her feel alive, like she was worth something. She hated him! And she never wanted to see him again.

"Dras…" she sobbed, giving in. Soundless cries of sorrow shook her body, and she trembled with grief.

Clutching her knees to her heaving chest, Rosalyn lay down on the couch and held the sofa pillow. She wanted the earth to open up and swallow her whole. Just so it would all be over. *When will it end?*

"He was quite the stud, wasn't he?"

Rosalyn squeezed her eyes shut, covering her ears and shaking her head.

"Please, just go away," she moaned.

The Strange Man implored, "What are you holding on to? Your friends are gone. Dras, Jeff… your mother. I'm the only one you have left."

"No," she refused.

The Strange Man sighed wistfully, gliding over to the window to look out at the empty street below. "How long will you cling to this life? How long will you cling to God, Rosalyn?"

Confused and angry at the accusation, Rosalyn looked up. "What are you talking about? I'm not clinging to God."

His back to her, she could see his reflection in the window. Only it was… different. Very different. His handsome features were gone, and in their place was something sickly pale with crooked, twisted teeth and sunken, glowing eyes.

Her breath caught in her throat, terrified.

The Strange Man, ignorant of the reveal or uncaring, continued, "You're either with God or against Him, love. If you do not choose me, then you choose Him. Is that what you really want?"

Still watching his gruesome reflection, Rosalyn stammered, unable to respond, until he finally turned to face her, his magnificent beauty restored. "What has God ever done for you? Your friends want to think He's loving, but if He were so loving, would He have let your father end his life and leave you and your sister alone? Would He have let your mother sell her soul to the bottle? There's devastation all around you, Rosalyn, and where is God?"

Rosalyn, momentarily forgetting the Strange Man's grotesque reflection, slumped on the couch, feeling an unnatural cold creeping up her legs.

The Strange Man continued, "I'm offering you truth, the mysteries that God would deny you in order to keep you compliant. I'm offering you power to take charge of your destiny. What does God offer you? He asks that you give up your will for His. That you subjugate yourself to His whims. He wants to make you a victim, but I will make you a conqueror. But you have to *choose*, Rosalyn."

She hung her head, knowing that he was right about at least one thing—she had to make a choice or else she would die in the cross-fire. She could not continue existing in this limbo between empty existence and total breakdown. The Strange Man approached. "It's time for you to choose."

After deafening seconds passed, Rosalyn asked the question of the hour. But this time she no longer asked out of annoyance or desperation. She asked because now, at the end, she was prepared to understand.

"What do you want from me?"

He smiled, seeing the change in her. "You're finally ready. Rosalyn, I want to set you free."

She looked to him coolly, beginning to believe. Or, at least, *wanting* to believe. The Strange Man reached behind his back and, as if by magic, brought out a strange fruit the likes of which she had never seen before. Not in a supermarket, not even on some exotic cooking show. No, this thing was wholly alien. It was bulbous and lumpy and reddish-orange, like a peach, yet unlike any peach Rosalyn knew. He offered it to her.

Rosalyn eyed it, hesitant to take it. "What is it?"

"My baptism," he said, still holding it out to her. "The gateway to a larger world."

It looked so full and juicy. Rosalyn wanted to bite into its tender meat, to see how it tasted.

Something inside told her not to take it.

The Strange Man sensed her reluctance and dropped to his knees, pleading with his dark, beautiful eyes. "You have no idea who you can become, do you? You've lived your whole life here, and what has it garnered you? They call you 'Trysdale Trash,' yes?"

She didn't respond. Only looked away. He leaned in closer, and she could smell him. He smelled so good.

"Now is your time," he told her passionately. "You can leave all of that behind. Climb out of the depths of mediocrity and become everything you were meant to be." He waited, but she remained silent. "Choose me, Rosalyn. Let me show you things. Let me make you something greater than you are."

Rosalyn looked to him, frowning. "But Dras…"

The Strange Man grew to his full stature, quietly outraged. He paced for a moment, unable to face her, and once more she saw his demonic reflection in the window.

Only this time she was not afraid.

The shadows in the room swelled as the Strange Man confessed, "I visited him that night, you know. Before he was arrested."

Rosalyn perked up, desperate to understand what had occurred between Dras and the Strange Man. To understand why Dras was sentenced to die.

"I told him who I was. He took it about as well as you did. Then I told him that you were special and that he was only standing in your way."

"What did he say?" Rosalyn boldly asked, feeling as though Dras were in the room, back with her. She craved his presence again. Even hearing the words he had spoken months ago would be a beam of light.

"He was angry. He was afraid that you would leave him." The Strange Man faced Rosalyn once more, his eyes lightless and earnest. "*That's* why he tried to warn you."

"He was trying to protect me," Rosalyn argued. "From you."

"No. He was trying to protect himself. He only wanted you as a comfort. He had no regard for what you wanted or what you deserved. He just wanted you for himself. To make him *feel better*. Dras wasn't intelligent, good-looking, or popular, but being around you made him feel like he was all of those things, and he didn't want to lose that. It was selfishness that led him to The Rave Scene that night, not love. Not sacrifice. *Yes*, I removed him. And, yes, it was harsh and cruel. But the things we are dealing with—the things I would teach you—are so much greater than human suffering. Greater than love. I had to remove him to release you from him. I know it's painful, and I know how much he means to you. But Dras was only keeping you from your destiny. If you are ever to achieve your true potential, then you *must* let him go."

He finished and remained standing before her, still holding the fruit. Still wanting to give it to her.

Rosalyn felt sick. The Strange Man certainly spoke like he knew Dras. Dras never wanted her to leave town. She remembered how he reacted when she tried to tell him that she wanted to go to Vermont. He wanted her to stay with him in Greensboro forever. To just "hang out" with him and never change.

But I have to change.

It was time now.

She had felt the distance between her and Dras growing even before he was sent to prison. They were drifting apart. Now it was time for her to find her own way. To find herself. Without him.

"But he shouldn't have to die for me," Rosalyn insisted, unable to fully break her connection with Dras. Jeff was gone. Her mother...any hope of having that perfect family was lost now.

But Dras...there was still a tug in her heart, one that whispered he wasn't gone forever. He could come back.

"With the power I can give you, you'll be able to save him. But—" His bewitching eyes glinted in the moonlight. "—you won't *want* to. You'll understand that sacrifices must be made. If he were to return, he would only get in your way again, and what you must do is too important. You'll have to sacrifice him to save yourself. It's the only way."

Rosalyn sat very still, her heart burdened beyond measure.

The Strange Man carefully placed the unusual fruit on the table before her.

"Time is short, Rosalyn," he said. "Greensboro is a different place now than the town you grew up in, and soon—very soon—the *world* will become very different, as well. Come with me, and you'll always have a place in it."

Rosalyn stared at the fruit, unable to decide.

Dras would want me to be safe, wouldn't he? Even if that meant he had to die? That's what he talked about that night at The Rave Scene. If this is the only way for me to really be safe, then it's what he would want me to do. Dras wanted me to put my faith in God, but God's not who Dras thought He was.

It all seemed to make sense. Greensboro was getting worse and worse by the second—that much was true. She could feel it in her bones. Something was coming.

But where is God? If He cares so much, why won't He come? Why won't He come for me?

Emerging from the shadows of the unseen realm, unperceived by Rosalyn's human eyes, a lone gremlin skittered into the room. It scurried across the floor, its scraping unnoticed by the mortal girl but not the immortal evil. The gremlin, climbing like a squirrel, worked its way up its master's side and perched on his shoulder. Using one clawed hand to shield its secrets from unwanted outsiders, the gremlin whispered an unforeseen development into the Strange Man's ear.

The Strange Man, broken from his temptation of Rosalyn, nodded, then plastered on his charismatic smile before turning back to the girl. The gremlin leaped from its master's shoulder and disappeared into the darkness as the Strange Man said, "Only you have the power to choose who you will become. You'll think about it. Right now, I have to go."

Rosalyn nodded automatically, her gaze fixed on the fruit, which silently beckoned her. Not once did she look up to see the rage building in the Strange Man's eyes.

"Something has—"

He bit his lip to hold in a curse.

"—come up."

The Committee, save Leonard Fergus, assembled in their private meeting hall, awaiting their visitor. The Strange Man entered the room, annoyed that he had been summoned as if he were a disobedient teenager caught in wrongdoing.

"You rang?" he drawled.

Mr. Hayden and the others approached their supernatural benefactor.

"What are you doing?" The mayor of Greensboro wasted no time on small talk. "Fergus is missing, our spies told us that Reverend Weldon is on his way here, and that wife of his just saved Millie Walker, but where do we find *you*?" Hayden, beside himself with anger, shouted, "No doubt flirting with that *trollop* of yours. Are you crazy?"

The Strange Man stretched his lips into a humorless smile. "Yes."

Hayden froze as if he just had cold water thrown in his face. He received an encouraging look from his counterpart and closest friend, Mr. Simms, and then, a bit more calmly, forged ahead. "Your *obsession* with that girl is distracting you from the threat at hand. We have been found out. Our very existence is jeopardized. If the entire town were to learn of the Committee, we'd all be ruined! What are you prepared to do about that?"

Mr. Hayden had all but pressed himself nose to crooked nose with the Strange Man, demanding answers as if he were in charge. He fumed, his face red.

The Strange Man didn't appreciate his attitude. "Let me tell you what I'm prepared to do, Mayor Hayden."

All gathered held their breath, waiting for the Strange Man's next words to come. But he did not respond with words. Instead he sent a claw to speak for him.

His sharp, marble talons glittering, the Strange Man flicked his wrist and with one quick strike removed Mr. Hayden's throat from the rest of his person. The Committee gasped and backed away in stunned terror, and Mr. Hayden, not yet realizing that he was a dead man, clamped his hand over the spurting, gaping wound in his neck and moaned before slumping to the floor.

Mr. Simms, his good friend, did not move to help him.

Nor did any of the other Committee members. Instead they stood paralyzed by fear, each dreading that he would be the next to feel the demon's retribution. The Strange Man, with Mr. Hayden's jettisoned blood spattered upon his clothes, wore a pleased expression.

"I've waited a long time to do that."

Then, outstretching his long arms and gesturing to the Committee, he announced, "There's a new mayor in Greensboro, boys, and that mayor is me. From now on the Committee will be following my orders and will serve me and the Dark Hour however I see fit. Any complaints may be voiced directly to me at this time. Anyone?"

No one breathed.

"Anyone?"

Drawing a Cheshire grin on his face, he looked to each pale-faced old man in the bunch, daring them to speak. Yet their tongues were still. "Well, now. Is that settled? Good. As for the Weldons, leave them to me."

CHAPTER THIRTY-FOUR

"OK, SOMEBODY WANT to tell me what's going on?"

Sheriff Hank Berkley drove faster, his burly hands gripping the steering wheel tighter with each look in the rearview mirror. So far they had eluded the tornado of jerking, chattering creatures, and he was eager to keep it that way.

To his right, in the passenger seat, Isabella Weldon braced herself between the armrest and the door. In the back, Annie cradled Millie, tears caught in her fear-filled eyes. Annie's knees shook and her teeth clacked together, but Millie seemed rather unruffled by the whole situation. After all, Hank mused, this was not her first run-in with the forces of hell. Millie lightly patted poor Annie's hand, as if to remind her that she wasn't alone.

In the front seat, Hank still waited for an explanation. Sweat dotted his face, and he removed one shaking hand from the steering wheel to adjust his hat and wipe the moisture away. "What are those things?" Hank spoke in a low tone, afraid to upset the kids any further.

"I don't know," Isabella answered, taking deep, controlled breaths. "They were just these..."

Hank turned to her, almost afraid of his own voice. "Gremlins?"

She spun to him. "Yeah. Gremlins."

His hands shook. *Gremlins.* He'd spent nearly two years receiving calls about their kind, nearly two years cleaning up after them, creating cover stories for their carnage. He'd even heard Dras fighting with them on the other end of a CB the night the boy was arrested. But never once had he actually seen them. Fear gripped him and held him close, because he knew now that they were real. Before, they were just words on paper. The things they did, the people they hurt, were just stories. It was always someone else they were after, someone else who had to face that last awful sight before being ripped apart by their hordes.

But now it was his turn to face them.

And for a moment he couldn't help but wonder if his "mysterious death" would be the next added to the ghost stories told around town.

A cold shiver clambered up his spine like a spider.

Isabella continued, "They just came out of the woodwork. They were after Millie and Annie when I came in."

Hank chanced a quick glance back to the girls cowering in his backseat. He knew that Millie must be the gremlins' target. He knew that such a fate awaited anyone who broke the silence in Greensboro.

But she's only five years old! Hank silently protested against the monster that Millie called the bogeyman. *Only a little girl!* The men behind the town's conspiracy were ruthless, to be sure, but to stand by and allow a little girl to be hunted by these *things*...Hank shuddered and wondered how many children, how many people, would be sacrificed to the Committee's Mr. Graves before it was all said and done. When would it be enough for the monster they protected?

That I protected, he glumly realized. *Merciful heavens, what have I done?*

"We need to find Jeff," Isabella announced. "I think...I think he's involved in this. I don't know how, but I just have this feeling..." She repeated into the night, "We need to find him before it's too late."

Hank's heart beat faster. *Jeff.* If these tiny devils were after Millie for wanting to change her testimony, then they would certainly be after Jeff too. Not only that, but Earl Canton and his makeshift army of vigilantes were also looking for him. Full of pity, Hank looked to Isabella and wondered if she knew the odds stacked against her husband. Sad as it was to say, Hank held little hope of finding Jeff in one piece. The armies of hell were hunting the poor boy. He didn't see how Jeff could defeat them all.

But Hank couldn't tell Isabella that.

The gremlins were far out of sight, and Annie sat unblinking. Millie watched as the older girl kept her eyes on the town as it flew by, as if expecting something to jump out at them. Millie, on the other hand, kept her focus straight ahead. She wasn't afraid. She was, however, quite concerned about her babysitter. Annie didn't know about the light like Millie did. *Maybe her mommy never told her.*

When Millie first heard about the bogeyman, she was afraid too. But that was before Mommy told her about the light that kept him away. At first she thought her mommy meant the candle's light. But when Millie saw Miss Isabella coming to save them, she saw a light inside of her. It was inside her eyes, beneath the surface. It made her whole face glow, and Millie knew that she was safe with her. The monsters were afraid of that light in Miss Isabella; Millie could tell these things.

As Millie rested in her young caretaker's arms, she felt Annie stiffen. With her head against the girl's chest, Millie heard Annie's heart hammer, as if it wanted to escape and scurry off to hide. Annie's breathing intensified, and Millie looked up at her.

"Annie?"

Annie's petrified, hazel eyes fixed directly behind them.

Millie turned to the front seat. "Miss Isabella?"

But Miss Isabella and the sheriff were busy discussing grown-up things. Millie redirected her worried pout to Annie. She *did* feel a bit of responsibility for her babysitter. She remembered Mommy's last words before she left for the night. "Take care of each other," she said, and Millie was resolved in her heart that she would do that.

"It's OK, Annie."

Annie shook, clutching Millie with all her might, her eyes frozen in such a stare that her tears dried in them. Suddenly she screamed, shattering the silence in the vehicle.

"They're coming!"

Isabella spun in her seat to peer past Annie and out the Jeep's back window.

She saw it. They *were* coming. In multitudes too numerous to count.

Isabella witnessed the things of darkness clamoring over themselves, tearing at each other's flesh to see who could get to the juicy spoils first. Like shadows come to life, the horrid monstrosities oozed slime, with claws that gleamed in the moonlight. Isabella's hands and feet went numb as the whirlwind of twitching, clicking darkness-crawlers spiraled toward them at a dizzying pace. Their teeth ground together in a frenzy that sounded like metal pushed through table saws, even from inside the Jeep. Nothing stood in their way. Trees were splintered and telephone poles were mowed down or simply uprooted by the might of their numbers. Power lines ripped free and dashed to the ground amid wild sparks of electric blue, casting every house the gremlins passed into cold darkness. The town was dying, street by street, house by house, all in the name of their wicked pursuit.

Hank fumbled for his shotgun bolted to the dashboard and worked the lock until it snapped free. Taking the weapon, he handed it to Isabella. "Do you know how to use one of these things?"

Isabella ripped the shotgun from his hands and gave it a quick, mechanical once over. "Mossburg Model 88, Maverick edition. Three-inch magnum rounds, double ought buck. Synthetic stock bead front sight. Six in the tube, one in the pipe. Put every pellet in a thirty-inch circle at thirty yards." She turned to him, ready for business. "Is it loaded?"

With eyebrows raised and mouth gaping, Sheriff Hank Berkley barely managed an "uh-huh."

"Good." She cocked the weapon with authority and started to ease into the backseat. "Don't look so surprised, Hank. I had four brothers. I can take care of myself." She patted him on the shoulder. "Just keep us on the road," she said and awkwardly climbed into the backseat.

He chuckled in awe. "Yes, ma'am."

Isabella slid into position and motioned to Annie and Millie. "Get down, girls."

They ducked onto the floorboard as Isabella shattered the back window with the butt of the shotgun. Taking aim, she trained the barrel on the dark mass, waiting for the first gremlin to make a move.

The creatures were horrifying to watch, and Isabella fought hard not to let their numbers intimidate her.

Where are you, Jeff?

He had to be mixed up in this somehow. All the late hours. The fear that he carried in his eyes. How he hid within himself and worked desperately to expose "something." This *had* to be that something. She had stumbled upon the truth he was chasing. But, ironically enough, it was coming after her.

He could be out there somewhere, another band of vicious things chasing him. He could be hurt, scared, alone.

He could be dying.

But Isabella shoved aside her fears. She prayed for God to take care of her husband, for that was all she could do anymore. As hard as it was for her to let go, she knew that if she didn't do her part right here, then she, Hank, Annie, and little Millie Walker would never live long enough to see any of their loved ones again. *This* was her responsibility now.

And right now, the Lord had provided her with a shotgun.

Narrowing her gaze, steadying her aim as much as possible in a speeding Jeep, Isabella cleared her mind. As the creatures obliterated houses and yards to get to them, she felt the rushing wind rustle her hair. A peaceful stillness rested over her body, and she knew beyond any doubt that God really was in control.

He was right here. He always had been.

Isabella faced the convulsing, repulsive devils only mere feet from her face, no longer afraid.

Bracing herself, she fired the first shot at the nearest gremlin. It shrieked in surprise as it blew back past its brothers and rolled to the pavement below. Isabella ejected the empty shell and replaced it with another live round.

She fired, and two more were caught in the blast, ricocheting against the other gremlins and collapsing to the ground. In the floor-board behind Isabella, Annie and Millie covered their ears from the boom of the cannon. The Jeep sped forward with a jolt; however, the breakneck speed did little to keep a safe distance between them and the gremlins. One by one the monsters pushed their feet against the heads of their brothers and dove forward, landing squarely on the roof of the vehicle. Annie yelped with blind terror as more and more landed with hard *thuds*, only to dangle from the sides, scratching the windows, trying to get in. Isabella took the butt of her shotgun and shoved it through the side window, shattering the glass *and* the nose of the gremlin that waited outside. It spiraled to the street and rolled over and over.

THUD! THUD! More on top.

The metal frame of the Jeep proved defenseless against their attack, and soon the edges of their tiny claws penetrated the roof. Bullets of moonlight shot down on those huddling inside as the creatures' talons poked more holes. Annie screamed. Millie screamed. Sheriff Hank Berkley screamed too.

Isabella kept her cool and fired at the gremlins that tried to get in through the busted back and side windows, firing again and again. A roar of grinding metal hurt Isabella's teeth as the tiny creatures peeled back the top of the Jeep, opening up the vehicle like a giant sardine can. Isabella and the sheriff ducked to keep from being decapitated as the roof of the Jeep went reeling back and skidding across the street behind them, exploding with sparks.

The gremlins swarmed the open Jeep, landing on seats and fighting with Hank for control of the steering wheel. He panicked and pulled out his sidearm, firing point-blank in the faces of the closest grem-lins. They squealed and flew backward, only to be replaced by more of their menacing brood.

Isabella continued to fire, holding off the swarm, until she used up her last shell. Swiveling the cannon around and grabbing its warm barrel, she gripped the shotgun like a baseball bat and swung without mercy, sending more gremlins to the road. More replaced those beaten back, joining the onslaught. Like a flock of angry, invincible ravens, they pecked and scratched and pulled at hair, toying with the humans. Annie and Millie screamed and batted gremlins away, the sheriff fired until he ran out of bullets, and Isabella smacked the little devils this way and that until her arms were scratched and bloodied, her clothes torn, and her hair hopelessly tangled. Still she struggled, refusing to give up. Chaos fixed itself atop the Jeep until it was nothing but a blur of teeth and terror and awful squealing like the sound of silverware caught in garbage disposals. The sounds of the monsters' devilish delight were paralleled by the sounds of the two girls wailing in the floorboard, clutching each other, in a nightmare without end.

Hank lost control of the Jeep, careening into the guardrail. Metal ground against metal and fire rain showered the night sky as the Jeep left the road and burst through the barrier, free-falling into the cold waters of Grover's Pond near Isabella and Jeff's old house. Gremlins, girls, and frightened sheriff alike spilled out of the open-topped Jeep and splashed one by one into the waters below.

Isabella broke through the water's surface, gasping for breath. The gremlin horde hovered overhead, clicking and screeching, as Isabella wiped her soaked locks from her face. She coughed and spat, then saw the demon army above her.

"No…" she wheezed.

Buzzing with bloodlust, the gremlins reared back as one unnamable thing and dove for the water. For Isabella. She had tried to fight them off, but it ultimately proved useless. Utterly helpless as she faced the black cloud with teeth coming down upon her, she realized she had forgotten the simple truth she told Dras when he faced these same monsters three months ago.

Scripture. *Demons fear Scripture.*

She'd been fighting them with *physical* weapons, but her battle was not against flesh and blood. It seemed God had protected her in her ignorance, giving her time to come to this realization. Now her awareness was attuned to the truth. She knew what she had to do.

Forcing herself to concentrate on her Lord rather than the demonic beings seeking to tear her asunder, she raised a defiant hand. "God did not give us a spirit of timidity, but of power!"

A bright, white-hot blast of supernatural light pulsed outward like an atomic God-bomb. Caught in the wake of 2 Timothy 1:7, the demons' numbers broke. Hissing and cackling like malevolent children, they immediately dispersed into the shadows of the night.

Once quiet settled again, the white light slowly dying down to darkness once more, Isabella relaxed, feeling vibrant and alive. *If I'd only done that sooner.*

Then she realized—"Millie!" She searched the still waters only disturbed by the dying gurgles of the Jeep. "Annie! Hank!"

Annie popped up next, crying hysterically, and Isabella flung arm over arm, swimming toward her. Gripping her firmly, nearly shaking her to remind her she was still alive, Isabella forced the girl to meet her eyes. "Annie! Where's Millie?"

"I don't know." Annie sobbed, her tears lost in the wetness of her face.

Isabella dove down into the icy waters, leaving Annie to swim for the shore on her own. After moments searching the gloomy depths, Isabella finally came up for air, empty-handed and panicked. "Millie? *Millie?*"

Annie sat huddled on the bank, her knees to her chest, rocking back and forth. At once she stood. "Isabella! Over there! There!"

Isabella followed Annie's wild gesturing to the other end of Grover's Pond. There little Millie Walker, carried by Sheriff Hank Berkley, emerged from the water. Both were alive.

Isabella and Annie cried in relief, ecstatic at the reunion of their friends. Annie jumped up and down in excitement on the bank of the pond, while Isabella swam to the sheriff and the child. Climbing out of the pond, she ran to the little one, fear reminding her how close she came to losing her. "Millie? Millie, are you OK?"

Millie was shaken and shivering, but she nodded despite it all. Hank smiled and handed the girl over. Isabella took the child in her arms and held her close, cradling her head close to her breast. Turning around, she saw Annie running toward the group. The teenager held out her arms and crashed into them. The three girls hugged, weeping and laughing, kissing the tops of heads and the sides of cheeks, rejoicing for their lives.

Hank stood back from the moment, sharing a warm grin with Isabella, but his expression soured. "We won't be safe for long. We'd better hurry."

CHAPTER THIRTY-FIVE

THE LINE OUTSIDE The Rave Scene coiled around the building as hundreds of Greensboro's youth excitedly sought access into the sin palace.

Across the street Jeff and Danny waited.

The two sat in Jeff's old truck, eyeing the club, knowing that therein waited their fate. To ease his worries, Jeff tried to imagine the morning after or a week from now, when things could be back to normal. When he could find Isabella, tell her everything, and begin to rebuild their shattered marriage.

But he couldn't see that far, and it worried him. Perhaps this was to be it. His final stand. Beneath The Rave Scene were the answers he was seeking, but also the monsters that the Committee was protecting. He couldn't have one without the other, and the very real notion finally broke through that he might not live to see another morning.

He might never see Isabella again.

Fear and regret filled him, and he thought to call her. To tell her everything he'd been too afraid to say before. To reveal himself to her.

That wouldn't be fair. It wouldn't be fair to be the husband Isabella wanted him to be, only to go on this last dark mission and die. To deny her the chance to live with the man she'd always believed Jeff could be.

As much as it pained him, Jeff decided it was better not to call her. Instead he hoped she would forgive him in death and maybe even begin to understand why he had to do the things he did.

I'm sorry, Iz. I love you.

"You don't have to do this," he quietly spoke to Danny, who furiously took long drags off a cigarette in a futile attempt to calm his nerves.

Danny turned to the fired preacher, taken aback. Jeff caught the expression and elaborated, "You've held up your end of the bargain. I couldn't have gotten here if it wasn't for you. You don't owe me a thing, Danny. You can take the money and get your family out of town. I *want* you to do that."

Danny looked back to The Rave Scene, thoughtfully puffing on his cigarette. "I think I've come too far to go back now, preacher. 'Sides, if something happens to you in there, they'll win. Can't let that happen."

"Danny," Jeff said forcefully, worried for the man he was now proud to call his friend. He marveled at how much Danny had changed in so few days. At their first meeting Danny wouldn't have cared whether good or evil triumphed in the end as long as he got his cut. Now he was different. But touched as Jeff was by Danny's metamorphosis, he felt guilty jeopardizing the young father any further and warned, "I'm not expecting to make it out of there unless it's in cuffs or a body bag."

But Danny carefully studied The Rave Scene, mentally preparing himself for the battle ahead. "Face it. You need me."

Jeff nodded solemnly. OK, so he and Danny would go down in a blaze of glory together. But there was one last thing to get straight first. "In that case," Jeff began, unsure of himself and how his next words would sound. It was ironic, as he'd spent nearly his entire adult life doing this very thing. "I need to talk to you about something."

"What's that?"

"You remind me of a friend I used to have. He was my best friend back in high school. His name was Kyle Rogers." Jeff cracked a grin, thinking of old times. "We...we used to get into a lot of trouble. I'm sure it would've been small-time to you, but for us, it was pretty wild. We used to go drag racing out on the Strip."

"*You?*" Danny asked incredulously.

Jeff was almost offended. "Yeah, *me*. I wasn't always a preacher, you know? What, did you think I came out of the womb with a Bible in my hand?"

Danny laughed. "Dunno. Guess I never thought about it."

"Nah, I was a punk. Had a hot temper, used to pick fights—"

"Now *that* I can imagine."

"Gave my parents a lot of grief back then. They didn't want me hanging around Kyle. Thought he was a bad influence, that kind of thing." Jeff paused, taking a deep breath. "Then our senior year we were out racing some motorheads on the overpass one Friday night. Kyle was driving, I was cheering him on in the passenger seat. We were racing from one stop light to the other—we were winning too—and, as we were coming down the overpass, we saw the light was yellow. We thought we'd blow by the motorheads. Showing off, you know? Only by the time we got to the light, it had turned red, and Kyle plowed right through it. We got creamed by a Buick. Spun us around, glass went everywhere. It was crazy."

Danny turned to Jeff, dreading the outcome of his story.

"Everyone was OK," Jeff quickly revealed, then chuckled. "But it really scared me. *A lot.* I started cleaning up my act, staying out of trouble, getting back into church…and I quit talking to Kyle." Jeff's face fell. "He was so mad at me. He was Trysdale Trash and didn't have many friends who weren't on dope. I was his only friend who was different from those guys. But I ditched him. Worse yet, I never told him *why* I was different. I never told him about God or what I believed. I was a kid, you know? Thinking about heaven and hell…that was the last thing on my mind."

"So what happened to Kyle?" Danny asked when Jeff grew quiet.

"We never spoke again. We graduated, I stuck around and worked for my dad in the ministry. Kyle moved to the City." Jeff felt his eyes burn with tears, and he swallowed the lump in his throat. "I heard about four years ago that Kyle was picked up for dealing. He died in Wexler State Pen. Hung himself in his cell."

Danny frowned. "Sorry, man."

Jeff kept silent for a long time, holding in a cry. "Me too…when I heard, I remembered all those times we snuck smokes or raced cars, and we had a blast, but I never told him about Jesus. I was always getting onto my brother because his friend Rosalyn was a lot like my friend Kyle. She needed to hear about Jesus, and I knew that if Dras never told her, if something happened to her like what happened to Kyle, sooner or later he'd wonder if he did enough. Or if maybe she was in hell because of what he *didn't* do."

The two sat silently for a moment in the truck, the sound of distant laughter coming from the entrance to The Rave Scene in the background.

Jeff said, "I've been thinking about Kyle lately. About things I left undone…how I failed the people that God had brought into my life. I don't want to make that mistake again with you. So, here goes. Danny, God loves you. All He wants in the world is to know you and help you. But because of the sinful nature that all humans are born with, we can't have the kind of relationship He wants with us. So He sent Jesus Christ to come, to break us free of that sin. He did it by dying on the cross, an innocent man taking upon himself the sins of all mankind. Now all we have to do is come to Him, confess that we're not perfect, and trust Him to forgive us, save us, and bring us before the Father as friends. Christ said He was the only way to get to the Father. Going to church won't cut it; being a good person won't cut it either. Only by following Christ in faith can we be redeemed and inherit heaven."

Jeff finished, not expecting a response from Danny. Right now the issue wasn't how Danny accepted the message or whether or not he even believed. Jeff knew it was just important that he took a stand and said what was on his heart. He was angry with God right now, didn't like His decisions or way of doing things, but that didn't negate the fact that God was still God. His Word still stood.

"I just thought you should know," Jeff concluded.

Danny rolled the smoldering cigarette butt in his hand ponderously. Before things got too awkward, though, Jeff turned to his partner. "Ready?"

Danny nodded, resolved.

Jeff faced The Rave Scene and breathed deep and bold. "Then let's do this."

Nearly bursting at the seams with dancing youth, The Rave Scene shook with its thumping bass as windows vibrated almost to the cracking point. Shrill techno sounds floated over the throngs of people, and the colorful lights blurred together.

Jeff walked through the crowd, oblivious to the revelry around him, sifting through the nameless faces. The steady beat resounded in his head, pounding in his chest, and he felt as though he'd walked out of the waking world and stepped into the forest of his night-mares. Ahead lay the forbidden unknown, calling out to him like a Siren on shore. Danny trailed behind him, struggling to keep up, but Jeff soon forgot about him—forgot about everything except the secrets that waited for him. Desperate now, he shoved through the crowd, dreamlike, some dark sinful part of him ready to leave the safety of his Christianity and enter the clearing where he could dance and howl and revel.

"Dude, you all right?" Danny asked from his side, his voice seem-ingly stretching across a cavern. "You don't look so good."

Jeff didn't feel so good. His skin felt tight and papery, his stomach growled with a hunger and thirst he feared he'd never be able to satisfy, and that incessant throbbing in his ears, driving him on like tribal drumbeats. He felt cold inside, right underneath his skin, wriggling like worms looking for an opening. Pain seized his chest, but he forced himself onward, ignoring Danny's concern as well as the shocked expressions of the young partygoers he pushed out of his way.

From across the room Larry the bartender glanced in his direction, and his eyes flashed with fear. As Jeff approached the counter, Larry offered, "Hey, Reverend, what are you doing here?"

Jeff moved to the bar and, without warning, grabbed Larry by the shirt collar and picked him up. With a heave he lifted the burly man off his feet and brought him down hard on the counter, knocking glasses to the floor where they shattered. Nearby customers eased away so as not to incur the same treatment. Taken aback, Larry shouted, "Reverend? What are you doing?"

"Haven't you heard, Larry?" Jeff leaned in, snarling. "I'm not a reverend anymore."

Saying it aloud made him feel liberated, free from the chains of his father, free from the responsibilities he had shouldered for so long. The brilliantly colored lights of the factory splashed across Larry's terrified face, and Jeff felt it.

Power. Real power.

Chilly, wet fingers of anger wrapped around his heart, smothering the warmth and love that had been there moments before when he had shared Christ with Danny in the truck. In a second he had turned. One last flicker of fear shrieked in the back of his mind, reminding him of Isabella and what she would say to look on his face now, delirious with rage, and he was frightened of the change, but he forced it aside. He needed to be changed. He needed to be a monster to fight the monsters.

He needed to see what was in that clearing.

Jeff shook Larry, growling. "Where are they?"

"Who? *Who?*"

"You *know* who." Jeff gripped Larry's collar tighter, causing the man to choke. "Where?"

"I can't!" Larry shut his eyes, fighting the pain, and Jeff was certain then that Larry was a part of the cover-up, as well.

"Tell me!"

"Reverend Weldon, please!"

Jeff looked up from the action for a moment. The partygoers had taken notice of the violent scene and grabbed their belongings, clearing out. However, the bouncers had noticed the action too.

Abandoning their posts at the doors, they headed to the bar.

Danny laid a hand on Jeff, his voice little more than a warble. "Jeff, hey, cool down."

But Jeff batted away at his friend. "Leave me alone!"

Danny's face paled. "Dude…" he whispered. "Your eyes…"
Darting to his reflection in the mirror, Jeff glowered. Froze.
His eyes were solid black.

No…

"Let 'em up!" Pete the bouncer hollered, a cadre of similarly shaped muscle men flanking him.

"Uh, we've got company," Danny said.

Jeff leveled his black-eyed gaze on the bouncers. Pete took a step back, stricken with shock. "What… what's wrong with your eyes?"

Jeff ground his teeth, obsidian orbs blinking back at the scared men. "Get. Out."

Without argument the bouncers stumbled into tables, heading for the exits. Jeff shut his eyes, fighting back the dull ache in his heart, and felt his mind slowly beginning to clear. Calmer now, but just as determined, he faced the trembling Larry once more. "Let's try this again. Where are they?"

Larry whimpered, "All right. I'll tell."

Jeff anxiously stood by as Larry punched in the keypad code in the storage room. A beep sounded and a section of the wall broke free, sliding back and to the side, revealing a stone staircase that led down a dark corridor dimly lit by candles lining the wall.

Larry backed away from the dark abyss, as if afraid of what secret monstrosities might dwell in those regions, and pointed. "It's down there."

Jeff remained standing, his mind calculating, assessing the situation.

Danny eased up to Jeff's side, and Jeff could tell that his friend was afraid of him. "You want me to come with you?"

Jeff spoke over his shoulder, "Stay here. Watch him," before finally crossing the threshold and starting down the staircase. Danny quietly called after him as Jeff entered the black.

"Good luck."

Jeff descended the staircase, and the darkness grew thicker, a stale, dead air filling his lungs. Breathing deeper, he waded through the blackness and followed the shallow light of the candles mounted to the wall. With his hand he guided himself along, feeling the chilly, rough stones. The staircase was creepy and medieval, in stark contrast to the lively, modern club above. He navigated the steep and narrow steps, pushing through to his mythic clearing, determined to have all his answers soon.

But would it be worth the sacrifice?

Jeff didn't know anymore.

After what seemed like an eternity, he reached the bottom of the staircase and stood in a long corridor lined not only with candles but with security cameras as well.

He was being watched.

It didn't matter now. He had come too far to quit. The Committee would kill him just as readily if he turned tail and climbed back up the stairs, retreating to the lights of The Rave Scene. No, he was down here with the darkness and whatever monsters it harbored, and here he would stay until he finished this thing.

He heard footfalls behind him.

Spinning on his heel, hugging the wall, he caught a glimpse of a bulky shape just as it rounded the corner. Panic seized him, and he hurriedly found a crevice in the labyrinth and scurried to slide his body into it.

Wedged in his hiding place, he waited as heavy steps sounded in the hallway, though the candlelight refused to reveal the shape's face or any other distinguishing features. The footsteps fell in long intervals, as if each one were carefully timed.

I've been found out.

Whoever was in the hallway was searching for him. By now someone must have seen the security feed and knew that he was in here. The Committee's security forces would be called in and would keep constant surveillance. All the exits would be sealed. He couldn't sneak out now, even if they *didn't* find him hiding. He had run into a dead end.

There was no way he was getting out of here.

As the footsteps echoed closer to his hiding place, Jeff doubted and thought to surrender. If he gave himself up now, maybe the penalty for breaking into the Committee's inner sanctum would be lessened. But the notion quickly faded. No, he couldn't surrender. That would be giving up, admitting defeat. He would not give up. All that would accomplish would be another trial; another son thrown behind bars and despised by all of Greensboro. He couldn't bear the thought of causing his dad that kind of pain. Or Isabella. He couldn't let her see him like that, ushered out by armed guards, just like Dras, with the crowd booing him and spitting at him. This was not about bringing more shame to the Weldon family name. This was about redeeming it. This was about redeeming *himself.*

Jeff had let down his brother, but he would make it right. Jeff would be the hero again. They would all be proud of him, just like they used to be. He would get his good name back.

Clutching his chest, trying to bury the sickening, smothering chill he felt flare up once more, Jeff brought his senses back to the here and now. He held in his breath, sucking in enough oxygen to last him a few precious moments as the dark figure brushed past him and continued its patrol. Jeff's eyes followed as the figure marched farther down the hall, its echoing steps still carefully timed. But he could not see the mystery guest's identity. He had to move before there were any more surprises. Exhaling finally, he eased out of his hiding place and stood in the hallway.

Then his cell phone rang.

With a sharp intake of breath, hoping that the guard, now a ways down the hall, had not heard the ringtone or his cry, Jeff fumbled to open the compact phone.

"*What?*" he hissed, walking in the opposite direction, away from his pursuer.

"What are you doing?"

It was Wrong Number. And he didn't sound happy.

Smartly Jeff shot back, "You're the one who seems to know everything I'm doing. What does it look like?"

"It looks like you're walking into a trap."

Turning his attention to other matters, Jeff explored the stony labyrinth, barely acknowledging Wrong Number as he spoke.

"This is a bad idea, Weldon. I don't think you know what you're getting yourself into. These are very powerful people! They don't play games!"

Jeff moved down the corridor, peeking around corners to assure each hall's safety before proceeding. "Neither do I."

"Well, aren't you the big brooding hero."

Jeff walked on, Wrong Number now becoming a nuisance. "Does this have a point? Or are you just trying to bug me? I don't even know who you are."

"Let's just say I'm your guardian angel."

Jeff softened just a little and said, "Look, I appreciate the sentiment and all, but I can do this myself."

"Oh yeah? Then where are you?"

Jeff was about to say he knew very well where he was, thank you, but a quick check around the darkness and nondescript walls told him otherwise. He slumped. "I don't know."

After a long hesitation Wrong Number said, "I'm going to really hate myself for this. Hang a right up here."

The compliance caught Jeff by surprise, and he froze in place. Listening carefully to make sure hopeful ears had not deceived him, he asked, "What?"

"You'd better hurry. They already know you're down there. Security is on their way, and you've got a lot of work to do if you want to get enough evidence to bring the Committee down. Now, hang a right at the next hallway."

Bursting into a mad dash, Jeff followed the easily laid instructions, desperately searching for his clearing in the woods where all secrets would be brought to light. Jeff rounded to the right at the next corner and Wrong Number immediately followed with, "Go straight past two more intersections, go left, then enter the third doorway to your left. You'll know it when you see it."

Jeff didn't bother to answer. The chase was on. He could feel himself humming with energy, as if he was getting closer to something powerful and real.

The truth.

The Committee locked it up in these stone walls, trying to keep it buried, but he was going to find it. He was going to set it free, and it was going to liberate all of them. And then they would know not to mess with Jeff Weldon. Then they would know that he was right and not crazy! Then they would know!

Jeff followed Wrong Number's instructions to the letter and entered through the designated passage. Stepping inside, he saw a large ceremony room. It was empty, save for lit lamp stands, and quiet, and Jeff suddenly felt very small in its stomach. He marveled at the size and design of the place. He felt like crying, having finally reached his end.

"Now you're there." Wrong Number's voice rang true from the phone.

Only it seemed to come from inside the room as well...

"So tell me..."

Jeff's eyes adjusted to the more adequate lighting in the room, and his attention was pulled to a man emerging from the shadows. But the man wasn't walking.

He was floating. And his shoes scraped across the floor.

With long, skeletal hands he politely applauded while using a leather-clad shoulder to press the phone to his winged ear.

"...is it everything you hoped for?"

Jeff's eyes widened in horror, and he dropped his phone to the floor with a dull clack that reverberated throughout the cavernous space. For coming out of the shadows, on the other end of his phone call, was the Strange Man.

CHAPTER THIRTY-SIX

SOAKING WET, YET glad to be alive, the small band of gremlin-fighters shivered on their way to the front doors of the Good Church of the Faithful.

The church was the first location past Grover's Pond that was readily accessible at this hour, and they all felt it was a good place to stop, gather their thoughts, and decide their next course of action.

Plus, the lights were on, and Isabella couldn't shake the hope that Jeff might be there.

Sheriff Hank Berkley carried Millie as Isabella led Annie by the hand, everyone huddling close for warmth. Exhausted from the battle, they mustered enough strength to climb the stairs, and Isabella opened the door.

Inside, the church was well lit and inviting, and immediately she felt relieved, as if coming home from a long trip. Annie left Isabella's side and flopped down in one of the pews, resting her worn legs. Millie perked up in Sheriff Berkley's arms, and he set her on her feet.

Will Baxter saw them and was quite surprised.

He stood at the pulpit, mouth open in mid-sentence and hands raised in the air as though Isabella had just interrupted him in the middle of a sermon. Perhaps he was preparing for his first service as the newly instated pastor of the Good Church of the Faithful. When he saw the impromptu congregation enter, he adjusted his glasses and hurried down the aisle.

"Uh...Mrs. Weldon," he stammered, his forehead creased with uncertainty. "What are you doing here?"

Upon seeing him, Isabella pushed past her tired troops. "Will, is Jeff here?"

Will stopped. "Uh...no. I haven't heard from him all day."

Will was acting strange, but she dismissed it. Her muscles ached, and the shallow cuts of the gremlins' claws stung her arms. She couldn't think clearly, fatigue fought to overwhelm her, and all she wanted was her husband. Kneading the beginnings of a headache, she turned away. "Great."

Will looked to his visitors, confused and uneasy. "What happened to you guys?"

Millie spoke first, her eyes round with wonder. "We were chased by monsters!"

Annie covered her ears, as if not wanting to hear about *them* anymore.

"Monsters?" Will turned to Sheriff Berkley to see if the girl's description was correct. Hank nodded sternly. Will raised one hand to his mouth and bit his fingernails.

Isabella paced, trying to prioritize. She needed a plan. She always worked better with a plan, a list, a strategy, a defined course of action. She didn't know where to begin. So much was happening. She had so many questions and so much new information.

The bogeyman is real.

Check.

He set Dras up for murder.

Check.

Now he was back with a vengeance.

Big check on that one.

But that left one really important question unanswered in Isabella's mind. What did he want? Was he after them or Dras? The church? Rosalyn? Or maybe it was something else altogether.

Where are you, Jeff? She wanted to scream. She could try calling him *again*, but somehow she knew that wouldn't get her anywhere.

Isabella looked to the two girls in her care—Annie slumping in a pew staring at the carpet and Millie standing in the aisle studying the picture painted above the baptismal. They both looked tired and pitiful.

Someone should take them home, but Isabella wasn't for certain they'd be safe there. Calling the police was not a viable option; Hank had been with her through the ordeal, and he was no more equipped to fight the monsters than she was. She felt alone. And cold. And wet.

She shook her head, growing impatient with the thinking process. If only God would speak to her, tell her what to do next.

The sounds of shotguns, roaring truck engines, and screeching tires met her prayers.

Isabella, Sheriff Berkley, and Will all moved to the windows and peered out to see a parade of pickups, sporting rifle-wielding men, pull up and park in front of the church steps. As they braked to a noisy halt, their roars and shouts of violent intent broke the serenity of the church's sanctuary.

Earl Canton stepped out of the lead truck with a pleased sneer on his face.

Isabella, Hank, and Will all ducked back in quickly. She hoped they had not been spotted. Worried, Isabella turned to Hank. "What do they *want*?"

Hank frowned. "Trouble."

"What do we do?" Will bit his nails all the more ferociously.

"We have to get out." Hank stated the obvious.

"They'll be in here before we can make it to the back doors!" Will shrieked.

Isabella's mind raced. "We can go upstairs. Hide in the bell tower until they go away."

Will was the first one to race for the stairs, abandoning the others. Puzzled, Millie asked, "What's going on?" but Sheriff Berkley didn't exhaust the precious time to explain. He scooped her up in his arms and followed behind Will.

Isabella rushed to Annie and pulled her to her feet. The teen's lip quivered and her panic threatened to return. "What's happening?"

"Let's just get upstairs." Annie made no move to protest, and the frightened five disappeared up the stairs just as Earl Canton threw open the doors.

Earl stood there, the church before him, and placed his fists proudly on his hips, grinning wide. Immediately his hungry pack of jackals trampled into the sanctuary and squandered no time in getting to work. Some used spray paint to give the church's walls a few personal touches. Others had axes and took them to the posts, walls, and pews. Still more threw potted greenery through stained glass windows and ripped out hymnal pages. Everything turned to chaos in a hurry as the men moved this way and that, destroying the church in a matter of minutes. Earl stood by to admire his men's handiwork, beaming all the while.

"Don't leave anything standing," he shouted over the ruckus. "We want to make sure the message is loud and clear."

Once all five were safely inside, Isabella closed and bolted the door to the bell tower, leaned her head against the door, and took a deep breath. Annie and Millie ran to the open windows and craned their heads outside. Will and Hank huddled together, both trying haphazardly to fulfill their obligation as men and think of a solution to the problem. However, when they came up empty, they turned to Isabella.

But Isabella was tired. Tired of it all.

Will frantically appealed to Hank once more. "What are we going to do?"

"We wait," Hank tried to calm him down. "Once they've had their fun, they'll move on."

"What do they want?"

Hank glanced to Isabella. "They want Jeff," he said delicately.

Will looked away, embarrassed, the conversation suddenly becoming an inappropriate one to have with Isabella in the room. But Isabella was beyond the point of offense. After her talk with Clancy, she had suspected as much. She rested against the door, her eyes shut tight, trying to block out the sounds of the ruthless men downstairs destroying the church where she and Jeff had invested their lives. "They think he forced Millie to change her testimony," she replied.

Hank nodded sadly. "I'm sorry, Isabella. I was there at Smokey's. I...I knew what Earl was planning to do, but I couldn't say anything." He hung his head. "I was too afraid."

"Maybe we can talk with them," Will squeaked.

Isabella turned to him, angry. "Do you really think they can be reasoned with?"

Will faced the sheriff, pointing a skinny finger in his face. "You're the sheriff! *Do* something!"

Isabella heard the crashes below and knew that soon there would be nothing left of the Good Church of the Faithful. A thousand memories washed over her. She saw Jeff preaching revivals, children making decisions to follow Christ, folks grieving together over their sick or dead. Beyond that, she saw after hours, when Jeff was alone, researching his sermon and Isabella would come to keep him company, so proud of him. She thought of the time they played hide-and-seek late one night. Just the two of them, grown adults, laughing and running like children until Jeff caught her and kissed her so sweetly. This was their church. It was as much a part of their marriage as their house on Grover's Pond.

Only that was gone too.

"Why is this happening?" she asked softly as she stared up at the ceiling, her heart breaking. "Why is everything so crazy in Greensboro?"

"They're called the Committee," Hank revealed at length.

Will struggled to hide both a shocked gasp and a betrayed glare aimed at Hank.

Isabella turned to Hank, alarmed. She suddenly had so many new questions, but she remained patient and lowered her gaze. "I'm listening."

He glumly continued. "A group of six men. Doctors, lawyers, old money, pillars of the community." He paused. "Men you know. Men you've known your whole life. You'd be shocked to know who they are. When the highway moved, they had to think of something. We would've lost everything. This man came—John Graves—and offered his help. It was only later they realized who...*what* he was."

Isabella listened intently, horrified. "Does Jeff know all of this?"

Hank nodded. "I think so. Most of it, at least."

How long had Jeff known, and why hadn't he said anything to her? Was this what he was involved in? Were these the people he was facing?

"They didn't know Graves was the devil, Isabella," Hank confessed. "When folks started disappearing..."

"Lindsey," she offered quickly.

Hank shook his head. "No. Long before that."

Tears froze in Isabella's eyes. "How...how long?"

"Year and a half." He hesitated. "Aw, heck, who knows how long that monster's been at it? But we've been a part of the mess since little Billy Potter. The Committee covered it up. We've all covered it up."

Isabella blinked, and a few scant tears slid down her tanned cheeks. "Even you?"

He nodded, ashamed. "Even me. Some of my deputies."

"The ones who attacked Dras. Those were the *Committee's* orders?"

"Yes."

"Who else?" Isabella found herself hungry for more, wanting to know who had lied to her. She wanted someone to blame. Someone to yell at. Someone to hit.

Hank continued, rattling on. "So many others, Isabella. Store owners. Teachers. Farmers. Even..." he abruptly halted, and his cheeks became rosy.

"Even what?" Isabella's heart skipped a beat.

"Even—" He looked away. "—even some of your own church elders. Leonard and—"

"*Leonard?*"

Then Hank looked to Will, damning him.

Isabella followed his gaze, her horror intensifying. She and Jeff were surrounded by liars! All these people, people they loved and trusted, people they cared for, had betrayed them!

Will saw her disappointment in him and marched up to Sheriff Berkley, wagging an accusing finger. *"Are you insane?* Do you have any idea how much danger you're putting us in by telling her all of this? What if *they* hear? What if *he* finds out? You'll kill us all!"

Hank stood tiredly, Will's words having no affect on him. "What does it matter anymore, boy?"

But to Isabella, Will's tirade was like a punch in the stomach. "Will…"

Will fell silent. Like Hank, he couldn't face her. He only looked at the tops of his shoes, like a child caught with his hand in the cookie jar.

Isabella's voice cracked with emotion. She didn't want to believe it. "How…how could you?"

"The Committee tried to reason with Jeff! They sent him the sermons and thought that if he just followed instructions, then he would never have to know and they would never have to…" Will trailed off, afraid to finish the sentence. "But he refused! He wouldn't listen to them. All he had to do was follow orders, but he wouldn't!"

"So they fired him from the pulpit to discredit him," Isabella concluded. "And you took his place."

"The church was *dying*, Isabella! You saw how many people we lost because Jeff couldn't disassociate himself from Dras! I did it to save the church!"

"Jeff was looking for the truth! That's all he's ever cared about!" Isabella backed her husband. "He wanted people to know the truth. Not some contrived, watered-down version of Christianity neatly gift-wrapped with a bow like *you* want to give them. He took *his* orders from God, not the Committee!"

Even though he was not there with her, Isabella felt closer to her husband as she stood up for him. They were kindred spirits once again; both of them felt the sting of treachery. These were their neighbors and families and friends, and they had given up everything to serve them.

For what? she asked herself bitterly.

Isabella only wanted to hold her husband close, to grieve with him over the loss of their innocence. She realized how much she had missed him. Not just tonight, but over the last few months, ever since losing Dras. Jeff had been struggling alone, keeping all his pain to himself and allowing it to slowly eat away at him.

Why didn't he tell her? Did he not want her to know? Did he not think she would understand, or did he just want to spare her the pain of learning the truth? She loved him for that, but hated him all at the same time, and just wanted to be in his arms.

Now the need to find him grew even greater. Since Earl Canton and his men were still laying waste to everything that Jeff had worked for in Greensboro, she assumed that they had not caught up to him yet; otherwise their thirst for vengeance would have been satisfied. So, in one respect, he was safe. But she could only imagine what plans the Strange Man—this "John Graves"—might have for him. Or this Committee Hank spoke about. If so many influential citizens of Greensboro were involved in the conspiracy, Jeff's allies must be severely limited.

There might not be anyone left to trust.

Please, God, stay with us.

CHAPTER THIRTY-SEVEN

No…" Jeff gaped in disbelief at the monster. The bogeyman. His stomach twisted in knots, and he felt queasy at the sight of the creature before him. The Strange Man closed the cell phone and tossed it into the shadows.

"Surprised?" He clicked his tongue against his green-stained teeth.

Jeff was speechless. Frozen.

The Strange Man moved closer, rubbing his inflamed knuckles. "Were you expecting someone else?"

Stuttering, not realizing he was even speaking, Jeff replied, "M– my guardian angel—"

The hideous fiend cackled. "Well, I was an angel. Once."

"It was you all this time?"

Seemingly bored, the monster answered, "Yes, Jeff. We've covered that already. Catch up."

"But I don't understand. Why?"

At that, the bogeyman stopped and turned in the opposite direction. With skinny arms he gestured to the expanse of the Committee's exquisite ceremony room and spoke loudly, his voice echoing, "Not much to understand, really. The Committee was getting on my nerves. I thought I would throw a monkey wrench in their plans, just for fun. That monkey wrench, my dear boy, was you. Whether you killed the Committee or the Committee killed you, I didn't really care. I thought maybe, just maybe, I'd get you *all* out of my hair!" He sighed as he droned, "Do you think I *enjoy* having those old codgers looking over my shoulder, questioning everything I do? As if I have to answer to them! I needed them for a while. However, the time has come when they are irrelevant."

"The Dark Hour," Jeff muttered, almost afraid to say it out loud.

The Strange Man stopped his theatrics and turned to Jeff, a trifle surprised. "Someone's spoiled my secret," he sang, his yellow eyes blazing.

For a moment Jeff almost thought he saw *fear* in the bogeyman's eyes. But the Strange Man quickly recovered. "No matter. My Master will still come."

Jeff shuddered at the sound of that. "Master?"

The Strange Man tittered, his voice a rattling wheeze, and Jeff shivered uncontrollably. "Of course." He exploded in shrill laughter. "Really, Reverend, did you think I was the Coming Evil? Oh, no, no." His merriment subsiding, he met Jeff's eyes and revealed his Cheshire grin. "You haven't seen *anything* yet."

"I won't let you do it," Jeff declared through bared teeth, feeling every bit the impotent spoiled child he sounded.

The Strange Man shook his head, amused. "I see that stubbornness runs rampant in the Weldon family. Dras was the same way."

Jeff tensed. "You don't get to say his name."

The bogeyman smiled and relaxed. Then, taking in a big, melodramatic swell of breath, the Strange Man held his arms wide and bellowed, "Well, here I am. Do what you will, Reverend. I'm the one who framed your brother and orchestrated his execution. Come on! Take your revenge!"

But Jeff remained standing firm.

Letting his arms fall to his side, deflated, the creature slithered up to the rogue preacher and breathed in his face the stench of warm garbage. "But you know better than that, don't you? You know that you can't hurt me. I'm eternal. You are *mortal*. So why fight so hard to get here? You knew you'd find me and not be able to do anything about it! Why try so hard?"

Jeff did not have an answer.

The Strange Man tapped his bony chin, thoughtfully. "I propose it is because you humans do not really want to *know* truth. You only want to pose the *question*. As long as you can keep that question between you and the answer, you will never have to accept the truth. Because in accepting the truth, you will be required to change, and face it, Jeff, you've never been one for change. Not many people are. But change must come." The ugly grin again, exposing his slimy, jagged teeth. "And I have come to bring it. Think of me as a catalyst. A prophet of a new age. I've come to prepare the way for one who will change the face of the world. And it will all begin with Greensboro."

Jeff closed his eyes, wishing he was dreaming. Wishing the things he was hearing and the monster before him weren't real. This bizarre conversation challenged everything he believed. Or maybe it reinforced it.

Maybe that was what scared him so.

Because if this thing—this devil—was real, that meant Jeff had turned from a God just as real to get his revenge. He had abandoned his principles because God had not done what Jeff thought He *should* do. And, because of that, more people had become victims of this monster.

What have I done?

"I'm not afraid of you." Jeff's knees grew tingly and threatened to collapse.

The Strange Man remained close to Jeff's face, circling him like a buzzard waiting for its prey to drop dead. "You don't need to be. Enough people are afraid of me already. No, Reverend Weldon, I don't want you afraid. I want you *angry*. I see it in your eyes. You're trying to keep the beast inside. You're trying to be the good Christian soldier when deep down you want to rage. You want to be violent."

Don't listen. He's trying to trick you. He's trying to get under your skin. Don't let him—

Yet Jeff felt something cold and wet inside, crawling, climbing, ready to claw its way into the world.

"You shouldn't keep it all bottled up like that," the monster encouraged. "It's not healthy for you. Let it go, Jeff. Let it go."

"Stop. Just stop it."

Jeff flinched and twitched, and the Strange Man's mouth eased into a grin. "Oh? Am I cutting too close to the wound, Reverend? Truth hurts, doesn't it? Now you may regret looking for it as hard as you have."

Jeff shook and couldn't stop. His head throbbed as it did before, after the night terrors. But this was different, stronger. There was something inside of him. A hate that he had harbored for some time. Now...it was growing. Changing.

Turning into something.

And he wanted to let it loose. The same rage washed over him that he felt when he threatened Larry, and he knew that his eyes had turned black once more. He was losing control.

NO!

"Well, my boy, you're here. You've found me. For three months you've forsaken all those who love you to pursue me. You wanted me so badly. Here I am! You want to take vengeance against me for what I did to your brother? Do your worst. I dare you."

The Strange Man stood back a few feet and stretched his hands before him to demonstrate his surrender, leaving himself open for an easy attack. But Jeff could only stand with his head hung low, his whole body trembling as the thing inside of him struggled to give birth to itself.

"Maybe I frighten you in this form." The Strange Man flicked his wrist, and the glamour appeared over him, shrouding his twisted, corpse-like body in a cloak of beauty. In the blink of an eye he looked just as he had in the weathered photo Leonard had shown him. John Graves.

"How about now?" the beautiful bogeyman taunted. "Shall I wear this mask for you? It never fails to please your friend Rosalyn. I can move amongst your town freely in this body, and they never know the evil in their midst. But one day soon they will know. One day soon the whole world will know." The monster that looked like a man smiled. "And they will tremble."

Jeff remained stoic, feeling the awful churning sensation inside of him growing.

Don't let it out...

The Strange Man's façade fell away like a drape, revealing his chalky white skull with glowing hot orbs for eyes. "Or maybe *this* is who you would *really* like to hit."

Turning aside, the Strange Man nodded to someone in the shadows. A figure approached. Jeff saw Deputy Ryan Stevenson.

The Strange Man backed away, giving the two men sparring space. "Maybe *this* is who you would rather take your vengeance on. After all, it was Deputy Stevenson here who came away with the most of your brother's blood on his hands."

Jeff and Stevenson faced off, each sizing up the other. Stevenson broke the moment and jeered, "I thought Earl would have caught up with you by now."

Jeff's heart raced, gearing up for a fight, and he felt the smothering rage inside take over. This time he did not fight it. Keeping his focus on the deputy, he spoke to the bogeyman. "So, why send *Stevenson* to kill my brother? Funny that you weren't the one to do it yourself. Did you just not have the power? Or does the Committee have you on a shorter leash these days?"

The Strange Man glowered, his cool calm momentarily broken. Slipping, he growled, "The Committee has no leash on me! They can't comprehend my power! *I'm* the new god in Greensboro!"

Jeff then turned to look at the Strange Man, his obsidian eyes unflinching. "Oh, I'm sorry. Am I cutting too close to the wound? Maybe now you regret looking for *me* as hard as you did."

The Strange Man roared—Deputy Stevenson's call to arms. The burly man stood tall, ready to brawl, as the bogeyman screamed, "My first order of business will be finishing with you what I started with your brother."

Stevenson's punch came hard and fast, and Jeff didn't have time to duck. He fell backward and landed with a loud slap across the steps leading to the doorway. Deputy Stevenson towered over him, massaging his red knuckles, patiently waiting for his quarry to return to his feet.

Jeff rolled over and pushed up on shaky arms, managing himself to a standing position, and brought his fists into a familiar stance, feeling the rage roll over him like cold fire. He had spent the last ten years of his life trying to suppress that rage, to hide it behind a normal life, a beautiful life, even the pulpit. But that wasn't the real Jeff. The real Jeff was angry and violent.

Now it was time to let the beast loose.

Jeff and Stevenson lunged like two steam locomotives and collided into each other, entangling their strong arms in vice-like grips. They became one furious, wrestling thing as they crashed to the floor. There they struggled for dominion, each one taking his turn.

Stevenson was first as he rose up and squeezed his large hairy hands around Jeff's throat. Struggling to breathe, Jeff kicked and swung wildly, only managing a few light punches, not enough to penetrate the brute's bulk. Jeff slipped a knee free and shoved it full force into Stevenson's groin. The wind left the deputy in a hurry, and he groaned and rolled off of Jeff.

The Strange Man watched the fight blissfully, clapping his hands. Jeff ignored the monster's pleased expression, as he was lost in the throes of battle.

Stevenson brought a broad palm across Jeff's right ear, causing momentary deafness and disorientation. Jeff staggered sideways, and Stevenson scurried to tackle him before he had a chance to regain his bearings. Jeff saw the charging bull coming after him just in time to sidestep and knock the deputy off balance. Fearlessly, Jeff leapt through the air and hit Stevenson with a full body football tackle that sent both men reeling to the ground. Jeff managed to get the upper hand as he climbed atop his fallen adversary.

Jeff punched hard and fast, busting Stevenson's lip on first impact. He hit again, and his arms felt stronger.

Jeff attacked Stevenson, feeling alive and powerful. Unstoppable. Like a machine. Forgetting everything that he was, everything he stood for, Jeff Weldon bashed a barrage of fists into Stevenson's broken face until finally the deputy quit struggling. Yet even then, even with the unmoving deputy below him, Jeff continued to fight, unleashing the fury and rage he had felt building inside of him for too long.

"*Jeff, don't!*" A voice cried out in his heart. It sounded like Isabella's voice, but he ignored it. What did she know? She was always bothering him, always wanting to *talk*. Couldn't she see he was busy? He had things to do! Things she wouldn't understand!

Why couldn't she just mind her own business?

He delivered more punches to Stevenson's face, bruising him badly, spattering blood from his busted lip, and cutting his eye with a knuckle. Still Jeff refused to let up. He deserved to have his revenge. To pay Stevenson back for what he had done to his brother! For what he had done to *him*! The blasted Committee had taken everything away from him! His home, his job, his good name! Everything! He deserved something back.

"*Take his life.*"

The voice came from nowhere—no, from somewhere inside. It replaced Isabella's voice, and Jeff didn't recognize it.

"*Kill him,*" the voice commanded again, louder this time, resounding in a cacophony that seemed to fill his skull. Now Jeff was unable to *stop* hitting Stevenson. He tried with all of his might to pull back, but to his horror, he could no longer control his own muscles. He felt the pounding in his head and the confusion that accompanied it, just like in the forest in his nightmares, only worse. Much, much worse.

"*Kill. Kill. Kill him. Spill his blood. You deserve it.*"

"No!" Jeff threw himself off of Stevenson and brought his hands to his head, pulling his hair, covering his ears, shutting his blacked-out eyes in concentration, *anything* to make the voices stop! Like a man on fire, Jeff thrashed on the ground, trying to make the din cease and relinquish its control of his senses.

"*Kill him. Kill him.*"

Tears welled in Jeff's eyes, and panic nearly drove him mad. But somewhere in the midst of it all, Isabella's voice rang true.

"*I love you.*"

The pounding in his head dulled to a low ache, and he rolled over onto his knees, tears of pain running down his bruised cheek. Breathing heavily, he tried to cool down, to gather his mind again while the voices were temporarily silenced.

"What's happening to me..." Shocked at his own savagery, he looked down at his hands, unable to believe the evil they had committed. They were sticky with Stevenson's blood. But there was something else covering his hands too. Something black and thick.

Something that *moved*.

Quickly, like stringy black worms with a will of their own, the black goo slithered up his arms, flailing out, only to snap back again, swallowing his fist first, then climbing its way up his arm. He fought against it, trying to shake it loose, but he could not. The slime-like substance was icy cold, and it constricted tighter and tighter. Jeff's shark eyes grew wide with terror as he felt himself being devoured alive but not consumed. No, this thing was not feeding *off* of him, but rather it was *feeding* him. *Just like Ray McCormick.* Faster and faster it fastened itself to his flesh. Bonding to him.

His mind flashed back to earlier tonight, in the North Woods. The lake had been calling out to him. He'd touched it, got some of its muck on his fingers. Now, like a parasite it attached itself, and he felt powerless to stand against it. The goo hissed and popped as it gurgled farther up his arm and into his shirt. It spread to his chest, and the tightening around his heart returned. The voices haunted him once more, and he understood that the strange organism was *talking* to him. Persuading him to do its bidding. Tempting him to give in to its evil impulses.

No, he realized. *Not its evil impulses, but... but mine.*

It was not putting evil into him but rather siphoning from him his rage and his hatred and magnifying that sin, only to feed it back to him, stronger and more concentrated. And like a baby sucking a bottle, he was guzzling down its milk. The milk of pride and anger and bitterness and unforgivingness. He was being corrupted. Changed.

As the freezing cold of the black, tar-like goo swallowed him, slurping its way up his neck, Jeff felt his heartbeat slow. He slipped in and out of consciousness and remembered the black creatures that shambled in his nightmares.

I'm becoming one of them.

Jeff forced himself to crawl away, to get as far from Stevenson's bloodied body as possible. He cowered, terrified by what was happening. He looked over at Stevenson and thought how easy it would be to finish him right then. To kill him.

The Strange Man hovered behind Jeff. "Ray McCormick sought the truth, as you do. His fear that he would never discover the fate of his daughter led him to me. His desperation made him a servant to my mysteries. Your search, however, is fueled by hate. I can feel your rage, Jeff. I can *taste* it. You walk about in the daylight, smiling and laughing and pretending to be the good son, but you and I both know that a monster dwells inside. You have struggled with the monster for so long, but now I can offer you freedom. Unleash it, Jeff. Kill Stevenson. Prove that you are finally ready to know the truth, and I will show you the secrets of the Dark Hour. You will know as *God* knows."

Jeff tried to ignore the Strange Man's words but was unsuccessful. He stared at Stevenson and the awful thing he had done, unable to put out of his mind what a few simple motions would be required to put an end to the deputy. He didn't want to let the evil inside control him, but he knew that he had little strength left to resist.

"No."

The Strange Man pushed further. "Give in to your anger. Can't you feel how powerful it makes you? You can be a god. Together we can reign over this town, and these people will never hurt you again. Those who rejected you and mocked you will cower before you and beg for your mercy! You will be their king! Just as you deserve."

"No."

"God has let you down. He's abandoned you. Give up! Why do you wait for Him when you know He will not come? I am right here! I can give you power *now*." The Strange Man thrust out his hand, as if Jeff were about to drown. "Take my hand, and you will gain the whole world."

The monster ceased his campaigning, waiting for Jeff's response. Jeff kept quiet for a long time. He hung his head, pressing his face to the floor, on the edge of vomiting or passing out or just dying.

"*I love you*," he heard Isabella say again in his head.

Only...

"*I love you.*"

It isn't Isabella, he realized.

"*I love you, My boy.*"

It was God.

Jeff opened his eyes, feeling the blackness there melt away, and looked at the Strange Man, seeing him clearly for the very first time. His anger receded, and he felt at peace. Jeff rose, and the black, slithering darkness began to leave him, shrinking away as though it were afraid of him.

No. Not afraid of me. Afraid of what's inside of me. There's sin in me, but God's Spirit is inside of me too.

"What does it profit a man if he gains the whole world and loses his soul?" Jeff asked the Strange Man almost dreamily, quoting Scripture.

The darkness shrieked and left Jeff in a blast, sending him teetering but never toppling over. It was time to stand firm now. Stand firm until the end.

The Strange Man backed away from the young preacher. "What?"

"*You* called Danny and told him to find me. You knew what he'd seen at the lake, and you knew he'd tell me and start me on the path that would lead to you. You've been helping me this whole time to learn the truth. But why? Why'd you do it? And I want the real reason, not that line about me being a monkey wrench." Jeff was amazed that his fear of the monster was evaporating.

God? Is that You? I'm sorry! I'm sorry I left You! I never want to do that again.

Feeling near tears, relieved yet exasperated, Jeff held on long enough to pose his question again. "Why did you help me?" though God was already whispering the answer to him.

"Make him say it, Jeff."

The Strange Man saw the newfound confidence in the young man's smile and snarled. "You really want to know?" He tried to muster his hungry wolf's grin again but failed. "To see your face. To see the hope die in your eyes when you discovered the truth and learned that there was nothing you could do about it. That, Reverend Weldon, that one look would make everything worth it for me. Just to see you defeated. Just to watch you lose."

"Tell him the truth, Jeff. You don't have to fear him. I'm here with you. I never left you. I will never leave you."

Jeff felt a fire ignite inside, not of anger, but of divine origin.

"I don't think that's it," Jeff began. "I think the truth is, you're afraid of me. Why else would you go to all the trouble to break me unless I was a threat? This is all about power. You want it; I have it. But not in myself. I get that now. You reminded me."

"That's right, son. I'm here."

Jeff walked forward, causing the Strange Man to inch away, and did something the creature would never expect.

Jeff held out his hand, to shake.

The Strange Man looked at Jeff's hand as if it were some alien thing.

"I suppose I should thank you for that," Jeff stated humbly, no longer afraid of the big bad bogeyman.

Outraged, the monster slapped the hand away and recoiled with a violent hiss.

Jeff remained resolved. "You're through here."

The dragon slain and the test passed, the hero turned to leave the labyrinth behind. On his way out, he spotted his discarded cell phone on the floor and considered for a moment the distraction it had become in his life.

Turning one last time to the Strange Man, Jeff smiled. "Keep the phone. I won't be needing it anymore."

Then Jeff walked into the dark hallway, leaving the Strange Man behind in the empty room, with only the unconscious Deputy Stevenson and the disowned cell phone serving as reminders to a humiliating defeat.

In anger, the Strange Man roared, and the rafters shook. Falling against the stone steps, finding himself weak and needing support, the demon sobbed. He had been bested. Still, though, in spite of his tears, he forced a vengeful smile to his lips.

If Jeff didn't want to play anymore, that was OK.

After all, there was still one more Weldon to contend with.

And he would show her no mercy.

Jeff emerged from the darkness and stepped into the light of The Rave Scene's storage room, feeling a thousand pounds lighter.

Danny still kept a watchful eye on Larry the bartender—who sat on the floor, his face in his hands—but upon seeing Jeff, he hurried to him. "Boss!"

"Let him go," Jeff said, gesturing to Larry, who looked up, confused and relieved.

"What?" Danny said.

Jeff moved toward Larry and helped him to his feet, even going so far as to dust the poor man off, as if to say, "Hey, no hard feelings." The bartender blinked back at the ex-preacher, waiting for the other shoe to drop. Waiting for more hitting.

Jeff only smiled. "Go on, Larry. Go home. I'm sorry."

Larry didn't wait for another invitation. He quickly hefted his weight and ran full force out of the club. "Go back to the Committee," Jeff called out to Larry's retreating frame. "Tell them it's over."

As if seeing his birthday party disbanding prematurely, Danny moved to Jeff. "What are you doing? He'll call the cops!"

"It doesn't matter, Danny. I know that now."

Danny stepped in closer, his expression intense, starving for answers. "What did you find down there?"

"The truth."

Danny looked ready to march into the dark abyss himself. "Well, what are we waiting for?"

"No."

Danny turned to his partner. "*What?*"

"There's nothing we can do," Jeff confessed, and he realized that he was OK with that. "Not yet, anyway. It's gone on too long, become too big."

"We can't just sit by while they do these things! What about Tabitha? What about my kids?" Danny's face turned red with frustration. "I thought you wanted to hunt demons, man."

"Danny," Jeff began calmly, "it's all about timing. God has a plan. I don't have any idea what that plan is, but right now, I have to believe He has one, because I don't. This is much bigger than I am, but God knows what He's doing, and when He decides that it's my turn to step up to bat, then I'll fight to the death if I have to. But right now—" Jeff nodded, affirming the statement for himself as well. "—we wait on Him. *He's* the Boss."

Danny cooled and his shoulders sagged, as if the air had been let out of him. "What am I supposed to do?" he asked, desperately seeking further purpose.

"I've gotta stay in Greensboro," Jeff said. "God's not through with me yet. But you don't have to. Nobody would blame you if you left. Take Tabitha and the babies and go away from here. Be safe. Just remember what you saw here. Remember that it starts in here." Jeff pointed at his own heart. "Don't let it get you like it almost got me. You want to do right by your family? Turn to Christ. He's the only one who can fix you in here, in your heart."

They stood in silence, parting ways, and Jeff felt as though he were saying good-bye to another brother.

Danny extended a dirtied hand in friendship. "Take care, preacher," he said, the coldness once heard in his voice long since evaporated.

Jeff smiled and shook his hand. "You too, Danny."

Then, most unexpectedly, Danny pulled Jeff into a hug. The two men held on, clapping each other on the back. Parting, Jeff turned and strolled to the doors of The Rave Scene, passing the patch on the floor where Dras had been beaten on orders from the Committee, and found himself smiling. He didn't know why God let Dras go through that. He didn't know what it would take to restore his town when so many bad things had happened. He *still* didn't have all the answers. But, for the first time, Jeff Weldon was OK with that.

He stopped, dug in his pocket and pulled out the keys to his truck. He tossed them to Danny. "Here. Take the truck and go get your family. I'm sure you can fit the babies' seats in there somehow. Leave the truck at the bus station, and I'll pick it up in the morning."

"What about you?"

"Looks like a nice night for a walk."

"Where you going?"

Jeff considered for a moment and turned to his friend. "I'm going to go find my wife." He added warmly, "I just realized that there's something I need to tell her."

CHAPTER THIRTY-EIGHT

EARL CANTON SMILED as his men tore apart the Good Church of the Faithful. With each pew that was split, each hymnal that was shredded, he sought to fill a void created nearly two years ago. Though, now that he was so engulfed by hatred, it was impossible for him to know if he was succeeding or not.

A year and a half earlier Earl Canton lost his only son. Without explanation Charlie was taken from him, killed because the boy jumped into the swimming hole with his friends and was the only one to break his neck on the rocks below. It was a senseless tragedy. At first Earl blamed the friends who were with Charlie that day. Then his anger fell on Sheriff Berkley for not doing his job and keeping those jumping cliffs off limits. When he still felt empty, Earl turned to the church.

Reverend Jeff Weldon was many years his junior, and Earl was a proud, proud man. Yet he pushed all that aside, only wanting solace, not caring from whom. When Earl came to the young pastor looking for answers, Jeff told him, "Trust in Jesus."

Jesus.

Church stuff. Like that was going to solve anything. *I should've expected that from a preacher.* They all said things like that, things that didn't help. They wanted to talk about God, but they couldn't explain where the Almighty was when his boy Charlie was climbing that cliff, ready to dive to his death. Why hadn't God stopped him? He was *God*, right? Couldn't He do anything He set His mind to?

Jeff had no answers for questions like those. No answers that meant anything to Earl, anyway. But now tragedy had struck *Jeff's* home. And now he was panicked, scrambling around town, looking for answers.

Where's all your talk now, Reverend?

Earl delighted in Jeff's maddening search for answers that only led to more questions. Jeff, who was so proud and held his head so high because he was *Jack Weldon's* son. And what did he have to boast about now, that royal prince? His father was dying, his brother was in jail, and his whole life was in shambles. *That'll show you!*

Gleeful vindictiveness afire in his heart, Earl stood at the front of the church and watched as his mob tore down the soul of Jeff Weldon's labors. Many of these people, he knew, had also lost friends and family over the last year and a half and were never given a proper explanation. They were all fed empty words of comfort and encouraged to look the other way. Told that time would heal their wounds. Their pain was never given a voice, never given permission to stand and be noticed.

And so it had come to this. They would make themselves heard. This whole town would know their pain. Their loved ones' deaths would not be buried in secrecy any longer, and at last the "good" people of Greensboro would acknowledge these tragedies.

Earl took an axe in his hand and hefted it high before bringing it down on the altar. *That'll show you, Jeff Weldon! That'll show You, God!*

The tapestries in the church dangled in tatters, the pews ruined, the stained glass shattered. The angry mob piled the loose boards and hymnals in the center of the sanctuary. From behind the pulpit Earl commanded, "Burn it."

Linus Branch adjusted his John Deere cap and pulled a lighter out of his back pocket. Hurriedly, he touched the flame to the edge of some sheet music for "Amazing Grace" and set it aflame. Everyone pulled back to hoot and holler at the flaming pyre, rejoicing in their devilry.

"I think he'll get the message *now*," Earl boomed loudly.

One of the few women in the crowd turned to Earl as if about to say something, then halted, speechless and terrified. "Be...be..."

"Julie, what's wrong with you?"

She waved her arms. "Be...be..."

Others turned to Earl to see what was upsetting Julie so much. When they saw, some shrieked, some yelled.

All of them ran.

Earl remained standing there, the axe in his hand and Julie below, stabbing at him with her finger. "*Behind you!*"

Earl turned around.

And dropped his axe.

Millie kept to herself by the window in the bell tower, watching the breeze rustle the lush trees outside. Annie rested next to her, and behind them Isabella, Will, and Sheriff Berkley continued to argue. Having grown up in a broken home, Millie had heard her fair share of shouting, and she just wished the grown-ups would stop acting like children.

Shifting her gaze to the church steps below them, Millie spotted a group of the angry men with guns and axes running from the church. Some jumped in their vehicles and peeled away. Some left the trucks behind and just kept running, screaming. The grown-ups with her couldn't hear the ruckus for all of their bickering, but from her position near the window and open air, Millie could.

Curious, she tugged on Annie's shirt. Annie looked bored with the arguing. At Millie's insistent tugging, though, Annie pulled herself out of her trance and looked down. Millie quietly pointed to the church steps, and Annie leaned out to see the men evacuating.

Millie whispered, "Where are they going?"

Annie shrugged. Then she frowned. "Do you smell smoke?"

"Fighting about this isn't going to solve anything," Hank tried to reason with Isabella.

Isabella pushed him aside, eager to get to Will. "He trusted you. Both of you! How could you?"

"We were scared. We didn't know what else to do," Hank admitted earnestly, defending not only Will but also himself.

Saddened, she turned back to Hank. "You could've taken a stand."

"Uh...guys?" Annie called from across the room.

Will begged Isabella, "You won't tell the Committee that I said anything, will you? I'll lose my job!"

Isabella wanted to give him a good hard punch in the mouth for her husband.

"Hey, there's something over here you might want to see," Annie called to them again.

Hank turned on Will. "Will you stop being such a coward? The Committee's not going to do anything to you."

"You don't know that!"

"Hey! Guys!"

The thunderous shout of little five-year-old Millie Walker brought everyone to attention. Annie stood back as her young companion commanded the room like a little general.

"Stop fighting." She was not asking.

Isabella softened. "We're sorry, Millie. We're just upset."

Annie took over. "Do any of you smell smoke?"

Hank and Isabella turned to each other. Come to think of it, Isabella *did*.

Then she thought of the angry mob downstairs. *What did they do?*

"Everybody out!" Hank said.

Will immediately charged the door to unlock it. Millie ran full force and jumped into Isabella's arms, and Annie rushed behind her. Sheriff Berkley took the rear, herding the girls. Will fumbled with the lock, his hands shaking, but he finally managed to throw the door open and run out into the hallway, nearing a blind panic.

Smoke filled the upstairs hallway, and Isabella heard the popping and crackling of flames in the sanctuary below. Immediately she and Millie coughed and pulled their shirts over their mouths to serve as poor breathing filters. The whine of the smoke alarms split her skull, making it hard to concentrate and next to impossible to communicate. Nevertheless, the five moved as one unit to the staircase, ready for anything.

Anything except the Strange Man.

Like a specter of death, the shadows lifted him off his feet as he ascended the staircase, revealing his white skull-like face and his leather straps and chains. At the first sight of him, the group froze, crippled by trauma.

All save Will. Screeching in abject terror, Will turned tail and scurried in the opposite direction to the other staircase. Hank's jaw dropped in awe and fright upon viewing the monster. "This was what Hayden was protecting," he breathed, as if unable to believe it.

Isabella too stood there, unable to speak. Unable to move. *This is Dras's bogeyman*, she finally understood. *This is what he faced. Alone.*

"Isabella, come on!" Hank hollered, racing to catch up with Will.

But Isabella remained, with Millie in her arms and Annie pulling at her shirt.

"Isabella!" Annie said. "Come on! *Come on!*"

However, Isabella's body had petrified. Even her tears were still in her eyes, transfixed as she was by the monster's stare. Floating up the stairs one by one, he drew closer to the three females. Extending his arms, the Strange Man flicked out his talons, touching the dry wood walls on either side of him. Trapping his intended prey, he moved closer to them, his long nails cutting into the wood, scattering shavings in his wake.

In a flash Isabella thought back to her earlier confrontation with the gremlins. Her faith had driven them away, but this thing—their king—stole that faith. She felt a warm fire ignite within her, bringing to her spirit a thousand scriptures she had repeated in times of loss and worry in her life, scriptures that had kept her focused on God's sovereignty and protection. But the demon's glowing eyes caused her soul to shrivel with uncertainty. What if he were more powerful than the gremlins? What if Scripture didn't repel him as easily?

Isabella didn't want to die. Millie squirmed in her arms, this precious person was in her charge, and she feared that if she failed, if her faith proved weak, then this child would die. Rather than stay and fight, Isabella chose to run, disappointing herself in the process. Seeing no way past the bogle-king, Isabella—with Millie in tow—turned toward the opposite staircase and pushed Annie ahead. Not that Annie needed much persuading. She raced for the stairs, leaving her friends behind.

Annie rounded the corner toward the staircase that Will and Hank had already descended. Daring only one look back, Annie looked past Isabella and Millie. Isabella too, despite every instinct that told her not to, glanced back to see the Strange Man hovering gracefully, his thin legs convulsing like those of a dead man on the gallows. He moved steadily, with a hideous, confident, green-slimed smile stretched across his chalky white face.

His unhurried pace terrified Isabella all the more. But ahead she saw—

"Annie, watch out!" Isabella cried.

Annie turned from her stare just in time to see a wave of flames split the trunk of a support beam, whistling with heat. A part of the pillar broke away from the roof and landed, flames and all, on the third step down. With a yelp, Annie jumped back, and Isabella helped her regain her balance before the hungry flames could burn her.

Hysterical, Annie turned to her guardian. "What are we going to do?"

Without explaining, Isabella grabbed Annie's arm. "Come on."

Isabella led them to her Sunday school classroom. It was one of the only other rooms on the second floor, besides Jeff's office, and it was the closest to them.

It also had a large window.

Isabella shoved Annie into the room without giving the Strange Man another look. That would only waste time; she had to act *now*.

"Here," she said, stern and out of breath, and handed Millie into Annie's trembling arms. Without missing a valuable moment, Isabella grabbed one of the sturdy bright yellow chairs that she fondly remembered sitting in while teaching kids like Matt and Terry Monroe, telling them about Jesus and His love for them. She heaved it toward the window. It bounced once and clattered to the floor. She picked it up again, her arms shaking with adrenaline and fear, and swung it with all of her might into the window.

The window shattered and shards of glass exploded to the fresh cut lawn below. Taking the chair in hand, she used its metal legs to break the jagged edges of glass from the window frame and then discarded the seat. She reclaimed Millie and motioned to Annie. "Climb out the window."

Annie stared at her. "Are you crazy? We're on the second floor!"

"It's the only way!" Isabella was losing her patience. "It'll be safe. Look!"

She and Annie moved to the window and looked out. A gentle roof sloped down from the window, and directly beneath its edge was a small brick wall that could, with a little effort, be reached by a frightened young girl's foot.

Isabella turned to the teen, forceful yet gentle. "It's the only way. You go first, and Millie and I will be right behind you." Annie was quaking down to her shoes. Isabella understood her fear, but there was no time for comfort now. "Annie, *please.*"

Taking a deep breath, Annie nodded. "OK."

Isabella smiled, proud of the girl, and helped her through the open window. Annie struggled but eventually found her footing. Slowly and carefully she climbed. Isabella watched her all the way down until she dangled from the edge of the roof. Reaching, Annie found her footing on the wall and then jumped the few extra feet to the soft grass.

With an accomplished smile, she looked back to the window. "I did it! I did it!"

Isabella, in the midst of war, felt the beginnings of hope. "I knew you could. We're coming down."

"*Isa—!*"

Before Annie had a chance to finish her warning, Isabella felt the cold, dead hand of the hungry lion that sought to devour them. In her arms, Millie screamed as the Strange Man spun both of them to face him. Isabella shrank back at the sight, feeling insignificant next to his terrible power.

With a hiss through his fangs, he tore Millie from Isabella's protective arms, placed his long, tapered talons around Isabella's neck, and gave a heave. Flipping backward, she sailed across the room and crashed into the building blocks with which she had helped her class build Jericho's walls not so long ago.

Now that Isabella was out of the way, the Strange Man turned Millie to face him. Placing her chubby chin in his skeletal hands, he lifted her face to meet the burning gaze of his haunting yellow eyes.

As if every scream inside of her had been removed from her mouth, Millie hung speechless with a blank, faraway look in her eyes.

The Strange Man smiled. "Millie? You broke your promise to me, child."

Millie could not talk. Not to apologize, not to defend herself, not to beg for mercy.

"Now you'll find out what happens to all bad little girls."

With bones cracking and tendons popping, the Strange Man's wicked mouth elongated like a cottonmouth snake, ready to swallow Millie whole.

Now the little girl screamed.

The Strange Man's tongue slithered and whipped around her small face like a sentient tentacle, leaving trails of green slime all over her skin. His fangs protruded from his swollen gums, extending for the kill. Millie kicked and screamed and punched at his bony frame with all of her might, but he would not budge. He pressed onward to his kill.

Until Isabella stepped in. "Put her down!"

Her cheek cut and bleeding from the fall, Isabella stood triumphant and tall.

The Strange Man regarded her with his inhuman, uncaring eyes. Isabella's valor faltered at that moment, her pride and heroic demeanor replaced by her concern for Millie's safety. Her eyes softened. "Please?"

Amused, the Strange Man cocked his head to the side.

"Please let her go. You can take me instead."

The Strange Man remained silent, and Isabella's heart raced. She didn't know if he was considering her offer, preparing to let Millie go free, or if he was just playing a game. Toying with her, only to kill the little girl right before her eyes.

She felt so powerless, helpless to do *anything*.

I can't save her.

Her muscles ached, and she suddenly felt tired. So tired. Fatigue wrapped its arms around her and squeezed. She wanted to give in, to collapse under the strain of this nightmare and let the world deal with its own problems. She wanted to fall fast asleep, never to open her eyes again until her Lord came to take her home. Frigid, green mist began to pool around her ankles, and Isabella just wanted to die.

So cold...

But then she caught the Strange Man smiling. There was a knowing sparkle in his eyes as he looked through the fog. And somehow she understood that *he* was doing this to her. It was his spell. He was *telling* her to quit. Trying to persuade her to look the other way so he could claim Millie's life.

Millie.

She looked to the youngster now. Millie's lips trembled, her eyes filled with tiny tears, silently pleading for Isabella to help. Her whole body hung in the air, supported only by the Strange Man's grip on her little chin. She hovered there, her life held in the balance.

Isabella steeled herself, forcing herself to concentrate on her victory at Grover's Pond. Calling on the Word of God to scatter the gremlin horde had been a last-ditch, knee-jerk reaction, brought on by fear and desperation. But it had *worked*. God was faithful to protect her when she reached out to Him. Isabella's mind calmed and sharpened into a deadly point. She was ready to strike down the devil, to show hell there was at least one Christian left in Greensboro, and she wasn't budging.

Feeling that fire inside her build into a ripple of electricity, she knew her weakness was making way for the Holy Spirit to work. Putting aside her own fear and doubt and exhaustion, Isabella made her heart ready to receive the power of the Lord.

After all this time, her own words to Jeff came back to her with perfect clarity.

Let God be God.

Isabella called upon the power of God in her heart, as from her mouth erupted a single blue-white ball of flickering flame. She spoke with authority and might, *"For God did not give us a spirit of timidity, but a spirit of power, of love and of self-discipline."*

The cool night air surged through the open window, whipping Isabella's hair and dispersing the green fog at her feet. The light of the Strange Man's glowing orb-like eyes dimmed, threatening to snuff out, as she repeated the seventh verse from the first chapter of 2 Timothy, just as she had done to drive away the gremlins, finally understanding that it wasn't the words that had power. It was what the words promised. God was here to protect His flock from the lion. The words were only meant to remind her of that, to open herself up to be used by God. The Strange Man recoiled, his own power and influence shriveling, revealing his impotence. He seemed smaller now, lacking any real strength. In cowardice, his shoulders reared up to protect his ears from Scripture, and he peeked out over them to hiss at Isabella.

Isabella could feel light emanating from her as she shimmered with a soft, warm blue glow, and the bogeyman shook with fear at the sight of it.

The Strange Man, still hissing in defeat, set the little girl down on the floor. Millie ran and collapsed into Isabella's arms. The woman squeezed her with a mother's tenderness then herded her out of the way. Standing taller now, seeing the Strange Man for what he was in the light of God's power, she felt invigorated.

Fear had left her, and Isabella felt strong. She again quoted Scripture, this time from James 4:7: "Submit yourselves, then, to God. Resist the devil, and he will flee from you."

Millie poked her head out from behind Isabella and screamed over the roaring wind, "Yeah! So go ahead! Flee!"

The Strange Man retracted his gaping jaw. He bared his horrible fangs and hissed at Isabella. "This isn't over, daughter of God."

With that the shadows swallowed him, and he was gone. The blue-white light faded, and the wind fell quiet. Isabella felt a hush in her soul, and she knew she was safe despite the blazing church below her. With a joy that she was unable to contain, she knelt to face Millie. "Are you OK?"

Millie nodded and hugged her hero tight.

Isabella felt the small child's heart beat next to hers, and she had never felt more connected to life. Millie suddenly pulled away. Her expression was curious, as if she needed to know the answer to a puzzling question.

"Mommy said the light keeps the bogeyman away. I see the light in *you*."

With an innocent awe, the child softly touched Isabella's face, gently pulling, as if trying to find the light inside of her eyes. "How did it get in there?"

Isabella laughed. "Jesus put it there."

Millie's eyes brightened. "Can He put it in me too?"

Isabella nodded, feeling her spirit quicken. "Yes. But you have to believe, Millie. With all of your heart, you have to believe in Jesus, and you have to trust Him."

"Like I do Mommy?"

"That's right."

"OK." Millie seemed eager to have the light.

"God can hear you, Millie. If you want the light, then you have to be the one to ask Him."

With the fire consuming the bottom floor and devouring its way to the top, little Millie Walker bowed her head. "Mr. God, I want to have the light inside of me like Miss Isabella. I want to listen to you like I listen to Mommy. Please, let Jesus put the light in me so I won't ever have to be afraid of the bogeyman again."

Isabella watched, incredibly touched. As Millie opened her eyes from her child's prayer, Isabella saw a change happening right before her. There was hope in the little girl's face—a hope of a future, a hope of change, a hope of making the world a better place. She stroked Millie's hair, kissing her head. "Good girl."

From below Annie called out, "Hey! Are you guys OK?"

Isabella remained by Millie's side but shouted over her shoulder, "Yeah!" Then she touched Millie's face. "Yeah, everything's great."

Elsewhere in the raging inferno once known as the Good Church of the Faithful, Sheriff Hank Berkley and the newly ordained Reverend Will Baxter scrambled for their lives.

Flames ate up the sanctuary, and the fires grew higher and higher, tasting the walls and taking bites out of the wooden support pillars. The roar was incredible and the heat blistering, peeling the altar layer by layer. The two kept their heads down, covering their faces to protect them from the heat and smoke, and fought their way through the chaos.

Hank turned to check on Isabella and the girls and felt sick to his stomach when he didn't see them following. They were right behind him. Had he left them? No. No, Isabella must have gotten them out. He had to believe that.

"I can't see anything!" Will looked back toward Hank as they both kept moving. Cautiously they continued, making every effort to avoid the walls of flame that shot up from the floor to meet the ceiling. They were caught in a battle between the flames and the church, desperate not to get caught in the middle.

Finally Hank managed to spot a glimmer of hope in the distance. It was the back exit, and it seemed untouched by the consuming fire. "There!" Hank hollered over the roar and pointed. Will followed his direction, and both shielded themselves and broke free of the fiery imprisonment.

Hank reared back, ready to bust down the door, but gaped as it opened of its own accord. On the other side, blocking their only hope of salvation, stood the Strange Man.

"Tsk, tsk, tsk. Shame on both of you for what you've done."

Will instantly wept, hiding his face in his hands with despair and shame. Hank looked at the young man, disappointed. The Strange Man remained in front of the open doorway, taking his time. "Did you really think I would not know?"

"I'm sorry!" Will pleaded. "I didn't mean to tell! Honest! It was a mistake! I'll never let you down again!"

"You have betrayed me."

Will whimpered, "I'm *sorry.*"

"I understand. These are confusing times. It's hard to know which side to choose."

Hank remained still, mindful of the flames behind him but too scared to move, scared to provoke the serpent into a strike.

The Strange Man came to a conclusion. "But the time for indecision has passed. A war is coming, and *everyone* must choose a side, once and for all. I'm giving you both one last opportunity to decide whose side you will fight for."

Will's jaw dropped; his eyes lit with excitement. The Strange Man gestured to the open door directly behind him. "I hold the key to your escape. No one is getting out unless he comes through me."

Hank knew there was no way they could overpower the Strange Man or outsmart him. The only way to get through that door would be to sell his soul to the devil, once and for all. There would be no going back. There would be no forgiveness or repentance.

It was time to fish or cut bait.

"What will it be, gentlemen? The flames or me? Life or death?"

Will shook in his shoes but finally stepped forward.

Hank started, "Will!"

Will, his eyes teary and red, turned to Hank with a defeated whimper. "I'm sorry, Hank. I don't want to die."

The Strange Man held out his hand, and Will took it. With his head hung in disgrace, Will pledged his loyalty by kissing the Strange Man's hand. "I choose you."

The Strange Man smiled and patted the boy on the head. "Poor Will, so timid and full of fear. I will make you bold as a king. Men will live and die by your command. Now go. I'm done with you this night."

The creature stood aside, and Will took off through the open door, lost in the darkness and never looking back.

The Strange Man turned his undivided attention to the sheriff. "Hank?"

Hank kept silent for a moment but finally took a deep breath and made his eternal choice. "I'm sorry too."

The Strange Man's smile widened.

Hank finished, "I'm sorry for ever listening to you. I'll take my chances with the flames."

Hank defiantly backed away from the bogeyman into the scorching fire. The Strange Man snarled and looked ready to chase Hank down and murder him himself. But then the demon regarded the flames and held back.

He's afraid of the fire, Hank noted with surprise.

"As you wish," the Strange Man sneered and left through the open door, abandoning Sheriff Hank Berkley to his own fate. A burning beam collapsed, blocking the door's opening, and sealing Hank inside.

Well, you've gone and done it now, Hank, the tired old sheriff told himself as he observed the burning church around him. The wood was losing in its war against the fire, and the hungry flames never seemed quenched, yet Hank pushed on. His shirt was soaked with sweat from the oppressive heat, and he could feel his skin cracking. He was burning up. Never one to kid himself, he knew that escape was impossible.

Hank was not afraid for himself, and he did not regret his decision. Even now he knew he had done the right thing, and that gave him peace.

But his thoughts turned to his daughter, Becky.

He thought of the day she was born, when he first held her. She was a tiny stranger then, but day by day he learned more about her until his love grew beyond the point he thought possible.

She was sixteen now. Blonde. Pretty. Popular. Boys were beginning to call on a more frequent basis, something Hank was still trying to get used to. She was growing up. Soon she would be off to college. She was nearly a woman, and he would have to send her into a world of monsters.

How would she know right from wrong? Had he done a good job teaching her? He'd taught her how to change a flat tire and pump her own gas, how to balance a checkbook and fill out her tax forms. He'd spent many a Saturday afternoon over this past year teaching her simple self-defense techniques as a little something special to surprise all the boys at college.

But now he wondered if he had done enough.

If he was gone, who'd be there to warn Becky about the evil around her?

As he fought through the heat of the flames, trying to make his way to an exit, the walls of the church broke apart. All about him the church caved in, and he prayed to God that Isabella and the girls had made it out safely and that maybe they could tell his daughter to be on the lookout for the devil before it was too late.

That would have to do, Hank surmised. He wished that he had taught her better, loved her more. But it seemed that the fire would claim him before he ever got the chance to make amends.

"Hank!"

Somehow over the whistling of the flames, he heard his name called. He could barely see through the smoke as he searched the blazes around him.

"Hank!"

There it was again. Isabella? No, it sounded like a man's voice.

"Hank! Over here!"

Turning from side to side, desperate to find the source of the shouting, he saw an opening in the side of the church where the walls had finally admitted defeat. There, standing amid the smoke and fire, was Special Agent Christopher Perdu. With his bright blue eyes sparkling, even through this conflagration, he smiled and gestured excitedly. "Hank, come on!"

Surprised by the sight of his friend, but not needing to be told again, Sheriff Berkley changed course and raced for the opening. The young man waved him on, encouraging him all the way. "You're almost there! Keep coming!"

The clear night behind the agent beckoned to Hank, promising cool breezes and another sunrise. The thought of living another day never tasted sweeter, and Hank pushed with all of his might to make it to the opening.

I'm coming, soft breeze! I'm coming, quiet streets! I'm coming, Becky! I'm coming, Doris!

Without warning, a burst of heat and flames exploded in his path. Shielding his face with his arm, he retracted in surprise, but Perdu's voice called out to him again. "You're almost there, Hank! Keep coming!"

Hank couldn't see. His eyes stung with smoke, and he could barely breathe here, oh so close to freedom! No. He would not give up. Not while his wife and daughter still needed him. Not while his friends still needed him. Not if God still wanted him here.

With his meaty arm still held to protect his watery eyes, Hank pushed onward blindly. He ran toward the opening, keeping his focus on Perdu's voice, trusting him to lead him to salvation.

"Keep coming, Hank! You've almost got it! Almost!"

Behind him Hank heard the church falling apart and felt the heat on his back. Yet he kept moving closer to the sound of the agent's voice and felt the cool summer's end breeze splashing across his face. Exhilaration filled him.

Finally he broke free of the flames' barrage and took his first step into the world, baptized by fire. A smile of accomplishment on his face, Hank removed his arm to meet the face of his savior. He found himself surrounded by Isabella, Millie, and Annie, all three laughing and rejoicing, jumping up and down, hugging him and kissing him on the cheek.

But Special Agent Perdu was gone.

"You did it!" Annie squealed.

She hugged him again, and Millie did not seem to want to let go of his leg, squeezing it with all her might. Despite the joyous celebration in his honor, Hank paused to look around. "Where's Perdu?"

Isabella stopped, confused, but still grinning with uncontrollable relief. "Who are you talking about?"

"Special Agent Perdu. The boy who kept calling me!"

Isabella explained, eyeing Hank strangely. "Hank, that was us. We were waving our arms and shouting. We didn't think you heard us, but then you looked our way and kept coming."

Hank stood open-mouthed. "But Perdu..."

"There was no Perdu, Sheriff."

As Hank struggled to understand, he glanced at a figure in the distance. It was Perdu. Hank stepped forward, excited to see him, eager to show the others. *Look!* he was about to say. *There he is!* But then Christopher smiled in that same way Hank's father used to when he'd made the winning basket in his youth, a mixture of pride and admiration, and gave a little farewell wave. Suddenly the agent who was no agent at all turned into a figure of brilliant blue light and shot up, straight into the sky, disappearing in the stars.

Hank stood, gob smacked.

A miracle staring him in the face, Hank turned to watch the burning church with the others, all of them reflecting on the night's adventures and the stories they would tell, and an unspoken bond formed between them all—a very special bond between an invigorated small-town sheriff, a terrified babysitter, an unlikely heroine, and a five-year-old girl, all of whom had faced their worst fears, stood up to the bogeyman, and lived to tell the tale.

CHAPTER THIRTY-NINE

O*K, BUTTERFINGER IS nasty.*

Danny came to this conclusion as he sat on the bench at the bus terminal and snacked on the not-so-tasty treat from the nearest vending machine. After coming to that revelation, he got up with a grimace of *yuck* and moved to the trashcan across the room. He tossed in the rest of the bar then also offered the trash can the remains from his mouth. Thanks to the nearby water fountain, the taste was soon washed away, and he felt much better.

Tabitha was at the counter with their twins, buying their bus tickets, while he muscled what little luggage they had into the cargo bay of the Greyhound. With that out of the way and the Butterfinger blessedly gone, he was left to wait for his sons and their mother.

He reached into his jacket and took out a small Bible that Nana Loraine gave him when he was seven. He never had much use for it in the past; it mostly slept undisturbed at the bottom of his underwear drawer. But with all that had gone on over the past few days, Danny found himself strangely drawn to its thin pages. Stranger still, he found himself reading.

Strangest of all, he found himself understanding.

A baby's cry from across the terminal interrupted his reading. Instinctively Danny tucked the Bible back into his jacket and prepared to go help Tabitha with the babies, when he realized it was someone else's baby crying. Another family. There were families all around him: mothers, fathers, children. A whole town full of people, he realized, who had no idea what was going on in the shadowed places of Greensboro.

Someone should warn them. Someone should help. He felt a pull in his heart, but he shoved it away. *No, not me. What good could I do?*

Maybe Jeff was right. Maybe it was best to take his family and leave town. No one would think less of him for it.

But somewhere inside *he* thought less of himself.

Danny Carpenter was not known to run away from a fight.

Raising babies, maybe, but never a fight. Greensboro was sick with something, and it was spreading fast. Right now he just wanted to take his family far away and let those better equipped than he stay behind to fight, those like Jeff Weldon.

A small part of him felt like he owed something to the preacher for helping him out. An even smaller part of him felt like he should stay behind and offer to fight beside Jeff, do something good with his life for a change. But he'd be a fool for staying. *You'd only get in the way. What good would you be to them? What good would you be to anyone?*

He sighed and slumped down on the bench, his heart torn with indecision.

"—coming live from Greensboro where authorities believe the latest backlash of the Greensboro Ripper trial has taken place. An unknown group of arsonists were seen vandalizing the church before escaping into the night—"

There was a newscast playing on the TV mounted in the terminal. Inside the glowing box, the displayed scene depicted the Good Church of the Faithful—or what was left of it—burning out of control as firefighters struggled to put out the blaze. Danny stood up, nearly in a daze, and moved closer to the TV.

The on-site reporter shoved past a hurrying emergency worker to get proper screen time and held the microphone close. "This latest act of violence has caused some residents to fear that the horror that began with the Ripper murders is far from over."

Danny watched as the cameras caught Jeff's wife, the sheriff, and two girls he'd never seen before being tended to by police and firefighters. Wrapped up in blankets. Taken to ambulances to be checked out.

Danny saddened, and he wondered if Jeff knew, if Jeff was OK.

"You ready, baby?"

Danny spun, startled, and saw Tabitha carrying a twin on each hip. She was all smiles, and he realized how much she glowed when she smiled. He stared in wonder at her beauty as he struggled not to hear any more of the broadcast behind him. "Yeah, I think."

They started off toward the bus, and as he walked beside her then, he felt like a man for the first time. He was finally taking responsibility for his life and his family, and it felt good. It was a happy feeling that he was prepared to ride all the way out of town.

But something about the burning church on the television brought him back, and he wondered if Jeff was in trouble again. *It could be the Committee. He might need my help.*

He shook it away and turned back to Tabitha as they headed for the Greyhound. One of his boys looked at him and reached out his tiny, pudgy hand, making a clawlike motion as if to say, "I want you, Daddy."

Then the baby smiled. Looked right at Danny and *smiled*.

Danny had never felt so good about anything in the world.

Maybe this was the power in being good. To bring light to a dark world. To change a life. To make a miracle. To love and be loved.

It was wonderful.

But there was something else—something that wouldn't let go of him. He felt it as they walked closer to the bus. Looking off to his side, he watched the families passing by the station. Families just like his that were staying behind, thinking they were safe. Being *told* they were safe by the Committee. The scary truth of the matter was that they had no idea what kind of hell was creeping around the edges of their haven, the same hell that claimed Ray McCormick's life. The same hell from his nightmares.

They're all going to die...and they don't know it.

He told himself that Jeff was still here. That he could help them.

But Jeff's just one guy. He needs an army of devil smashers.

Maybe I...

Tabitha climbed the steps of the bus when Danny reached out and gently tugged at her arm. She turned to him, playfully surprised. "What is it?"

"I can't."

"Can't what?"

Danny noticed the other passengers behind him, not-so-patiently waiting to board. He tugged a little harder, and Tabitha followed his lead, getting off the bus so the others could make their way inside. His stomach felt hot and his hands sweaty, but he felt a peace in the midst of it all. A peace that told him, *I'm proud of you.*

It was that peace that kept him going when he felt like crying.

"I can't go with you."

"What?" Tabitha was shocked, panicked. "Why not?"

"It's not right. This town is in trouble, and I can't just leave knowing that. I have to stay behind and do what I can to help."

Tabitha lost herself in his eyes. He wondered if she thought the Danny she had known for years had been replaced by some kind of clone. The Danny she knew who used to drink and swear and beat on her. *But I'm a new man now. The man you always deserved. Only now I can't go with you.*

"You're staying?" Her brow wrinkled, her eyes tearing up.

"I have to. I've done so many bad things in my life, and I can't keep running, Tabby. I have to face my decisions and take responsibility for them, and maybe even do something to make up for them. I have to…I have to be a man and do the right thing."

She kissed him, suddenly and deeply. They had lived together for years, had made two babies together, but today at the bus station, Tabitha kissed Danny like she never had before. It was a kiss not born of passion or lust, but of real, honest love.

She loved him. At once he knew that she *really* loved him.

He held on to her, wanting the moment to last forever, though he knew that soon he would have to go back into the war zone. He didn't know what he was going to do, but the fire inside him told him that his role in this battle was important. God had chosen Danny. God had handpicked Danny Carpenter—a worthless man—for this one assignment.

And Danny would not refuse.

He kissed Tabitha long and hard, hoping to live a lifetime of love in one fleeting moment. When they parted, they both had tears in their eyes. Turning to each baby, Danny felt a lump in his throat, and he lost his breath. He kissed his sons on heir fuzzy heads, a deep shuddering in his chest almost unbearable.

"Daddy loves you," he croaked, eyes stinging with tears. "I'll always love you."

Tabitha began to sob, but Danny used every last bit of strength he had to remain strong. "I want you to cash in my ticket. Take the money and use it. Just stay in Watcher's Grove with your mother, all right? Don't come back here. It's not safe. I want you to start a new life, Tabitha. If…if I can, I'll come and find you. But most importantly, I want you to take this." He paused and pulled the small Bible out of his jacket. He slipped it into Tabitha's purse, and her eyes grew wide.

"Where did you get that?"

"My Nana Loraine gave it to me a long time ago. Listen, I've been…flipping through it, you know? And the preacher's been talking to me a little and…I think he's right. I'm starting to believe that what's inside of this little book is really the only hope that any of us have."

"I don't understand."

"Read it, OK? Talk to God. Follow Jesus, and you'll find me someday. Promise me, OK? Please?"

She paused, sniffling back tears. "I promise."

"Teach our babies too. Make sure they follow Him, so I can see them one day too."

"I love you, Danny."

"I love you, Tabby. And I'm sorry for everything that I ever said that made you cry and for everything that I ever did that made you hurt. Please—" He cupped her soft face in his hardened hands, tears finally breaking free and rolling down his cheeks. "—forgive me."

She nodded and kissed his hands. "I do."

I do. Like a wedding vow. The closest thing to a wedding vow that they shared, and he cherished it.

The bus engine started. It was time for Danny to face the future and trust God, no matter where the road led.

"You need to go," he told her, though his heart screamed at him to say otherwise.

He pulled his family close for one last embrace, touching his babies' arms, their legs, their sweet faces. Kissing their soft lips and button noses, smelling them deeply and rubbing his whiskers against their necks. These were his sons, his baby boys. He wasted so much time that he could have spent with them, time that was no longer his to give, and he regretted it now. It felt like dying, saying good-bye to them. Finally he kissed Tabitha one last time. It was nearly impossible for her to let go, and she held on to him for a moment more. Before she pulled away, she whispered into his ear, "You're my hero, Danny Carpenter."

She kissed him on the cheek, turned around, got on the bus, and never looked back.

The doors closed and the bus left the station.

Danny only took a few moments to weep, his chest heaving with silent sobs. When he was done for now, for he'd cry every night until he saw his babies again, he raised his head to the heavens, and the clouds seemed to roll away, setting the moon free.

Free. The thought sounded good to him.

"OK, God," he whispered to the night sky. "I'm all Yours. I don't understand one crazy thing that's going on around here, but, I'm with You. Got it?"

The quiet night stared back at him, and Danny nodded.

"OK. Then let's go score one for the good guys."

CHAPTER FORTY

WHAT WAS THAT thing, Earl?" Linus Branch clutched his rifle, referring to the dead-like creature hanging in the air that broke up their "peaceful" assembly at the Good Church of the Faithful.

But Earl Canton honestly did not know. He'd seen monsters before, three months ago at Smokey's during what some folks called in whispers "Gremlin Night." This new character was something wholly different and far more horrifying than those little creatures. He struggled with the implications of such a beast. Earl had never been one for believing in the supernatural, but after seeing the man-monster-thing…he found himself confronted with the reality of heaven and hell.

And yet, where was God? Twice now Earl had seen what he could only describe as "a devil," but God remained shockingly silent. No miracles, no wonders, and, most importantly, no answers.

My boy died, and where were You, God? What do You really care about any of us?

Unable to answer the great questions of the cosmos and still uncertain that God fit into the world he knew and understood, Earl turned his thoughts back to the monster. His posse needed him to lead, to come up with some way to fight back. They stood staring at him, waiting for an explanation.

"Earl," Linus's buddy Milton Wilbanks prompted, "do you know what it was?"

"I don't know. But I can tell you one thing."

The crowd moved closer, eager to hear what their fearless leader had to say. They were confused. Scared. They needed someone to explain things to them.

Even if it was Earl.

"How long are we going to be afraid?"

Dumbfounded, the people stared at him. "This isn't the first strange thing you've seen in this town. We've all heard talk about things going on in the North Woods that have no explanation!

We've all seen what's been happening in Greensboro ever since that big storm tore through here last spring. How long are we going to stand by and let our town officials and the sheriff's men push us around and bully us into keeping quiet? This is *our* town, and it's about time we took it back. Back from people like our mayor, who wanted all these disappearances to be a secret from the voters in last year's elections. Back from people like Sheriff Berkley, who—unless I'm the only one who noticed this—didn't seem too bothered by closing our people's cases so quickly. Back from people like Reverend Jeff Weldon, who stood by the side of Dras Weldon, a convicted murderer and..." Earl paused, gathering his hatred, "if you ask me, probably killed *all* those missing people!"

The people looked to each other, as if never piecing any of it together before. As if they hadn't noticed how many people had disappeared without explanation over the past year and a half. Earl knew they hadn't. The people of Greensboro had kept their heads in the dirt so long they didn't know daylight from darkness. They were blind, but he was not. *He* thought about these things. He wasn't stupid. He knew that *something* was going on in Greensboro, something that the well-to-dos and elected officials were in on, but he just didn't know what.

Yet.

"That Reverend Weldon," Earl began anew, talking as the people's friend, as someone who could identify with their pain. Someone who knew their sorrow firsthand because he felt it too. "He's not going to help you. We've let those Weldon boys get away with a lot because of their daddy's name, but no more. If Jeff Weldon wants to support the monster that killed Lindsey McCormick and TJ Walker, then I say we treat him no better than a monster! I say we show him the same judgment that Ryan Stevenson showed his brother!"

One lone man raised a trembling hand, breaking Earl's pace and drawing every eye to himself. "Uh...Earl? Isn't that...a little much? I mean, shouldn't we let the sheriff and his boys handle it?"

"The *sheriff*? Let me tell you something about ol' Hank Berkley. That man does nothing in his office all day but sit on his thumbs. And that's all he's good for. He's a coward who can't muster up enough courage to stand up to a loudmouth like me." He cracked a smile, admitting a fault, which won him even more followers as some of the braver few chuckled at his good-natured expense.

A bit more lightheartedly, but with the same passion, Earl continued, "If we want justice in our town again, we have to stop sitting by and doing nothing. We have to quit lying down and taking what *they* give us! We have to become the law. And I say we start with Jeff Weldon. Let him be the example."

"But that's pushing it a little far now, Earl. Haven't we already done enough?" Milton whined.

Another said, "Milton's right. We already burnt the man's church to the ground. What more do you want?"

"You afraid?" Earl accused.

The man shrunk back. "Well...yeah. You saw that monster! What if it came because of what we did? You know, like punishment?"

"Fine! Go back to your wives, if you're afraid. We don't need no boys here; we need *men*! Men willing to fight for what they believe in—assuming you folks still believe in something. Go back to sitting by the phones waiting for a call from the police that *officially* tells you what happened to your kin. But my boy is dead for no good reason, and I can't let that go."

Earl finished his charge and remained facing them, out of breath. The crowd looked to one another, each person waiting to see someone else's reaction before he decided on his own. Earl saw the fear in their eyes, the complacency that cursed their town long ago and that had been there ever since the highway moved. Maybe even long before that. These were timid people, too afraid to cause a ruckus. Too afraid to get things done, to take a stand and make a change.

But not Earl.

He waited as, one by one, they made their decisions. When the moment passed and the final votes were in, every man stayed, more determined than ever to fight, leaving them with only one question.

"So, what do we do, Earl?" asked one, and the others echoed him, ready to deal out their judgment, ready to finish the business that they had all set their minds to do.

Earl grinned. "We go pay the good reverend a little house call."

After what was possibly the longest night of his life, Jeff Weldon finally made it home. Walking to his apartment on the East Side that night, having lent his truck to Danny, Jeff felt freer than ever. He was confident now that God was in control of Greensboro's problems and had his heart set to wait on God to deal with the town.

In the meantime, Jeff had to fix things with Isabella.

Beaming with joy and a newfound peace, Jeff rounded the block and discovered his apartment. The old rundown place had never looked so good. Without wasting a moment, he jogged up the front steps, about to burst with excitement, longing to tell Isabella every-thing he had learned, wanting to share with her his heart and his love and, more than anything, just needing to spend some time with her mending their friendship.

Reaching the top of the stairs, he flung the unlocked door open. "Hey! I'm home!"

However, the brownstone was quiet and dark when Jeff entered.

Immediately, all exciting revelations were stilled, and he was on the alert again. He had an awful feeling that his long night was not quite over. Fumbling for a lamp in the darkness, he called out again.

"Sweetie? You home?"

No answer. And where was that lamp? He struck something in the darkness, on the floor. It startled him, and he bent down to feel for the object. It felt familiar. Like a lamp.

Groping for the switch, he turned it on, and everything was made horribly clear.

The television set was busted. Dressers were overturned, their drawers snatched from them, and spilled out all over the floor. The couch was split open and stuffing covered everything. The drapes were torn to shreds, the windows busted, and obscenities were spray-painted all over the walls. Threats. Warnings. Curses.

Jeff's heart sank to the floor, and he felt his whole body grow limp. His mouth hanging open in disbelief, he fought to find the words to describe his feelings.

Moving forward, he heard crunching beneath his shoe and stopped in his tracks to see a discarded picture frame on the floor. Crouching down, he carefully picked up the frame and looked at the frozen memory. It was he and Isabella. Their wedding picture, now cracked.

Panicked now, he shouted, "Iz?" and started rummaging through the house, racing up the stairs first. "Iz!" he hollered, each time growing more and more terrified, worried that the Committee had retaliated for his actions. When no reply came, he flew back down the stairs and entered every room on the first floor, dreading discov-ering her dead body somewhere. *Please, God, not like that. Don't let it end like that.*

"Isabella? Are you here? Answer me!"

The house was empty, and he spun on his heel, ready to tear into the night to find his wife when he met the grinning face of Earl Canton in his open doorway, backed by a crowd of angry followers.

"Welcome home, Reverend."

The church lay in smoldering ruins as the fire department shut off their hoses and the last of the embers died away. The ambulance had arrived, and the paramedics had wrapped Annie and little Millie Walker in fuzzy blankets. Now they sat in the back of the vehicle, being treated for minor scrapes and burns. Millie watched as Annie gesticulated outrageously with her free hand, relaying the *entire* night's fill of events to Ginny via a borrowed cell phone. Sheriff Berkley left the presence of deputies Roy Miller and Carter Ross, having finished telling them the story of the church that once was, and found Isabella pacing nervously.

Before Hank could speak, she answered his question. "I'm worried about him."

"We're almost done here, and then we can go look for him."

"No." She stopped and faced him. "Something's wrong. I can feel it."

Hank thought to argue, but after what he'd seen tonight, nothing was too odd for him anymore. He signaled to Deputy Miller. "Get us a car."

"Earl," Jeff eased, backing away from the door and the mob outside, "what are you doing?"

"Having us a little party." He chuckled. "You're the guest of honor."

"Where's Isabella?"

"No clue. She wasn't here when we worked the place over, if that makes you feel any better. We've been looking for you all night, Reverend. Got some things to discuss with you."

Jeff tried to break the tension with a nervous smile, immensely relieved to hear that Isabella was OK. "Well, I hope it's not about your choice in decorating, because I've got to be honest with you, I'm not liking it."

"Cute," Earl drawled bitterly. "You Weldon boys were always real cute."

Earl motioned for his two good ole boy lackeys, Milton Wilbanks and Linus Branch, to enter the house. "Get him."

Jeff stepped back in retreat. "Let's talk about this."

"Nothing left to talk about."

"I don't want to fight you, Earl."

Earl sneered. "That's OK. You just stand there, then."

Earl broke the holding pattern and charged the young man with a growl, swinging his fists. Jeff dodged, evading rather than attacking. Earl recovered quickly and came at Jeff again. In an attempt to duck the blow, Jeff stumbled and collapsed onto his already broken coffee table, bringing it to its final demise.

Outside, the mob edged closer to the open doorway, watching the scene but not moving in, not daring to interfere unless their leader called for them.

"Listen, I understand—" Jeff began.

Earl threw another punch, and this one connected. Jeff's nose broke for the second time in his life, and blood sprayed everywhere. He went down hard, and Earl stood even taller, satisfied. "You *understand*? You don't understand anything!"

Jeff pleaded, gargling through the blood in his throat. "Earl, please..."

Earl grabbed Jeff by the collar and lifted him to his feet. Jeff felt dazed, realizing that even *Stevenson* had not hit him so hard. He met Earl's eyes and found sadness and desperation.

Earl flung his victim across the room and chased him down. Climbing on top of him, Earl beat at Jeff's face, splattering blood.

"Uh...Earl..." Milton ventured to intervene. "Shouldn't we...uh...I mean, I think he's learned his lesson."

"Quiet!" Earl snapped, his voice shrill.

Jeff felt his teeth loosen and wondered if he'd be the next Weldon son rushed to the emergency room. Maybe he'd even be operated on in the same room as Dras. If he survived that long.

I'm going to die, he thought, and felt himself falling. Actually, it wasn't so much that *he* was falling but that time and space and the ages themselves were *whooshing* past him, and for a brief sickening instant he saw the slick, black beasts of his nightmares and the town that gave itself over to a dark god.

Jeff snapped to attention as Earl yanked him up and threw his broken body toward Milton and Linus. "Take him." He wiped spittle from the corner of his mouth.

After seeing the savagery of their leader, Milton and Linus didn't stop to argue, and Jeff wasn't able to fight or resist. He slipped in and out of his dreams, seeing horrible visions of monsters standing in the town square, worshiping the monument with the strange circular sigil. The two men dragged Jeff's body to the hungry crowd outside, who clamored in victory.

After escorting their prisoner down the front porch, Milton and Linus tossed him to the ground as Earl stepped out of the house.

"What do we do now?" Milton said.

"We hang him."

A few shocked gasps rose from the crowd.

"We can't do that!" one man protested.

"Are you nuts?"

But Earl did not listen. "It's either them or us! What's it going to be? My son is *dead* because of him! You all have lost people too. He murdered them, and none of you are willing to do anything about it!"

By now some in the crowd were hesitant to act.

Linus wrung his hands. "Uh, Earl? Jeff might've scared Millie Walker into changing her testimony, but even the courts said that *Dras* was the killer. Not Jeff."

The crowd faced Earl, as though he'd gone insane.

"Quit looking at me like that!" He marched down the steps. "He's guilty, I tell you!"

"I don't know, Earl," Linus spoke up again.

With rage building, Earl pushed the man to the dirt. "Then leave! All of you! I can do this myself!"

Without waiting for a response, Earl stormed to his truck and jerked it into gear before parking under a tree. *This ends tonight.* Getting out in a flash, leaving the door open, he ran to Jeff and hefted him up. Jeff moaned, barely conscious, as Earl yelled to Milton, "Help me!"

Milton, too afraid to say no, hurried over and helped Earl heave Jeff's battered body onto the bed of the truck. Their cargo dropped, Earl reached for a rope that lay near Jeff's feet. Throwing a looped end over the thick branch above, he tied off a secure knot and carefully made a noose.

The crowd watched in horror.

"Stop it!" some began to shout.

"Let him go!"

Earl finished the noose and wrapped it around Jeff's neck. He yanked once on the rope to make sure it was taut. "Shut up!"

They began to boo him. To throw things at him. Anything small and loose they could get their hands on. They shouted, and one brave man even jumped onto the tailgate of the truck to climb in. However, his heroic attempts were met with Earl's boot to his face. With a yelp, the man flopped backward onto the ground, useless.

Earl hopped out of the truck bed, and the crowd rushed him. He fought them off, strong in his rage, and made his way to the driver's side. Climbing in, he revved the engine loud enough to wake the whole block. Grinning like a wild man, he showed them all that he was ready to shift the truck into DRIVE and pull forward, taking Jeff's platform out from under him and leaving him to hang from a tree.

The crowd roared in protest, and Earl revved the engine all the more to drown out their cries. Finally a shotgun blast quieted them.

Earl took his foot off the gas pedal, and hushed faces fell on Sheriff Hank Berkley. Behind him Isabella Weldon stood, her eyes brimming with horror at the sight of her husband nearly hanged, a hand to her mouth to stifle a scream.

"Cut him down," Hank demanded, having never looked firmer.

Earl smiled at the command. "I been wondering if you'd be coming around here." Putting the truck into PARK but leaving the engine running, Earl stepped out, and the crowd shuffled to make way for him.

Hank cut a hard look at the crowd. "I ought to haul every one of you in for having a hand in this."

Immediately all heads lowered in embarrassment. Some people dug their toes into the ground; some looked the other way. *Cowards.* Earl Canton remained defiant. *They can't get away with this anymore. I won't let them.* "Why don't you just go back the way you came, Hank? Looking the other way is what you're good at."

Hank didn't budge. "Not anymore, Earl. Now, you'd better cut him down now, or—"

"Or what?"

Hank held the shotgun steady, pressing the barrel to the man's nose.

"You wouldn't dare." Earl snarled.

Hank cocked the gun. "Try me."

Humiliated, Earl gave up and raised his hands in surrender. Hank set the shotgun down and brought out his cuffs. The same crowd that once sought Jeff's blood now cheered as Earl was apprehended.

Isabella pushed past the mob with purpose, leaping onto the tailgate and going to work at untying the noose around her husband's neck. She struggled against the knot, her hands trembling with excitement until, finally, the rope's hold on Jeff was broken and he collapsed into her arms.

"Oh, baby," she sobbed, holding him close and stroking his hair, covering his bruised face with soft kisses. "I thought I lost you."

Jeff looked up to her. "Hey…"

She laughed through her tears. "Hey."

"I've been looking for you. Where've you been all night?" Jeff chuckled, then winced in pain.

Eager to care for him once more, Isabella shushed him. "Careful."

He gazed at her, his green eyes becoming clearer, and smiled. "Our house is a mess, Iz."

Isabella almost turned to their brownstone there on the East Side, but she understood that wasn't what he meant. "Maybe..." she began timidly, "...maybe we can put it back together again? If...if you'd be willing to try."

He beamed in response, and she hugged him close as he lay there in her arms, but he gently pushed her away. Surprised, she looked down at him.

"Isabella," he paused, catching his breath. "There's something that I've needed to tell you for a long, long time."

She studied him carefully, bracing herself for the truth he solemnly attempted to tell her. "What?" she asked, fearful of his next words.

"I hate meat loaf."

And there they were. Those precious words Isabella Weldon had longed all seven years of their marriage to hear.

Her lips quivered and she bit them to hold in her tears, but she found she couldn't. She burst out laughing and crying and pulled him close to her again, loving him so much, kissing him powerfully. She knew then. It didn't matter anymore. Whatever stupid things they said to each other, whatever hurt they caused in the past, they could work through it. He was her best friend. Her soul mate. They belonged together, and now they were finally reunited.

Thank You, God, she prayed, weeping and kissing her husband's neck and shoulders as she embraced him. *Thank You...*

Above them, heaven watched and smiled.

EPILOGUE

WE WERE FIVE *years old, and it was our birthday.*
That was the first real, clear memory Rosalyn had of Dras Weldon.

Only Dras wasn't here anymore.

Instead she was alone, sitting in her darkened apartment, gazing out at the solemn night sky. Looking down, she stared at the folded note and continued to roll it over in her hands. The note Dras gave her. Still unopened.

Would she open it tonight? A part of her yearned to read it and understand what was so important that Dras felt he must sacrifice everything to tell her. She felt along the edges of the note, worn from where she'd fondled it for so long. It had taken some work to find it. She had successfully buried it underneath years of photographs she had removed from the walls after Dras's arrest. But there it was, at the bottom of the shoebox. Still waiting for her.

However, the fruit sat silently on her coffee table, waiting for her as well. The fruit that *he* gave her.

Rosalyn looked from the note in her hands to the fruit on the table.

Which one do I choose?

What did it matter what the note said? Dras was gone. Soon he would be executed. He wasn't coming back for her, despite what she held on to in her heart. It was over. It was time to move past it and discover who she could be without him. It was time to be on her own.

She laid the note on the windowsill and marched toward the fruit. Squeezing its plump flesh, she raised it toward her mouth, ready to eat it, then stopped.

Is this wrong?

She looked back to the note that lay on the windowsill. Maybe it held some great cosmic answer, something that could stop the Strange Man, something that could save her. Maybe if she just read it, Dras would speak to her through the words on the page and everything would be all right again.

Sighing heavily, Rosalyn shut her eyes, the fruit still in her hand.

Enough, Roz. Just do it.

Bringing the fruit to her lips, she opened wide and bit into its meat without hesitation. Warm juices burst forth, dark and viscous.

Black, sticky goo invaded her mouth and filled her completely, and Rosalyn dropped the fruit to the floor, grasping her throat and choking as the goo assimilated her from the inside. She gurgled, struggling to scream, but it was too late.

Before her, the Strange Man flickered into existence. He had been there all along, she finally understood. Watching and waiting for her. Now he reared back on his haunches, cackling like a wild, ancient god as the lost girl collapsed to the floor.

In a heartbeat, it was over.

Rosalyn Myers was lost to the devil, and not a soul in the world noticed.

It is coming.

To Be Concluded...

Choose for yourselves this day whom you will serve.

—JOSHUA 24:15

COMING FROM
GREG MITCHELL
IN 2013

Dark Hour

Book Three in The Coming Evil Trilogy

PROLOGUE

Truth is nowhere to be found, and whoever
shuns evil becomes a prey.
—ISAIAH 59:15

LL IN ALL, Dras Weldon mused as he finished a bite of instant
potatoes, *prison is a whole lot like high school.*

While matriculating in Wexler State Pen—the City's
maximum security prison—for the last ten months, Dras couldn't
help but make the comparison. Prison had its cliques too. To his left,
Dras spotted the black guys, in their makeshift congregation, flexing
their biceps and sizing each other up, looking to be the biggest and
baddest. To his right, the rough-looking Mexicans, bad-mouthing
everyone else in Spanish and looking pretty cocky about it. Somewhere in the middle were the white guys, throwing gang signs all
their own, tattoos coloring their shaved heads. Each racial section
was trying to out-show the "competition."

And at a secluded table—like the senior class, the kids everyone
wanted to be—sat the lifers. Most importantly, Old Nick. Old Nick,
a lifer who looked like Santa Claus's evil twin in a prison uniform,
lounged. He and the other long-term convicts who surrounded him
were like a pride of lions lazily keeping their watch over the other
inmates. As Dras observed, no one went to the lifer table. Old Nick
and his crew were legends in Wexler, content to rule their makeshift
kingdom inside these stone walls. In prison, the food chain went up
pretty high, and a man had to claw his way from minnow to great
white. Old Nick was a great white.

Dras was a minnow. Minnows were easy pickings.

"Hey." A gruff voice snapped just over Dras's head as a very large
and scowling Mexican with long greasy hair draped over broad
shoulders interrupted his lunch. The man shadowed over him like

a mountain, and Dras, his spoon hovering in front of his mouth, turned to the imposing figure with nonchalance.

"Can I help you?" Dras recognized the man. Scuttlebutt was that the guy was Raul "Machete" Rodriguez—a new arrival and close friend to the penal system—who was nicked after a botched convenience store robbery. No doubt he was looking to establish his rep pretty quick, especially with Old Nick taking notice of the scene.

Machete Rodriguez said, "You're in my seat."

Dras looked down to his chair. "Am I? Sorry 'bout that."

Dras kindly stood and gathered his tray, ready to leave. But Machete grew red in the face and slapped Dras's tray away. Dras frowned at the sight of his instant potatoes sailing across the cafeteria. *Bummer.*

Turning back to his new friend, Dras remained unfazed. Machete sneered down at the wiry young man. "You disrespecting me, small fry? Trying to make me look like a chump?"

Dras shrugged. "I generally don't try to make people look like chumps until I've known them for a while."

A few snickers rippled through the surrounding tables, and Dras saw that even Old Nick found the exchange amusing. Machete must have spotted it too. Outraged, the ogre seized Dras by the collar and hoisted him to eye level. "You laughing at me?"

Dras brightened when he saw Rhino headed across the cafeteria.

"This guy bothering you, Jesus?"

George "Rhino" Beasley lived up to his namesake. He was a stocky dark-skinned man with drooping jowls and rolls of fat hanging off his thick frame. When he charged, anyone with good sense knew to get out of the way. Rhino huffed up to Dras and Machete, backed by an entourage of equally hungry-eyed predators. "You OK?"

Machete turned around to see the troop of muscles marching his way and nearly gulped. Dras looked over the Mexican's shoulder, indifferent. "Yeah, I'm all right, Rhino." Dras nodded to the floor, where the remains of his lunch lay splattered. "I really had my heart set on those potatoes...but other than that, I'm fine."

Machete turned back to Dras, his stony expression giving way to a hint of anxiety. Dras raised his eyebrows. "Right?"

Machete nodded, slowly and deliberately. "Yeah...sure."

Rodriguez turned back to the imposing figures behind him, saw Old Nick and the rest of the lifers laughing in hysterics, then gave one last menacing snarl to Dras in a vain attempt to salvage his reputation.

"But this isn't over," he said.

Dras sighed. "I was really afraid you'd say something like that."

Machete left, his fists clenched, wincing in humiliation as he passed the other inmates. Dras watched as the Mexican slammed the doors and left the dining area, then released an honest-to-goodness breath of relief.

Rhino said, "If he gives you more problems, you come to us."

"Will do. Thanks, Rhino."

"Anytime, Jesus." Rhino clapped a sweaty, meaty palm on Dras's back then nodded toward the boys. With a few grunts, the men retreated back to their corners until they were needed again. When the two were alone, the burly inmate turned to his younger counterpart.

Dras laughed, a bit embarrassed. "I told you to quit calling me that, big guy."

Rhino shook his head, good-natured but defiant. "I see Jesus in you. So, you as close to Jesus as I'm gonna know."

The two shared an amiable moment before—"Weldon! You causing trouble again?"

Dras wheeled about as a salt-and-pepper-haired man in a beige uniform, flanked by two more uniformed gorillas twice his size, stomped full force toward him. Heat immediately flushing in his face, Dras scratched the back of his messy blond mop top. "Uh, hey, Sergeant Winters."

Winters, the leader of the trio, already had his nightstick in hand. "Can't turn my back on you for one second."

Under the cold stare of Winters, Dras shifted unpleasantly, noticing that the rough-and-tumble convicts around him were quickly finding other places to be.

Sergeant Winters had that kind of reputation.

Rhino stepped in between the imposing authority figure and the small inmate. "He wasn't startin' nuthin, Sarge."

"Shut it, Rhino. I didn't ask you to be a character witness." In an instant, Winters had his nightstick pressed up against Dras's chin, lifting his face to size him up. "I say you just earned yourself another night in solitary."

Dras's smirk sank as Rhino protested louder. "He ain't done nuthin'!"

Winters leveled a glower at the husky prisoner, his hardened face the antithesis of compassion. "You looking to spend time in Blackout with him, tough guy?"

Rhino puffed out his chest. "You bet I am!"

"Rhino, no," Dras interrupted, patting his burly friend on the chest. "It's not worth it. I'll be all right."

"But—"

"Really," Dras nodded, trying to look braver than he felt. "What's one more night, right? I've got this one."

Dras appreciated his friend taking up for him. Rhino was a good man who had a bad day once, coming home from work early to discover his wife in bed with another man. So enraged was he that Rhino strangled the other man to death before realizing that that man was, in fact, his own brother. Broken and wrought with grief at what he had done, Rhino put up no fight as he was arrested and later sentenced to life imprisonment. Despite that one moment of wrath, Rhino was a softhearted man deep down who always watched out for Dras. But, as Dras had learned since his arrest, there were some things he had to do on his own.

Winters's expression was stone as, with a jerk of the chiseled chin, he wordlessly ordered his men to take Dras into custody. The guards escorted Dras out of the cafeteria while Winters stayed, fixing Rhino in place with a harsh glance.

Dras heard his friend still sticking up for him. "You know he ain't done nuthin'. That's Jesus. He always innocent."

Eyeing the bold man, Dras saw as Winters's granite features threatened to crack. Then he stiffened suddenly. "Stay out of it, Rhino," he said and followed Dras.

The buzzers sounded as the security doors parted. His armed chaperones solidly gripped each elbow, keeping Dras to his path. The familiar *click click click* of Sergeant Winters's polished shoes grew louder until the man caught up with him, grouchy as always.

"I'll take him the rest of the way," Winters muttered, and the two behemoth guards left to attend to other business. Using his faithful nightstick, Winters prodded the small of Dras's back, herding him down the lonely cement corridor that led to solitary—"Blackout." It wasn't the first time Dras had spent the night in Blackout. And thanks to Winters, who seemed to derive some sick pleasure from punishing the "new kid" at every available opportunity, Dras worried it wouldn't be his last.

"You know I wasn't hurting anybody, Sergeant," Dras defended. "Why are you putting me in Blackout? I mean, what have I ever done?"

Winters's craggy face split into a real smile. "What can I say, Weldon? You must have that kind of face. Just ticks people off."

"Yeah," Dras groaned. "Story of my life."

Winters led Dras to an all-too-familiar door and opened it with a creak. With a mocking bow, Winters presented, "Your room, sir."

"Where should I check my luggage?" Dras feebly retorted, hoping a little humor would lighten the mood.

"I'll have the bellhop up in a minute. Don't you worry about that."

Dras entered the dark bay of solitary, resigned to his fate. "Guess this is 'good night,' then, Sarge."

"Don't let the bed bugs bite," Winters humorlessly responded, shutting and locking the door, sentencing Dras to his solitude, leaving him to reflect for the thousandth time on the events that led him here.

Prison was the last place in the world Dras Weldon ever imagined himself winding up. The closest he ever came to the Big House in his crime-free life was an old Clint Eastwood movie he watched with his dad when he was ten.

Those first couple of months in Wexler, Dras had been isolated, bandages all over his body, jaw wired shut with some horrifying brace. He assumed he looked like some kind of B-movie horror monster—which in theory sounded sort of cool to him—and most inmates stayed away from him early on. He was locked up in a cell, mostly lying down, sometimes sitting in silence, healing.

After he started recovering, though, when the bandages came off and Dras's trial started, he was introduced into the wonderful world of prison life, a clumsy, baby-faced boy who had made the—what some might consider *unwise*—decision to stand against a centuries-old evil force looking to steal the soul of his best friend.

Rosalyn. He thought about her every day.

Settling in for the rest of the afternoon, Dras sat down on the cold floor of Blackout, leaning his head against the wall. He wondered how Rosalyn was doing these days, if she'd read his letter, if she'd withstood the Strange Man.

As he often did when Winters stuck him in solitary, Dras reached into his pocket and pulled out the small Bible that once belonged to his brother, Reverend Jeff Weldon. On the night Dras went to his short-lived war with the Strange Man, he'd taken the pocket Bible as a weapon. Upon his prison sentencing, Dras had asked only for that Bible to keep him company in lockdown. Now, by the slim light of the food tray slot in the steel door, Dras cracked open his brother's old Bible, thumbing through its worn pages. Multicolored

Greg Mitchell

notes scribbled on tattered pages served as warm reminders of the spiritual journey Jeff had taken in studying this book. Now they functioned as a map for Dras, guiding him to discover the truths of the old manuscript for himself.

Finding familiar passages, Dras read them aloud, taking comfort in the sound of his own voice. In keeping with his normal routine, he knew he would continue to do this until "lights out," when the darkness rolled in. Then he would recite the scriptures from memory, warding off the terrible loneliness as long as he could before sleep finally overtook him. But nighttime was still a few hours off. He could still read, could still focus on *something*, anything, to keep his mind off the unending quiet of solitary.

Setting aside the Bible verses for the moment, Dras removed a handwritten letter from his brother, tucked between the pages. After unfolding it, Dras held the note to the sliver of light, eyes poring over Jeff's sloppy cursive.

> *Hey, freak—*
>
> *Just wanted to give you a little update on things at home. First off, Dad's doing well. I mean, he's not getting better, but he's not getting worse either, so thank God for small favors, right? Mom's constantly hovering over him, as usual, and she keeps asking if you can get DVDs in prison. She thinks you'd be happier if you had one of your crappy movies to watch.*

"She'd be right," Dras glumly muttered.

> *I keep telling her that they already give you TV privileges, which sounds pretty cushy to me. Why don't they just let you serve your time at home if they're going to feed you and give you free cable? Ah, I'm just kidding. You know that.*
>
> *Iz and I are doing all right. She's still working at the Laundromat, and I'm doing pretty well for myself at the hardware store. I guess all those years working with Dad on roofs finally paid off... or royally screwed me up for life, I can't tell which. But we're making ends meet. Which reminds me; they're almost done building the new church. It won't be like Dad's church, though. I keep hearing talk that it's going to be a Universal Church or something like that. Iz and I are thinking*

326

about becoming Catholic and going to Father Joe's church in Russellville, ha ha. He's a pretty good guy, as we've gotten to know him. You know Mom would kill me, though, if I started saying "Hail Mary" and all of that, ha ha.

Anyway, I want to get serious for a minute. Things are getting strange in town, and you know what I mean. I don't know how much is safe to say, but just know that it's getting harder here. There're not many people left who believe like we do, so we've had to start sticking together. We're holding Bible studies, but I can't say where. People are starting to disappear around here, and our numbers are growing shorter. They're looking for us, Dras. So far we've stayed ahead of them, but we're starting to have to get creative. Some folks have already asked Iz and me if we can help them get out of town, but we've got to be really careful. Usually I'd say that I wish you were here, and you know I do, but at the same time, maybe you're safer where you are for the time being, as crazy as that sounds. I believe God's taking care of you in prison. He's got a plan for you yet, little brother. Keep following Him, and I'll write you again when I can.

—Jeff

The letter was dated four months ago, and it was the last. Since that time, no contact from Jeff. No phone calls, no visits, nothing.

"What happened, man?" Dras asked the quiet dark surrounding him. "Where'd you go?"

It worried him greatly. Another thing that bothered him was that he *still* had no word on Rosalyn. Jeff seemed to purposefully exclude her from his letters, and whenever Dras asked about her during his phone privileges, Jeff always got real twitchy and would say things like "Ah, you know, Rosalyn" or "She's going through a tough time." Dras didn't blame Rosalyn for not wanting to come see him in prison. Sure, it was painful not to see his best friend—his soul mate—but he could understand it if Rosalyn didn't want her last memory of Dras to be of him in an orange jumper behind bars.

But to go so long without hearing about her, without knowing that she was safe from the Strange Man...it was thousands times worse than solitary. And now, added to that uncertainty, was his brother's recent silence.

Dras slipped the letter back in the Bible, closed the cover, and shut his eyes, anxious for his friends.

What's going on in Greensboro?